Seasons
of
Change

Seasons

of

Change

by

Cheryl Okimoto

*To Micah & Sigrid
Thank you for all
you do. May you always
be richly blessed.
Cheryl*

Lulu.com

Seasons of Change

© 2009 Cheryl Okimoto

Published by Lulu

ISBN 978-0-557-25426-2

Printed in the United States of America

Visit www.cherylokimoto.com

Not only so, but we also rejoice in our sufferings, because we know that suffering produces perseverance; perseverance, character; and character, hope.

Romans 5:3-4 (NIV)

With grateful thanks to my wonderful readers: Anne, Annie, Cari, Cheryl, Gloria, Jaime, Lisa, Ray and Vickie, and with special thanks to my husband for all his patience, encouragement and help. I couldn't have done this without you.

This book is set in Hawaii, which has a culture quite different from any other place. That culture comes through in a number of places in this book. For my Mainland readers, I have included a "Notes" section in the back of the book to help you get the most out of the story while still maintaining a good deal of authenticity.

For my kamaaina readers, please understand that I toned down some of the pidgin and culture for my malihini readers. For example, how do I explain Steve's Filipino gardener? When you get there, kamaaina reader, know that Heather and Greg asked about it and had fun with it.

Chapter 1

*T*he sun was warm on Steve Jeremiah's face and the trade winds brought a hint of what Hawaii thinks is winter, the brush of a barely cool breath against the skin. The sky was a deep, aching blue that reminded him of his sister Jenni's eyes. The mist of the blowhole drifted away on the breeze and he heard the surf crash against the rocks below.

He only heard the surf because he didn't hear what he wanted to hear, the rumbling purr of two hundred fifty-five horses under the hood of his BMW Z4 convertible.

"Lord, this is a forty-five thousand dollar automobile," Steve groaned as he listened to the click of his key in the ignition. "It should be roaring to life. What's up?"

He tried again. Click. Click. No response.

"This cannot be happening to me!" Steve laid his head on the steering wheel and groaned again. After seven years of professional football, there had been very few things he had not gotten pretty much as soon as he wanted or needed it. He was spoiled. He admitted it but really, he didn't want that much. He had his house up on Alewa Heights, his convertible and the offseason leisure to enjoy Oahu, this paradise that shouted of God's glory.

This morning he had come out here because he wanted to admire the sunrise and read a book beside the Pacific while occasionally watching for the blowhole to spout off and maybe even catch a whale in the distance, spouting its own blowhole even when the tide was low. Now he was ready to move on to Waimanalo and see if the waves would challenge him in a run on the beach.

As usual, he had been denied the whales and now he would also be denied Waimanalo. Unless perchance she had just been coy before. He turned the key again, firmly depressing the clutch. Not coy, dead.

Steve gripped the steering wheel as he stared into the distance, seeing the dark days of his past rather than the smudge of Molokai rising from the blue waters of the Pacific. A poor boy from the wrong side of the tracks in Abilene, Kansas, the only car he'd ever had to drive was his mom's old Mercury station wagon, held together by baling wire and duct tape. He'd always been too preoccupied with football to pay any attention to how Uncle Joe fixed it. That preoccupation had paid off with a lucrative pro football contract but it wasn't doing him a bit of good now.

With a groan, Steve popped the hood and climbed from the butter-soft leather seat. "If only" ran through his head as he peered under the hood, clueless about what he was looking for. If only he had paid more attention when Uncle Joe tried to teach him about cars. If only he'd taken Mr. Markel's auto shop instead of hanging out with the girls in Ms. Holland's home-ec. If only he'd already joined a traveler's club. If only he had any clue how to call a tow truck without a phone book or the internet.

Hopefully Pete was at home. Flipping open his cell phone, Steve speed-dialed his best friend who was also his only friend on Oahu.

"Hey Steve," Pete came through loud and clear as usual. "What's happenin'?"

"It's more like what's *not* happenin'," Steve slammed the hood of the car. "This 'marvel of German engineering' that you convinced me was the best thing this side of heaven isn't running."

"It's not? What's wrong?"

"If I knew I wouldn't be calling you, now would I?"

"Guess not," Pete's chuckle was much too happy for Steve's sour mood. "What *are* ya callin' me for?"

"Well, I'm stuck out here at the blowhole by that beach where you tried to get me killed last winter."

"You mean Halona Blowhole by Sandy Beach?"

"That would be the one."

"So whatcha want me to do? I can't fix it, brah."

"Believe me, I'm well aware of that fact," Steve rolled his eyes at the thought of his friend's even greater ineptitude with cars. "But I don't have a number for someone to call. I was hoping you'd get one for me."

"Ah, so ya didn't join –"

"No, I didn't," Steve sighed, "and I don't need your 'I told you so.' Just give me a number for a tow truck and a place for it to be towed to."

"No prob. Hang on a sec and I'll get the number to the garage that keeps my marvel of German engineering running smoothly. They can tow it and fix it."

A short time later, Steve settled down on the rock wall above the blowhole to wait for the tow truck that the receptionist at the garage had guaranteed him would be on its way "soon."

"A car, a car, my kingdom for a car," Steve muttered, paraphrasing Shakespeare's King Richard. "I guess I should thank you, Lord, for reminding me that I'm not in control and I can't have everything I want, but if you don't mind, I don't feel like being thankful right now. I finished my book. There are no whales out there. There's not even a sea turtle. I can only take so much blowhole at once. There's not even anyone to talk to out here this morning. If you've got a plan in all this, I'm not seeing it."

Steve tried to settle back and enjoy the incredible beauty of the place. The Pacific stretching out before him to the far horizon was that deep, deep blue that caressed with a soothing embrace. The tide was going out and the surf rolled with gentle swells only occasionally breaking with force against the brown-black lava rocks below, sending white foam splashing over the rocks and mist sputtering from the blowhole. The sun was still in the Southern half of its spring journey and it hadn't yet gained the sub-tropical summer strength that it would have in just a few short weeks, so it kissed his cheeks gently. The coastal road perched precariously on the side of Koko Head Crater, but he was too close to the stately mountain to appreciate the full beauty of its leeward crest, windward collapsed lip and peaceful green valley nestled well below the summit. He was nicely set to enjoy watching the action at Sandy Beach, but surprisingly, there wasn't anything interesting there.

He was no longer content to just enjoy the beauty of Hawaii right now. He knew that all across the Mainland, people were still cold on this late February day and most of them would love to trade places with him, busted car and all. Even here on Oahu, where everyone enjoyed beautiful weather almost every day of the year, most of the residents would also take his place instead of being trapped at work on this incredible day that cried for attention. He could give the day the attention that it demanded but he was tired of doing it here at the blowhole with the inactivity of waiting. He wanted to enjoy this day in Waimanalo.

It kind of underscored his life. Since he'd achieved his dream of becoming a Chicago Grizzly, he'd fallen into a waiting pattern. Now his thirtieth birthday was rushing at him like a middle linebacker on a blitz but he was still waiting. He was waiting to find Jenni again sixteen years after she'd run away. He was waiting to find the love who teased his dreams like the rainbows teased the mist at the blowhole. He wasn't just waiting idly, he was actively looking for both, but God wasn't helping any and Steve was getting tired of waiting.

He looked at his watch. Whatever the receptionist had meant by "soon" wasn't even close to what Steve thought it meant. It was almost an hour already. Steve got up to pace the sidewalk. After a few minutes, he realized that pacing was only increasing his frustration. He plopped back down on the wall. He crossed his right leg over his left, propped his elbow up on his knee, and dropped his chin on his hand. He stared at Koko Head, carefully inspecting the foliage growing out of the rocks. Something entered his peripheral vision. Turning his head to the left, he saw the tow truck pulling off the road and into the parking lot. His sigh of relief turned to a groan when the driver stepped out of the cab. No way was this tall gangly kid touching his Beamer!

"Keys in the car?" the youth growled, striding purposefully toward Steve's midnight blue convertible.

Steve nodded, trying not to glare at the youth. Pete said they were the best on the island. If he was wrong, he would pay!

"What's the problem?"

"It won't start."

"You wanna be a little more specific?" Steve could swear the driver rolled his eyes. "Don't usually get called when they do start."

Steve felt the heat rising in his face. "Nothing happens when I turn the key."

"You depress the clutch?" The youth unzipped the top of his coveralls and whipped out a thin towel, draping it over the leather seat. "All the late models have built in safety measures, ya know. Can't start 'em without the clutch depressed so they don't jerk 'cause they're in gear."

"I've had this car for a year. I know how to start it." It was Steve's turn to roll his eyes.

"No need get all huhu, brah, just checkin'."

"Who who?"

"Hawaiian for grouchy." He slipped behind the wheel and turned the key. "Yep, it make."

"Mah-kay?" Steve was beginning to feel a little stupid.

"Hawaiian for dead." The youth slid off the seat, knelt beside the car and twisted to feel under the clutch with his left hand. The partially unzipped coverall pulled tight over his right shoulder and gapped open over his left side. Steve saw curves under the driver's black t-shirt. "He" was a she.

"Ah-ha! Spent three days figurin' it out on Uncle Pena's car last year, but there she is." She smiled as she stood and turned, holding something tiny in her hand. "I got good news and bad news."

Steve stared at the hand holding a small piece of what looked like a rubber plug. It was definitely a woman's hand. A woman who worked with her hands, but a woman nonetheless. He could now clearly see that what he had thought was a tall gangly teenaged boy was actually a very tall, slender woman with hints of curves in all the right places under her coveralls.

"Hey mister, you in there?" Steve forced his attention back to the matter at hand when she waved a hand in front of his face. "Your car, brah."

"Yes, my car," Steve looked at his car rather than at the woman. "You have good news about my car?"

"I've got bad news too." Her smile grew a little as she recognized that look. Most guys were bowled over when they realized they were being rescued by a woman. It was especially gratifying this time because she had recognized the man waiting on the wall and it had taken her breath away.

As far as she was concerned Steve Jeremiah was the hottest thing on the football field. She'd only become a fan because he played for her team but then she had become a Jeremiah fan just like her family. She admired number ninety-five even if she did resent that he got such a fat paycheck. When she'd seen him needing her to rescue him, the admiration surged and the resentment waned. It had taken every ounce of fortitude she possessed not to gush over him when she climbed out of the truck. Now he was trying not to gush over her. How cool was that?

"So what's the bad news?" He kept his gaze trained on his Beamer.

"First the good news. It's an easy fix. This manini piece of rubber is part of the clutch safety system and it broke."

Steve decided that manini must mean tiny. He wasn't going to ask because he didn't want to look stupid in front of this intriguing woman. At least not any stupider.

"So then what's the bad news?"

"It'll be at least two or three days before I can get it fixed," she grimaced and gave a small shrug of her shoulders.

"Two or three days? Why?" Steve glared at her, shocked out of his distraction over her gender.

"Two problems." She bounced the offending piece of rubber in her hand. "I don't have this particular part in stock because I don't get much call for it, in fact only once before. And surprising as it may seem to you, you aren't number one on my list yet."

"Excuse me?" Steve thought he detected a bit of sassiness in her tone. Did she know who he was?

"I've already got four cars in my queue." She quickly decided not to let on yet that she knew he was a superstar defensive end. "You may have a forty thousand dollar automobile, but that doesn't make you more important than the jobs I already have."

Okay, that wasn't unreasonable but it was darned inconvenient for him.

"So what am I supposed to do?"

"Well, as I see it you've got three options. There's TheBus –"

"Not a chance," Steve emphatically shook his head.

"Or you can get a friend to chauffeur you –"

"Possible, but not attractive."

"Or you can rent a car for a few days."

"That's definitely doable," Steve nodded, "but how do I get to the car?"

"I don't suppose you joined some kind of preferred driver club?" She used her shapely eyebrows as a question mark.

"Never saw the need for it," Steve sighed, crossing his arms and leaning back against the car. "Lots of things I should have done that I didn't do yet."

"Well, plenty time for that later," she smiled, "but for now, let's get your car towed to the garage. You can call the rental agency and I'll give you a ride down there."

"You can do that? You won't get in trouble."

"I'm the boss," she grinned. "No one to give me trouble."

"Not even a husband," Steve grinned back.

"Nope," her grin faded quickly and she snatched work gloves out of her pockets. "Let's get this beast turned around so I can load it on the truck. You steer."

"I am not sitting in this car while a woman pushes it!" Steve rose to his full height and planted both fists on his hips.

"Didn't think you would," she tossed over her shoulder. "You're gonna push and steer at the same time. It's a whole lot harder than giving a little shove from the front."

"Before I push and steer, tell me, you got a name?"

"Heather," she growled. "Now let's get this beast moved."

Steve tried to keep his attention fully on getting his car lined up for the tow truck rather than wondering what was up with this peculiar woman. He couldn't figure out if she was friendly or not. One minute she smiled like a siren, the next she was growling like a grumpy old man. Was she attracted to him? Did she know who he was?

It didn't take very long at all before she was tightening up the tow bar around the front tires.

"By the way, I'm Steve –"

"I know who you are," she grunted and turned away. "Get in the truck."

Chapter 2

Steve sat in the cab of the tow truck trying to decide if he was supposed to make conversation with his suddenly surly driver. He couldn't figure her out. Heather had worked with efficiency and strength while loading his car on the truck but now there was something about her that cried out with vulnerability. The fingers of her left hand tapped a nervous beat on the steering wheel and she was chewing on her lower lip, paying more attention to the road than he suspected she needed to. Heather had said nothing after ordering him into the truck, but he was pretty sure she wanted to say something. He couldn't decide if he wanted to hear what she had to say. If he did, how would he encourage her?

Lord, I don't know what you're doing here, but I know you, so I'm sure you're up to something. Please give me some wisdom.

Heather wasn't happy with herself. She didn't like being confused and unsure. She needed to be in control. The sudden presence of this man in her life was confusing and therefore a threat to her control. She wasn't sure what to do about it.

When he'd asked if she had a husband, reality slapped her in the face. Heather didn't have, and would never have a husband because she wasn't wife material. That didn't bother her anymore because she had a full life, a life she really liked. But for some reason, when Steve Jeremiah asked if she had a husband she suddenly longed for one, something that hadn't happened in a long time. It must be because Heather kind of had a crush on him and yet he also made her mad. She'd noticed that sometimes her brother Luke had that effect on his wife. Maybe her mind was trying to trick her into thinking she was in love. She certainly felt like she'd known him for years.

Heather had known who Steve Jeremiah was even before he became a Grizzly, while he was still in college in Oklahoma. Her younger brother Greg had dreamt of the Grizzlies picking Jeremiah in the draft, certain he was just what the team needed. Greg had written and told her all the reasons why, and when he'd been right about his pick, he had spent endless hours reading about Jeremiah on the internet, then sharing stats and facts. With number ninety-five's first pre-season game, Greg had started very carefully reporting every great play that Steve Jeremiah was in on, just in case she missed it.

When Greg's own dreams of playing college football were unrealized and life intruded in his near obsession, the rest of the family was already fired up about Steve Jeremiah. Of course, it hadn't been a hard feat since they were all Grizzly fans anyway.

While she'd been in the Army for the start of the Jeremiah passion, Heather had caught it vicariously through letters, emails, and phone calls. She had also picked up some of it firsthand when she was able to watch Grizzly games. Then she'd come home and seen how old and tired Dad was getting, how hard her family all had to work just barely scraping by. Her teenaged brothers talked about how much Steve Jeremiah was getting on his new contract. A tiny bit of resentment began to creep into her heart, resentment that he made a shocking amount of money for a game while her father couldn't get a steady paycheck for his important prison ministry. Still she couldn't help admiring Jeremiah because he lived well off the field as well as playing well on the field, so she felt guilty for her resentment and then she resented him more for her guilt.

Now he was sitting in her truck and she could see that for all the money, all the hero worship, he was just a regular guy. And she felt like she should apologize, but he couldn't possibly know why. And she was really, really bad at explaining things, so she was afraid she'd mess it up if she tried but she had to say something.

"My father went to bible college right out of high school," Heather kept her eyes on the road as she began to speak. "That's where he met my mom. He was a year ahead of her, so he took a job as an associate pastor close to the college after he graduated. They got married two weeks after she graduated."

Heather paused to drink from the can of diet cola in her drink holder. Steve was intrigued and he hardly breathed in the hope that she wouldn't be diverted from her story.

"They spent two years as itinerant preachers on the Mainland, raising funds for the mission to Africa that they planned to go on. My older brother Luke was six months old when they landed in Africa, I came along not quite three years later, my brother Greg two years after that. Mom was from Hawaii, so they came back here after ten years in the mission field because she was dying. Within four years, Dad was widowed, remarried, had another son and became a prison chaplain. I guess we should have felt neglect, resentment or something but we never did. Dad was so full of God's love that we didn't feel any emotional need but we felt the financial need."

Heather sighed and shook her head. She propped her left elbow up on the window ledge of her door and began to massage the back of her neck. Steve waited quietly for her to continue, knowing that she was sharing something very important but not at all sure why.

"Dad worked in the prison for almost fifteen years. He never was able to make more than just enough to get by. Not because he wasn't capable but because he was devoted to serving God and others. When he died last year, his health was broken and so was his wallet."

She sighed again and shook her head. "I admired my dad more than any other man I've ever known. That's why I resented you making all that money just for playing football."

Steve wanted to sink through the seat and disappear. Heather was bringing up the bane of his existence, the irrationality of the astronomical sum he received to play a game, but she wasn't done with her story.

"I had a hard time understanding how a man could make that kind of money for a silly game. You play with a graceful power that's beautiful to behold, but still ... millions of dollars a year? And my dad didn't even get a salary as a prison chaplain. He had to go out and beg for every dollar of his support. It's not right."

She was correct, it wasn't right. Steve felt guilt rise with every word she spoke. He began to massage his temples with his left hand splayed across his face, hoping she wouldn't see the effect her words were having on him.

"I was angry that my family so loved to watch you play football, even while we were watching my dad die. I felt bad that *he* loved watching you play football. Then my two youngest brothers came back from the prayer breakfast before the Superstar Game, talking about you. And they kept talking about you."

Heather glanced over at her passenger who looked like he was trying to shrink his big body into a little ball. She was shocked that her words were having such a powerful effect on this world-renowned athlete.

"Hey man, no shame! I'm so sorry. I am so bad at this!" She slapped the steering wheel. "I should have started with the end. You made a real difference with my brothers. Dad was wasting away from the cancer, and Tim and Robert were starting to act out in school, cutting classes, not doing homework, all that kine stuff. But they came home from that prayer breakfast talking all, 'Jeremiah told us about his dad being an alcoholic. We sure have been blessed to have our dad.' And 'Jeremiah said it's important to do the right thing and do it well.' They kept talking about you and I was ticked off because Dad had been saying those kine things for years and they hadn't listened to *him*."

Heather gave a little laugh and shook her head. "Dad told me to lighten up, that's just the way some people are. Even he had to hear 'fatherly' advice from someone other than Grandpa before it sunk in. He told me that you were using your God-given talents in a mission field of your own."

Steve grunted in disbelief, and Heather laughed outright.

"That's exactly the noise I made when he said that! But he was right. I've heard it from other boys and their parents too. And I've learned about some of the other things you do, helping people with your money instead of using it all on yourself."

Steve stared out his window for a moment, then he harrumphed and turned to face her. "So why don't you like me?"

"It's not that I don't like you," Heather began to blush. "I just don't know how to act around you. You confuse me because you aren't what I'd come to expect when I was angry and yet you aren't quite the hero far above us all either. You actually seem likeable, but I don't want to gush all over you like some crazy fan."

"Gushing isn't all that bad," Steve said dryly.

"I'm sure it's better than being pummeled, huh?" She grinned sheepishly.

"Quite a bit better, actually," he agreed emphatically.

"Seriously, I'm sorry," Heather slowed the truck to make the right turn into the garage. "I didn't mean to make you feel bad. What you do is good, very good. You're doing God's work."

"Thank you," Steve gave her a small smile. "I appreciate your honesty."

"Not everyone does," Heather shrugged, "maybe because I don't often communicate it kindly."

"Yeah, you might want to work on that," Steve said dryly.

"I'll start today," Heather laughed. "Why don't you go in and have Malia help you get your car rental arranged while I drop your car and get it queued up? Then I'll give you a ride to get your rental."

"Sounds like a plan," Steve agreed.

When Heather left the truck, Steve sat for a few moments, taking some deep breaths. That was quite a story. This stranger had waltzed into his life and quickly touched him in a way no one had done since his grandma died.

Lord, am I really doing your work? Am I stewarding your resources wisely? Are you pleased with me?

He didn't get an answer, but then he hadn't really expected one. Maybe God was talking to him in another way. Steve sent up another prayer for guidance as he climbed out of the truck.

Chapter 3

I've got good news and bad news," Steve smiled at Heather when she entered the office a short time later.

"Start with the good news," she sighed.

"They can give me a man-sized car."

"Very good. We wouldn't want you crammed into an economy-sized toy car." She gave some papers to Malia and turned to face him. "What's the bad news?"

"It won't be available until after three, so you're stuck with me for four hours."

"Four hours!" Heather frowned. "I can't have you hanging around the shop for four hours. No one will get any work done. What am I going to do with you?"

"Having lunch would be great," Steve sighed. "I'm hungry but I have no wheels, so if you don't want to do lunch I guess I won't be having it until after three."

"You do need to have lunch," Malia suggested helpfully to Heather, "and it won't hurt you to take a few hours off."

"We both need to have lunch," Steve said hopefully.

Heather had to smile a little at his imploring attitude. It reminded her of her young nephews. She studied him for a moment. He really did seem like a nice enough guy. She wouldn't see him again after he picked up his car, so she supposed a few hours with him couldn't hurt.

"Let me wash my hands and get out of these coveralls, and your wish is my command."

Watching her walk toward the back room, Steve began to grin. As if sensing his thoughts, Heather turned and shook her finger at him.

"Within reason," she arched her eyebrows. "I have veto power."

She turned and took two more steps, then turned back again.

"Oh Malia," she said, "feel free to gush and ask for an autograph!"

Steve saw the twinkle in her eye as she turned again and disappeared behind the closed door.

"Oh wow!" Malia, Heather's cousin and receptionist, did indeed gush. "You're really here. Steve Jeremiah of the Grizzlies. You touched my desk. I'll never work anywhere else now that I've seen you in this office. Can I have your autograph?"

"I'll be happy to," Steve turned his most dazzling smile on the exuberant young woman. "Do you have paper and a pen?"

"Oh, oh! Yeah, yeah, yeah," Malia fumbled around on her desk, giving a cry of triumph as she came up with a pink sticky pad and a green pen.

"Please tell me you will never show this to anyone else," Steve held the pink pad rather gingerly.

"Oh! Right!" Malia snatched the pink pad away and thrust a yellow one at him. She sighed. "Sorry about that."

Steve wrote a quick note and handed the pad back to her. Malia read it aloud with a sigh.

"'Malia, your smile warms my heart, Steve Jeremiah, #95.'" She sighed a very gushy sigh and clasped the pad to her breast with both hands. "I'll smile for you any day, Steve!"

"I said you could gush, not drool," Heather said drolly as she strode into the room.

"She wasn't –"

Steve's mind went blank when he turned and saw his mechanic. She did have curves in all the right places!

Without her coveralls, cap and sunglasses, she was obviously feminine. Delightfully so. It was embarrassing to think he'd even for a moment mistaken her for a boy.

Her hair was still pinned up for work, but Steve could now see that it was glossy black, probably long and curly too. She was dressed simply in a black t-shirt and shorts that flattered her figure without being too clingy and revealing. Her legs were very long and well-muscled like a biker or a dancer. Because she wore flip-flops, he could see that she had toe rings. Four of them. Her eyes were hazel, tending a little more toward green and they were suddenly curious under arched brows.

"You have a problem with my slippers?" Heather lifted her shapely right leg and wiggled her foot. "What's wrong with my prom slippers?"

"Look who's drooling now," Malia muttered under her breath, just loud enough for Steve to hear. He tried not to blush.

"Prom slippers? What?" Steve ran his hand through his hair. "No, no. It's not your flip-flops, it's your toe rings. I've never seen so many. Never seen any, come to think about it."

"Malihini," Heather rolled her eyes at her cousin and sighed. "If you're going to spend the off season in Hawaii, you're going to have to learn some culture, malihini."

Malia giggled and nodded vigorously in agreement.

"Mala-whatie?" Steve looked from one grinning woman to the other.

"Mah-lee-hee-nee," Malia pronounced it distinctly.

"Newcomer." Steve didn't miss Heather's slightly disparaging tone. "If you've been driving that BMW on the roads of Oahu for a year, you should know a little something about the place where you've been driving it."

"About that," Steve ran his hand through his hair again and had the grace to look sheepish at being caught in his exaggeration. "You know I haven't actually been driving it that much since I was on the Mainland for the last eight months."

"Oh really?" Heather smiled wickedly, acknowledging that she'd caught him. "Did you hang around with any kamaaina last year?"

"Kama-whata?" Malia giggled again and Heather rolled her eyes.

"Kamaaina. Locals. Obviously not," Heather shook her head.

"Not really," Steve looked down at the floor. "I pretty much hung around the house, getting settled in, lounging in my pool and healing up."

"Oh that's right!" Malia gasped in sympathy. "You had some ribs cracked in the Championship Game when you got hit with that illegal block."

Steve smiled at her sympathy.

"And bruised your ego when you lost the game," Heather smirked.

"Thanks for the reminder," Steve's heavy sigh was only partly to make Heather feel guilty for her remark. It did still hurt that he had made it into the Championship Game and lost.

Heather eyed him skeptically, not sure how serious his apparent pain was, but Malia was full of sympathy.

"Heather, that's so mean," Malia stood and frowned at her cousin with fists planted firmly on her hips.

Heather caught Steve's small smile as he snuck a look at her without rising from his dejected pose. She rolled her eyes and stepped forward, grabbing his arm and shushing her cousin.

"First lesson, malihini," she said as she dragged him out the door, "these are slippers, not flip-flops and not thongs. These particular ones are rubber, hence they are 'rubber slippers.' Even the drug store ad says so. This pair happens to be my 'prom slippers,' relatively new and gently used. After lunch, we'll stop and get you a pair."

"Where are we going for lunch?" Steve was willing to have Hawaiian culture lessons, but first things first.

"You buying?"

"Of course."

"Good," Heather smiled as she led him toward a very old BMW. "'Cause I only have five bucks on me. If I was buying, it was going to be hot dogs and soda at Costco."

"Are we riding in that?" The car could probably be green but it was badly faded and had countless rust spots so he couldn't be sure. Steve had serious thoughts about not being caught dead in such a vehicle.

"Relax," Heather grinned as she opened the driver's door. "I'm a mechanic. It runs like a dream and the front seats are almost as good as yours."

"Why does the outside look like the car should be in a junk yard?" Steve glared suspiciously over the roof of the car, crossing his arms over his chest in an obvious refusal to touch the door handle.

"Look, I've only had the car a few months," Heather shook her head. "First things first. Mechanically, it's better than your car right now."

"That remains to be seen," Steve scowled.

"Get in and you'll see," Heather followed her own advice and slipped into the car. Steve bent down to glare at her, arms still crossed.

"Where are we going?" He raised his voice to be heard through the closed window.

"I know this great sushi place," was the muffled reply.

Steve jerked the door open and leaned in with his left arm on the roof of the car.

"You did *not* just say sushi, did you?" He glared at her.

"You don't like sushi?" She looked at him with innocent eyes.

"I've never had sushi and I'm not sure that I'm ready for raw fish." Thinking about eating a catfish raw, Steve shuddered. Gross.

"Sushi is not raw fish, that's sashimi," Heather smiled sweetly, "but we'll save that for another time. You like shrimp?"

"I love shrimp."

"Then Bubba Gump it is. Get in and let's go." She waved her right arm to encourage him to get into the car.

"What's Bubba Gump?" Steve asked as he slid into the car.

"Bubba Gump Shrimp Company. It's Forrest Gump's restaurant."

"Really," Steve paused with his seatbelt halfway across his chest. "That's a real place, not just something from a movie?"

"Very real, delicious, and fun for a movie buff," Heather wagged her hand for him to hurry up. "Get your seatbelt on so we can go. My mouth is watering just thinking about it."

Steve clicked his seatbelt and jerked in surprise.

"You have a dog," he said, noticing the canine net for the first time.

"Brilliant deduction Sherlock." Heather rolled her eyes as she turned to look over her shoulder as she backed the car. "What was your first clue?"

"The dog net, of course," Steve grinned proudly. "What do you have, a Rottweiler?"

"Nope."

"A pit bull?"

"Wrong again."

"A bull dog?"

She shook her head.

"German shepherd?"

"Fourth down turnover."

"You have a Chihuahua!" Steve feigned shock. "What kind of junk yard has a Chihuahua?"

"First off," Heather frowned. "I don't have a junk yard. I have an auto repair shop. They are vastly different. I don't deal with junk."

"Present car excepted," Steve snorted.

"Present car *not* excepted," Heather patted the dashboard. "Don't you listen to him, sweetie. You aren't junk, you were just abused."

"I stand corrected," Steve tried not to let her lighthearted comment drag him back to a time when he was trying to learn that he wasn't junk, just abused.

"With a little TLC, she'll be better than she ever was before." Heather's tone was gentle, as if she knew his hidden pain. If her brothers had read all about him and told her what they'd read, maybe she did.

"She's already come a long way." Steve knew he was talking about himself as well as the car. "You were right about her running better than my car right now."

"And she'll be even better in the coming months," Heather smiled softly.

And so will I, Steve sent up a silent prayer. *Thank you, Lord, for the reminder that you aren't done with me yet.*

"But," Steve took the conversation back into safer territory, "your Chihuahua will still be a Chihuahua!"

"No, he won't," Heather raised her chin haughtily, "because my Chihuahua is actually a Golden Retriever."

"You have a Golden!" Steve was delighted. Grandma's Golden had given him many great memories in a very sad childhood. "What's his name?"

"Moose," Heather laughed. "My nephew was learning his animals when I got Moose. Every furry four-legged animal was 'moose' to him, so it kind of stuck."

"How old is he?"

"My nephew or my dog?" Heather asked.

"Both!" Steve grinned. "Start with the dog, but you may as well tell me what the moose lover's name is too."

"Moose just turned three," Heather did a quick mental calculation, "so that means that Germy is almost five now."

"Germy?" Steve looked horrified. "What kind of parents give a child a name like 'Germy'?"

"Microbiologists," Heather said smugly.

"You're kidding, right?" Steve was shocked. "Please tell me you aren't serious!"

"I'm not," she laughed. "His parents named him Jeremy but his big brother, only two years older, dubbed him Germy."

"And that stuck too," Steve sighed with relief.

"Yeah, so I guess Moose was a kind of pay-it-forward thing," Heather smiled brightly.

"Good thing the dog can't escalate," Steve shook his head in wonder. "Seems like you have quite a family."

"I have a great family," Heather agreed. "My mom, four brothers, two nephews and a niephew on the way."

"What's a niephew? Is that another Hawaiian word?" Steve hadn't learned so many words in one day since he was in kindergarten.

"No, that's a mom word," Heather smiled with the memory. "Back in the dark ages, before it was easy to tell the gender of a baby before it was born, my mom made up the word combining niece and nephew. It was her verbal shorthand."

"And it stuck too," Steve grinned. "Lots of sticky things in your family."

"With two curtain climbers, you better believe it!"

"Your mom sounds cool." Steve glanced out his window as he struggled with the lump in his throat. "You're lucky to have her."

"You have no idea," Heather said softly, then remembered his orphaned state. "Oh I'm sorry. I guess you do, having lost your own."

"I keep forgetting that my life is an open book," Steve was a little embarrassed. "Is there anything you don't know about my life?"

"Everything Tim and Robert have read about you, they've shared with me. So no, I don't suppose there's anything I don't know."

"Does that mean you're as big a fan as they are?" Steve asked hopefully.

"I'm a big fan of the Grizzlies," Heather emphasized. "You're a side benefit."

"Ouch! There goes my ego!" Steve scrunched down in his seat and pretended to pout.

"Wow, that's really studly!" Heather laughed loudly. "If you're going to act like that, why bother having an ego?"

"Touché," Steve sat up and stretched his left arm across the back of the seat. He immediately realized that while it was much more comfortable, his hand was only inches from the nape of Heather's long, elegant neck. The temptation to touch her was great but he couldn't see a way to withdraw his arm without being obvious about his sudden attraction.

"Since you already know everything there is to know about me, let's talk about you," Steve said. "Why do you have a Golden Retriever instead of a junk yard dog?"

"Watch it, mister," Heather glared. "You're treading on thin ice."

"Yes ma'am," Steve acted properly chastised, "but seriously, why the Golden?"

"Moose is a therapy dog," Heather said.

"A therapy dog? I'm impressed."

"Don't be," Heather sighed. "I got him for purely selfish reasons."

"Oh? What are they?"

Heather frowned and shook her head slightly, more to herself than to him. She suddenly became very interested in the traffic, too interested to answer his question.

Steve's curiosity was really piqued now. There was a real story there but she had just shut down, blocking him like a superstar offensive lineman protecting the quarterback. He'd figure out some way around the block. He always did.

Chapter 4

*S*teve surrendered his fork and leaned back in his chair, stretching his legs out and sighing contentedly. "This was a great lunch. Thank you for bringing me here."

"Even though you flunked the Forrest Gump quiz?"

"Even with that," he nodded.

"I can't believe you forgot Forrest played football," Heather snickered.

"An inconsequential game for fools," Steve replied haughtily, eliciting a hearty laugh from his companion.

"Well I wouldn't go that far," Heather smiled into her Speckled Lemonade. "The game's not really inconsequential!"

"But it is for fools?"

"I didn't say it, you did."

"But you didn't have to agree," Steve smiled across the table and found himself wishing he had the right to hold the hand that was playing nervously with her glass.

"Ah, but I'm a painfully honest woman, remember?" Heather blushed as she ducked her head and looked at Steve through her thick, smoky eyelashes.

"How could I forget?" Steve replied with a heavy sigh and a sad, slow shake of his head. "You're a cruel, cruel woman."

"But I can make up for it by helping you look local," she smiled brightly. Too brightly. He wasn't sure he trusted her.

"What're you going to do to me now?" Steve asked cautiously.

"We're already at the shopping center," she replied pertly, "and you still have over two hours before you can get your rental car. No time like the present to get you some rubber slippers, board shorts, and a couple aloha shirts."

"Whoa there, little filly," Steve drawled, "this Kansas boy doesn't need anything but his t-shirt, jeans and boots."

"*If* you were still a Kansas farm boy that would be acceptable," Heather corrected him, "but you're not in Kansas anymore, Toto. You're now an island boy. You can't run around here dressed like a Kansan. Besides you're not even wearing boots, you have on jogging shoes."

"Nope, no way." Steve crossed his arms very firmly over his broad chest, tucking his hands in and compressing his lips like a little boy rejecting broccoli.

"Yep, yeah way," Heather leaned across the table, challenging him by pushing into his space. "It's what Pete Kalaau wears when he's on Oahu."

"Yeah, but that's Pete." Steve knew he was going to lose this one, but he was going to take it to the fourth down before turning it over.

"Malihini," Heather hissed.

Okay, maybe he'd punt instead of turning the ball over on downs.

"I get veto power?" he asked hopefully.

"Only on the *specific* item," Heather grinned as she stood, "but I'm telling you what types of things you need."

ALL TOO SOON, Steve found himself downstairs in a clothing shop filled with a bewildering array of aloha wear. Heather flew through the store, shaking her head and grumbling about the selection of material. Before he could actually focus on a pattern long enough to see what was in it, she was already out the door.

"Wait," Steve followed hot on her heels. "I thought we were going to get me some aloha shirts."

"We are, but not from there," Heather sniffed disdainfully. "Those are all much too 'old man.' You need something bolder."

"Define 'bolder,'" Steve said cautiously.

"You'll see when we find it," Heather smiled smugly.

"It" was indeed bold. Two stores later, Heather finally found ones that she liked. He was doubtful about the three shirts, one black, one navy blue and one a bold orange. All three had large leaves and flowers and something he was pretty sure was supposed to be leis splashed across them. When he tried them on, he wasn't sure until he saw the approval in Heather's eyes when he stepped out to model them for her. Oh yeah, he was getting these, and wearing them. But the board shorts and rubber slippers?

"Do you know how *white* my legs are?" Steve whispered to Heather when she started sorting through the board shorts.

"Do you know that you have a secluded backyard with a swimming pool?" she whispered back. "Hang out there until you're decent enough to be seen in public."

"But why?" Steve tried to repress the whine that wanted to come out with his plea.

"Because I said so," Heather said with an amazingly straight face.

"But I don't wanna," Steve let the whine out.

"Malihini," Heather hissed.

"You know that's not going to work for long," Steve glowered.

"I know. But it works today, doesn't it?"

"Okay, okay. But I'm *not* trying these on here," Steve growled. "Just get me what you want in a size you think will fit. If it doesn't, I'll donate it to the Salvation Army."

Steve also refused to take off his shoes to try on rubber slippers, so when they finally headed back to the car, he had three aloha shirts that definitely fit, and four board shorts and two pair of slippers that might fit.

As they strolled along, Steve was trying hard not to think about what Heather would do if he held her hand. She suddenly stopped in the middle of the sidewalk.

"What's up?" Steve looked quizzically at her.

"Is that weird for you?" She nodded at the window of the store they were standing in front of.

"Is what weird?" Steve turned and saw the jersey in the window of the sports store. His jersey. "Yeah, that's weird. But not as weird as seeing myself walk away from me."

He nodded toward a rather large man who had just passed them wearing a Grizzlies' ninety-five jersey.

"Let's get out of here before someone puts two and two together," Steve took Heather's arm and practically dragged her down the walkway.

"Lighten up and don't be so obvious," Heather pulled her arm from his grip. "Act naturally and they're less likely to focus on you long enough to connect the dots."

Steve looked askance at her. "It almost sounds like you've had some experience."

"Does it?" she replied curtly as she walked purposefully past him. Why did she have to say that? She didn't want to talk about her past with him.

She was definitely hiding something, and Steve was getting that feeling he sometimes had. There was something God wanted to do here. He wasn't sure what was going on, but he did know that he needed to get her to talk. He caught up with her quickly and grabbed her arm again, pulling her toward the food court.

"How about some dessert?" he said as he hauled her over toward an ice cream counter.

"I don't want any," she tried to snatch her arm out of his grip but this time he wasn't letting go.

"Sure you do," Steve stopped and smiled with narrowed eyes, "and if you don't, I'm going to make sure that everyone notices us."

"Why?" she challenged.

"Because I want to know what you're hiding," Steve replied softly but firmly.

"What makes you think I'm hiding anything?"

"I'm not stupid, Heather," Steve said softly. "I know the signs. I once had secrets too."

"I guess it's only fair," Heather grumbled with poor grace. "Since I know all your pain you may as well know mine. Fine. Give me the bags. I want something with lots of chocolate. I'll be over there."

HEATHER FOUND A seat at one of the few two-seater tables in the food court and sat so she could watch Steve as he waited in line at the ice cream counter. How had she let the man get under her skin so quickly? She wasn't exactly a private person but neither did she dive right into relationships like she had today.

Not that she was calling this a relationship. It wasn't. It wouldn't, couldn't be. But somehow Steve Jeremiah was turning out to be a man who was much too likeable and she was having a hard time keeping him out. He made her want to think about possibilities, made her want to trust him. Maybe it was the shock of seeing her number one hero sitting on the wall at the blowhole, waiting for *her* to rescue him. He was certainly turning out to be everything she had imagined, and then some.

It had to be the confusion over whether to admire or resent him. Steve was stressing her and she always tended to speak without thinking clearly when she was stressed. It was as simple as that. He wasn't really getting under her skin. She was simply stressed and therefore talking too much. She wasn't starting a relationship after just a few hours with the man, especially since she'd started off so poorly. When he picked up his car later this week, she'd be done with him, so she'd just take today as it came.

He was so much more gorgeous in real life, Heather acknowledged to herself as he headed her way with the tray of ice cream easily handled by one very large hand. Those eyes made her think about laying on her back in the sand on a warm summer day, staring up into the blue, blue Hawaii sky. His hair was a brown so dark it was almost black and it was thick with just a hint of a curl. And he was so very big. She had known he was six foot eight. Greg had given her that stat years ago, but it had become real today when he stood beside her and towered over her own six foot frame. No one but her older brother Luke and her dad had ever come close to making her feel that small. Actually, even they hadn't because Steve was much broader, so well-muscled. Heather stifled a sigh as he sat across from her. Why was she wondering how it would feel to slip her hand into the warm safety of his very capable hands?

"Ah! Chocolate smothered in hot fudge," Heather pretended her sigh was only over the chocolate delight Steve place before her.

Steve stretched his very long legs along the outside of the table, effectively but not subtly blocking her in. Obviously he wasn't going to let her slide.

Heather ate a couple bites of her sundae before she realized that Steve wasn't eating his. He was just staring at her, waiting.

"I'll talk," she sighed again. "Eat your ice cream before it melts."

Steve picked up his spoon and waited expectantly. Heather wrinkled her nose and started talking.

"It really isn't a big secret. You could actually Google me and find out everything for yourself." Heather said hopefully.

"The details maybe, but not why it bothers you so much," Steve motioned with his spoon for her to go on.

"Okay, you asked for it," Heather fortified herself with another bite of chocolate. "I went into the Army shortly after high school. I was a wheeled vehicle mechanic because I love the work."

Heather scooped up another spoonful of ice cream, half hoping that Steve would comment so she could get sidetracked. He just smiled enigmatically and deliberately filled his mouth with another spoonful of his sundae.

"To make a long story short," Heather sighed, "my third tour of duty I got stationed back here in Hawaii and soon found myself in the sandy desert instead of on sandy beaches."

A quick glance at Steve revealed a flicker of sympathy in his eyes. He guessed where this was going. She took a deep breath and dove deeply into her story.

"It was supposed to be a routine pickup. A convoy had been attacked a few days earlier and two vehicles were left behind. Intel said the area was free of enemy activity and we were cleared to retrieve the disabled vehicles. Intel was wrong. We had just headed back to base when we came under enemy fire. We were lucky to make it back alive. I was wounded."

Heather took another deep breath, pushing down memories of the sound of gunfire and men and women screaming, the smell of gunpowder and blood, the searing pain and rising panic. A large warm hand covered her suddenly cold one. The war receded into the distance when she looked into the deep blue pools of sympathy staring at her from across the suddenly too small table.

"I'm sorry," Steve murmured softly. "I didn't realize."

"It's okay," Heather reluctantly pulled her hand from beneath his and picked her spoon up again. "My counselor says that talking about it some is good. That's how I'll break its power over me."

"There's more, isn't there?" Steve picked up his spoon too. They both fortified themselves before Heather resumed her story.

"Since my injuries were serious enough to prevent me from returning to combat duty," Heather continued, "they eventually shipped me back to Hawaii. My command made me out to be a hero and since I was both kamaaina and stationed at Schofield Barracks, I became a local media sensation."

Steve grimaced in sympathy.

"So suddenly strangers knew who I was," Heather shook her head, "and I heard hundreds of people telling me how I was a hero. They made all those brilliant observations about how tall I am, what a role model I am for women, how proud they were, yada-yada."

"I get the picture," Steve saluted her with a spoonful of ice cream.

"I know you do. But it gets even better," Heather swallowed and blinked, trying to control the tears that threatened. "This was the same time my dad's cancer came back. Some enterprising reporter found out and decided it made a good human interest story."

Steve winced and shook his head. "You mean, 'Wounded War Hero Watches Father Die' stuff?"

"Pretty much," Heather nodded, "and they went on and on. So then Dad and I both got it, especially when we were together. They played out Dad's cancer and my struggles to recover for everyone to see. Soon we began to get the well-meaning Christians who wanted to pray for us, as if we couldn't or wouldn't pray for ourselves."

At Steve's frown, Heather amended her statement.

"It's not that we didn't need or want other people's prayers," Heather scraped up the last of her sundae. "It's the way they would talk. Some of them acted like we had some secret sin blocking our prayers. Or there were the comments like 'Do you believe that God can heal anything?' or 'By his stripes you are healed.' My dad was a *minister* for more than thirty years and they acted like we knew nothing about God and prayer."

"They meant well," Steve reached across the table and once again covered her cold, trembling hand with his warm, solid one.

She took strength from his comforting touch and smiled tremulously. "I know, but that didn't make it hurt less."

"Listening to your story," Steve directed his frown at the table. "I feel like my worries and pressures are so petty and unreal."

"Oh no, Steve," Heather stacked her right hand on his. "They're very real and not petty at all. I can't begin to imagine how much it hurt to lose the Championship Game. I'm a fan. I watched the game and it hurt to lose. It must have been agonizing for you, pouring your heart out on the field and still coming up short."

"Yeah, but it isn't life and death like you faced," Steve shook his head in disagreement. "It's just a game."

Heather stared at him and suddenly all her earlier confusion washed away. Steve Jeremiah was so much like her father, humble and devoted to God. She knew that he financially supported men and women of God in their ministries but he was also a minister of the gospel in his own right, touching broken lives and pointing them back to Christ. Somehow she had to make him see that.

"No, it's not just a game," Heather leaned forward and passionately pled her case. "It might be for some professional athletes but not for you. You've taken a part of our culture and used it for God's glory. Sure there's no eternal significance to who won the Championship Game any given year but you have bartered your fame from playing to become something of great significance."

In her earnest desire to encourage Steve, Heather was oblivious to the fact that she was narrowing the gap between them.

"On the field, you play with a rare combination of skill, speed, raw talent and heart that gets people's attention," she fiercely defended his life, "and off the field you live with an intentional moral goodness that inspires people because you got their attention on the field. You use that attention to point them to Jesus. You plant seeds of eternal life in countless young people's lives. What you do has much more eternal significance then me saving a handful of lives over in Iraq. Your life isn't petty."

Steve stared into hazel eyes that flared green with passion. Suddenly he was fully cognizant of the fact that her lips were mere inches from his and he desperately wanted to kiss those lips.

Heather realized the precarious position her passion had placed her in. Quickly she snatched her hands away from Steve's and sat back.

"I think we should go get your rental car now." For a moment she looked wildly around her, trying to gather her equilibrium again. "What did I do with my purse?"

"You didn't bring a purse," Steve laughed gently as he stood with the tray.

When he returned from dumping their rubbish, Steve took the bags from Heather and offered her his arm. She ignored the offered arm and stalked out of the food court in front of him. If she had been a cat, her tail would have been twitching furiously.

It was going to be a challenge getting to know this woman but she was definitely worth the effort.

Chapter 5

*B*y Saturday morning, Steve was doubly sure that Heather Shepherd was worth the challenge of getting to know her and that it was going to be twice as hard as he had first thought.

He had looked her up on the internet on Thursday evening and discovered that she left out a good chunk of the story. She hadn't just been made out to be a hero, she had been nominated for the Medal of Honor.

The reports said that when her small retrieval convoy had come under fire, Sergeant Heather Shepherd had taken charge of the machine gun on one of her disabled vehicles. She provided covering fire while the eight soldiers in her squad, five wounded, three seriously, took cover, trying to save the lives of the wounded while waiting for a helo extraction team to pick them up. Only after all her team members were safe did she leave her post.

She received her first wound in the first round of gunfire, a flesh wound to her upper right arm. Then she was also wounded in her left side and hip. The last wound, nearly fatal, she received as she was running to the extraction helo. The round pierced her left shoulder at an angle just right to slide under her body armor and do some serious damage.

If she received the Medal of Honor, she would be the first living recipient in the Iraqi Conflict and only the second woman to ever receive it. They hadn't made her out to be a hero, she was the genuine article.

And she was avoiding him.

On Friday evening, just before six, Malia had called and told him his car would be ready by ten in the morning.

"Come on down," she had sung cheerfully into the phone. "Someone will drive your rental back for you."

He had hoped that "someone" would be Heather, but no such luck. Apparently she was much too busy to do more than give him a nod from the maintenance bay. Instead, a young man built like a linebacker met him in the office. He was Heather's younger brother Greg and he was willing to take the car back.

"Only thing, brah," he seemed a little chagrined to ask, "can you give me a ride after we pau? I got no wheels down there."

"I think I can do that," Steve agreed cautiously, "if you'll tell me what 'pow' is supposed to mean."

Malia giggled behind him and Greg grinned.

"Sorry, brah," Greg smirked. "I forgot you one malihini. Pau, spelled p-a-u, is done. Finished. Kaput."

"I'm beginning to think I need some foreign language classes," Steve ran a hand through his hair, "and I'm still in America. Go figure."

They all laughed. Greg promised to be ready in a minute or two, so Steve found himself standing by Malia's desk, wondering if he should talk to her or pick up a magazine and have a seat. The door opening behind him solved that question.

Steve turned hoping that it was Heather. Instead it was two very tall youths who appeared to be in their mid teens. They looked vaguely familiar. They also looked nervous.

"Ask him, Tim," the younger one poked the older one in the back. "Go on."

"Quit pushin'," the older one snapped back.

"Ask what?" Steve grinned, suspecting these were the youngest brothers Heather had mentioned before.

"Will you sign our pictures?" Tim asked. Both boys thrust pictures at him. Tim had a Sharpie marker in his other hand.

Steve took the picture from Tim and smiled. The prayer breakfast last year. Now that he saw the pictures he even remembered these particular boys. There had been something so sad about them, even though they were very excited to meet professional football players.

He squinted at the picture and tried to clarify the memory. Lost in thought, he sat on the corner of Malia's desk.

"During breakfast, you asked me," Steve pointed at Tim, "how I kept my faith in the locker room. And you," he looked at the younger boy, "you're Robert. You were concerned because I have no family."

Steve remembered how touched he'd been by the boy's genuine concern for his loneliness. Most teenaged boys wouldn't have even realized that he was alone, much less been concerned about it.

"You remember us," Robert stepped up and sat next to him on the desk.

"Of course I remember," Steve looked into eyes that were a whole lot like Heather's. "I had breakfast with you."

"But there were a dozen other guys at our table," Tim said in awe.

"And it was over a year ago," Robert said.

"And you meet a lot of people," Malia was standing at his right elbow.

"But you guys reached me here," Steve tapped his chest right over his heart. "I recognized something of me in you that day."

Greg joined the others, awed that this multi-million dollar, superstar football player was touched by their average lives.

"I didn't know at the time but Heather told me the other day that your dad was dying at this time," Steve swallowed hard, pushing back tears. "You were hopeful, fearful, resigned, just like I was."

Steve closed his eyes and sighed.

"You were what, thirteen, fourteen?" He looked at Robert who nodded. "That's the same age I was when my father died. The circumstances were vastly different but the emotions weren't."

He stared down at the picture of him with his arm around Tim who was grinning broadly. He knew with sudden clarity that Tim was still struggling with his father's death. He felt that particular nudge from the Lord telling him that he had a connection with the teen, an understanding that could give him comfort. He prayed that God would direct his words.

Most of the story they'd already heard since it had been part of his testimony at the prayer breakfast – his father's alcoholism and abuse, his death when Steve was still a teen. He didn't keep those things secret, knowing that many young people would be encouraged by his triumph over those things, encouraged to break the cycle in their lives too. But there was a part that few people knew. That still small voice was telling him that Tim needed to hear it.

"I kept on hoping that the old man would change but I feared he wouldn't. When my sister ran away, something broke in me and I resigned myself to the loss of a normal life. Then my father died and I was angry. Angry at Mom, angry at my sister, at Dad, at God, but mostly I was angry at myself. I thought that if I hadn't given up hope, my dad would have changed and lived."

The silence rang loud when Steve finished speaking.

"You do know," Tim whispered, looking down as he blinked away tears.

"But I was wrong," Steve bent down to make contact with the boy's downcast eyes. "I was wrong to be angry at anyone, even myself."

Tim lifted hopeful eyes and Steve again heard that whisper in his ear. He knew that Tim too felt guilty about his father's death.

"My father didn't change because he didn't know any other way of life and he didn't care anymore. That's why he got drunk, got in that car and thought he could beat a train. My lack of hope didn't contribute to his death in any way."

Steve stood and put his hand on Tim's shoulder.

"Your dad died because he got cancer and God called him home," Steve spoke softly and firmly. "He did not die because you got angry at him for being sick. Your anger did not contribute to his death in any way."

Tim's eyes filled with tears and he pressed his lips together tightly. A sob bubbled up and his shoulders shook. Steve stepped up and wrapped the boy in a warm embrace. Tears ran down his own cheeks as he held the sobbing boy.

Suddenly other arms were embracing them.

Greg's voice rose in prayer. "Father, thank you for sending this man of God to speak healing words into my little brother's life. You are indeed an awesome God and I'm amazed anew that you care enough about us to set answers in motion even before we know enough to ask for help."

With an amen of agreement, Steve released Tim and stepped back. Clearing his throat, he held up Tim's picture. "I'll autograph these on one condition."

"Sure. What's that?" they chorused.

"You have to promise to give me copies of these pictures."

"THAT WAS A really cool thing you did for my brothers," Greg told Steve after they had dropped off the rental car and were headed to Greg's mom's house. "You're the real deal, Steve Jeremiah."

"Thanks, but I think you all are the real real deal," Steve replied.

"Especially my sister, huh brah?" Greg said slyly.

"Especially your sister," Steve blushed. "She's pretty special."

"She'll be a tough nut to crack," Greg warned.

"Why's that?"

"Well first off, she's barely on speaking terms with God since Dad died. She hasn't been to church since the funeral almost a year ago."

"She hasn't lost her faith, has she?" Steve asked. "It didn't sound like it when we talked Thursday."

"No, she hasn't lost her faith," Greg sighed, "but she hasn't processed all the pain and loss of the last few years."

"This too shall pass," Steve suggested hopefully.

"Sure it will," Greg nodded, "but if you're wanting to court my sister, you've already been handicapped by a dozen or so idiots in her past."

"How's that?"

"She has decided that she isn't intended to ever marry."

"How did she come to that conclusion?"

"Well first there's the freshman punk she had a crush on. She signed up for auto shop because he was taking it and then she turned out to be a natural. She was at the head of her class, even helped him a time or two. He said she was a freak, not a real girl because girls can't be mechanics."

"He certainly was a punk but surely she's learned better since then," Steve suggested.

"Surely you jest," Greg snorted. "The guys in her mechanics' class in the Army didn't like her because she ended up being the distinguished honor grad. She can't help it that she loves to fix cars but guys have a hard time handling being rescued by a woman."

"She rescued me already," Steve said. "I'm not having a hard time with it. In fact I find it very attractive that she can keep my car running."

"She's also sworn off dating because she's had way too many guys ask her out only once because they didn't like the fact that she towered over them," Greg grinned. "She's freakishly tall, you know."

"No, I don't know," Steve grinned back. "Actually, I thought she was rather small."

"Then there's the cooking thing," Greg said. "My sister's idea of high cuisine is grilled cheese on wheat and a bowl of Campbell's Tomato Soup, made with milk of course."

"That's rather interesting," Steve laughed.

"I'm serious," Greg shook his head. "When we have family get-togethers, which we have just about every Sunday, she always brings green bean casserole because it's the only thing she can fix. She has the pizza place programmed into her cell phone so she won't starve."

"Amazing!"

"Amazing?" Greg snorted. "Every guy who hasn't dumped her because she's a mechanic or because she's freakishly tall, has dumped her when he found out she not only can't cook but she has no desire to learn."

"Amazing," Steve grinned as he pulled up in front of the house Greg pointed out to him. "Absolutely amazing, because she's the perfect woman for me."

"Get outta town!"

"I took home-ec in high school because I got to hang out with the girls," Steve laughed again. "Turns out they were all disgruntled when I was the best cook out of the whole bunch. I love to cook and I don't like anyone messing around in my kitchen."

"Brah, you have my permission to date my sister," Greg slapped him on the back. "If you can convince her."

"Any suggestions?" he asked.

"Yeah, come on in and meet Mom," Greg said. "She'll invite you to church and Sunday dinner and I'll be truly innocent when Heather asks me why I invited you."

"Sounds like a plan," Steve climbed out of the car and followed Greg in to meet Mom.

Chapter 6

*S*teve was as nervous as if he were on a first date. In a sense he was because he hoped this service would lead to a long-term family relationship, even if he never got the girl.

Yesterday, Mrs. Shepherd, or Aunty Gloria as she'd told him to call her, had insisted that he stay for lunch. She had gently grilled him about his Christian life.

His team bible study met with her approval as did his daily bible reading and journaling and also his Sabbath rest, but Aunty Gloria was not pleased with his church attendance policy here in Hawaii. He had a home church in Chicago which he attended as regularly as his profession allowed, but he didn't have one in Hawaii where he spent the offseason.

"I've been attending various larger churches," he had explained. "I generally slip into the back about ten minutes after the service starts and leave right after the message."

"Why would you do that?" Aunty Gloria frowned.

"Because I've found that my presence is usually a distraction," Steve shrugged. "I'm uncomfortable being the center of attention at church."

"For shame," she shook her finger at him. "You need a place to grow. You come to our church. You won't be the center of attention and you won't be a distraction more than a week or two."

So here he was, feeling very nervous about going to church. The strangeness was part of it. This church met in an elementary school cafeteria not a traditional church building. His attire was not what he would call traditional either. Though his aloha shirt and jeans weren't too bad, the rubber slippers where very strange. Since Heather had insisted he buy them and Greg had assured him that many of the men and women at church would be wearing them, he decided he might as well wear them too but it felt weird.

Most of his nervousness was about spending the day with the Shepherds. He truly liked Heather's family. They made him acutely aware of his loneliness but they offered a remedy at the same time. Even if his relationship with Heather never progressed beyond a simple friendship, he would still like to call this family his friends.

Halfway up the walkway, Tim and Robert met him with two small boys in tow. He greeted the teens with handshakes and one-armed hugs and squatted down to say hello to the little guys.

"You must be Matthew. I'm Steve." He offered his hand and the older boy shook it shyly.

"And you must be Jeremy." The younger brother didn't take his offered hand. Instead he reached up and tugged on Uncle Robert's arm.

"He don't look like one grizzly," Jeremy whispered loudly as Robert stooped to talk to him.

"He's a football Grizzly, Germy."

"I know that," the four year old rolled his eyes and sighed with disgust. "Where his helmet and his shirt?"

"I only wear them when I'm playing football, Jeremy," Steve smothered his laughter. "The rest of the time I look like any other guy."

"No you don't," Matt said solemnly. "You're a giant like my daddy and Uncle Greg."

"I am kind of big, aren't I?" Steve struggled to keep a straight face. "But I won't hurt you."

"Giants don't hurt little boys," Jeremy told him. "They give them horsey rides. Will you give me a horsey ride?"

"Jeremy, you know better than to ask before it's been offered," a deep voice spoke above them. Steve smiled at the man who must be Heather's older brother Luke whom he'd heard about yesterday at Aunty Gloria's.

"Your daddy's right," he told Jeremy, "but I'm offering now. Only how about we wait until we get to your grandma's house later today?"

"You going to Grandma's?" Jeremy asked excitedly.

"She invited me to lunch," Steve assured him, "and I hate to turn down dates with pretty ladies."

Jeremy frowned at him. "You going out with Aunty Heather?"

Steve quickly stood up and looked heavenward, hoping the little boy wouldn't see the grin that split his face or notice how his uncles were shaking with suppressed laughter.

Luke was much more adept at maintaining a straight face around his sons, so he quickly scooped up Jeremy and took Matt by the hand, heading back into the building.

"He was talking about Grandma, not Aunty Heather. Don't you think Grandma is pretty?"

"Yeah, but she's old!" Jeremy said as they disappeared into the cafeteria.

Steve looked at Tim and Robert and all three howled with laughter. Steve leaned against the support post for the walkway awning as the teens' laughter fueled his own. They also leaned against the post, one on either side of him, shoulders touching his arms.

The camaraderie touched Steve deeply. A sudden longing to permanently have this in his life curtailed his laughter. He dropped his arms across the teens' shoulders and pushed away from the post. "Come on guys, let's go see if we can find the pretty lady."

"She probably won't be here," Tim choked on his laughter.

"So we better just look for Mom," Robert finished for him.

If Steve had wanted to enter church unnoticed, he failed miserably because their laughter preceded them. Everyone turned to look but the Shepherds had obviously primed everyone for his arrival. No one pointed, stared, or whispered, but everyone came over to shake his hand and welcome him. No one asked his name.

After meeting a seemingly endless parade of people whose names he could not remember, Tim and Robert finally led him to where the other Shepherds sat.

"We have to sit in the back row," Robert said proudly. "One day when Pastor had one of the elders preach, he sat back here and realized we block everyone's view when we sit up front, so he banished us to the back row."

Steve looked at the teens and for the first time realized how big they were for their age. Tim was sixteen and Robert wasn't quite fifteen and both of them were well over six feet. Tim was already almost as tall as Greg.

"You are pretty big. You just might end up bigger than me," Steve grinned.

"You think so," Robert stood a little taller and grinned at his brother.

"I don't expect to be able to call either of you 'little' brother much longer," Greg agreed with Steve.

"But I'll always be able to take you down, no matter how big you get," Luke assured his youngest brothers, then looked right at Greg. "All of you."

"In your dreams," Greg grumbled.

"In your nightmares," Luke shot back.

"I'll give you nightmares," Greg threatened.

"When and where?" Luke demanded.

"Mom's just as soon as you drag your chicken self on over there after church."

"You're on."

"Alright! Royal Rumble," Tim grinned.

"Clash of the titans," Robert high-fived his brother.

"This I gotta see," declared Steve.

IT TURNED OUT he didn't just "see" the clash of the titans, he was one of the titans!

Steve was pretty sure that the message had been a good one but he hadn't been able to focus much. That didn't happen very often, but then again he also had never before been swept up into Christian brotherhood so quickly and so exuberantly.

Luke's wife Nalani had been the worship leader. The pastor's message was about living the joy of the Lord and Nalani had chosen her five worship songs to fit it. Her family matched her enthusiasm and Steve got caught up in it too, clapping and singing joyfully.

When the last worship song was introduced as "the dancing song," Steve was surprise at the Shepherds' reactions. With whoops of joy, they pushed their chairs up close to the row in front of theirs and stepped out of their slippers, sliding them under the chairs.

Steve stepped back because they obviously needed some room. When Nalani sang about walking in victory, they walked energetically. She sang for them to dance, and they vigorously danced. She sang "jump" and they jumped high and hard. When she sang "shout," Steve couldn't even hear her they shouted so loud.

He was thoroughly enjoying the worship when a sudden bubble of joy burst in his chest with shocking force. The power was overwhelming and it took his breath away. He stumbled out the door and slumped against the wall, hands on his knees. This feeling was good but shocking in its strangeness. As he hunched over to catch his breath and corral the surging joy, a small hand rested on his shoulder.

"Are you alright, Steve?" Aunty Gloria's voice was laced with concern.

He rocked back and smiled at her with joy-filled eyes.

"I'm way more than alright, Aunty Gloria," he whispered fiercely.

"That's awesome," she grinned with delight.

"Thank you. You were right," Steve tucked her small hand in the crook of his arm.

"About what?"

"About me needing a church home," Steve smiled toward the door from which sounds of exuberant joy pulsed. "About this being the place."

"Shall we go walk in victory?" Aunty Gloria laughed and motioned toward the door with her free hand.

"We shall."

And they did. As Nalani and the worship team sang the song a third and final time, they walked, danced, jumped and shouted with enthusiasm but little grace. What bits of the message Steve was able to tune in on only fueled his feelings of joy. For the post-message worship, they danced, jumped and shouted with even more abandon than they had before.

All that joyous energy had to go somewhere, so when he realized that the clash of the titans included all four of the Shepherd men not just Luke and Greg, he eagerly accepted their challenge to join them. And challenge it certainly was because Heather's brothers were big men.

Luke was about an inch taller but twenty pounds lighter than Steve. Greg weighed at least as much as his older brother but stood about four inches shorter. Though Tim and Robert hadn't yet started to fill out in breadth, they both already topped six foot. Tim was almost as tall as Greg, and Robert was right behind him. Add to their size the fact that they had been wrestling each other pretty much all their lives, and Steve, the superstar professional athlete, had no real advantage in this clash of the titans.

Soon he was glad he had followed Greg's advice and traded his aloha shirt for an old t-shirt. The clash of the titans was a vigorous wrestling free-for-all. Nobody cut him any slack as the newcomer and his new shirt would have been ripped to shreds in no time. His borrowed t-shirt had already suffered at least one tear. It would have been worse if it weren't so tight that it was hard to get a handful of it.

Matt and Jeremy made a very enthusiastic cheering section. They were so vigorous in their screams of delight and encouragement that their cries of "Moose" didn't register at first. Steve had Luke pinned facedown in the grass and was trying not to be overwhelmed by the other three Shepherd men. Suddenly a furry golden head pushed between him and his victim.

"It better be Moose licking me and not you, Jeremiah," Luke bellowed.

Moose meant Heather had arrived, so Steve gathered his full strength and with a mighty grizzly roar, he pushed himself fully under and then into his three attackers, sending them sprawling on the ground. Bending his knees to maximize the strength of his powerful legs, he quickly grabbed a fist-full of Luke's t-shirt and the seat of his denim shorts. With another grizzly roar, he swung the big man onto his brothers before they could get up.

He raised himself to his full height and shot both arms into the air in the classic victory pose.

"Goliath beats the Shepherd boys," Steve bellowed joyously.

He turned and trotted toward Heather with a grin. Out of the corner of his eye he saw that the defeated Shepherd boys were gathering for a rush. He did what any brave titan would do.

He ran and hid behind Heather.

HEATHER WAS SHOCKED to find Steve Jeremiah wrestling with her brothers in her mom's front yard. She was accustomed to seeing her brothers wrestling, but Steve wasn't even supposed to be here to say nothing of the fact that seeing him in that t-shirt was disconcerting. It was much too small, fitting him like a second skin, and it had been generously ripped. His well-developed torso was enhanced, not concealed by the flimsy covering. Watching his muscles bulge and ripple as he'd thrown her big brother had taken her breath away. Seeing him sprint toward her with that smile had done serious damage to her resolve to avoid him.

Her heart thudded dangerously in her chest as he bobbed back and forth behind her, pointing over her shoulders at the dish in her hands. "Green bean casserole. Watch out for the green bean casserole."

One of her brothers had told on her and he was going to pay when she figured out which one.

"Matt, take aunty's casserole dish for her," Luke stalked closer.

"No!" Jeremy cried, flinging his arms around one of Steve's legs.

"No!" Steve cried, stepping closer to Heather and wrapping an arm around her, covering the casserole with his big hand.

"Woof," barked Moose, putting himself between his mistress and the advancing horde.

"Coward," hissed Heather, shifting slightly to her left to look at Steve. She instantly regretted it as it put her much too close to a kissing position. Quickly she shifted forward again.

Steve whispered in her ear. "Absolutely. They're killing me."

The Shepherds continued to advance, spreading out to flank him.

"Hold that dish tight," Steve warned.

She only had time to pull the dish a little closer to her body before she was suddenly swept up in a pair of very strong arms.

"You wouldn't hurt your sister," Steve whined as he clasped her to his chest.

"Oh we wouldn't, would we?" Greg smirked, creeping closer.

Steve held Heather tighter, hoping Greg was only bluffing.

The blood pounded in her ears and Heather fought the urge to toss the casserole dish and wrap her arms around Steve's neck. It wasn't fear that he might drop her that drove that urge.

"Boys, time to come in and wash up," Mom called from the front door. "Oh good, you're here Heather. Bring your casserole in so we can eat."

Mom walked back into the house, totally unfazed by the sight of her only daughter in a stranger's arms.

"You're going to pay for this, Jeremiah," Greg warned as he stalked past.

"Big time pay," Luke promised.

When it was clear that they were indeed going into the house and not gathering for a sneak attack, Steve set Heather carefully back on her feet.

"Do you make it a habit of being rescued by women?" Heather snapped, trying not to be disappointed to no longer be in his arms.

"Lately, yes!" Steve laughed, apparently not bothered by her observation. Interesting. "Aunty Gloria has perfect timing and so do you."

Aunty Gloria already. So he wasn't a stranger to Mom.

"When did you meet Mom?" Heather asked suspiciously.

"Yesterday when I brought Greg home. She insisted that I stay for lunch," Steve grinned proudly.

"And then ...?"

"She invited me to church today."

"And Sunday dinner," Heather shook her head and moaned softly to herself. Her plan to avoid him had so backfired. She shook her head sadly. "Welcome to my ohana," she grumbled.

"Hey, I heard that word in church," Steve grinned happily, undaunted by her bad attitude, "lots of times when people at church were greeting me. It means family or something like that."

"Exactly that. Family," Heather sighed in disgust and turned to go into the house.

"Hey, wait a minute," Steve reached out and tugged the back of her shirt. Her practice jersey. Her number ninety-five which she always wore over her swimsuit when she left the beach. The jersey that boldly said "Jeremiah" across the top.

"I thought you weren't a personal fan." She could hear the smile in his voice. "I thought you were just a fan of the team."

"Oh, this old thing?" She feigned disdain. "The twerps gave it to me for Christmas a couple of years ago, so I must wear it."

With a long-suffering sigh, she raised her chin and stalked up the walk into the house. She didn't have eyes in the back of her head, but she knew Steve was grinning like a Cheshire cat.

LUNCH WAS SERVED buffet style and everyone took plates out onto the lanai or into the backyard. Steve managed to slip into the line right behind Heather who strongly suspected that her family had maneuvered to give him that position.

Steve helped himself to salad, chicken wings, rice, macaroni salad and a big helping of green bean casserole. She snickered when she saw him point to the last dish.

"What's that?" he asked suspiciously as he eyed rice wrapped in what looked like green paper.

"That is sushi," she said sweetly as she dropped a piece onto his plate instead of hers. "This one has avocado and shoyu tuna. And this one has shoyu Spam."

Steve stared at his plate. The two pieces of sushi stared back up at him.

"This white stuff looks like rice, but what's that?" Steve poked at the dark green wrapping.

"Nori," Mom told him.

"Seaweed," Heather grinned wickedly and strutted out to the lanai.

"Seaweed and Spam?" Steve moaned as he sat down next to her and poked at the sushi as if it would bite him.

"You don't have to eat it," she said sympathetically, then softly hissed, "Malihini!"

That got the desired response as Steve glared at her and followed her lead, popping the whole piece of tuna sushi in his mouth at once. He chewed gingerly for a moment then raised his eyebrow and nodded once.

"Not bad," he said as he swallowed, "but I'm pretty leery about the Spam."

"Leery about Spam? Sacrilege!" Luke scolded as he sat down on the other side of Heather.

"Spam is our official state meat," Heather said in shock.

"It is not," Mom shook her head fondly.

"It should be," Greg sat down next to Steve.

"We eat more cans of Spam here in Hawaii than any other state in the union," Nalani got into the fun as she sat next to her husband.

"Spam, rice and eggs for breakfast, oh yeah," Luke said.

"Spam musubi," Greg added.

"Spam stir fry," Heather smiled.

"Spam and cheese sandwiches," Luke suggested.

"Mom's Honolulu cheese steak!" Robert called from the picnic table in the yard where the teens sat with the little boys.

"Melicious!" cried Nalani.

"Brok' da mout'!" Greg agreed.

"So ono!" Luke exclaimed.

"What did they just say?" Steve implored Heather.

"They all said it's delicious," she replied with a twinkle in her eye.

"They did? In what language?"

"Hawaiian," she pointed her fork at Luke. "Ono means good. Brok' da mout' is pidgin, 'broke the mouth,'" she enunciated carefully. "It doesn't really help to put it in proper English so forget that. It means super delicious."

"And the other?"

"Melicious? That's a mom-ism. Something like 'maliciously delicious.' It's especially used for brok' da mout' foods that are particularly high in calories, cholesterol or other not so healthy stuff."

"So what makes this Honolulu cheese steak meliciously ono?" Steve asked, pronouncing the last two words carefully.

"Spam sliced thin, cut in strips and sautéed in butter with mushroom, onion and garlic," Luke sighed and sniffed as if smelling it being cooked.

"Covered with melty Provolone cheese and topped with thinly sliced avocado, local kine," Greg added.

"On grilled sweetbread rolls," Heather said. "Slathered with Mom's secret sauce."

"It's only secret to you, sweetheart," Mom said. "Everyone else in the family knows how to make that secret sauce."

"Mayo, shoyu, and wasabi," Tim called from his table.

"Okay, mayo I recognize," Steve didn't even bother to look at Heather this time. Someone had definitely told about her ineptitude in the kitchen. "But what about the rest?"

"Shoyu is well known to malihini as soy sauce," Heather said haughtily.

"Wasabi is a green paste," Mom explained. "You could call it Japanese horseradish."

"That Honolulu cheese steak does sound interesting, but I'm not sure about brok' da mout'," Steve issued a subtle challenge. Heather wasn't biting but that traitor Greg did.

"Next week, Mom," he grinned wickedly at Heather. "Next Sunday, we serve up Honolulu cheese steak for the skeptic."

"I'm here," Steve saluted her brother with a forkful of rice.

"I'm sure you are," Heather muttered dryly as she glared at her brother who just grinned broader.

Chapter 7

*T*he next few weeks were difficult for Heather. She had her reasons for not wanting to risk a relationship with anyone, much less with Steve, and they were good reasons. Slowly but surely Steve was demolishing those reasons and she wasn't happy about it.

He had thoroughly enjoyed Mom's Honolulu cheese steak and had even declared himself an official Spam lover. He had proven that love by bringing his own dish the next Sunday, a Spam jambalaya that her brothers approved of with "brok' da mout'." Far from being bothered by her lack of culinary instincts, Steve seemed delighted by the knowledge that she would never have her feelings hurt because he could make a better mac salad than she could. He'd even had her mom teach him how to make sushi!

Her family had accepted Steve with open arms. Her brothers were teaching him to surf. Mom had started taking him to the retirement home for her biweekly volunteer days, where they of course loved him. He played football with her brothers, teaching Tim and Robert some techniques. According to Matt and Jeremy, he had become their number one horsey. Even Moose, the traitor, seemed to prefer Steve over everyone else. He ran to Steve as soon as she let him out of the car at Mom's on Sundays, wrestling joyfully, following him around, and pouting in his doggy way when she called him so they could leave.

She personally had done a pretty good job of avoiding Steve except at Sunday dinners where she tended to come late, leave early and stay as far away from Steve as she possibly could. But two days ago he had called her and asked her what she knew about motorcycles.

"Not much," she said cautiously, not sure where this was going. "Except that they have two wheels and a combustion engine. I've never worked on any. Why?"

"I was thinking about getting one for here in Hawaii," Steve said, "but since I'm only here three or four months out of the year, I don't really need a new one. I was hoping you would give me your expert opinion on some used ones."

Heather pulled the phone away from her ear and checked to see if she still had a connection. She did. She hadn't imagined what she just heard. She put the phone back up to her ear.

"I'm sorry," she said. "I think we have a bad connection. Say again."

"I wanted to use your superior mechanical abilities to make sure I don't get a used lemon," Steve said clearly and distinctly.

Heather was so shocked that she didn't think about her answer. Forgetting that she was trying to ignore him, she blurted out, "Give me a few days to read up on them, and sure, I can check some out with you."

"Great," Steve sounded overjoyed, "as soon as we get back from Hilo next week, I'll start scoping out some we can look at. Will Wednesday or Thursday be better for you?"

"Wed– ... Wait a minute! What's this when *we* get back from Hilo?" Heather knew for sure she had a bad connection. She was going to the Big Island with her family for Grandma's eighty-eighth birthday. Steve Jeremiah wasn't.

"Your brothers didn't tell you that they invited me, too? That must have been after you left on Sunday. I'm sorry, I thought they told you." Steve didn't sound apologetic at all. He knew good and well that they hadn't told her.

So here she was sitting in the interisland terminal with Luke guys and Mom, waiting for the rest of her brothers and Steve. She was more than a little disgruntled that she was going to be spending the better part of four days with him. Since the boys were on spring intersession, they weren't coming back until Tuesday, and they were all staying in Grandma's big house. It was going to be very difficult to avoid Steve when they were going to be together all day Saturday, Sunday, and Monday, plus tonight and whatever time they had on Tuesday. She was definitely not a happy camper.

Steve certainly was. There he was, laughing with her brothers as if he didn't have a care in the world. He probably didn't. He seemed to be perfectly content with her family's efforts to throw them together.

Greg said something and suddenly Steve stopped and shook his head. He motioned at the group of them sitting at the gate then at her younger brothers behind the two men. Greg shook his head and shrugged. Steve shook his head in reply and strode over to the attendant at the gate. Greg grinned and motioned for them to come over. Mystified, Luke, Nalani and Heather headed that way while Mom and the twerps stayed with their gear.

"But I don't just need four upgrades," Steve was saying as they came up behind him. "Look at this crew, don't you see six very tall adults? They're not going to scrunch up in economy class even on a short flight like this one."

Heather noticed Tim and Robert look at each other and grin. Steve had included them in the adults. Drat the man. Her heart wasn't going to be able to take this kind of talk. She couldn't very well argue with him about doing this either, not without deflating her little brothers.

"I'm sorry, sir," the woman was trying to be helpful, "but we only have eight total first class seats and four are already taken. One by you and three by other travelers. Four upgrades are the best I can do for you."

Steve looked at her brothers, looked at Heather and then back at her brothers.

"Do you mind this time, Heather? They *are* bigger than you," Steve's eyes begged her to understand. "I hate to ask it since you're .... Um, since I .... Since you're older than them, but do you mind if they sit in first class this time?"

Out of the corner of her eye, Heather saw her little brothers grow at least an inch when Steve said they were bigger than her. She decided to ignore his fumble, pretty sure he'd almost declared her to be "his girl," right in front of her family. The man was infuriatingly sensitive to the fatherless teens but she wasn't going to fall for him.

She smiled brightly in spite of her determination to keep him at a distance.

"I think we got some of the front economy seats anyway. There's lots of leg room there," she saw his relief at her understanding. She could have sworn he was going to stroke her cheek, so she broke eye contact and turned to glare at her brothers. "But I'll make you pay this weekend, brats."

They grinned and laughed, more than willing to pay whatever price she came up with. Steve turned back to the airline attendant and made the arrangements for the upgrades. She went back to sit with Mom and the little guys, telling her about the sudden flight modifications.

After a few minutes, Tim and Robert came bounding over and flopped down beside her, bursting with news.

"Steve is changing our return flights now," Tim grinned.

"But there was only one available upgrade for our original flight time," Robert picked up the story.

"So Mom and Luke guys are coming back a little early, on the 4:15 flight," Tim said.

"And we're coming back on the 5:30 flight with Greg," Robert grinned.

"When am I coming back?" Heather glared suspiciously.

"At our original flight time with Steve," Tim said innocently as he stood up to let Nalani sit.

"In the seat right next to him," Robert whispered in her ear as he too darted away from her long arms.

Steve was still working with the attendant, but everyone else was grinning at her. Not one of them looked chagrined when she gave them stink eye.

THE NEXT MORNING, Heather was awakened by the heavenly smells of coffee brewing and Portuguese sausage frying. She loved coming to Grandma's house because it was one of the few times she got good breakfasts now that she lived on her own. She threw on her terrycloth robe and made a quick stop in the bathroom before heading on into the kitchen.

She hit the door and froze. How had she forgotten that Steve was here? For a moment she was mesmerized by his deft wielding of the spatula, flipping pancakes and fried eggs without a single mishap. The smell was divine. Wisdom told her to retreat and get properly dressed.

She started to step back when suddenly Jeremy caught sight of her and sang out, "Aunty Heather."

Steve turned quickly and promptly dropped the carton of orange juice he'd just picked up. He'd never seen her with her hair down, running amok in all its wild glory. The look in his eyes would have been gratifying if she was trying to get his attention. But she wasn't, so when Steve looked down at the mess he'd made, she slipped from the room.

"I'm sorry," she heard him say. "I don't know what got into me. I usually lose things, not drop them."

"I think I know what got into him," Greg said behind her. She whirled and gave him stink eye.

"Don't sneak up on me like that," she pressed her hand to her heart.

"I'm not what has you all flustered," Greg said. "When you gonna face facts and let God bless you, Boss?"

"What facts are you talking about?" Heather crossed her arms over her chest.

"The fact that he's crazy about you and you're crazy about him."

"Am not," Heather snapped.

"Are too," Greg laughed.

"Oooh, men!" Heather turned and stormed off.

When she reappeared ten minutes later, she was properly attired in a t-shirt and jeans with her hair once more controlled by a braid. Steve didn't look at her less adoringly than he had before and he pretty much kept it up all day.

Late March in Hilo is still cold by Hawaii standards and it rained a lot, but they were still able to put in plenty of sightseeing over the weekend. Grandma's birthday was Sunday and they had a big party planned at a local restaurant that evening. That left Saturday and Monday to take Steve to see as many tourist sites as they could.

Saturday they went to Volcanoes National Park. It was a favorite outing when the Shepherds came to Hilo and there was somewhat of a ritual around it. First they had to stop at KTA, the local grocery store. Greg, Tim, Robert and Matt were riding in Steve's rented SUV. As soon as Matt saw that they were pulling into the KTA parking lot, he got excited.

"I never knew a kid could get excited about a grocery store," Steve looked at Greg in surprise.

"The Shepherd boys get excited about coming to KTA," Greg assured him.

"Are you going to keep me in suspense?"

"It's simple really. One of my mom's classmates works here. We started visiting Grandma every summer after we moved to Hawaii. When Grandma took us to KTA the first time, I guess I was about seven or so. When Aunty Mitsue saw me, she fell in love with me, as everyone tends to do." Greg ignored Steve's eyeroll and continued his story as he helped Matt get out of the SUV. "She gave us all candy. Course, Luke and Heather only got it because Aunty Mitsue had to be nice to them but she loves me best. Same with the punks and the twerps when they came along later."

"Don't tell me she still gives you candy!" Steve shook his head in wonder.

"Of course she does!" Greg grinned back. "I'm even better looking now then I was when I was seven."

"So you have to come to KTA when you come to Hilo?"

"We're actually getting snacks for today," Tim clarified, "but just you watch, if Aunty Mitsue is there, Greg, Matt and Germy will end up with some candy too!"

Tim was right. Aunty Mitsue was there and it didn't take much effort before she was leading the beggars back to her office to raid her candy jar. Of course, Tim had left out the part where he and Robert were still not too old to beg for candy also. Steve tagged along with the Shepherd boys while the rest of the family did their shopping

Aunty Mitsue had a bewildering array of treats in her candy jar. Some of it Steve easily recognized from the familiar chocolate bar wrappings, but much of it was unfamiliar. He was leery about the white wrappings for some of the candy. The pictures on the wrappers clued him in that they were at least loosely related to fruit but the Japanese writing left the contents too much in doubt.

He found something in a clear wrapper with English writing. He didn't understand what "ume" meant but he could see that it was a honey-colored hard candy wrapped around something.

Greg saw what he was holding. "You don't want that! I'll take it."

Steve jerked his hand away with the candy still firmly clutched in it. He glared at Greg. "Why not?"

"You won't like it," Greg assured him with a very serious face. It was much too serious.

Steve looked at Tim and Robert who shook their heads with equal seriousness. Steve didn't trust any of them. He noticed Matt stuff a couple pieces of the same candy in his pocket.

"How about you let me decide for myself?" Steve frowned and tore the small bag open. He popped the candy in his mouth.

He tasted the sweetness immediately. It was kind of like honey. Then the salt hit his taste buds too. He blinked rapidly and swallowed convulsively. He fought the urge to pull the candy from his mouth.

Greg dropped his head on Tim's shoulder and shook with laughter. Tim and Robert tried to keep a straight face, but they just couldn't hold it in. Aunty Mitsue looked up from where she was helping Matt and Jeremy pick out their favorite candies. As soon as she saw Steve's face, she knew.

"You gave that poor man ume candy," she scolded.

"We told him not to eat it aunty, I swear!" Robert tried not to grin as he protested her scolding.

"It's not so bad," Steve said bravely. "What's on the inside?"

"Dried salted plum," Aunty Mitsue told him. "It's an acquired taste. Hang around these rascals and you'll be eating Li Hing Mui before you know it."

"That's the dried plum without the candy," Tim enlightened Steve with a huge grin, patting Greg on the back as his big brother wiped away tears of laughter.

"I think that might take awhile!" Steve frowned at his friends, determined not to spit out the candy, even if it killed him.

When they joined the others Luke was upset that he'd missed the fun but Heather wasn't sure if she should scold her brothers or encourage them. She was half hopeful that they'd scare Steve off, but she didn't really want to see it happen. She wasn't interested in a romantic relationship, but she was really beginning to like Steve as a friend.

As soon as they left KTA, they headed down the road to the park and spent the rest of the day hiking around the volcanoes. Steve carried either Matt or Jeremy on his shoulders most of the time. As usual for the Shepherd family, between Nalani, Gloria and Grandma, someone caught almost every minute on camera, both still and video.

By the time they made it back to the cars, Heather couldn't help but notice that Steve's hair was adorably mussed from the wind and grubby little hands. His nose was slightly sunburned too. Jeremy was draped over his head, sound asleep with arms dangling, and Steve very carefully removed him so that he didn't wake up.

As he buckled her dirty little nephew into his booster seat, Steve smoothed some curls off his forehead and stroked his cheek gently before leaning over to kiss his forehead. The look of love and longing tore at Heather's heart and she quickly stepped back, firmly pushing away the love and longing that she refused to feel for this gentle giant.

When she turned she ran right into her younger brother, bouncing off his broad chest. Greg looked at her sadly and shook his head.

"When you gonna let go Boss?" he whispered.

Now, her heart cried, but she just shook her head at him and went around the car to slide in next to Jeremy in the back seat.

When they got back to Hilo, everyone was in the mood for loco moco. They discovered that Steve had never had the island delight so that sealed the deal. He enjoyed the simple fare of a heaping bowl of rice, hamburger and fried egg smothered in gravy. Long before he was done, he was discussing alternate recipes with Mom and Grandma.

Back at Grandma's house, Luke and Nalani disappeared upstairs with the boys to get them bathed and ready for bed. The rest of the adults went out on Grandma's lanai to enjoy the star-studded night for awhile. Heather was stretched out dozing in her deck chair and hadn't noticed that everyone but her and Steve had gone inside. He gently nudged her knee with his.

"What's up?" She smiled softly at him, assured that he couldn't see her clearly since the moon was a new moon and Grandma had no lights on the lanai.

"I wanted to ask you something," Steve said quietly.

"Sounds serious," Heather sat up and twisted in her chair to look at him.

"It is kind of," Steve leaned forward, putting his elbows on his knees and clasping his hands. He stared out at the ocean in the distance. "But I don't want to make you mad or anything."

"I can't imagine you would," Heather was puzzled.

Steve didn't say anything for a few minutes, then he finally looked over his shoulder at her.

"Why don't you go to church anymore?" he said softly. "I know you love the Lord, and I can't understand why you would stay away from his house. But I want to understand."

"You couldn't start with something easy and work your way into that?" Heather sighed. She got up from her chair and leaned against the rail, staring out into the night and listening to the cacophony of the coqui frogs. After a few minutes, Steve rose and stood behind her. Hands in his pockets, he didn't touch her but she felt his presence nonetheless.

"Are you mad at God?" he asked.

"Am I mad at God?" Heather thought about it for a moment. "You know, I was at one time, but I don't feel it anymore."

She thought back over the past few years. She thought about the war, her injuries, the loss of her father, watching her family's pain, and finally surrendering her dreams of a husband and children of her own. She'd had lots of anger at God, but something happened along the way. Even before Steve came into her life, she had begun to regain some of her awe about God and his creation. The incredible power of the waves crashing upon the shore. The exhilaration of riding one of those powerful waves on her boogie board. The sweet smell of pikake. Her nephews' amazing ability to see elephants on the H1 and their giggling over nothing at all. In so many ways, God had quietly and certainly brought peace and joy back into her life after three years of physical and emotional pain. Could she let go of the need to know why he had allowed so much sorrow?

"I remember that I used to hide in my closet when my father came home drunk and angry," Steve spoke as if he knew what was on her heart. "I would beg God to make it better, but nothing happened. Then I started asking God why and he never answered. When I was thirteen, just after I hit my growth spurt and started to get as big as him, Dad started in on Mom one night and I couldn't take it anymore. I lit into him, but of course I was just a gangly kid and he was much stronger than me. So he soon had me down on the ground."

Heather heard his heavy sigh, felt his pain at the memory.

"In that moment, as I lay on the floor and he kept going at me, I had a revelation. Call it a boyish fantasy if you want, but I knew that Jesus was with me. He was crying with me and he was sheltering me, not from the blows to my body but from the blows to my spirit. At that moment I quit asking God to change my circumstances or to tell me why it was happening. Instead, I asked him to give me strength so that I could survive and bring him glory."

Steve sighed softly and took a step closer to Heather. "I felt real peace for the first time in my life. I felt God's arms around me and I knew he had heard and answered my prayer. My father stopped suddenly and walked away. Through all the things that happened after that – my sister running away, my dad, mom and grandma dying, even losing the Championship Game – I have never totally lost that peace though it has been seriously challenged."

Heather knew her tears were as much for herself as they were for the big man standing behind her.

"It's waxed and waned," Steve's voice was a rumble that touched her soul, "but it's always there, and the knowledge that I gained that night also stayed with me. Even when I don't feel God, I know he's there, sheltering me from the blows to my spirit because it belongs to him. Even when I had no hope for a better life, I still had that peace that passes understanding because I knew that God was with me in the darkness. I know he won't leave me, that he suffers with me. I know that he has a plan for whatever pain I do have to go through, a plan that will bring him glory if I keep my focus on him instead of myself and my pain."

Heather took a deep, cleansing breath and let it out.

"I think I'll go to church in the morning," she said quietly.

"I think I'll fix you breakfast before we go," Steve replied.

She felt his big hands settle gently on her shoulders and a feather-light kiss touch her hair, then he turned and walked away.

Alone, by the light of a million stars, Heather went down on her knees and asked God to give her the strength to make her life count.

She didn't see the two older women standing by the lanai door, didn't hear them as they wrapped Steve in a group hug and cried for joy.

Chapter 8

*B*eing back in church was much more fulfilling than Heather had expected. None of her family made a big deal of the fact that she showed up in Grandma's kitchen in a blouse and jeans instead of her usual Sunday wear of swimsuit, board shorts and Jeremiah practice jersey. But they all made sure that they gave her encouragement with a quick kiss or a gentle touch.

Heather was glad her first time back to church wasn't at their home church on Oahu where everyone would have made a fuss over her being back again. Though she knew many of the people at Grandma's church, they knew nothing of her estrangement from God. They all greeted her just like they greeted the rest of the family.

It was obvious that God had known she was coming back and he had prepared a service for her. The church's halau had prepared a special dance to "Only For the Weak" by Avalon that incorporated both Christian hula and creative sign dance. The beauty of the dance had her furtively wiping away tears that were fueled in part by her desire to be likewise dancing again.

Then the pastor preached from Acts 9, about Saul on the road to Damascus. He spoke of how Saul was a very religious man who had grown up in the Jewish faith. He knew his bible and he knew he was a powerful defender of the faith. Or so he thought, but he had known God without truly seeing him. God stopped his religious life on the road to Damascus and afflicted him. If he had hardened his heart and not obeyed when God told him to go to Damascus and wait, if he had kicked against the Lord's will, he would have remained in his blindness. God's word would still have gone forth but through someone else. Thankfully Saul obeyed and ultimately gave up his religion to faithfully follow the Christ.

As the pastor brought his message home to his congregation, Heather knew he was talking to her.

"It is easy," he pointed out, "for those of us who grow up in the church to be so religious that we lose our focus on God. But he will meet us on our Damascus road. When we're ready for the scales to be removed from our eyes so we can follow Christ in faith instead of simply in religion, he will send our Ananias to bring the words, the touch that will restore us to God. Only then will we go onward, serving the Lord in true power as we serve from our weakness and God's strength."

Heather was weeping silently, long before the message was done. Sandwiched between Greg and Steve, sitting in their usual place at the back of the church, Heather felt sheltered from all eyes, safe to confess to God how wrong she'd been, how she had resented the suffering and pain that was the very thing to bring her into closer fellowship with her Savior.

As her tears began to fall, Steve quietly offered his hand, palm up in the narrow space between them. Heather didn't hesitate to slip her hand in his and lean against his powerful shoulder. As she thanked God for her restoration, she thanked him for sending Steve, her Ananias, speaking the words that caused her scales to fall away.

When they stood for the final worship song, Heather gave Steve a hug, slipping away quickly before he could return the embrace. She turned to her brother and gave him a fierce hug. As she clung to Greg, Steve felt of stab of rejection. Then he saw Greg look at him in surprise over Heather's head. His surprise gave way to a slow grin and a wink as he hugged his sister back. Steve stepped out into the aisle to allow Heather to precede him as they left the service. Greg threw an arm across his shoulders.

"Time, my friend," Greg said in a low voice, "time, patience and persistence. That's all you need." Then he was off down the aisle, following Heather out to where the church served lunch for newcomers and visitors, leaving Steve to hope and pray that he was right.

Though Heather was profoundly grateful for the part Steve played in bringing her back to God, she still didn't know what to do about him. She certainly liked him and wanted him for a friend, but until she determined for sure that a potential romance with him was God-approved, she needed to keep her distance. When it was time to leave the church, she made sure she climbed in the back of Grandma's car rather than getting maneuvered into Steve's rental.

They spent a lazy, rainy afternoon in Grandma's living room, playing board games and enjoying the fireplace. In the evening, they went to Grandma's favorite restaurant with all the Big Island relatives. Through it all, she quietly watched Steve, saw his gentleness and genuine care for others, and she wondered what she was supposed to do about the stirrings in her heart. She often felt his eyes upon her, and when she would glance his way, he'd smile tenderly with a gentle patience.

The next day they went around the island to Kailua-Kona. Steve was intrigued by the desolate lava fields, the donkey crossing signs, and the Painted Church, but the highlight of the day for him was Puuhonua O Honaunau, the City of Refuge. It was fascinating to see a slice of life from ancient Hawaii, but the place itself held a deeper spiritual attraction for him.

Heather joined him as he stood alone and gazed out across the bay in a rare moment when neither of her nephews were climbing on him or demanding his attention.

"How did they know?" Steve mused as she walked up beside him. "About the city of refuge? How did they know?"

He turned toward her and made a sweeping motion with his left hand, pointing to the village behind them.

"The kapu system, the kii statues, the mana of the dead chiefs, it's all so pagan, and yet they got this," Steve pointed toward the actual sanctuary. "They got this so right. It's too close to the Hebrew cities of refuge to be merely a coincidence, and yet the ancestors of these people had left the Middle East long before God gave the plan for the cities of refuge to Moses. They didn't even establish them here until long after God himself came as the high priest whose death gave us an eternal city of refuge."

"Some people claim that God prepared these islands for the arrival of the missionaries," Heather shrugged, "maybe this was all part of it. Hints at what had been done. Suggestions that there was a better way."

"'The Lord moves in mysterious ways, his wonders to perform,'" Steve said as he reached out and brushed a stray strand of hair off her cheek, tucking it behind her ear.

"He always completes what he starts," Heather whispered.

"In his time," Steve dropped his hand and smiled softly. "Always in his time."

"Uncle Steve! Aunty Heather!" Steve stepped back, startled at hearing their names coupled like that. Then he smiled again and turned toward her nephews who were rushing over to drag them off so they could have lunch.

As he turned, Heather thought he whispered again, "In his time. Always in his time."

Back in Hilo, the little boys had an urgent need to burn off some of the energy that had been bottled up for the hour-long drive from the Kona coast via Waimea. Everyone but Grandma and Mom agreed that a game of football would be just the thing.

"So where's the football?" Greg asked Steve.

"Why are you looking at me? I don't live here," Steve shrugged.

"But you're the pro football player, aren't you supposed to keep one in your back pocket or something?" Luke said.

"Sorry guys, but I try to carry as few things as possible," Steve told them.

"Why's that? Because you have a platinum charge card and you can get anything you need?" Tim asked.

"Nope. I leave most important things at home so I don't lose them," Steve laughed.

"What's this?" Heather walked up in time to hear Steve's revelation. "Why didn't you ever tell me about this, punks?"

Tim and Robert looked at each other and shrugged.

"I don't remember reading anything about it," Tim said.

"Me neither," Robert agreed.

"Ah, so you do have secrets we don't know about," Heather smiled slyly. "Do tell!"

"Nothing to tell, really," Steve shrugged. "I just have a bad habit of forgetting things."

"Like what kind of things?" Luke asked.

"I've left a few things behind in hotel rooms," Steve said evasively.

"For instance?" Heather demanded.

"Three cell phones, four pair of jeans, two pair of running shoes, and six books," Steve smiled sheepishly, "and more razors and toothbrushes than I can count."

"Do you ever get them back?" Robert asked.

"Sometimes, but most of the time someone at the hotel just keeps them as souvenirs."

"Why would anyone want a pair of your shoes for a souvenir?" Greg mused.

"How about to use as a boat for kids to sail across a pond?" Heather suggested.

"A doorstop?" Tim contributed.

"A planter?" Greg asked.

"I know!" Robert cried. "A football!"

"Yeah, that's right," Luke looked down at Steve's sneaker clad feet with a gleam in his eyes. "A football."

"Oh no you don't!" Steve took a step back.

"Ah, come on Steve," Tim said, "be a sport."

"Yeah Steve, be a sport," the rest of the Shepherds chorused.

"Okay," Steve glared at them through narrowed eyes, "if you can get one, you can use it as a football!"

"Alright," the brothers grinned at each other and spread out to flank him.

Steve took a step back and tripped over Heather's outstretched leg. Since he was already off balance, she plowed into him and took him to the ground. As her brothers attacked Steve's feet, Heather whispered, "You should have worn your rubber slippers."

Steve started to roll over and toss them all but stopped when he saw two small heads pop up behind Heather.

"You don't play fair!" he accused.

When one of Steve's shoes was liberated for the football game, Heather stood up with her nephews still clinging to her back. She reached back and tickled them until they fell off giggling. Then she smiled down at Steve who was leaning on one elbow. She offered him a hand up. When he was upright again, she stood on tiptoe and whispered, "All's fair ...."

Then she ran off to join her brothers, leaving him to finish the saying, "... in love and war," and wonder.

A small hand tugged at his and Steve looked down into Matt's upturned face.

"If you take off your other shoe and your socks, you can play too," he earnestly informed Steve.

"Will you be on my team?" Steve knelt to untie his remaining shoe.

Matt looked at him thoughtfully and then leaned close to whisper, "Are you really any good?"

"I think so," Steve whispered back.

"Okay, then," Matt agreed, "let's go play."

Even if Nalani had wanted to, Luke would not have let his pregnant wife play so she sat on the sidelines as a very enthusiastic cheering section. The rest played vigorously, but all the guys were careful of Heather and little boys. Steve hadn't asked, but from the way Heather's brothers played around her, he guessed she had some lingering fragility because of her wounds. His suspicion was confirmed when Robert accidentally put a shoulder in her left side. Heather cried out in pain and twisted away, but she tripped over her brother and fell hard.

"Why don't you be careful, you klutz?" Greg pushed his little brother away and knelt next to Heather who was having trouble getting her breath.

"Sometimes you're like a bull in a china shop, boy," Luke snapped as he knelt at Heather's other side.

"Chill guys, he didn't mean to do it," Steve snapped as he pushed his way in and took Heather by the shoulders, lifting her enough to cradle against his chest. "Take it slow, sweetheart. Take it easy. You're okay, right?" He leaned down to look in her eyes. "Is it just pain from the old injury or are you hurt again?"

"Just pain," she croaked out, clutching his arm tightly, "and lost my breath."

"I know it's hard, but try to relax against the pain," Steve encouraged. "I promise it will help."

She looked long and deep into his eyes, drawing strength from his quietness. Everyone watched silently as her breathing gradually returned to normal. Steve felt her grip on his arm loosen and he knew she was going to be okay. Until that moment, he hadn't realized how tense he was inside.

Suddenly Heather's left hand snaked out and grabbed Greg's shirtfront, pulling him close.

"You apologize," she cut her eyes over to Luke, "you too."

She took a deep breath and looked up at Robert.

"It was an accident." She sighed heavily. "I shouldn't have even been playing with you jerks. If it's anyone's fault, it's mine."

Heather winced again as she tried to sit up straighter.

"Maybe you should take her inside," Greg suggested to Steve.

"Maybe you should apologize to Robert like I said," Heather snapped at him.

"She's right, brah," Greg grabbed Robert in a hug. "I was way out of line. Please forgive me?"

"Me too," Luke said. "I was just scared. It wasn't your fault."

"Help me up," Heather whispered to Steve while her brothers were reassuring Robert.

He stood and helped her to her feet. She laid her head against his chest for a moment, relishing the feel of his arms around her. Then she turned and called her nephews.

"Hey boys, let's go sit by your mom for a while," she took a few ginger steps and winced against the pain. Steve quickly stepped up and swept her into his arms, carrying her over and setting her down carefully next to Nalani.

Nalani smiled slyly at Heather. "Did he ask if he could do that?"

"No my dear, he didn't," Heather winked at Steve.

"Oh, your honor has been besmirched," Nalani complained loudly and melodramatically. "What are we going to do about that?"

"Boys," Heather reached out to Matt and Jeremy. "I *really* think you better sit over here by Mommy and Aunty."

"You don't mean –?" Steve groaned softly.

"Oh yes, we do," Nalani smiled encouragingly.

"It's just what I need to feel better," Heather insisted.

Steve looked over his shoulder and saw the forces gathering behind him. He went down on one knee, laid his left hand over his heart and bowed his head before the women.

"We who are about to die salute you," he said with a twinkle in his eye.

From his kneeling position, Steve rolled over his left shoulder and came up in a three-point stance, ready for the attack.

No CLASH OF the titans can go on very long. Just like always, in about fifteen minutes all five men were winded and they agreed to call it a draw. Heather looked sympathetically at Steve as he dropped in the grass beside her, laying on his back with his head cradled in his hands and his eyes closed.

"Poor baby," she crooned, "would you like some ibuprofen? You got beat up pretty bad out there."

"Me! Beat up?" Steve huffed. "Woman, I don't know what's wrong with your eyes, but you should see an ophthalmologist. I was the one doing the beating."

"Ha," Luke said as he flopped down by Nalani. "I did the most beating."

"I got beat but good, and I'm not afraid to admit it," Tim shook his head. "Come on, Robert, let's go in and see if we can beat Mom or Grandma at a board game."

"You gonna come too, brats?" Robert asked Matt and Jeremy.

"We're not brats," Matt said as they jumped to their feet and followed their uncles.

"Are too."

"Are not."

"Too."

"Not."

"Too too too!"

"Not not not!"

When the sounds of their argument died away, Greg groaned and pushed himself to his feet.

"It's getting harder and harder to beat those boys," he sighed. "You think we're getting old?"

"Speak for yourself," Luke growled.

Greg laughed and headed for the house. "Catch ya later, old men."

"Darlin', you think you can carry me into the house and give me a real good massage?" Luke looked imploringly at his wife.

"I certainly won't carry you but if you get yourself to the bedroom I'll give you that massage," she promised with a wicked smile, "maybe even more."

"That's an offer I can't refuse," Luke rolled over and pushed himself up gingerly. When he was upright, Nalani slipped under his arm and together they walked into the house.

"How're you feeling?" Steve flashed his baby blues at Heather.

"Very well, thank you," she smiled down at him.

"Good, I'm really glad," he closed his eyes for a moment.

"Psst." Heather looked down at Steve who was peeking at her through barely open eyes. "Is everyone gone?"

"Yes," she whispered back.

"Good," he sighed. "Then can you get me some of that ibuprofen? I don't think I'll move from here for three days. Your brothers hit hard!"

"I guess I owe you one," Heather stood up. "I got you into it, didn't I?"

"Yes you do, because you certainly did."

Heather laughed and headed into the house but when she returned a few minutes later with the ibuprofen and some water, Steve was sound asleep. She went into the house and got a book to read, then went back outside and waited for Steve to wake up.

Two chapters later, he was still asleep and she wondered if she should wake him since it would soon be time for supper. She looked down at him and was suddenly struck by how sad and lonely he looked. When he was awake, he was always interested in what others were doing but while sleeping, he seemed to be acutely aware that he was indeed alone in this world.

She reached out and brushed a lock of hair back from his forehead. For a few seconds she was sorely tempted to kiss him. She pushed back the temptation, very mindful of how much Steve had to lose if they attempted to take their relationship beyond friendship and it didn't work. She would only lose him, but he would lose the family who loved him and filled an empty place in his life.

"Steve," she said softly and gently nudged his shoulder.

"Yes, love?" he asked sleepily.

Heather stifled a sob, suddenly wishing that she could give him her love, but she wasn't there yet. She couldn't give him all that he deserved.

"Hey Steve," she nudged his shoulder again, "you need to wake up and take your ibuprofen."

"How long have I been sleeping?" he asked without opening his eyes.

"Oh, about half an hour, forty-five minutes."

"Couldn't be," he said, rolling over onto his left side and propping his head up on his elbow. "I'm not old enough to need more than a power nap."

Heather giggled and dropped three ibuprofen into his outstretched hand.

"Just think of it as three power naps, compressed together."

"That's a thought," Steve looked at the three pills in his hand. "How did you know I needed three?"

"Well, two barely do for me and you're a bit bigger than I am, so I guessed three would do."

"Wise woman," he said. He popped the pills in his mouth, then held out his hand for the water. "You know that these aren't going to work fast enough to get me up from the ground anytime soon, don't you?"

"Sure, but I figured that a big strong guy like you would 'suck it up and drive on.' That is what they say in the pros, right?"

"Yes, that's what they say," Steve affirmed with a grimace. "I hate that saying."

Heather's laugh rang out and Steve looked around, suddenly realizing that they were still alone. He passed the water to Heather and sat up the rest of the way, his legs at forty-five degree angles and his elbows propped up on his knees.

"Were you out here the whole time I slept?"

"Yes," Heather handed him his glass of water again.

"You know people will talk if you do stuff like that," Steve warned.

"They already do," Heather said dryly, nodding toward the window in the living room. Three faces that had been pressed against the glass disappeared when he looked that way.

Steve laughed and shook his head. "That wasn't the little guys, was it?"

"No," Heather affirmed his suspicion. "It was Mom, Grandma and Greg."

Steve took another drink of water then set the glass down in the grass.

"Do you think there's any chance that this might become more?" Steve asked as he stared at the glass between his feet.

Heather drew her knees up to her chest and wrapped her arms around her legs. Though his question was rather obscure, with no obvious frame of reference, she knew exactly what he was talking about.

"I think there's a chance that there might be a chance," she said, "but I'm not willing to give up this for something that tenuous."

Steve grunted softly, and Heather nudged his shoulder with hers.

"This is really good," she explained quietly, "and if we try for more and don't make it, won't we lose this too?"

"I guess that's a good point," Steve agreed grudgingly. "So you're saying there's a chance, but not yet."

"I need to learn how to listen to God again, Steve," Heather smiled sadly. "It's been a long time, and I sure don't want to mess this up."

"Neither do I," Steve agreed. He tossed back the last of his water, then stood to his feet in one fluid move. He reached down and pulled Heather to her feet. She rested her hands on his chest and looked up at him.

"You did that pretty smoothly," she said suspiciously. "Have you been playing up your pain?"

Steve leaned his forehead against hers.

"Every fiber of my being screams in pain," he sighed, "but I'll suck it up and drive on because I'm a pro, and that's what we do."

He pressed a kiss to her forehead, then turned, tucked her hand into the crook of his elbow and led her back to the house.

THE NEXT DAY, the whole crew drove up to Laupahoehoe where Grandma had lost her cousin in the 1946 tsunami. They wondered around on the grounds, reading the plaques and walking in the place where the school once stood. Heather sat on the crumbling foundation of one of the buildings and stared off across the bay. After a while, Steve came and sat quietly beside her.

"Do you think any of them knew?" Heather mused. "When they got up that morning, did they have a clue that they would face eternity that day? Did the friends and family of the victims know that they would never see them again? Did the survivors know their lives would be forever changed?"

It was a thought that deserved careful consideration, so Steve took his time before he offered an answer.

"I guess we'd like to think they did," Steve squinted against the sun, "but in my experience, most of us get no premonition, no idea of the change coming. I know I never have and I've had quite a few life changing moments."

"Except for Daddy dying," Heather said, "I haven't either. Although with Dad, you can't call it a premonition. We all knew it was going to be any day, so we made every day count. I hope some of them made their last days count."

They sat in comfortable silence for a while until Luke came to tell them that everyone else was ready to go. When they got back to Hilo, they visited the tsunami museum and learned more about both the 1946 and the 1960 tidal waves.

After lunch Heather's grandma asked if they'd gotten any omiyage yet. She explained to Steve that in Japan, it's a social duty to return from a trip with gifts of food. Those gifts are called "omiyage." It had become a widely accepted tradition in Hawaii, so Steve needed to take something back for his friends, family and co-workers on Oahu. There were a couple good places in Hilo to get omiyage, but the Shepherds went to KTA first to say good-bye to Aunty Mitsue and to support her store. They also stopped to get some chocolate-dipped shortbread cookies to take back to Oahu.

All Steve's friends except Pete and his parents were with him so he didn't have to get much omiyage, but Steve decided he wanted some treats for himself as well. After his experience with the ume candy, he didn't have any interest in the more eclectic snacks available at the stores. He ignored the other men completely and carefully followed Aunty Gloria's suggestions about what he might like.

As soon as they finished shopping for omiyage, it was time to take Mom and Luke guys to the airport. While they were unloading the luggage, Grandma said she'd have to say good-bye so she could go to her Tuesday afternoon quilting group. Heather's other brothers announced that they wanted to stay at the airport since their flight was just an hour later than Mom's and Luke guys' flight. It didn't make sense for Steve to leave with them and bring them right back. Besides, they would be a big help entertaining Matt and Jeremy in the long wait after they got through security, and Hilo's lounge area was extremely comfortable for waiting, even for their oversized bodies.

Heather knew what they were doing. While Tim and Robert were helping Steve and Luke unload the luggage, Heather punched Greg on the arm.

"I know what you're up to, punk," she accused.

"Don't know what you're talkin' 'bout, Boss," Greg played innocent.

"Yes you do!" Heather sighed. "Look, I'm trying, okay. Can you give me some time?"

Greg studied her face for a moment then gave one quick, hard nod. He grinned and wrapped an arm around her shoulders, pulling her close enough to whisper in her ear. "But don't wait too long. You're gettin' kinda old ya know."

Heather elbowed him in the gut, hard. She smiled sweetly when everyone looked their way as Greg doubled over, groaning with pain. "I guess his kimchi at lunch disagreed with him."

Chapter 9

*A*ll too soon Heather found herself alone with Steve in Hilo for three hours, plus two hours at the airport and a flight just shy of an hour. Almost six hours with a very attractive man with whom she wasn't sure she should be falling in love, not a pleasant prospect.

When they left the airport, Steve didn't ask where she wanted to go. He drove with purpose and at first Heather was content to just wait and see where he was going, but she soon started to get suspicious. He was driving much too confidently for a man who had never been to Hilo before.

"Where are we going?" she asked warily.

"Somewhere your mom suggested," Steve feigned intense interest in his driving. "She gave me directions."

Heather saw the old hospital up ahead and made an educated guess. "You know it's already afternoon. We won't see any rainbows."

"I know," Steve acknowledged, "your mom told me that, but she also said it was still worth the trip."

Rainbow Falls. Her mom had suggested Rainbow Falls, a place she knew Heather thought was very romantic. She wasn't sure if she should be frustrated or intrigued. Now she knew that not only Greg wholeheartedly approved of Steve, but so did Mom. That was worth thinking about, especially since both of them had already spent more time with Steve than she had.

Obviously she needed to remedy that situation if they were going to have a chance at something else, but was a romantic place like Rainbow Falls a good choice? It was a moot point now because they were there already. She may as well enjoy the scenery.

They walked side-by-side down the path until they reached the overlook point. The beauty of the waterfall, the deep pool, the lush vegetation stirred her heart as it always did. She listened to the music of the waterfall, closed her eyes and held her face to the mist that was more mauka rain than waterfall. Then she sighed and deliberately turned away. She leaned back against the rail, her right foot draped over her left, arms crossed at her waist. Steve continued to watch the waterfall.

"You remember the first day we met?" Heather asked.

"Can't hardly forget," Steve observed.

"Specifically, do you remember when I said I had veto power?" Heather continued to look at her feet.

"Yes, I do," Steve sighed.

"I'm going to need to invoke that right for an indefinite period."

"Okay, I'm not arguing," Steve turned and matched her pose, "but may I ask why?"

"It's complicated."

"It usually is," Steve observed wryly, "but we have plenty of time."

"Alright then. First, you really love my family and my family loves you."

"Agreed."

"You think you might love me." Steve started to say something, but Heather quickly threw up her hand to stop him. "We're going to leave it at that." She took a deep breath and let it out in a soft sigh.

"I think I might want to love you," her voice was low and husky as she blushed a little, bit her lower lip and looked off to her right.

"Excuse me?" Steve sounded a little too pleased.

"You heard me," Heather said calmly. She looked back down at her feet. "But when I fall in love, I want it to be strong and true, not based on emotions invoked by jaunts to romantic settings."

She sighed and rubbed her forehead.

"Romantic love leads to marriage," her voice was low and shaky, "and marriage is life for real. It's everyday life, day in, day out, with very few romantic settings like this."

She finally looked directly at Steve.

"If a couple can't build romance in their everyday lives before they get married, how are they going to do it after the honeymoon is over?" Heather said sincerely. "Life changes in so many ways after the wedding. The ability to build romance out of everyday life has to already be a constant in their relationship."

Steve look thoughtfully at Heather for a long moment, then nodded. "I see your point."

"But here's the other thing, Steve," Heather pushed away from the rail and faced him. "Remember that first thing I said, about you and my family?"

He nodded.

"Well, if we manufacture romance, like this," she waved her hand toward the falls, "and it doesn't work, one or both of us will get our hearts broken, and you lose my family and we all lose you."

Steve looked stricken at the thought.

"But if we try to build romance out of everyday life and it doesn't work," she smiled tremulously, "we'll still be ohana. And even if it hurts, it won't be the deep kine hurt. It will heal and someday we'll dance at each other's weddings, as brother and sister, not as brokenhearted lovers."

Steve turned and stared at the falls, mulling over her words. Finally he nodded and turned back to Heather. "How did you get so smart about love and romance?"

"It's got to be God," she laughed, "because I don't remember ever consciously thinking about it before!"

"Fair enough. Can't argue with God," Steve agreed. "We won't try to manufacture romance the easy way, but you need to understand something."

"What?" Heather looked at him warily.

"You may be right that I might not actually be in love with you yet," Steve said, "but I know that I'm headed that way. It's where I want to be and I'm not going to back off from it."

"Okay," Heather whispered faintly.

"I accept your challenge," Steve laughed at her startled look. "Oh yes, it's a challenge. I will fight to build romance in everyday ways and win your love. Understood?"

Heather opened her mouth and closed it again without a sound, then looked down at the ground with a blush. Steve took that as an affirmative.

"Shall we go?" With a small smile, he motioned toward the path.

Heather studied her feet for a moment, struggling with the strong surge of attraction she felt for Steve. His declaration put him in a very vulnerable position. She fought a shiver as she realized that he had willingly, lovingly given her a tremendous amount of power in their relationship. *Please Lord, guide me in this relationship. I don't want to be outside your will.*

Heather closed her eyes and took a deep breath. She looked up at Steve with a tremulous smile but steady eyes. She nodded and without a word, turned and headed up the path.

When they climbed back into Steve's rental, he started the car then looked over at her.

"Liliuokalani Park?" he asked.

"Do you promise not to stop on any of the bridges and try to kiss me?" Heather teased him.

"Scouts honor," Steve promised.

"You weren't a scout!"

"But I do have honor," Steve winked. "We'll walk fast, like we're exercising. You can tell me stories about Moose and I'll tell you stories about Grandma's Golden, T-Rex."

"T-Rex! Who would name a Golden Retriever T-Rex?" Heather exclaimed.

"Me," Steve grinned.

THEY SPENT A wonderful afternoon talking story and getting to know each other better. It wasn't until they were on the plane that Heather got serious again.

"I had a wonderful time today, Steve," she sighed heavily.

"So I did," Steve said with concern, "but you don't sound happy about it."

"I'm not sure if I am or not. I guess we'll see," Heather stared out the window at the baggage handlers. Steve waited patiently.

"It seems like what we talked about at the Falls today is entirely possible," Heather turned and looked at Steve. "So to be fair to you, I need to be upfront about something."

Steve felt a cold hand clutch at his heart.

"The human body is wondrously resilient," Heather still faced Steve, but she looked at a point just below his chin rather than making eye contact. "Part of the reason for that resiliency is the redundancy in the body. Two eyes, two ears, two kidneys, two lungs, two ovaries. If one is down, the other can take up the slack while it heals."

Heather sighed and blinked back tears.

"I lost some of my internal redundancy when I was wounded in the war, and had some non-redundant organs damaged." She swallowed hard and continued to stare at Steve's throat.

"Specifically I lost my left ovary and have some scaring on my uterus," she whispered. "The doctors aren't sure if I'll ever be able to get pregnant. If I do, I might not be able to carry the baby to term. I just thought you should know, before, you know, you might .... I just thought you should know."

Steve didn't answer, couldn't answer. He leaned his head against the seat and closed his eyes, processing what Heather had told him. Suddenly he heard a ding and the flight attendant was leaning over him.

"Sir, ma'am, we're getting ready for take off. Please be sure your seatbelts are securely fastened and your seats are in the upright and locked position."

Steve allowed the quiet bustle and hum of the taxi and take off to distract him for a while. When they were airborne and leveling off, he reached over and took Heather's hand.

"For the last ten years or so, I have waffled between the desire to have a boatload of kids and the fear that I would be a father like mine was." Steve sighed and shook his head. "That desire for sons and daughters of my own is very strong but so is the fear. Would children be a trial that I couldn't bear, that would drive me to drink? I guess that's a real possibility."

Steve looked at Heather, sitting with her shoulders slumped and her head drooping. Steve tilted her chin up with his free hand and looked into her hazel-green eyes.

"It seems to me that we both have issues," Steve very deliberately raised her hand to his lips and pressed a kiss on it. "I guess we'll just have to trust God and see what he has in store for us."

Heather smiled shakily. She felt her heart begin to fall as she took in the love and acceptance in Steve's eyes. When her tears started to trickle down her cheeks, Steve raised the armrest and wrapped his arm around her, cuddling her against his chest. Safe in his embrace, she cried in earnest.

After a few minutes, Heather's sobs began to taper off. Her breathing deepened and her arm wrapped around Steve's waist as she snuggled closer. Steve shifted a little so her head was in a more comfortable position. He pressed a kiss against her hair and stared out into the night as they winged homeward.

Heather's nap wasn't very long. Fifteen minutes later, the captain announced that they were beginning their descent into Honolulu International Airport, so Steve gently woke her.

She sat up with a jerk and rubbed her eyes with the heels of her hands. She slid her hands slowly down her cheeks and grimaced when she touched her chin. Heather reached out gingerly and touched Steve's shirt front at the dark, wet spot that wasn't there when they boarded.

"I drooled on you," she began to blush.

"Hey, don't be embarrassed," Steve said softly. "I'm not complaining."

"No shame," she smiled.

"What?" Once again Steve had trouble keeping up with her.

"No shame, dat da pidgin for 'don't be embarrassed.'"

"No shame," Steve tried it out. "It's certainly more efficient."

"Not all pidgin is," Heather laughed.

"Like what?"

"Stick around and you'll see."

"Oh, I plan to," Steve drawled.

Heather pretended to be busy making sure everything was ready for landing as she desperately tried not to blush yet again. Steve's chuckle assured her that she'd failed. What was her problem these days? She was blushing and weeping like a sixteen year old with a crush.

Steve easily handled both of their carry-on bags as they left the terminal and headed to baggage claim.

"Are we still on for tomorrow?" Steve asked.

"Tomorrow?" Heather was having trouble remembering what to do right now, much less what she was supposed to do tomorrow. "We're doing something tomorrow?"

"Motorcycles," Steve said as he reached into his right pocket. "You're going to help me look at motorcycles."

"Oh that. Sure, I guess," Heather watched curiously as Steve frowned and shifted the bags to his right hand. He plunged his left hand into his other pocket then stopped and looked at the ground around where they stood, then looked at the ground behind them. Realization dawned on Heather.

"Your cell phone," she snickered, "you've lost your cell phone."

"I guess," Steve grimaced and shook his head.

"When did you last use it?"

Steve groaned and smacked his hand to his forehead. "In Hilo, of course."

"Where? At Grandma's? In the car?"

"The airport. At the gate," Steve said with certainty. "I called Pete to let him know we were on schedule."

"Why Pete?"

"He's our ride," Steve groaned again. "He's at the cell phone waiting area, waiting for my call."

Heather made a show of pulling her cell phone out and handing it to him.

"Here. Use mine." She started walking again, shaking her head.

Steve followed as he punched in the number. It rang four times and went to voice mail. He hung up and redialed.

"He better pick up this time," he grumbled.

One ring and a cautious, "Hello?"

"Pete!"

"Steve. You lost your phone again," Pete laughed.

"How'd you guess?" Steve said dryly.

"Strange number when Steve is supposed to be calling me. It's a dead giveaway," was the loud cheerful reply. Heather could hear everything and she wasn't restraining her mirth. "Is this a stranger's number or should I program it into my phone?"

"Might as well program it," Steve grinned at Heather's quick blush. "Name's Heather."

"Oh, a lady friend! Fess up, brah."

"Just come and pick me up," Steve rolled his eyes. "I'm already in baggage claim."

He snapped the phone shut and handed it back to Heather.

"No goodbye?" She tsk'd. "How rude."

"Let's watch for our bags," Steve put down the carry-ons and turned toward the baggage carrousel.

"You get them while I retrieve your phone," she flipped open her phone.

"How're you going to do that?"

"Give me your number and you'll see."

She dialed the number. When it went to voice mail, she hung up and hit redial. Again voice mail, again redial. A third time. This time Heather was gratified to hear, "Airport Security."

"You found my phone!" she cried happily. Steve stepped closer and leaned down to listen in. "Thank you so much."

"Uh, where are you lady?" Heather pictured him looking around the terminal seating area in the upper corridor.

"I'm already in Honolulu. Can you help me get my phone back?"

"How you want me to do that?" The voice on the other end sounded wary.

"My grandma lives up on Kapaka Street. I guess she can pick it up if you tell me where it will be."

"Who's your grandma?"

"Pua Nakanishi."

"Aunty Pua is your grandma?" Heather grinned as if she expected that response. "She goes to my church. She makes the best haupia pie."

"That's my grandma," Heather affirmed. She noticed the bags on the carrousel and shooed Steve over with her free hand. He shooed her back, wanting to hear how this played out.

"Tell you what I'll do," the security officer said. "We got those mail-it-home boxes for contraband stuff. Give me your address and I'll mail it to you."

As Heather started to give him her name and shop address, she stepped deliberately away from Steve and pointed toward the baggage carrousel. He frowned but went to get the bags anyway.

"Thank you very much," Heather was saying as Steve came back with the bags. She picked up her carry-on and walked out of the terminal, fully expecting Steve to bring the rest of the bags. "What's your name? I'm going to have Grandma make you the biggest and best haupia pie you've ever had."

When she hung up the phone, Steve shook his head in wonder.

"I'm going to get my phone back, huh?" She nodded. "But why did you have him send it to you instead of to me?"

"Oh please," Heather rolled her eyes. "Church friend of Grandma's or not, I'm not tempting anyone with the knowledge that they have Steve Jeremiah's phone."

"Good thinking," Steve motioned toward the dark BMW X5 SAV that had just come around the corner. "There's Pete."

Chapter 10

*P*ete pulled up to the curb and popped the back end of the SAV. While Steve was loading the bags, he opened the front passenger door for Heather. Steve glared at him before climbing into the back seat on the driver's side.

"So, Steve hasn't told me about you, Heather," Pete said.

"Oh, he probably just forgot," she said airily.

"Yeah, he has a habit of forgetting things."

"I'm beginning to see that," Heather tried to sound innocent.

"Did he ever tell you about the road trip when he forgot all his –?"

"No!" Steve virtually shouted. "She doesn't need to hear about it."

"No, I guess she doesn't," Pete laughed. "But did you hear about when we went to get off the plane in Dallas one time and he couldn't find his shoes?"

"Where were they?"

"Back in the terminal in Chicago, under his seat!"

"No kidding? He walked onto the plane in his socks?" Heather giggled and Steve grunted.

"No kidding," Pete shook his head in amazement. "And then there was the Sunday in December that he nearly froze when we got home because he'd left his jacket hanging in the hotel in Tampa."

"Oh really?"

"Really. And there was my birthday party incident."

"Oh? Do tell," Heather encouraged Pete.

"Please don't," Steve begged from the backseat. They ignored him.

"Yeah, Steve set up this great surprise party for my twenty-fifth birthday. At the end of the evening, when everyone else had already left the restaurant and the waitress came with the bill the surprise was on Steve when he discovered he'd left his wallet at home. I had to pay for my own birthday party."

"Oh you poor man," Heather commiserated.

"Poor man, my foot," Steve growled. "I paid you back! And I still am."

"Yes he did," Pete grinned at Heather. "That's not the kine stuff he forgets."

"He just forgets things," Heather suggested.

"Not all things," Pete said. "He never forgets his –"

"Pete!" The driver's seat suddenly jerked forward violently as Steve shouted over his friend.

"Steve, behave. He's driving," Heather scolded.

"Somethin' wrong with your leg, brah?" Pete feigned concern.

"Something's wrong with your brain, my friend," Steve retorted. "Let's not go there."

"Why not?" Pete pretended to be puzzled. "It's not some dark secret, it's just a strange personality quirk."

"That Heather doesn't need to hear about yet," Steve warned.

"Why not?" Pete seemed genuinely puzzled this time. "I don't think it's gonna freak her out or something. She seems cool."

"But what if it does?" Steve muttered.

Heather looked over her shoulder at Steve. In the light of the street lamps, he looked like he was pleading with his eyes. Pleading for what? Her understanding?

"I'm intrigued," Heather mused.

"It's actually kind of endearing," Pete said. "Unfortunately, he's had some bimbos laugh at him when they found out. Kind of embarrassing."

"Really embarrassing," Steve grumbled in the backseat.

"I'm really intrigued now!" Heather said.

"Like I said, it's no big deal," Pete grinned, "but Steve has a thing for toys."

"Toys!" Heather was delighted, but Steve slunk down in his seat.

"Lots of toys," Pete continued. "Tonka trucks, Hot Wheels, Legos, Lincoln Logs, trains, G.I. Joes. And he doesn't just collect them, he plays with them. All except the –"

Pete's seat jerked again. He looked up at Steve in the rearview mirror.

"Right. Sorry, brah," Pete apologized.

"Sorry about what?" Heather asked, looking from one man to the other.

"Nothing," Steve's garrulous friend had suddenly clammed up. Heather was very intrigued.

"Later," Steve said. He looked out the window and muttered, "Much later."

Heather decided to let it drop for now, but she did want to know more about the toys Pete had already talked about.

"So he really plays with the toys?" she asked Pete.

"Not just him, everyone who comes over," Pete laughed. "He likes to have play dates with the team kids."

"Oh yeah?"

Steve shook his head as he listened to his best friend tell the woman of his dreams all his secrets. He felt like banging his head against the window. He looked out the window again, suddenly realizing that the landmarks sliding by were much too familiar.

"Pete!" He interrupted Pete's story about a Lego challenge. "Where are you going?"

"Your house, brah," Pete suddenly groaned and looked at Heather. "But you don't live there. Where do you live?"

"Not at the top of Alewa Heights," Heather said drolly.

"I'm two blocks from Steve's house," Pete shook his head. "And you live ...?"

"In Kaimuki," Heather said.

"Oh, dumb, dumb," Pete groaned.

"Turn around, Pete," Steve said.

"Where do you live?" Heather asked Pete.

"Hawaii Kai!"

"Steve, it's ridiculous for Pete to go all the way to my place, come back here to drop you off and then drive right past me to get home," Heather turned to Pete. "Take him home then drop me off."

Steve couldn't effectively argue since Pete was pulling into his driveway.

Even though Steve was fully capable of getting his own luggage, Pete climbed out of the SAV to help him. He stepped up to close the back end before Steve could slam it shut.

"Hey braddah, I'm really sorry," Pete said. "I wasn't thinking."

"She's my girl, Pete," Steve glared. "If you mess with her, I'll ...."

"I get the message," Pete put up both hands in a defensive posture, "but this is me you're talkin' to. Brah, you sound really jealous."

"Insanely so," Steve sighed.

"But it's only a fifteen minute ride," Pete seemed genuinely puzzled.

"I know," Steve groaned, "but man, I so don't want anything to ruin this."

"Wow, you got it bad," Pete whistled. "Does she know?"

"She knows, but not how far I've already fallen," Steve said.

"How far is that?"

"As long as Heather Shepherd is in this world, I couldn't possibly love another woman."

"Okay," Pete said, "she's my sister."

He turned back to the SAV, but Steve reached out to stop him.

"Don't tell her, Pete," Steve said quietly. "She can't know."

"Why not?"

"Because then she'll try too hard to make it real for her," Steve said. "I don't want her to have that kind of pressure."

Pete nodded in agreement and walked to his door.

"Pete," Steve called as he got ready to climb in. Pete straightened up and looked at him. "I'm sorry man, for, you know .... I was out of line."

"Yeah, I know," Pete grinned and slid into the driver's seat.

Heather didn't ask what they had talked about because she strongly suspected they had been talking about her and Steve. She had heard Steve's apology and knew that he was disturbed about Pete being alone with her, but he also knew he didn't need to be upset.

They rode quietly for awhile but Heather wanted to talk about Steve with his best friend.

"So, you've known Steve since you joined the team six years ago," Heather observed. "Were you friends from the start?"

"Yeah, right off," Pete said. "Are you a fan?"

"Of the Grizzlies? Only all my life! My dad's from Illinois and my mom discovered she loved watching football with her husband so I was indoctrinated from my mother's womb."

"And of Steve?" Pete asked.

"Who wasn't enthralled with him from his rookie year?" Heather replied. "The big defensive end who moved like a panther and hit like a speeding locomotive. He led the league in sacks! What's not to like?"

"I know. That was my senior year," Pete said. "Watching him made me seriously consider changing my position. I wanted so much to be like him."

"Are you glad you didn't?"

"Playing middle linebacker to Steve's defensive end?" Pete grinned. "Oh yeah, you better believe it!"

"I'm glad too," Heather agreed.

"Why? Because otherwise you probably wouldn't have gotten to meet my adorable self?" Pete grinned.

"No Pete! I'm a Grizzly fan, remember?" Heather rolled her eyes. "Together you two took Grizzly defense back to the powerhouse it's supposed to be."

"Yeah, but we still haven't won a championship," Pete sighed.

"Next year, brah," Heather smiled. "Next year."

"I think we just might, if our o-line can protect our hotshot quarterback," Pete agreed.

When they were finally Diamond Head bound on the H1, Pete looked over at Heather.

"Steve's a great guy, ya know," he offered.

"Yes, I do know that, Pete," Heather sighed, "and if I ever forget my family will remind me. They've accepted him as ohana."

"So why the sigh?"

"I truly don't know," Heather sighed again and thought for a moment. "Maybe it's partly because I feel like everyone is pushing Steve at me. But I have four brothers so I was very young when I learned that I couldn't let people push me around."

"Brothers can certainly be pushy," Pete agreed.

"And because I was a girl who liked football and auto shop, lots of people were always trying to push me into more girly pursuits. I got into the habit of pushing back and doing my own thing. It's pretty deeply ingrained now. The other side of the coin is that I really like my life the way it is. I don't want to give up my home and my shop and move to the Mainland if Steve and I ...."

"Your shop?" Pete said. He glanced quickly at her, then back again. He smacked his hand to his forehead. "I'm so lolo. You're my mechanic. That's why you look familiar! You towed Steve's car when it broke down. You're Greg's sister. You look different out of the shop."

"Right on all counts," Heather smiled. "I didn't realize you didn't know who I am. Steve didn't tell you he's been hanging around my family since the week I fixed his car?"

"Nah, the buggah didn't," Pete shook his head. "He hasn't been hanging around my place as much, but I hadn't realized he had a ..., um ..., was ...."

"Yeah, I get your point," Heather bailed him out. "I wonder why he didn't mention me to his best friend."

Pete heard a hint of hurt in her voice. "Hey sistah, no worries. Steve's a pretty private person when something's really important to him."

"I'm not worried," Heather said haughtily.

Pete just snorted. "Yeah, right. Your exit Sixth or Koko Head?"

"Sixth Avenue. I'm a block behind the shop."

Pete paid close attention to his driving as he made his way over to the right lane to exit.

"Seriously though, Heather," he finally said. "Steve's a great guy. You can depend on him."

"Seriously though, Pete," Heather replied. "I know Steve's a great guy. He's not the problem, I am."

"Why do you think that?"

"You're a Christian, aren't you?"

"Sure am. Six years now."

"Are you a trying-to-do-God's-will Christian or one who's satisfied just having salvation?"

"I try to do God's will."

"I am too but the problem is that I haven't been talking to God for almost two years, except to tell him how mad I am at him," Heather smiled sadly. "I'm not sure how to hear him anymore."

"I think I understand," Pete said as he pulled up in front of the house she'd pointed out. "But do me a favor? Please try not to break Steve's heart. Give it a fair chance."

"I'm trying, Pete," Heather climbed out of the SAV and waved to Pete who waited in the drive until she'd unlocked her door.

Once she was safely inside, Heather watched Pete's taillights disappear around the corner. She laid her forehead on the cool glass and sent up a silent plea that neither she nor Steve would get their hearts broken.

Chapter 11

*T*he next day, Steve showed up at the shop promptly at eleven-thirty to take Heather to lunch. It was very ordinary, just plate lunches in foam containers from a local fast food joint, but they enjoyed each other's company and Heather had to concentrate very hard to not feel romanced.

Steve had lined up three motorcycles for them to look at. The first one was right there in Kaimuki. Heather took a quick look at it and vetoed it right off.

"So what was wrong with it," Steve said as they drove off. "I kind of liked it. It sounded good."

"Sure it did," Heather frowned at him. "It was big and shiny and rumbled like a little boy's dream, but it wasn't safe for you."

"Why not?"

"The tires and the shock system were getting too old," Heather frowned. "You outweigh that guy by at least a hundred pounds. You would have put a lot more strain on the bike than he does. Within a hundred miles or so, things would start giving out, maybe with you on it. Leave that one for a little guy."

Steve felt childishly pleased that Heather called him a "big guy," even if in an offhanded way. People often called him that, but coming from her, it sounded more like an affirmation than an observation. He grinned and Heather deliberately ignored him.

Heather was cautiously optimistic about the next bike. When she gave Steve a nod, he turned to the seller who had introduced himself as Mike.

"You mind if I take her out for a spin?"

"Sure," Mike replied. "I would expect you to."

Heather was surprised by Steve's boyish grin of delight. He popped the trunk of his car and pulled out a leather jacket, helmet and gloves.

"I'm glad to see you use proper safety gear," Heather said with a smile.

"Have to, sweetheart," Steve winked. "It's in my contract."

When Steve took off, Mike glanced sideways at Heather. "Is that really Steve Jeremiah from the Grizzlies?"

Heather looked at the man, enigmatic behind her dark sunglasses. "What if he is?"

"If he is," Mike half-laughed. "I'll be tempted to just give him that bike. He's saved my virtual football team more than once."

Heather stared at the man for a long moment, then she gave a quick twitch of a smile and turned to watch the road where Steve had disappeared.

"Looks a lot like him, doesn't he?" she said noncommittally.

When Steve returned, he thanked Mike for the ride, complimented him on the bike, and promised to call after he looked at the last one and made his decision.

Heather grinned at him after they drove off.

"What's funny?"

"That guy asked if you were you?"

"And you said ...?"

"'Looks a lot like him, doesn't he?'"

Steve burst out laughing. "That's great!"

After they laughed together, Heather looked at Steve with her elbow on the window ledge, cheek propped on her fist.

"But seriously, Steve," she said, "what am I supposed to say when people ask? And what about my family, did you discuss it with them?"

"Best thing is to follow your gut," Steve shrugged. "Some people it's okay, others, not so."

"Okay, but did you talk to my family too? You hang around enough that someone's going to see you with one of them and ask," Heather said. "Do you trust Tim and Robert to have the discernment?"

"Would you?"

"Honestly? Right now, probably not," Heather shrugged. "They're too young and innocent still, at least when it comes to knowing the jerks from the good guys."

"They might be wiser than you think," Steve suggested, "but I'll defer to your judgment on this. Thanks for caring enough to ask, it means a lot to me."

That was a major understatement. Steve was impressed that she had stopped to think about his feelings rather than just take pleasure in Mike's reaction to meeting him. More and more he saw her as perfect for him.

The seller of the last motorcycle was Sarah, a woman nearing middle-age. She stood sadly in the open garage and answered their questions with either simple answers or noncommittal shrugs.

The motorcycle looked solid and safe. It was a three year old Harley Softail Deuce in an intriguing black cherry. It was well cared for and fired right to life with the classic Harley rumble. This time, Heather was the one who asked if Steve could take it for a spin. Sarah frowned.

"You ride much?" she asked.

"I've been riding since I was fifteen," Steve answered. "That's almost fifteen years."

"What did you ride, dirt bikes, sport bikes?" She almost sounded suspicious.

"Street bikes or cruisers."

"Where?"

"Country, city, open road. Kansas, Oklahoma, Illinois, and a summer trip through the Midwest." Steve knew he was providing his letters of reference. Sarah wasn't going to adopt this baby out to just anyone. "I lost count sometime after fifteen thousand miles about five years ago. Never had an accident."

Sarah studied him thoughtfully for a moment, then looked at the bike. With tears in her eyes, she gave a quick nod.

As Steve got his gear from the trunk, he looked at Heather with a raised eyebrow and a small nod sideways to where the woman stood. Sarah scuffed her toes at small bits of gravel on her paved driveway, hands in her pockets, not looking at them or the bike. Obviously she didn't want to see Steve drive off on it.

Heather understood Steve's wordless request. She gave him a slight smile and a slow blink as a nod.

As the sound of the Harley's throaty rumble faded off in the distance, Heather walked over to Sarah who still stood in the open garage. She took off her cap and sunglasses, hoping to make a connection with the hurting woman.

"You don't really want to sell this bike, do you?"

The woman shook her head slightly and shrugged.

"Whose was it?" Heather asked softly.

"My husband's," she whispered.

"What happened to him?"

"Killed in the line of duty last spring," Sarah choked on her words. "He was a cop."

"Was he the detective shot by the kid on ice at the convenience store in Makiki? In May?" Heather felt a stab of pain.

The woman nodded and suddenly Heather wished she had kept her sunglasses on. She knew her own anguish had to show in her eyes.

"That was right after my dad died," she whispered.

"I know," Sarah whispered back.

"You do?" Heather was surprised.

"Rick really admired you," Sarah explained with a nod. "He had been in the first desert war and was also injured. He said you were a real hero, not just because of what you did over there but because you came back here and picked up your life and really lived it."

Sarah paused to pull a packet of tissue from her pocket, taking one for herself and offering one to Heather. She took it gratefully. "So many young people today act like the world owes them something, but you not only tried to live a normal life in spite of your combat experience, you also gave back to the community."

Startled, Heather stared at Sarah.

"Rick was a detective," Sarah smiled. "When something caught his attention, he detected. He knew about you and your dog. Moose, right?"

"Yeah, he's a Golden Retriever," Heather was shocked and beginning to wonder what God was up to.

"Rick went to your dad's funeral," Sarah whispered. "He felt so bad for you."

Suddenly Heather needed to sit down.

"He said he wanted to hug you, you looked so sad," Sarah smiled sadly. "But he didn't know you, so he just shook your hand and said he was sorry for your loss, just like everybody else."

Heather pressed her hand to her temples and swayed gently.

"Oh dear," Sarah cried with concern. "You don't look so good. Come in and sit down."

She led Heather through the garage and into the kitchen where Heather collapsed into one of the chairs. Putting her head between her knees, she breathed deeply. Sarah set a glass of water on the table beside her.

"I'm sorry. I didn't mean to bring up painful memories," Sarah sat in the chair beside Heather's.

"I'm shocked that my painful memories are so intertwined with yours," Heather said. "If he told you all that, it was one of the last things he said to you. He died that night!"

"Yes, he did," Sarah grabbed a couple tissues from the box on her table and handed one to Heather. "He came home for dinner like he usually did. He would talk about his day before going back out."

Sarah paused to blow her nose. "That night, he talked about the funeral. About how he wished he'd known your dad. He said he felt a burden to encourage you but he didn't know how."

She stopped and grabbed another tissue.

"I said," she cleared her throat. "I said he'd find a way in God's time …. Then I said, 'Bye, I love you,' … and watched him ride off on his bike …. He was already dead by the time I got to the hospital."

Heather knelt beside Sarah and held her as they both cried. After a few minutes, Heather pulled away and Sarah grabbed some more tissues, sharing them with her.

Steve suddenly loomed large in the doorway. Sarah looked at him, then back at Heather.

"I think God's time is now," Sarah smiled. "Come dear."

Sarah led them back into the garage. As Heather slipped past him, Steve raised his eyebrow in question.

"Later," she whispered with a small shake of her head.

Sarah was reaching for two helmets sitting side by side on a shelf in the garage.

"Here. One of these should fit you, dear," she offered them to Heather.

"For what?" Heather was genuinely confused.

"To wear while he packs you for a ride, of course," Sarah said.

"No!" Heather jerked her hands to her chest and stepped back from the helmets. She stepped into the hard wall of Steve's chest.

"Yes," he murmured in her ear.

"You don't technically have motorcycle safety gear," Sarah said, "but your work boots and denim coveralls are close enough."

"I don't ride," Heather croaked.

"No time like the present to start," Sarah insisted, pushing the black helmet with silver trim at her. "Rick's is probably going to fit best, but you might want to unpin your braid."

"No," Heather shook her head insistently.

"Oh yes," Sarah said. "I know it seems scary to you, but you'll love it."

She looked down at the helmet and blinked back tears.

"Rick used to pack me whenever he could," she smiled. "He loved taking me to church on the motorcycle." She sighed and smiled up at Heather and Steve. "It was one of the ways we built romance out of everyday life."

Heather felt Steve's grunt of surprise. Hearing her own words coming from this lonely widow, she knew she was being nudged by God. She reached up and began to unpin her hair.

Sarah helped her with the helmet. She smiled thoughtfully.

"Perfect fit," she said. "I guess Rick gets to encourage you after all."

Sarah gave Heather some quick passenger tips. Lean when Steve leans, relax, don't wiggle around or make any sudden movements, relax and trust Steve. Heather tried to concentrate but all she could think about was that she was going to climb onto a totally open vehicle with nothing but denim and a helmet between her, the road, other vehicles and any stray objects that happened to fly her way.

"Don't hurry back," Sarah told Steve. "Ride around town some until she gets comfortable, then take her out to Makapuu Point. You need to know how it's going to handle two-up before you decide to buy it."

Heather had a death grip on Steve when they first started. They didn't crash in the first five minutes, so she relaxed a fraction. As Steve drove carefully through the streets of Hawaii Kai, she felt more comfortable. When she sat up enough that her helmet wasn't scrunched tightly up against Steve's, her neck was no longer pushed painfully back and she relaxed even more. She was actually beginning to enjoy the ride when Steve pulled into Maunalua Beach and parked. He took off his helmet, so Heather did too. Steven half turned and grinned at her over his shoulder.

"You need to get off first, or I'll end up kicking you," he said.

"Oh. Okay," Heather climbed off. "Are we pau already?"

"You almost sound disappointed," Steve set the bike on its kickstand, then dismounted, turned and sat sideways on the seat.

"I almost am," Heather said in surprise.

"We're not pau yet," Steve grinned. "I just wanted to give you a break and make sure you're ready for the next leg."

"Oh. Thanks," Heather said.

For a moment, Steve watched Heather watch the boats in the bay.

"What happened back there?" Steve asked. "With Sarah?"

Heather thought for a moment, trying to decide how much to tell him.

"I'm pretty sure it was a God thing," she finally said.

Steve waited patiently. Heather continued to watch the boats.

"Whatever it was, it was intense and I need to think about it before I can talk about it," Heather glanced at Steve out of the corner of her eye and saw he was dejected by her reply. She stepped closer and Steve looked up.

"I'm having fun right now," Heather grinned. "I don't want to talk. I want to ride."

Steve smiled, slow and easy.

"Then let's ride. But first," Steve raised his right index finger, "a rider's brief."

"But Sarah already gave me one," Heather said.

"And you," Steve tapped her lightly on the nose, "were too terrified to listen well. Now you will. You need to because, as you well know, the road to Makapuu has lots of curves. You have to sit right or we just might take a swim."

"Okay, I'm listening," Heather said.

"Sit back a little and don't hang quite so tight," Steve grinned. "Not that I don't like you up close, but when you hold on that tight, it's a little awkward."

"I noticed that," Heather said. "Awkward is bad on a motorcycle, right?"

"Very bad," Steve agreed. "Next, when I lean, you lean too, but not as much. Don't lean outside of me."

"So, follow your lean," Heather quipped.

"The pun is sorry but the thought is right," Steve laughed. "You also need to look over my shoulder if you can without leaning around me. That helps you see when I'm going to stop so you aren't surprised."

"I can do that," Heather sighed, "but it would be easier if you didn't have such big broad shoulders. They're kinda distracting."

"Focus, Heather," Steve choked back a laugh. "You also need to remember not to wiggle around back there. In a car you can move pretty much whenever you want, but if you do it at the wrong time on a motorcycle –"

"I know!" Heather was feeling a little too giddy. "'We just might take a swim.'"

"Good, you're listening," Steve grinned. "Now, most important, relax and trust me."

"I think I can trust you," Heather wondered if he knew she wasn't talking about just for this ride.

"I'm glad," Steve smiled softly. "I'm going to ride here in Hawaii Kai some more until you're ready to go on."

"How will you know I'm ready?"

Steve reached over and tucked a wisp of hair behind Heather's ear. "You can tap me on the shoulder and point toward Hanauma Bay."

"But how will I know when I'm ready?" Heather asked.

Steve wondered if they were just talking about today's ride.

"When you begin to feel like you can trust me not to crash and burn with you," Steve stood and smiled down at Heather. He knew he wasn't just talking about today's ride. "When you're into the joy of the ride instead of worrying about getting to our destination alive, you'll know you're ready."

"Okay," Heather smiled. "That sounds good."

AFTER TEN MINUTES of prowling the streets of Hawaii Kai, Heather realized she was looking forward to the open road. When Steve slowed for a stop sign, she tapped him on his right shoulder and pointed toward Hanauma.

Steve nodded and flipped on his right turn signal. Soon they were turning left onto Kalanianaole Highway. Steve accelerated gently but steadily. They were climbing up the back of Hanauma Bay with Koko Head standing sentinel to the left. Heather's heart soared and a laugh bubbled up inside her.

Heather's mechanic side assured her that the motorcycle ran well on the long straight rise, even with their combined weight of almost four hundred pounds. There was no hint of any potential mechanical problems.

Her playful side leapt for joy. The sky had never been so blue, the mountains more inspiring, the flowers on trees and bushes more beautiful. But when Steve topped the rise at Hanauma Bay's park entrance, for a moment Heather was tempted to clutch Steve tightly in fear. She knew this road well, knew the sharp left with the steep descent.

Just trust, a small voice whispered to her soul. *Trust me. Trust Steve.*

Heather let go of her fear and laughed for joy. Over Steve's right shoulder she saw the blue of the Pacific against the mixed green and brown of Palea Point on the shoulder of Hanauma. Then they were flying around the curve, leaning left.

With Koko Head's bulk on their left and the deep, deep blue of the ocean beckoning to the far horizon, Heather felt another bubble of joy burst over her in a flood. They dipped and surged up, swayed left and then right. Sometimes nothing but guardrail and the steep drop was between them and the blue Pacific. Sometimes lava rock formations loomed, close enough to touch.

The ride was much too short. Soon they were climbing the last rise before Halona Blowhole, where the road would straighten out and level off, with just a few gentle curves before the long straight climb up to Makapuu's scenic lookout. As she gazed out at water so blue it hurt the heart with its beauty, Heather saw something. She squealed with joy and tapped Steve on the right shoulder, pointing urgently to the blowhole parking lot.

When Steve pulled into a parking stall, Heather was so excited she could hardly wait for him to stop before she was off the bike, removing her helmet as she dismounted.

"Whales," Heather cried, almost dancing with excitement. "Hurry, there's whales out there."

Steve grinned at her excitement. He put the kick stand down, and reached for the key to turn off the engine. He was much too slow.

"Hurry up!" Heather said with frustration. She darted to the fence to the right of the blowhole where people were pointing and "oohing."

Steve had never seen whales in real life. He was intrigued but he wasn't excited. He took the time to lock his helmet on the bike rather than take it with him as Heather had.

She had found a space at the rail to squeeze into. Steve walked up behind her and saw the most magnificent sight he had ever seen.

About a hundred yards off shore, a large dark sleek body rose gracefully out of the water, hanging there for a long breathtaking moment, rotating about a quarter turn before slapping back into the water. A very large, two-winged tail slapped the water just beyond him, sending up a large spray.

Steve heard himself "aahing" with everyone else. He now understood Heather's excitement. The couple to their left squeezed together and gave Steve some room to step closer to the rail.

He propped his left arm on the rail and angled his body into the narrow gap between Heather and her accommodating neighbors. She nudged him with her left elbow, pointing with her right hand at a whale that had just breached. He laid lazily in the water, then rolled slightly to his right before disappearing. Suddenly his big tail broke the surface, rising high before it slapped the water. They stood there with the small crowd, pointing and laughing, expressing their amazement and enjoyment of the impromptu show.

After a while, Steve began to be more aware of the woman beside him than the whales out in the ocean. He suddenly realized that his hand was resting on Heather's shoulder. Her head was inches from his. She turned to say something and they were virtually nose to nose. Steve's heart began to pound.

"I think we should go," he whispered huskily. "This is a little too romantic for me."

Heather knew exactly what he meant. She gave a quick nod and stepped away from the rail and Steve. She turned and looked for her transportation, suddenly having no clue how she'd gotten to the blowhole.

Steve tapped her on the shoulder and pointed over at the motorcycle, then he handed her the helmet she'd left at the rail. As he watched her walk away, fumbling with her helmet, Steve threw a prayer heavenward.

Oh Lord, I hope this is your will. It's way too late for me to not get my heart broken.

Chapter 12

*S*teve arranged with Sarah to come back for the motorcycle that evening after he'd contacted his insurance agent. Heather was picking up Moose from Malia's house where he'd enjoyed playing with her little brothers and sister while Heather was in Hilo, so Steve called Greg and confirmed that he would be available to take him to Sarah's.

Heather made a deliberate effort not to see Steve the next day, but then his cell phone was delivered to her shop in the afternoon. That's when she realized she didn't know Steve's home phone or email or any other way to contact him except by cell phone. She called Greg.

"Hey punk," she said cheerfully.

"I love you too, Boss," Greg replied just as cheerfully.

"I need some help, Little Big Man."

"With what?" Greg asked warily. The trouble she'd gotten him into over the years was legendary.

"I just need to get in touch with Steve," Heather said.

"No prob, I've got his cell number," Greg replied.

"I'll do you one better. I've got his cell phone."

"How'd that happen?"

"It's a long story," Heather laughed.

"I have time," Greg hinted.

"I don't right now," Heather countered. "Do you have a home phone or email for him?"

"Nope, sorry."

"I know where he lives," Heather said. "Come over at six-thirty and go with me."

"How do you know where he lives?"

"That's part of the long story."

"Why do you need me?"

"Because I'm not going to his house alone," Heather said.

"Good thinking," Greg said. "I'll do it on one condition."

"What's that?"

"You tell me this long story on the way."

"You got a deal," Heather said.

"You want me to come by the house or the shop?"

"The house. I'll change before we go."

She hung up as she heard his laugh. It wasn't what he was obviously thinking. She wasn't changing to be clean and attractive for Steve, she was changing for her own comfort. She didn't like to smell like motor oil all the time.

WHEN GREG AND Heather got to his house that evening, Steve came to the door in his at-home clothes, old Dockers shorts and a well-worn, generously ripped Oklahoma practice t-shirt. The first thing Heather noticed was his muscles, the second was that he wasn't winter white anymore. She was doubly glad Greg was along to help her flee temptation.

"Hey, how did you know dinner was on?" Steve asked with a grin.

"We brought your phone," Heather said quickly, pushing the box at him, ready to bolt.

"Why didn't you call?" Steve said. "I would have come to get it rather than you coming all the way up here."

"Only had your cell number, brah," Greg walked through the door and sniffed appreciatively. "What smells so good?"

He gave Steve a handshake and one-armed hug.

"Put a decent t-shirt on, man," he whispered with a laugh.

Steve looked at Heather who was still standing on the front stoop, very obviously not looking at him.

"I wasn't expecting company," Steve explained needlessly.

"Based on the smells comin' from your kitchen, I'd say you better start expectin' it more often," Greg grinned.

"Come on in. Make yourselves at home," Steve said as he walked across the room, leaving Greg to hold the door for his sister. "I'll be back soon."

When he disappeared around a corner, Greg turned to Heather who had ventured in only after Steve left the door.

"Do you want to stay for supper?" he asked quietly.

"No! Yes! ... No! ... I don't know!" Heather was torn between the desire to play it safe, to run from her growing attraction to Steve and the almost instinctual need to not let him get away.

"I guess that means we stay," Greg said wryly.

"Punk!" Heather stuck out her tongue and deliberately looked away from her brother.

Something about the pictures hanging in koa wood frames near the door caught her eye. She stepped closer and gasped in surprise. They were framed pictures of Tim and Robert with Steve. She recognized them as the prayer breakfast photos from the year before. They were autographed by her brothers!

"Did you know about this?" She looked over her shoulder at Greg.

"Yeah," Greg said slowly. "You didn't?"

"No, I didn't."

"I guess you left family dinner too early that day," Greg shrugged.

"Family dinner?"

"Yeah, two weeks ago or so. The boys gave him the pics after dinner," Greg explained. "Steve asked them to autograph them."

"Why did they give Steve pictures?"

"He asked for them."

"When? Why?"

"When? The day he picked up his car," Greg said. "Why? Probably because he's a man who knows what a broken heart needs."

"What do you mean?" Heather asked sharply. "Who's heart?"

"Tim's."

"What?" Heather was surprised. "What was wrong with Tim's heart?"

"Turns out Tim was blaming himself for Dad's death," Greg said. "God revealed it to Steve and he helped Tim see it wasn't his fault."

"Why did he think it was?"

"I talked to him later," Greg stared sadly at the pictures. "He said that when the cancer came back, he got mad at Dad. Figured Dad must not have obeyed the doctors. Somehow when Dad died, he decided that he was being punished for being angry at Dad."

"But he never said anything," Heather's heart broke to think of her little brother carrying such a burden alone. "The better part of a year he was hurting like that for no reason. Why didn't we see it?"

"Maybe because we were trying to deal with our own pain," Greg rubbed the back of his neck. "Maybe we just hurt too much."

"Why Steve?" Heather barely breathed the question.

"Maybe because he belongs in our family," Greg said just as quietly.

"I hope you're right, Little Big Man," Heather used her childhood nickname for her brother. "'Cause I think he's going to be hard to dig up."

Heather looked up at him over her shoulder. Greg grinned in understanding, then he nodded his head toward the wall to her left.

"Did you see the fireplace?"

"No! Where?" Heather turned to look. "Wow! That's great."

The fireplace was made of rugged stones. The chimney rose unbroken by a mantle but shelves winged off to either side. On the left side sat a stylized crystal statue of three people with mouths open and arms raised in praise, on the right, a well-used softball on a small pedestal. A semicircle of flagstones in front of the fireplace provided a fireproof barrier to protect the hardwood floor.

A white plush rug kissed the edge of the flagstones and several pillows ranging from body pillows to neck rolls were scattered over the rug.

Built into the wall adjacent to the one with the fireplace was a hutch. Heather wasn't surprised to see that it held a number of toys. Next to the toy hutch was the backside of a room which Heather guessed was either a bathroom or closet. Maybe it was a pantry since she saw a dining table just past the wall that created a short hall on the other side of the mystery room and extended about five feet to the left of the hall.

On a line with the table and just to the left of the front door an armchair and a couch sat at right angles to each other, open to the dining area and to the large set of shades that covered what would be the makai wall. The shades started about four feet from the corner of the living area and extended all the way around the corner into the dining area, ending by the kitchen counter. The open-beam, peaked ceiling unnecessarily gave height and airiness to a room already vast.

"What do you think is behind the shades?" Greg asked.

"I don't know, probably windows," Heather said.

"Maybe it's Steve's 'Portrait of Dorian Gray,'" Greg said melodramatically.

"It is 'picture,' not portrait, and it's neither," Steve said from behind them. Wherever he had disappeared to, he now matched their attire, jeans and a regular t-shirt. Heather thought his t-shirt was too small. "Sorry to disappoint you, but it's just Honolulu."

Steve pressed a button on a wall panel and the shades began to roll up into a recessed hiding place. Behind the shades was a wall of glass, floor to ceiling, from the front living area all the way around into the kitchen. The shades had hidden a spectacular view that didn't disappoint at all.

Diamond Head was a dark shadow off in the distance to the left and the lights of Honolulu defined the shoreline. From here, Heather could see where Aiea and Pearl City took over, and that was probably the lights at Barber's Point, tiny in the distance where the very last light of the setting sun was winking out for the night. During the day, she could probably look down into Punchbowl, pick out landmarks on Waikiki and maybe even spot Mom's house far below them.

"Why did you close them?" Greg asked, impressed with the view.

"Sometimes it's too distracting when I'm cooking," Steve shrugged. "So I close them. Tonight I watched the sunset then closed the shades when I came in to fix dinner."

"There's a lanai," Greg noticed the sliding glass doors where the living and dining areas met. "Can we go out there?"

"Sure," Steve said, stepping toward the doors.

"No!" Heather cried, stepping back from the doors.

Both men turned to her with questioning looks. Heather couldn't think of an excuse, only the truth. She had to tell them something or they would insist on going out. She blurted out the truth, glaring at Steve.

"If we go out there, the view and the breeze are going to give me chicken skin," she didn't bother to take a breath. "I'm going to shiver and you're going to put your arm around me to warm me and I'm going to fall in love and I'm not ready to fall in love yet."

Blushing furiously, she finally took a deep breath. Planting her left fist on her hip, she shook her right index finger at both men. "And I told you both that already!"

Steve stared at her, bemused. He wasn't sure if he was supposed to shout "Hallelujah" or laugh. Greg laughed. Heather stalked over to the panel where Steve had pressed the button that raised the curtains.

"Is she often like this?" Steve asked Greg while he watched Heather.

"Like what?" Greg asked. "Bossy or brazen?"

"Both. Either."

Heather ignored them as she tried to find the button Steve had pushed. There were lots of buttons and the room was rather dark because Steve only had lights on in the kitchen and by the front door.

"Most of her life," Greg told Steve. "She's very dramatic ..."

Heather frowned and pushed a button. Lights in the living room slowly rose.

"But she can't lie worth a darn ..."

Heather pressed her lips together and snorted softly, pushing another button. Fans began to whisper overhead.

"So she blurts out the truth then tries to cover her embarrassment ..."

Heather told herself not to blush as she jabbed at another button. Soft music, something classical and soothing. She wasn't soothed. They were laughing at her.

"By diverting attention somewhere else."

A long arm reached around her and the shades began to descend.

"Oh this is so much better," Heather said sarcastically as Steve stood behind her with his right arm around her, casually restoring everything she'd done. She thought he was close enough to feel his heart thumping. Or was that her heart? She looked for a distraction. There, stairs to the right.

"What's down there?" Ducking under Steve's arm, she stalked to the stairs.

"That's the rest of the house," Steve motioned for Greg to follow his sister. "Shall we take a quick tour? Dinner will take care of itself for a while."

"Got to keep her out of trouble," Greg shook his head as his sister disappeared.

The stairs made a right angle with the end of the hall. They were lit by the light from the kitchen as the top half of the wall was open on this end. Steve flipped a switch and light flooded the rest of the stairs.

Halfway down the stairs the walls ended and railings began. They descended into a large room. Another set of sliding glass doors was directly across from the foot of the stairs and a laundry area filled the right side. The matching frontloading washer and dryer were flanked by clothes sorting bins on the washer side and a large folding table and hanging clothes arm by the dryer. There was plenty room for more, but the only other furnishings were an ironing board and iron.

Another set of stairs went down to the left along the back wall, an open rail overlooking them. The hall that went off to the right was flooded with light when Heather found the switch. Three bedrooms opened off the hall, one at the front, two along the same wall as the laundry.

"Since this house is built into the mountainside," Steve explained. "It has to go long and narrow, not boxy, except of course, the top level. This level and the one below are 'L' shaped."

They stepped into the first bedroom which wasn't furnished yet.

"The bedrooms all have private baths and walk-in closets," Steve said. "This room and the one next to it mirror each other. This is the smallest room, the next is slightly larger. The one at the end of the hall is almost as big as the master bedroom. It stretches the width of the house."

"Do they all have a lanai?" Greg nodded at the one visible through the sliding glass doors.

"Just like upstairs, it's one big lanai that wraps around," Steve said. "They all open on to it. There's a set of stairs going to the upper lanai at the front and down to the back patio at the other end, by the laundry room. Shall we go down?"

"Are the bedrooms all unfurnished?" Heather asked as they turned to leave.

"Except the master bedroom, yeah," Steve shrugged sheepishly. "Seems a waste to have all this and not use it, doesn't it?"

The stairs to the lower level were open on the left, protected by the same sturdy wooden fence-like rail that was on the upper stairs and overlooking this flight. The room the stairs ended in was at least twice as big as the laundry room just above it. Another fireplace graced the back wall of the family room which had a pool table, big screen TV and a large comfortable couch. The other side was a large weight room. The outer wall was solid glass, with patio doors off both the family room and the weight room. There was a door on either side of the back wall.

"What's behind door number one?" Heather pointed to the one on the right.

"That's the bathroom," Steve smiled slightly. "The master bedroom is behind door number two."

Heather didn't want to see it. She turned deliberately to the glass wall. In the darkness, they could only see their reflections.

"What's in your yard?"

Steve turned a knob and gas tiki torches came to life all over outside. They lined the patio and the privacy fence, outlined the flagstone walk and the kidney shaped pool. Beautiful. Very romantic.

Heather deliberately turned toward the stairs.

"I'm hungry. Let's go eat," she demanded.

"Bossy, I tell you. Always has been," Greg whispered to Steve. "You sure you want to get into this?"

"Watch it punk," Heather glared from the stairs.

Greg started up the steps behind her.

"I'm not a punk," Greg whined childishly. "If you don' quit callin' me that, I'm tellin' Mom."

"Punk," Heather said clearly and distinctly. "Punk, punk, punk."

"I'm tellin'," Greg warned.

Steve grinned as he turned everything off.

"Oh, I'm sure," he said to himself as he followed the squabbling siblings up the stairs.

Chapter 13

*D*inner was grilled chicken marsala on a bed of vermicelli. Broccoli drizzled with a light garlic cheese sauce and French bread completed the meal. Greg declared it brok' da mout'.

"You eat like this every night?" he asked.

"When I'm home, sure," Steve shrugged.

"You always fix so much?" Greg was beginning to plot. "What do you do with the leftovers?"

"Freeze it in single serving portions and eat it when I don't have time to cook," Steve said. "My freezer is full of them."

"I'm guessing," Greg grinned, "that you should be dressed for company at suppertime more often. You just might have some help keepin' that freezer from gettin' fuller."

"You're welcome anytime," Steve grinned back. "I'm home most nights."

They ate in companionable silence for a while, then Greg put down his fork and sighed.

"That was so ono, brah," he said. "Thanks for the invite."

"Did I invite you?" Steve asked, puzzled.

"Sure," Heather piped in, "when we were standing at your front door."

"Ah yes! I forgot."

"So Steve," Greg leaned his elbows on the table, "what do you do with yourself in the offseason? Other than Sundays, which you now mostly spend with us. And Saturdays too, I guess."

"Yeah, learning to surf is fun," Steve said. "I'm glad you guys invited me."

"Learning to surf is an optimistic description of what Steve does," Greg told Heather. "A natural he is not."

"Why don't you come with us, Heather?" Steve asked.

"Yeah, come with us," Greg said. "It's been a long time."

"No," Heather said firmly.

"But why not?" Greg could still whine like a little boy when he wanted something from his big sister.

"Because ...," Heather had two good reasons, neither of which she wanted to share with either man. Greg would certainly get overprotective if she told him her left hip couldn't take the strain anymore so she had downgraded to a boogie board. Steve would think she was in love with him if he knew how disturbed she was by the thought of him in nothing but a pair of board shorts. No way was she confessing. It was time for a diversion.

"So Steve," she said mimicking Greg's earlier posture and question. "Other than surfing and cooking excellent meals, what do you do with your time?"

"Actually, I like to hang around the house and read," Steve said.

"Speaking of hanging around the house," Greg said, "do you take care of it by yourself? It's pretty big for a bachelor pad."

"The house I take care of by myself, but I have a gardener who comes once or twice a week to take care of the yard."

"What? The Kansas farm boy doesn't garden?" Greg teased.

"This Kansan wasn't a farm boy, he lived in town," Steve said, "and no, he doesn't garden."

"But he does clean house?" Heather asked. "How's that work?"

Steve stared thoughtfully at his guests for a long moment. He finally shrugged. "Dad was alcoholic. Mom was depressed. If Jenni and I didn't take care of the house, it didn't get done. When she left, I did it all."

"Jenni's your sister, right?" Greg asked. "Didn't she disappear when you were kids?"

"She was fifteen, almost sixteen, and I was fourteen," Steve said sadly. "I haven't seen her since then."

"Did your dad abuse her too?" Heather asked quietly.

Steve carefully studied her, wondering how much honesty she wanted. He finally looked at Greg and saw compassion that matched Heather's. He sighed heavily and looked down at the table. "I haven't told anyone but Pete. Everyone else assumes she was kidnapped or something, but she ran away. Yes, he abused her too but not as often or as violently. In the last year before she left, I don't think it was just physical."

"You didn't suspect at the time, did you?" Greg asked.

"Not at the time, but I put two and two together later. Why do you ask?"

"Because you're here to tell about it," Greg looked at him steadily. "If someone had done that to Heather, I would have killed them or died trying."

"I think that's why Jenni left," Steve agreed. "She knew once I figured it out I'd get hurt even worse than I had ever been before. I wasn't big enough to defend myself. Our father was almost as big as I am now and when he started, he was merciless."

"Childhood isn't supposed to be like that." Heather frowned fiercely.

"But I guess in the long run it works out for you, Steve," Greg wanted to get back to a lighter conversation.

"Why would you say such a thing?" Heather was appalled.

"Other than 'all things work together for the good of guys who love God'?" Greg smugly paraphrased. "It's a good thing Steve can keep house because y– Ow! Why'd you kick me?"

"Kick you?" Heather said with saccharine sweetness. "I'm sorry, it's those darn leg twitches."

"Leg twitches, my left foot," Greg groaned.

"Actually, it was the right," Heather said.

Steve laughed, surprised at how quickly their silliness pulled him out of dark memories.

Heather decided to take the conversation back to safer ground. She couldn't believe that her brother had almost told Steve he would make a good "househusband" for her. Sure she didn't keep house to Mom's standards, but hers was more than just livable. Besides, she wasn't ready to be thinking about marriage to Steve.

"So, you read, cook, clean house, ride motorcycles and surf," she said, propping her elbows on the table. "What else do you do with your time?"

"I also like to golf," Steve replied.

"I've only gone a few times," Greg said. "I keep hoping one of these days I'll start getting the hang of it."

"You a serious golfer?" Steve asked.

"You mean like throw a club when I hit in a water obstacle?" Greg laughed. "Nah, I like golf for the fun of it."

"Good, we'll have to play sometime," Steve took the last piece of bread from the basket. "What about you, Heather? You golf?"

"Never have," she said.

"You want to learn?" Steve asked.

"I wouldn't mind," she shrugged.

"I'll teach you," Steve smiled slowly.

Heather had a vision of herself wearing a skort, a sleeveless women's golf shirt and a visor, like she'd seen on TV. She saw Steve wrapping his arms around her, trying to help her with her grip. She'd seen that in a romantic comedy or something.

That was not happening.

"No way," she blurted out. "Not until our honeymoon."

Greg sprayed his soda across the table, Steve choked on the bite of bread he'd just taken and Heather's hands flew to cover her dark red face.

"I didn't say that out loud," she muttered. "I did not say that out loud."

Greg's roar of laughter assured her she had. The twinkle in Steve's eyes as he coughed behind his hand confirmed it. Heather jumped up from the table and stalked catlike into the living area, muttering about men and misunderstandings. A distraction, she needed a distraction.

"Your house is naked Steve," she said.

Steve looked at Greg who just shrugged. They followed Heather into the living area of the great room. Steve looked around and saw what she meant.

Other than his lounging area in front of the fireplace which he used frequently as nights were often cold up here, the place was bare. No pictures on the wall except Tim's and Robert's, no knickknacks except the crystal statue and Jenni's softball. No area rugs, coffee tables or coasters for drinks.

"I guess I could hire a decorator," Steve suggested with a shrug.

"Oh, no need," Heather said sweetly. Too sweetly. "We'll help."

"Yeah, I know where all the thrift shops are," Greg agreed.

"Salvation Army," Heather said.

"Goodwill."

"Ooh, Price Busters."

"Don't forget Ross."

"Savers!" they said together.

"This does not sound good," Steve muttered.

"Relax, brah," Greg comforted him with an arm around his shoulders. "Haven't you heard of 'shabby chic'?"

"What do you think, Greg?" Heather suggested. "Some of those Hawaii picture frames for those mostly empty shelves?"

Greg stroked his chin as he contemplated the built-in bookshelves on the short wall perpendicular to the hall.

"The 3-D ones with the dolphins will go well up there," he mused. "The palm trees down there."

"One of the bobbling hula girls for sure," Heather said.

"Nah," Greg corrected. "The hula pig!"

"Oh yeah! Perfect," Heather agreed.

"I think not," Steve said.

They ignored him.

"A velvet Elvis," Heather exclaimed. "It would be great on this wall."

She pointed to the wall shared with the bathroom. Steve thought it would be more appropriate on the other side.

"How about some wrestling posters over there?" Greg suggested.

"Some of those milk crate thingys for end tables," Heather said.

"Do you think Aunty Connie still has that crib box?" Greg asked. "It'll make a great coffee table."

"Oh yeah," Heather agreed. "Especially if she has some of those big diaper boxes. They'll make great legs."

"No," Steve said, unsure if he should be annoyed or amused.

"No worries, brah," Greg comforted him with a hearty slap on the back. "We'll cover it with Contact Paper, the wood-look kine. No one will ever know it's not the real thing."

"We'll have a decorating party on Saturday," Heather decided. "You got a picture phone, yah Greg? Let's take pictures. We can email the distress call to everyone and include pictures so they know what we're up against."

"I'm perfectly capable of doing it myself," Steve tried to stop the train, but it apparently had no brakes.

"Too late," Heather said. "You've already had this place for more than a year and done nothing with it. Take pictures Greg."

"You snooze, you lose brah," Greg grinned at Steve as he pulled out his cell phone and started snapping pictures.

"We'll be here at eight in the morning, with starter gifts," Heather told Steve. "You have plenty food for breakfast, lunch and dinner."

"And plenty cash," Greg said.

"What? I have to fund my own execution?" Steve grunted in disbelief.

"Of course," Heather said. "Make sure you have some small bills too, we'll need them for garage-saling."

Steve was beginning to hope they were serious about the decorating but not the redneck trash.

"It'll be fun, brah," Greg said.

"Yeah, lighten up," Heather grinned at Steve who stood frowning, feet firmly planted, arms crossed over his chest. "It'll be fine."

Steve just glared at her, so she sidled up to him, slipped her hand between his rock-solid chest and tree-trunk arms and leaned her head against his shoulder. It was a well practiced gesture that had always worked with her dad and her brothers. Unfortunately, it was having an effect on her too this time.

"Give it up, Steve," Greg laughed. "When she does that it's going to happen, one way or another, whether you like it or not."

Heather felt Steve's muscles flex beneath her cheek and her hand. She quickly stepped away, blushing and trying to think of anything but the man beside her.

She tried to focus on what Greg was saying about Saturday. She couldn't. Thoughts of Steve, how he was so big and strong, flooded her brain. Think of something else. What was Greg saying?

"Hey Boss, where'd ya go?" Greg was looking at her strangely. She still tried not to look at Steve.

"I ... I'm ... just," Heather couldn't get her thoughts in order. Nothing acceptable would come to mind. Don't say it, she told herself. Don't blurt out your thoughts. Don't! You can do this. Just don't look at Steve. She looked.

He stood there watching her with blue eyes questioning. His dark hair was getting a bit too long and looked a little messy right now. Adorably so. His black t-shirt strained over his muscles. Those rock hard muscles.

"I'm wondering," she blurted out. "If I would love you if you weren't so ripped, so big and strong."

Steve's eyebrows winged up to his hairline and he grinned broadly. Greg just roared with laughter. Heather smacked her forehead with the heel of her hand, twice.

"I've got to stop doing this," she cried.

"Please don't," Steve disagreed.

"It's part of your charm," Greg suggested slyly.

"I've got to go," Heather looked around. "Where's my purse?"

"You didn't bring one," the men chorused.

Heather stalked to the door, but they were closer. By the time she got there, Greg was already going down the walk and Steve was leaning against the doorframe, crowding her space way too much.

"Sure you won't stay for coffee and dessert," Steve tucked a stray strand of hair behind her ear, brushing her cheek with his fingertips.

"Save the coffee for Saturday morning," she smiled sweetly then turned to head for the car.

Steve realized something was amiss.

"Heather!" he called softly.

She turned and he bent down to pick up her slippers.

"You forgot something," Steve said, holding them out to her.

Heather looked down at her still bare feet and blushed. She walked quickly back.

"It must be contagious," she said with a smile as she reached out for the slippers. Since she was already moving that way, she went up on tiptoes and kissed Steve quickly on the cheek before running back to the car, slippers in hand.

As he watched them drive away, Steve rubbed his cheek thoughtfully. He couldn't wait for Saturday.

Chapter 14

*S*teve went all-out for breakfast on Saturday. By the time Aunty Gloria came with Tim and Robert just before eight, he had fixed much more than coffee. Fresh cut fruit and three kinds of juice were chilling in the refrigerator. The biscuits and cinnamon rolls were almost ready to come out of the oven, the rice was done, the sausage gravy was simmering, bacon was frying and Spam was sliced and ready for the skillet. The only thing left was eggs to order.

Shortly after eight, Steve's large great room seemed small and he was delighted. Luke's family was there and so was Malia's – Uncle Kenji, Aunty Hannah, thirteen year old Nick, ten year old Alex and seven year old Brianna. Uncle Pena hadn't brought Aunty Connie and baby Leilani, just eight year old Suzie and five year old Jeremiah.

Steve had met everyone at church but he didn't know the aunties and uncles very well, so he was enjoying this opportunity to spend time with them. The laughter was plentiful and many hands made light work in the kitchen. Steve had already surrendered the spatula to Aunty Hannah, Malia's mom, when Uncle Pena got his plate.

"Stevie-boy, your table's not big enough," Pena observed. "You want we should find you one bigger one? They haven't picked up the big rubbish yet. Bet we find you one."

"Hey, we saw chairs on Judd," Robert piped in.

"Yeah, dey got no seat," Tim confirmed, "but cardboard an' duct tape, dey fix anyt'ing."

"I saw one toilet," Luke volunteered. "It'll make one great umbrella stand for da front door."

"You know you need one up here," Aunty Gloria volunteered helpfully. "It rains too much up here, people gonna need umbrellas."

Steve was enjoying the good natured ribbing when the front door opened again. Even though he was in the kitchen and couldn't see the door, he knew his sunshine had just walked into the room. Greg's bellow confirmed it.

"Hey Steve! Heather and I saw one bed on the corner of Mamalu. You may need to fumigate the mattress but hey, the price is right."

Suddenly Moose was standing there grinning up at him and Heather was reaching past him to snag a cinnamon roll from the basket on the counter behind him.

"Umm, is that biscuits and gravy?" She smiled up at him. "I love biscuits and gravy, but can you make 'em as good as Dad did?"

"Yes he can," Tim cast his vote. "Better hurry and get some."

All her immediate family except Greg heartily endorsed Tim's approval.

"Here, you judge for yourself." Mom handed Heather a plate which Greg intercepted.

"Hey!" Heather complained. Before Greg could grab the fork, Steve snatched the plate back and gave it to Heather. Arm up to block Greg, he turned his big body to shield her from her annoying younger brother.

"Hey!" Greg grumbled. Heather looked over Steve's arm at him and stuck out her tongue, then she smiled up at Steve before picking up the fork.

"Umm, melicious," she sighed with the first bite and leaned back against Steve's chest. "Have I died and gone to heaven?"

"I don't know," Steve rumbled softly, "but this feels like paradise to me."

"Behave," Heather elbowed him gently.

"You first," Steve said.

Heather realized she was leaning against Steve and straightened up with a guilty start.

"I went on line yesterday," Steve said offhand, "and checked out golf courses in Hawaii. Did you know that there are over a hundred?"

Heather felt herself beginning to blush.

"That many!" Greg said straight-faced. "That'd take months to go through all of those."

"Think someone could teach someone else to play golf after visiting that many courses?" Steve wondered.

Heather stalked over to the stove, ignoring Greg and Steve.

"You doing one over medium for me, Aunty Hannah?" she asked.

"Right here, honey,"

"I guess that would depend," Greg told Steve, "on whether you were devoted to golf or you had other pursuits too."

Heather ignored them and the blush that was creeping up her neck. As soon as she got her egg, she went out to eat on the lanai in peace. A couple minutes later, the door slid open again. She didn't look up until she heard Luke's voice.

"Are they picking on you, Shadow?" Her big brother stood with two cups of coffee in his hands, smiling knowingly.

"Unmercifully," she smiled and reached for a cup. "One of those for me?"

"One sweetener, just the way you like it," Luke handed her a cup then sat down next to her.

"Seriously, how're things going for you?" Luke asked.

"Other than the fact that my brain turns to mush whenever he's around?" Heather asked.

"Whew, that bad?" he shook his head. "Yeah, other than that."

"I'm scared, Big Man," she said.

"About what?"

"Well, for one," Heather sighed, "what if I'm just infatuated with a massive set of muscles, a pair of gorgeous blue eyes and a Grizzly uniform?"

"That's not the case," Luke assured her.

"How do you know?"

"First off, you wouldn't be fascinated by just any old muscles because they're commonplace in your life," he flexed his own and Heather started to giggle.

"Watch it, brat!" Luke cautioned, giving her stink eye.

"Okay, you're right. No worries on the muscles," Heather stifled her grin.

"As for the Grizzly uniform," Luke said. "You've been working on Pete's BMW for five years now, every spring, regular as clockwork. You haven't lost your mind over him."

"I haven't lost my mind over Steve," Heather objected. Luke just looked at her with raised eyebrows. "Okay, maybe I have. So what about the gorgeous blue eyes?"

"I can't think of any way to reassure you on that point," Luke conceded, "but two out of three ain't bad, yah?"

"You're right, Big Man" Heather sighed. "No worries in that direction. But how will I know if it's God's will for my life?"

"Oh Shadow," Luke said. "I don't think it's a matter of 'if' anymore for you two. It's a question of 'when?'"

Hearing that from Luke, Heather's heart soared free of her fears. He'd always been a rock in her life, always understood her even before she did. Since Dad died, he was the one she'd always known she could depend on.

"So how do I know when?" she asked. "How did you know with Nalani?"

"When the thought of losing her drove me to my knees in anguish," Luke said, staring off across Honolulu Harbor. "When I knew I would give up anything but God for her, that's when I knew it was time."

Heather thought about Luke's relationship with Nalani. They'd known each other for years as friends at church. It was only after she went to California for college that Luke began to seriously court her. They saw each other during Christmas and summer breaks, spending more and more time together. Letters, phone calls and emails had been the bulk of their courtship.

Luke made Mom go along as chaperone when he went to propose to Nalani during spring break their junior year. Luke had told Heather that he couldn't bear the thought of Nalani leaving without him at the end of the summer. Heather had graduated from high school that spring, and she'd spent a lot of time with them before their wedding in July, just before she shipped off for basic training. They'd gone back to California as man and wife. He'd stayed four years with Nalani in California until she finished her psychology doctoral class work, putting off his own studies in law and criminal justice to help her get her schooling. Now at thirty-two, he had just passed the bar exam while Nalani was already a successful counselor.

"Did you ever resent it?" Heather asked. "Putting off your life for hers?"

"Not for one minute," Luke said, "because I never saw it as putting off my life. It was becoming one with Nalani in a new life. But if I had pushed into marriage with her too soon, I probably would have come to resent it."

"I know that if I ... you know ... with Steve," Heather couldn't bring herself to say the "m" word yet. "I'm also going to have to leave Hawaii, at least for a season. And then there's all the media attention too. I really ... like Steve but I don't think I'm ready to sacrifice like that for him yet. How will I know when I am?"

"It'll grow on you and one day it'll hit you like a ton of bricks," Luke had that special smile that only crazy-in-love marrieds get. "You'll know."

"What if he's not there?" Heather expressed the other worry on her mind.

"Oh Shadow, don't you worry about that," Luke grinned and stood up, taking her now empty plate. "He's gonna be there long before you are. He's almost there already."

"You really think so?" Heather frowned as she stood.

"I know so," Luke assured her.

"So, Big Man, how did you deal with the ... you know ... temptation?"

"By fleeing just like you are," Luke grinned.

"What do you mean?" Heather said. "I feel like I'm sitting in the fire, not fleeing anything!"

"You're surrounding yourself by family when you're with him," Luke said. "You're making sure you aren't alone with him."

"But isn't setting up something like this so I can spend the day with Steve kind of using you guys?"

"Of course it is, but that's what we're for. No one objects at all," Luke assured her. "In fact it's kinda fun."

Heather thought for a moment, then grinned. "You and Nalani used me, didn't you?"

"Shamefully so," Luke didn't bother to try to look ashamed, "and you were clueless."

"And here I thought you guys just liked my company!" Heather tried to think of a tactful way to ask her last burning question. "I know you guys did spend time alone, especially as you got more serious. Did you ...?"

"You mean, did we 'did' or did we 'didn't'?" Luke kind of clarified her question.

"Yeah, did you 'didn't'?"

"We did not!" Luke said. "Not until the wedding night."

"So how were you alone and not do it?" Heather said. "When I was in Iraq, it seemed like everyone who got alone with anyone did it."

"We were never really alone, except in the car," Luke said, "and we never parked anywhere but home or our destination. As soon as the engine was off, we were out of the car."

"So when you weren't with the family, and now I see why you wanted time away from us," Heather said, "you were out in public places only?"

"Yes," Luke affirmed. "I learned more about Honolulu in that last summer before we got married than I had the first ten years I lived here. I think we walked every square inch of the public parts of the city."

"Thanks Luke," Heather said. "I really feel better about this whole thing."

"Good, because I think we need to get inside and rescue your beloved from our crazy family."

"Do you really think he needs rescuing?"

They heard a roar of laughter through the closed lanai door.

"Oh yeah, he needs rescuing," Luke said wryly.

Chapter 15

*W*hen Luke opened the door, another roar of laughter greeted them. Heather saw Steve running his hand through his hair, looking bemused. He definitely needed rescuing.

"There you are, dear," Mom said. "I think it's time to get this rowdy bunch on track for today's mission."

"Yes ma'am," Heather gave Mom a two-finger salute. Robert was on the floor by the door, so she nudged him with her foot. "Hey brat, get their attention, will ya?"

"You mean ...?" Robert grinned at her and gave her a mock salute.

"Just like I taught you," she nodded.

Robert handed her his plate and scrambled to his feet. He stood straight, shoulders back, chest out, stomach in, took a deep breath and bellowed, "At ease!"

Immediately silence descended over the room. Then Steve began to snicker. Everyone started to laugh, and Robert shrugged apologetically at Heather.

"Don't worry, it's not your fault," she gave Steve stink eye. "It's the new recruit. You did fine."

She patted Robert on the back then pointed at Steve who was barely trying to control his laughter.

"You can give me twenty," she said, marching toward him. He reached into his back pocket for his wallet.

"Not dollars! Pushups!" She smacked him lightly on the chest. "Just for that, give me forty."

"Yes ma'am," Steve gave her a very sorry salute. "You want them one-handed? Elevated? With a clap between?"

"Don't be a showoff," she frowned, pointing at the ground. "Just do it."

The man needed some bigger t-shirts, Heather observed as he dropped at her feet and began to do perfect pushups, way too easily. His back and arm muscles threatened to split the seams of his too tight t-shirt as he rose and fell.

Heather realized that everyone was watching her watch Steve. She blushed and deliberately turned her back, walking over to stand before the fireplace.

"First thing on the agenda today," Heather started. "All males thirteen and over are cleaning the kitchen."

"Awe, why us?" Greg complained.

"'Cause I da boss," Heather said haughtily. "But before that —"

"How can you have a 'before that' before a 'first thing'?" Tim asked.

"Yeah, that don't make sense," Robert agreed.

"You punks want me to narrow the range on that kitchen duty?" Heather gave them stink eye.

"No. Go ahead," they backed down.

"Okay. First, the first thing —"

The front door opened, interrupting her again. "Oh for Pete's sake, what now?"

Pete stuck his head around the door. "You called?"

"Hey, who invited the riffraff?" Steve complained from where he leaned against the dividing wall, arms and legs crossed.

"I did," Heather said. "I thought you could use a friend today."

"Who needs a friend," Steve was puzzled, "when I've got you all?"

Laughter burst out around the room. Heather glared at him, feebly trying to control her own laughter.

"That, you will pay for, mister," she promised.

Steve looked down at Aunty Gloria who was standing just inside the dining area. "That didn't come out right, did it?"

"No," she laughed, "and they won't forget it for a very long time."

"Like forever," Luke promised.

"Or even longer," Greg warned.

"And it they forget, I'll remind them," Hannah grinned slyly. "I got the whole thing on DVD."

"Be careful what you say and do Steve," Greg warned. "I told you that when the family's together there's usually a camera on somewhere."

Heather spoke over the rumble of laughter. "In spite of the fact that we're not friends of Steve —"

"Except for me," Pete interrupted with a wave from the back wall.

"Except you, Pete," Heather agreed. "We have gathered for a mission that will still go on. Phase one —"

"Is this the first thing or the thing before the first thing?" Uncle Pena asked.

"Forget the first thing," Heather gave him stink eye. "Focus on the phases."

"Focus on phases. Focus on phases," Matt said. "That's cool! Is that a rhyme Aunty Heather? We're learning about rhymes in school."

"Actually twerp, it's more like alliteration because the repeated sound is at the beginning of the words," she explained, "but this is way off track. Can we get back to the matter at hand?"

"Sure," Matt said helpfully. "Focus on phases everybody!"

"Phase One will be the giving of gifts to our non-friend back there. The rule was," Heather explained to Steve, "nothing bought new. It had to either be handmade or something already in their home."

Steve assumed that the gifts were in the motley collection piled up by the door. There were bags, boxes and strangely shaped packages wrapped in brown grocery bags or newspaper.

"We can't present anything with him standing over there," Hannah said.

"Yeah, bring him in here and grab a chair," Pena commanded.

"Make him sit on the floor," Luke suggested. "He's the one who has no furniture."

"Excuse me," Heather spoke over them all, "but I do believe I am still in command of this mission. I will give the directions."

"Yes ma'am," Luke said.

"Pete," she instructed, "please bring that armchair over for your friend."

"Will do!"

"Kids," Heather addressed the six little ones sprawled at her feet. "Go get Uncle Steve and bring him over here to the chair Uncle Pete is bringing. See if you can make friends with him, okay?"

They scrambled up and swarmed over to Steve. Suzie and Jeremy grabbed one of his arms while Matt and Jeremiah got the other.

"Come on, Uncle Steve," Matt said. "Aunty Heather wants you over there."

"What if I don't want to go?" Steve asked.

"You have to," Alex shook his head. "She's bossy like that."

"I think that's why I don't want to go," Steve pretended to pout.

"We'll have to push him," Brianna told her brother with a heavy sigh.

As they slipped behind him, Steve stood to his full height and slowly flexed both arms, lifting the four kids on his arms so that their legs dangled in the air. Luke and Greg snatched up their little cousins and deposited them on his back, helping them hang on with arms around Steve's neck.

"This isn't even a challenge," Steve said. "No one's clinging to my legs!"

Robert nudged Nick and they started to rise.

"Later," Hannah commanded. "Precious cargo."

Steve strode easily to the chair and gently set down the children who were clinging to his arms, then reached up and plucked Alex off. When he had Brianna in his arms, she smiled up at him.

"Are we your friends now, Uncle Steve?" she asked.

"Yes. You all are my friends," Steve deliberately included all six of them but no one else.

"Goody," Jeremiah said. "Can we help with you presents?"

"I'd like for you to," Steve said, "but you'll have to ask the commander."

"How about you give him your presents first?" Heather suggested. "Then everyone else can let you know which ones you can help with."

There was a small flurry of activity as the parents helped the children find the bags that their gifts were in. The four younger ones had refrigerator art, for which Steve was going to need some magnets. Alex gave him a clay pencil holder he'd made in school, Suzie a felt trivet. Robert's long handled metal dustbin and Nick's still-life water color were also school projects and to Steve's delight were surprisingly well done.

Uncle Pena gave him a small tool box with hammer, wrench, pliers, and some tools Steve didn't even recognize.

"Hey this is great," Steve thanked him. "I don't have any tools."

"So how'd you hang our pictures?" Tim asked.

"That was me," Pete said. "I came over to help the poor friendless waif."

"He's not friendless now," Matt said. "He's got me."

The laughter and banter continued while Steve received the rest of his gifts. From Tim he got a pack of toilet paper with a bold note, "Because a guy can never have enough." Connie had sent a serving platter which was a duplicate wedding gift that she still had stashed away. Pete gave him a Grizzly nightlight, Greg, a well-thumbed *Bathroom Reader*. Malia presented him with a potted aloe plant which certainly comes in handy for a cook. Hannah gave him a local cookbook and a set of aloha print potholders, Kenji, a fishing rod, with the promise to take him out if they ever became friends.

Nalani pointed out one of the two genuine gift bags to Jeremy and told him to give that to Uncle Steve.

"This is almost as good as a birthday party, isn't it?" Jeremy said as he leaned over the arm of the chair to watch Steve open it.

"I don't really know, Germy," Steve said without thinking. "I've never had a birthday party."

You could have heard a pin drop. Everyone stared at Steve, stunned.

"You've never had a birthday party?" Heather whispered.

"Not even when you were little?" Greg was bewildered.

As Steve looked around the room, he was struck by how different his life had been from the one this boisterous, lovable ohana shared. Suddenly he felt like crying, but he just shook his head and shrugged.

"Not even with the team," Gloria looked accusingly at Pete, "after you became a Grizzly?"

"My birthday's in the offseason," Steve said, "so everyone was off doing their own thing."

"When is it?" someone asked.

"April seventeenth."

"That's my birthday!" Jeremy leaned across the arm of the chair and whispered like it was a wonderful secret.

"It is? How old are you going to be?"

"Five," he held up his left hand with fingers splayed wide.

"Oh, I'm going to be older than that," Steve grinned, "so I guess we can't be twins."

"Course not, silly," Jeremy giggled.

"How old will you be?" Nalani asked.

"Thirty."

"That's pretty old," Jeremiah frowned up at him. "You still gonna play football?"

"For a few years still, buddy," Steve grinned.

"Hey, hey, time's wasting," Heather snapped her fingers at them. "Let's finish up Phase One."

"Focus on the phases," Matt giggled.

Nalani's gift was a quilted sunflower pillow.

"When I made that a couple years ago," she explained. "I didn't know why I was making it. I don't know anyone who likes sunflowers, but I thought it was pretty. When I got Heather's email, I went online to do some research because I had no idea what to give you. I discovered that Kansas is the Sunflower State, so that was for you."

"That's so cool," Steve fingered the yellow yarn looped in a fringe around the edges of the pillow. "Thank you."

"Here's Grandma's," Matt gave him the other gift bag.

It was a framed needlepoint that said, "There's no place like home," with Dorothy's feet at the top, heels clicking together. Instead of the traditional ruby slippers, she was wearing bright red rubber slippers, with hibiscus blossoms instead of bows.

"You made this yourself?" Steve asked in surprise.

"My own design," Aunty Gloria smiled at him. "Made specially for you."

"I'm deeply touched," Steve said. "Thank you. Thank you all, this has already been a wonderful day."

"Wait a minute," Greg said, "don't be gettin' all emotional on us yet. You still got two more."

"Matt," Luke directed, "give him the one from Daddy."

"You're gonna like this," Matt said. "I helped Daddy with it."

"So did I," Jeremy swung on the chair arm again. "Hurry an' open it."

It was a beautifully framed and matted picture of the whole crew up in Volcanoes National Park.

"You helped with this?" Steve asked the boys.

"Well, mostly we watched," Matt said, pointing to the mat, "but we got to tape the picture to the back of that thing."

"We got to push down those things on the back," Jeremy turned it over and pointed at some clips. "See, I pushed down these and Matt did those."

"And you did a great job," Steve said. "It's perfect. Thank you very much."

"One last one," Heather sounded a little nervous. "Alex and Matt, carry that big one very carefully over to Uncle Steve. ... No, turn it the other way. Take the paper off from the back. You have to see it all at once."

Steve heard gasps of surprise as the paper fell away. He grasped the top of the frame in the center and the boys let go so he could turn it.

He stared at an incredible oil painting. The artist had captured a grimace of pain through the facemask of the Berserkers' quarterback. He and Pete were the cause of the pain. Pete was hitting him in the right side of his ribs, driving him up into the flying tackle of number ninety-five.

He was amazed by the artist ability to capture the moment. He could almost hear the quarterback's grunt of pain. Then he noticed the signature.

"You?" Steve looked up at Heather. "You're the artist?"

"I dabble in it, yes," she looked relieved. Did she think he wouldn't like it?

"Thank you," Steve choked out. Heather saw the tears in his eyes and decided he needed a distraction.

"Okay, enough of this mushy stuff," she clapped her hands together and walked across the room, effectively diverting most of the attention to herself. "To complete Phase One, we need to get the gifts all over here, neatly and carefully placed on the hearth so that they're out of the way for now."

Steve insisted upon taking care of the painting himself but the children were allowed to carry the rest, with plenty warnings to be careful. When they finally finished and settled back on the floor, Steve leaned against the wall by the hutch, watching Heather as she transitioned into Phase Two.

Chapter 16

*P*hase Two is scheduled to start at zero nine thirty," Heather explained. "This is the search and rescue phase. In this phase we will 'search' for the things that will 'rescue' this pitiful, friendless man and his barren house from their drab existence."

"Looks to me like Steve thinks he's already found that," Greg said to Luke in a stage whisper.

"Ain't that the truth!" Luke replied.

Heather chose to ignore her brothers, Steve's grin and the family's laughter. She charged on like a general directing her troops.

"Everyone ten and under will be staying here at the command post to take care of Moose and Nalani and to help Aunty Connie with Leilani when they get here. Uncle Kenji and his pick-up truck will also be here, waiting for calls to get items too big to carry in the other vehicles.

"Steve's car, as sweet a ride as it is, is useless for this venture as there is no room to put anything in that two-seater. Greg's hatchback is barely better. They will remain here. That makes our drivers Luke, Mom, Uncle Pena and Pete. We'll have teams of three in each car."

"Excuse me, captain," Gloria interrupted, "but I would prefer not to drive. You take my car and I'll ride with Pena."

"I'll ride with Heather," Steve quickly said.

"Oh, there's a surprise," Luke nudged Greg.

"Yeah, didn't see that one coming," he replied.

"Okay, and so will Robert," Heather agreed with Steve as if her brothers hadn't spoken. "Mom and Uncle Pena can try to keep Greg out of trouble. Luke will take Malia and Nick. Pete, you get Aunty Hannah and Tim."

"What are we getting?" Hannah asked.

"I'm glad you asked. Here are specific things each squad must get." Nalani handed Heather a sheet of paper and she began to read. "Refrigerator magnets, appropriate for attaching refrigerator art."

"That's what we gave you, Uncle Steve," Matt said. Heather frowned at him. "Sorry, I'll shut up now."

Heather continued over the snickers. "Every squad must return with at least two entire place settings, including drinking glasses, plates, bowls, coffee cups and flatware. They do not have to match but they do have to be free of damage. No chips, cracks, etc. You must also find at least one area rug, one throw pillow, one wall decoration, one shelf ornament and one toy. Those are all the required items. Anything else that makes a house a home will be welcome. Like serving dishes, towels, blankets, lamps, etc."

"May I interject?" Steve asked. Heather frowned.

"Let the man speak," Luke said.

"It is his house, Heather," Mom scolded gently.

Heather tossed her head, sighed dramatically and threw out her hands. "Speak if you must!"

"I must," Steve grinned. "My kitchen needs no cooking utensils, not even a musubi maker or coffee grinder. I have pretty much everything a man, or woman, could want in a kitchen. I also have a sweet gas grill and all the implements to go with it, which we will be using for dinner tonight."

"So let me understand this," Kenji scratched his head. "You have everything to feed an army, but you have nowhere for them to sit and nothing for them to eat off of?"

"Hmm, when you put it that way, it does seem strange, doesn't it?" Steve acknowledged.

"Like I said, he belongs in this ohana," Greg said wryly.

"May we get back to the mission at hand?" Heather asked.

"Focus on the phases," Matt and Suzie said together. When the laughter died down, Heather pretended she'd never lost control.

"Except for furniture, all items are majority rules for your squad. Does each squad have someone with a camera phone?" All three of the other squads gave her an affirmative. "Good, Steve has a camera phone too, so when you find furniture candidates, send pictures to Steve's phone," Heather looked at him. "You do have your phone, don't you?"

"Yeah, it's –," Steve's right hand came out of his pocket empty. So did his left. "Just a minute."

Everyone laughed as Steve took off down the steps. Heather continued the briefing while Steve tracked down his phone. "When beds are acquired, we will inform the other troops of the size so that bedding can also be obtained.

"We will attack this mission with a zone defense. Zone One, which I will take with my squad, is Diamond Head of Punchbowl Street. Zone Two, Uncle Pena's zone, is between Punchbowl and Puuloa. Luke, Zone Three is yours; it's everything Ewa of Puuloa. Pete, take your squad into Zone Four, the Windward side.

"Phase Two ends at twelve thirty when we reassemble here at the command post for lunch. Phase Three will commence after we eat. It will include the unveilings and the actual transformation of this pitiful excuse for a home. Any questions?"

Steve strode back into the room with a triumphant grin.

"Here," he handed his cell phone to Heather. "You be my keeper today so I don't forget it somewhere else."

"Yeah, but if she's with him," Greg asked Luke, "who's going to make sure she doesn't forget it?"

"Better give that phone to Robert," Luke suggested.

Heather stuck her tongue out at her brothers and pocketed the phone. "Any legitimate questions?"

"Yeah, what if we end up getting the same thing someone else got?" Pena asked.

"No worries," Steve said. "I'll just give it to the Salvation Army since that's where you got it from anyway."

"Oh, the boy's learning," Kenji laughed.

"It's almost as if he belongs in our ohana," Hannah winked at Heather.

"Okay, let's hit the road. Time's wasting," Heather said with a frustrated sigh. Family could be so aggravating.

STEVE'S HOME WAS greatly transformed by evening. Kenji had kept busy well into the afternoon picking up all the furniture they'd found. Pena's tool box was put to good use, hammering in nails for pictures and putting together beds, shelves, and even a dining room table that sat twelve.

Some furniture wouldn't be delivered until Monday or Tuesday, but everything had been found. Bedding, blankets and towels were washed, dried, and put to use or put away.

They fired up Steve's gas grill and timed everything to have dinner ready at seven-fifteen because everyone wanted to watch the sunset shortly before seven. After some joking questions about whether the upper lanai could take the weight of all twenty-three of them, they decided to split up. The view on the lower lanai was only slightly less incredible than the upper one, so the oldest and the youngest stopped there while the others went upstairs.

Luke and Nalani took the new patio swing at the stairs end of the lanai. Greg, Pete, Malia, Tim, Robert and Nick sat in a cluster at the front corner. Heather found herself sitting with Steve on another patio swing at the other end of the lanai.

The view was spectacular and the evening was cooling quickly as the sun sank. Heather felt the chicken skin dimple on her arms. She shivered. Steve put his arm around her and tucked her close to the warmth of his big body. She sighed and laid her head on his chest.

"We shouldn't be doing this," she observed.

"You want to stop?"

"No."

Steve rubbed his cheek against her hair. Heather was tempted to raise her face for a kiss but she didn't. Instead, she wrapped her right arm over his rock hard abs and around his waist. They sat like that for a few minutes, watching the sun sink deeper, knowing that their hearts were also going deeper.

"This morning, did you really think that I might not like your painting?" Steve finally asked.

"Yes," Heather answered after a long pause.

"Why? It's incredible. How long have you been painting?"

"Just about all my life."

"Who taught you?"

"No one really."

"You've never had lessons?" Steve was even more amazed.

"A unit on painting in eighth grade art class is all."

"Wow! That's an incredible raw talent you have."

"But I've been taught so little," Heather sighed, "that I feel like I don't know anything."

"But you obviously know a lot."

"I hope so. I want to," Heather said, "but I know how much training I needed before I became independently proficient at auto mechanics. I know how much I thought I knew when I hardly knew anything at all, so I'm sure that an art critic would tear apart my paintings."

"Why don't you take lessons?"

"Because I have to make a living. I keep telling myself someday I'll make time for lessons but I really like my life the way it is now."

"You do, huh?" Steve's question was thoughtful.

"Yes, and that's why we shouldn't be doing this."

Steve knew she was talking about falling in love, not just watching the sunset together. "Because I like my life and you like yours."

"And if we fall in love, one or both of our lives are going to change drastically," Heather said with a sigh. "Do you want it to be yours?"

Steve gave it serious thought.

"Honestly?" he finally said. "Not really. I want you in my life the way it is, not a different life."

"Me too."

"So what do we do?"

"We wait," she sighed, strangely sad to keep what she wanted.

"Wait for what?"

"We wait until we're both ready for a new life ... and hope we both get there at about the same time."

They sat quietly, watching as the twilight continued to fade. Already in its descent to the horizon, the three-quarter moon grew brighter and brighter. It seemed almost close enough to touch. They heard laughter on the patio two floors below.

"Shall we go help get dinner on?" Steve finally asked.

"We better," Heather pulled reluctantly away from Steve.

When she stood, she realized that everyone but Pete and Greg had gone downstairs. They were still sitting in the front corner, talking quietly and unobtrusively chaperoning her and Steve.

"Thank God for wise friends and family," Steve said softly.

"Amen to that," Heather agreed. She loved being with Steve so much that she knew it wasn't wise to be alone with him. She hadn't really needed Luke's earlier advice but it was good to be reminded. Suddenly she had an idea.

"Hey, you ever been up Diamond Head?"

"The volcano over there?" Steve pointed to the east. "No, I haven't."

"Let's go on Thursday," she said.

"Okay," Steve said slowly, "but why?"

"Because we'll get to be alone together without being alone, silly," Heather said. "One mile up, one mile down. Lots of time for talk story, but way too public to do anything stupid."

"Sounds like a plan, I guess," Steve said.

"You don't sound so sure. It'll be great. I love Diamond Head." She frowned and feigned concern. "I hope at your advancing age you have the physical stamina to make it up and back down. You're too big to carry."

Steve threw back his head and laughed.

"I have a hard time resisting such a challenge," he said.

"So you'll go for sure?"

"Yes I'll go, my dear," Steve gave her a firm commitment.

"Good. It's going to be fun, being with you without my family but in a place where you still have to behave," Heather said.

Steve stopped with his hand on the lanai door handle and looked down at her with surprise. "Me behave? Correct me if I'm wrong, but I think you're the one who has already proposed."

Heather blushed a dark red and stared at him, speechless. Steve slid the door open, laughing as he walked into the kitchen, asking the aunties if they needed him to carry anything down.

Chapter 17

*S*teve showed up in Heather's office at the shop at nine on Thursday morning, ready for inspection. Heather gave him a careful once over. He wore hiking boots, short socks, khaki shorts for comfortable walking, snug but not tight, another too small t-shirt, this one pale blue. It made his Pacific-blue eyes even more intense. She sighed.

"Don't you have any t-shirts that fit properly?" Heather asked with a frown.

"What? This fits fine," Steve rubbed both hands across his chest.

"It's too tight," Heather said. "They do make them bigger, you know."

"But in warm weather, I like them tight," Steve explained. "They absorb the sweat quicker and therefore cool me quicker."

Well, they distracted her but Heather decided to keep silent on that subject today. Instead, she demanded to inspect his backpack.

"You have all the things I told you to bring?"

"Yes ma'am," Steve pulled the items out of the pack as he named them. "Water bottles, two each, trail mix, camera, cap, sunglasses, sunscreen, extra batteries for both the camera and the flashlight. Tell me again, why a flashlight?"

"For the tunnel," Heather said, "like I told you before."

"Ah yes, the tunnel, something I normally experience on a hike."

"This isn't just any hike," Heather said proudly. "This is Diamond Head! A unique experience."

"Darlin'," Steve drawled, "every experience with you has been unique."

"Um, yes. Well ... shall we go," Heather motioned toward the door.

"After you, m'lady," Steve said with a courtly bow.

In the outer office, Heather stopped to make sure Malia had everything squared away for the day. She assured them that she had the office under control as usual and that Greg had already arrived to supervise the shop and drive the tow truck if necessary.

Fortunately, Greg was already too busy to do anything but throw a wave and a "don't do anything I wouldn't do" their way.

"You know, I don't think I've ever discovered what Greg actually does with himself, other than being a general pest and surfing," Steve observed when they pulled out onto Waialae Avenue.

"That's because as much as he talks, he doesn't talk about himself," Heather said.

"You're right," Steve was surprised. "I never realized that. Has he always been that way?"

"I think so," Heather said. "Even as a child I had to drag things out of him, but I always knew when something was wrong with him."

"You two are pretty close," Steve said.

"Yes, and Luke too," she agreed. "I guess it's because most of our childhood we were the odd ones out. In Africa we were much too light-skinned to not stand out and when we moved here, we weren't local enough, even though Mom was."

"So," Steve returned to his original question, "what does Greg do?"

"He works two part-time jobs, as a lifeguard and as a waiter," Heather said. "He took classes at the community college and he finally got his associates degree last year."

"When did he start?"

"Right out of high school," Heather explained. "Yes, it took seven years because he wanted to do it on his own. He wouldn't live with Mom and Dad. Even though he has a roommate, living on your own in Honolulu is expensive. He's only been able to afford to take one or two courses a semester."

"No scholarship, huh?"

"Not for Greg," Heather laughed. "He's never been a very good student, in spite of his intelligence. He learns well and uses what he learns, but school and him don't get along."

"What are his long-term goals? Or is he stopping with the associates?" Steve asked.

"He's enrolled in the bible college now. This is his second semester," Heather said proudly. "He's going to be a pastor."

"I think he'll make a great one," Steve said. "Is he getting through bible college the same way as the community college?"

"Even though it'll probably take him another seven years, yes," Heather said. "He doesn't have a lot of options."

He might have more options than he knows, Steve thought to himself as he pulled into the Diamond Head parking lot.

IT DIDN'T TAKE long for Steve to see the wisdom of the supplies Heather insisted upon, all except the flashlight. Even in early April, the interior of Diamond Head was hot and still so drinking water and sun protection were a must. The crater was huge, both wide and high, and the trail would be both beautiful enough to use the camera frequently and long enough to possibly need the reinforcement of the trail mix. The trail looked easy enough when they first started out from the comfort station.

Since Heather had said she wanted to do this so they could talk story, Steve wasn't at all surprised when she started asking questions just a few minutes into their journey.

"Do you have a real college degree or did you go to Oklahoma just to get into pro football?" Heather asked.

"I actually do have a degree in English," Steve said. "It was a close call because I changed my track from Literary and Cultural Studies to Writing halfway through my junior year. I had to take some extra courses to get my degree."

"English? Seriously?"

"Since I love to read, it seemed like a no-brainer to me," Steve shrugged.

"Did you take it just because it seemed like an easy way to keep the academic standing to play football?"

"Honestly? Yes," Steve confessed, "at least for the first two years, but in my junior year I started thinking about the possibility of life after football. I asked myself if I could see myself using the degree I was working on. I realized I couldn't, but I sure could see myself writing. So I changed my track."

"Do they normally let you do that?" Heather asked.

Steve thought for a moment.

"I don't know," he was surprised at the realization. "When I was in college, I didn't get much argument from my advisor over anything. I said I wanted to change my track and the next semester he approved the classes for the writing track."

"So did you find out if you're any good at it?"

"I'm pretty sure I am," Steve said thoughtfully, "but if I'm going to be honest, I'd have to admit that at this point it wouldn't matter if I was or not. As soon as I decide to publish a book, someone will snatch it up."

"Have you written one yet?"

"No," Steve said. "I've written three. They're all on my hard drive waiting for me to decide to put them out there for the world to see."

"Why haven't you gotten them published?"

"Because I don't want to find out that I'm really not any good, just famous," Steve answered shortly.

"Why would –?"

"No," Steve said. "No more questions until I get to ask some."

"But why?" Heather snorted. "You've know my family for what, a month now? You know the whole Heather Shepherd saga."

"I know the high points and I know what they think about your life," Steve said. "I don't know much at all from your own lips."

"I'd rather talk about you," Heather grumbled.

"And I'd rather talk about you!" Steve retorted. "I've already talked about me, so now we talk about you for a while. Why don't you surf anymore?"

Heather walked on, not responding. Steve walked quietly beside her. Knowing she would eventually tell him, he was content for now to give some more attention to the trail which had grown steeper and was beginning to switchback up the mountainside.

"I haven't told anyone else," Heather finally sighed, "because my brothers tend to get overprotective."

"So I'm sworn to secrecy?"

"Well not a blood oath or anything but I'll be really, really upset if you tell them."

"Fair enough," Steve said. "As long as it really is none of their business."

"It's not like I'm dying or anything," Heather said. "I just have to adjust my lifestyle some. The physical therapy did a lot to restore virtually all my muscle tone and strength in my left hip and side, but my hip still tends to give out when I strain it too much. Surfing is one of the things that strains it."

"So you don't surf anymore," Steve said quietly.

"Not long board, but I can boogie board," Heather said. "It's very low impact, as long as I stay out of the bigger stuff."

"Okay," Steve agreed. "I won't tell your brothers. Next question, what do you do besides boogie board, fix foreign autos, and paint?"

"Hey," she looked at him sideways. "This sounds a lot like the question that got me in trouble at your house last week."

"I guess it is," Steve smiled down at her. "I answered it, now it's your turn."

"I read, watch movies, bicycle, play with Moose and eat a lot of frozen pizza," Heather said. "There, now you know it all."

"Hold on, not so fast. What do you read?"

"Books. I don't like magazines. What about you? What do you read?"

"I'm a compulsive reader. I even read the back of cereal boxes. What kind of books do you read?"

"Mostly fiction, Christian. I really like suspense novels. What books do you read?"

"I also like Christian suspense novels but I read a bit of everything too. What's your all time favorite book?"

"*Green Eggs and Ham*, by Dr. Seuss. And you?"

"'I do not like them in a house. I do not like them with a mouse.' Yep, that's a classic," Steve agreed. "Mine would have to be *The Shepherd of the Hills*, by Harold Bell Wright."

"Never heard of it," Heather said.

"Most people outside of Missouri usually haven't."

"But you're from Kansas."

"My mom was from Missouri. It's Kansas' eastern neighbor," Steve explained. "Apparently when she was little, teachers in most of the schools in the Ozark area if not in the whole state read the book aloud sometime around third or fourth grade."

"And she read it to you?" Heather asked.

"Yeah, it was one of my earliest memories," Steve said. "Jenni would be curled up on one side of Mom, me on the other. Mom loved that book. It was one of the few things that would animate her."

"There's more to that story, isn't there?" Heather touched Steve's arm lightly. He had slowed almost to a crawl and was mentally somewhere far away.

"Yeah," Steve said softly.

"But you don't want to talk about it right now, do you?"

"Not really," Steve agreed.

"Okay, let's talk about something else for now," Heather smiled understandingly.

"Thank you," Steve gave her a quick one armed hug as they ambled slowly along.

"Do you like movies?" Heather asked.

"Only almost as much as books," Steve said.

"Do you have a favorite?"

"Man, that's a tough one. Give me a genre."

"Okay, fantasy."

"You would pick that one!"

"One of your favorites, huh!"

"Oh yeah."

"So, let me guess ... *Lord of the Rings*?"

"Good start."

"*Chronicles of Narnia*?"

"Right again."

"*The Princess Bride*."

"Three for three. Did you sneak a peek at my DVD collection?"

"No. Mine!" Heather laughed.

"We enjoy the same movies," Steve grinned. "I think I like that."

"Okay, let's see how good you are," Heather said. "'Some things in here don't react too well to gunfire.'"

"*The Hunt for Red October*," Steve said promptly. "Sean Connery said it to Alec Baldwin in the engine room of the nuclear sub when he was going after the cook."

"Very good," Heather said. "Now you give me one."

"'Is it too much to ask for a little precipitation?'"

"Awe, too easy! Steve Carell in *Evan Almighty* when the flood hadn't come at the prophesied time," Heather smiled slyly. "I bet I get you on this one. 'I ... am ... that ... hero!'"

"You just made that up."

"No, but it isn't exactly a movie," Heather acknowledged. "So I did kind of cheat."

"What's it from?"

"That's Larry Boy, from the VeggieTales."

"VeggieTales?"

"Don't tell me you don't like cartoons," Heather said.

"I love cartoons," Steve corrected her. "*The Iron Giant* is awesome, but I've never heard of VeggieTales."

"Matt and Jeremy will fix that for you if you mention it on Sunday."

"So they like VeggieTales."

"No. They love VeggieTales," Heather pointed to a manmade formation to their left. "Let's stop at the lookout before starting up the steps."

They walked over and sat on the wall. The view was pretty incredible, but Steve was more interested in the sights right there in the lookout.

"Did you ever want to go to college?" Steve asked after a few moments of enjoying the view.

"Not really," Heather said. "The only two things I ever wanted to do with my life were being a mechanic and an artist. I didn't see how college would help me with either, especially since the Army taught me how to be a mechanic and I never seriously considered being an artist as a profession."

"How did you get started on European made cars?"

"My first tour of duty was in Germany," Heather said. "I didn't drink or cat around like most of the other soldiers, so to fight the boredom during the week when I couldn't roam around the country, I started hanging out at one of the local garages after work. The owner was really cool. He took me under his wing and taught me as much as he could. When I got out and started my own shop, it was only logical to work on BMWs and Mercedes."

"Do you always call it BMW? Ever call it a Beamer?"

"Never! And don't you do it either. Herr Schneider hated that nickname. Said it was disrespectful to an incredibly well crafted vehicle."

"Okay, I got it," Steve laughed. "I drive a BMW."

"Did you always want to play football?"

"From the time I held my first football," Steve said. "I was in third grade when my mom enrolled me in the parks department's flag football. I was hooked. I've played it every year since then."

"Did you come to Hawaii because of Pete?"

"He's the guilty one," Steve said. "Since my grandma died when I was still in college, I've never had any family as a Grizzly. Being from Hawaii, Pete didn't have much family around during the season. When we had time off, we started hanging around together. When he went to his first Superstar Game, he took me home with him. Eventually I decided I could do a lot worse than living in Hawaii during the offseason, even if it meant seeing his ugly mug most days. So here I am."

"I'm glad you are," Heather smiled then nodded toward the path. "You ready to hit the road again."

"Sure," Steve said. "I'm game if you are."

"We're almost to the summit now," Heather told him. "Most of the rest of the trail is stairs."

"Not a problem," Steve said. "I kinda like stairs."

"I guess if you didn't, you wouldn't like your house," Heather observed.

"Which means it wouldn't be mine, it would be someone else's!"

"You have a point," Heather laughed.

The stairs were too narrow for them to walk abreast, so Steve was following Heather. When they reached a landing halfway up, Steve glanced up and froze. "What's that?"

Heather heard something that almost sounded like panic in Steve's voice. She turned to look at him, then turned back to see what he was staring at.

"That's the tunnel," she said, puzzled.

"No," Steve shook his head. "No, no."

"I told you about the tunnel," Heather walked back down a couple steps to stand eye to eye with Steve. There was definitely panic in his eyes. Over his shoulder she saw that no one was coming up the trail.

"Turn around and go back down," she commanded quietly. "Let's go to the lookout point at the foot of the steps."

When they got to the lookout point, Heather walked to the rail facing out over the switchback path that had gotten them to this point. She wanted to keep their conversation as private as possible.

"Steve, I told you about the tunnel," Heather said gently. "I told you to bring a flashlight for the tunnel."

"I thought you meant it like using headlights in the Likelike Tunnel," Steve groaned softly. "Unnecessary for yourself but helps others see you coming."

"It is unnecessary," Heather said, "unless by some strange fluke the lights go off. I always bring the flashlight because I've seen sudden power shutdowns in Hawaii more than once. The tunnel is well lit as tunnels go."

"No it isn't," Steve hissed. "I saw the yawning black mouth. That tunnel is way too small."

Realization dawned on Heather. "Are you claustrophobic?"

Steve just stared at her with anguished eyes and tense body. Two groups of hikers passed by, one going up, one coming down. Heather waited until they were out of earshot.

"It's okay, Steve," Heather spoke softly, soothingly. "Do you want to go back?"

"No," he shook his head emphatically. "I want to make the summit with you."

"And I with you," Heather smiled and lightly stroked his arm, "but if you go all tense like this in there, you're going to lose it."

"I know," Steve ran his hands through his hair in frustration. "I feel like such a wimp."

"You're not a wimp, Steve," Heather whispered fiercely as another bunch of hikers passed by. "Claustrophobia is actually a lot like PTSD. It can happen to anyone and it's treatable."

"You think?" Steve hissed sarcastically. Immediately he was repentant, even before he saw shock register on Heather's face. "I'm sorry, so sorry. That was way out of line."

Steve put his hands on her shoulders and inclined his head toward hers.

"Please forgive me for speaking to you like that," he asked softly, as anguished over his harshness with her as he was over the tunnel.

"I forgive you," she whispered, still mindful of the hikers who suddenly seemed more prevalent.

"Thank you," Steve said and pulled her into a hug.

Heather felt Steve's heart thundering under her hand pressed against his chest. She pushed back enough to look up at him but stayed in the shelter of his arms. They were close enough to speak very softly and still hear each other in the quiet on the mountainside. It had the added benefit that few people were likely to try to eavesdrop on lovers stealing an embrace.

"Obviously you know it's treatable," Heather said a little sarcastically to help lighten the mood. "Does that mean you've gotten treatment already?"

"Two counselors," Steve said. "One in Chicago, one here in Honolulu. Both Christian."

"Has it helped?"

"Yeah, but with my childhood, there was a lot that needed help," Steve smiled sadly. "Claustrophobia wasn't a priority."

"When did you start counseling?" Heather could feel the tenseness slowly draining from Steve.

"About four years ago, I guess."

"What made you start then? You already had it made as a Grizzly. You were pretty much guaranteed the Hall of Fame," Heather kept her voice low and soothing, her conversation anything to distract him from the tunnel.

"Yeah, I realized that," Steve said, "but I also realized it wasn't how I wanted my life to be defined. I didn't want to be a Hall of Famer whose home life stunk. I wanted to be a superstar husband and father, but I had no clue how to do it."

Steve breathed deeply and smoothed back some wisps of hair from Heather's cheek. Under her hand, she felt his heart rate returning to normal, even as hers was beginning to thunder.

"I realized I had trained for football all my life, way before I ever had a chance at the pros," Steve continued, "and I decided to train for family life too, even before I had a chance to get one."

Steve studied Heather's face as she stood there, almost breathless. His eyes suddenly grew smoky. Heather could feel his heart begin to beat faster again. He wanted to kiss her. She wanted the kiss.

Heather deliberately stepped back, out of his embrace.

"So you want to make the summit?" Heather meant more than the top of Diamond Head.

"If you're serving God," Steve wisely put his hands in his pockets. "You have to shoot for the top. He deserves our all in everything we do."

"When you're ready, we'll go up," Heather said. "We'll go in together. I'll go first and you follow close behind. If I start to get too far ahead of you, tap me on the back, okay?"

"I can do this," Steve said. "I've already learned to ride in almost any elevator, even though some still give me the creeps. Like the one at the Sears Tower. Can't do it!"

"Your reaction earlier was probably the unexpectedness of it," Heather said. "I should have been more specific about the tunnel."

"It's not your fault, it's mine. You would have told me about it if I had told you about the claustrophobia," Steve reassured her. "I think I'm ready to go now."

"You're sure?" Heather asked, studying his face for any signs of his earlier panic. "No dark thoughts ready to pop out?"

"Sweetheart," Steve drawled. "Right now all I'm thinking about is kissing you."

Heather blushed furiously. "Then I guess we should go. When we get through the tunnel, we're going to go left. There's another lookout there, okay?"

Steve nodded his approval of her plan. They climbed the stairs and Heather started talking, hoping to keep Steve's mind off the upcoming tunnel. "Do you guys ever run the stadium stairs like I've seen on commercials?"

"Sometimes."

"Then this will be like a walk in the park for you," Heather said, then she giggled.

"What's funny?"

"Well, technically this is a walk in the park, the Diamond Head State Park," Heather said. "So it's a walk in the park for everyone."

"Clever," Steve said dryly.

"Anyway, there's two hundred eighty steps going up to the top. A stadium has how many?"

"It's not the steps I'm concerned about," Steve muttered, seeing the tunnel looming large in front of Heather.

"You're not supposed to be thinking about the tunnel."

"Should I be thinking about kissing you?"

"I would hate to answer that with a 'no' right now," Heather sighed. "We're both going to have to duck because it is pretty short, but you're going to be able to see just fine after your eyes adjust from the bright sun to the lower light. Stay close and let me know if you start to stress, okay?"

They entered the tunnel. Heather could hear Steve breathing hard behind her.

"This is really small," Steve grumbled.

Heather looked over her shoulder and saw how much Steve was hunched over, how close he was to her. She faced forward and began to giggle again.

"I don't see how you can laugh at a time like this," Steve complained.

"I'm sorry," Heather said, "but I just realized that if we were using those flashlights, we would look like the cover of a Nancy Drew novel. Nancy forging ahead while Ned hovers protectively at her shoulder."

Her giggle felt like a breath of fresh air to Steve. He still felt the walls looming over him but without the crushing power that he had expected.

"How're you doing?" Heather looked over her shoulder again.

"Still thinking about that kiss," Steve gave her a small smile. She quickly faced forward, trying to think of something else to say. Nothing came to mind.

A shadow blocked the light at the head of the tunnel. Someone was coming. Heather looked back at the big man filling the tunnel behind her and she wondered how they would all fit. Apparently the person at the head of the tunnel wondered the same thing.

"Wow! That guy's huge, Martha," a man's voice said. "Go back up, we aren't squeezing past him."

Heather was delighted to hear Steve's snort of laughter. They heard the man at the head of the tunnel, warning someone else they should wait. Apparently they disregarded his suggestion because shadows darkened the wall again. A small figure appeared around the curve with a man behind her.

"Is he a giant, Daddy?" the little girl's voice carried easily.

"Probably not, punkin," a man replied, "but I think he's too big for Daddy to get past. Come on back and let's wait for him to come out."

As Steve and Heather drew closer to the mouth of the tunnel, they heard other warnings to wait. Suddenly Steve reached out and tugged on Heather's t-shirt. Concerned, she turned quickly but Steve didn't look stressed. He looked slightly amused.

"It sounds like there's going to be a lot of people looking at us when we get out of here."

"Yeah, so what?"

"Someone's probably going to recognize me."

"Oh," Heather said quietly.

"Are you okay with that?"

"Do I have a choice?"

"We can turn around and go down."

"And not make it to the summit?" Heather said with a heavy sigh. "Let's go on."

She started walking again, none to happy about a bunch of tourists with cameras realizing that Steve Jeremiah was in their midst. It was going to happen sooner or later. It may as well be sooner.

Chapter 18

A few minutes later, Heather stepped out of the tunnel into the bright sunlight. She timidly smiled at about twenty people, some sitting on the steps to her right, others standing to the left, in her way.

"Excuse me," she said quietly, hoping to get out of this without any attention, then Steve stepped out of the tunnel and straightened up.

"Wow, he *is* a giant, Daddy," the little girl said.

"That's Jeremiah, honey," one young man whispered to the woman next to him. She looked at him in surprise.

"The Chicago Grizzlies' Jeremiah? Really?" She turned to Steve. "Are you?"

"Guilty as charged," Steve raised both hands and shrugged his shoulders.

"Cool," the young man said. "Are you here on your honeymoon too?"

"No such luck," Steve laughed. "I just live here in the offseason."

"I can see why," an older man looked suggestively at Heather.

Steve turned his head slowly and stared coldly at the man. He shuffled his feet nervously and said to the woman and teenaged boy with him, "Come on, let's go."

"But Dad," the boy said.

"Let's go," the man snarled. "You don't need his autograph anyway."

Steve frowned at the man and tensed, instinctively knowing that the man was cut from the same cloth as his father had been. Heather put her hand on his arm and he looked down at her. She smiled sadly and shook her head slightly. She was right, there was really nothing he could do about it. Except pray.

"Can I have your autograph, Mr. Jeremiah?" the little girl asked.

"I would love to give you one, honey," Steve said, "but I don't have anything to write with."

"I might have something," one woman said as she began to root around in her bag.

"I'd like to have your picture even more," the young husband said.

"Not a problem," Steve answered, "but how about we go over into the lookout so we're not blocking the traffic."

It turned out that they blocked traffic anyway. People coming up and going down wanted to see what all the commotion was about.

Steve smiled generously and patiently through dozens of pictures with the ocean in the background. He signed autographs on Diamond Head flyers, receipts, and scraps of paper dug out of pockets and backpacks. Then one elderly Japanese couple made it clear through halting English and generous hand gestures that they wanted not only a picture of them with Steve but also with Heather. They had Heather and Steve stand next to each other, then they stood in front while the young husband took the picture.

When Steve realized that he could easily rest his elbow on the man's head, he could barely stifle a laugh.

"I sure would like a copy of this one," Steve whispered to Heather.

"That's doable!" Heather reached into her pocket for her digital camera. When the couple started to walk away, she stepped around them and put her hands out to stop them. Setting up her camera, she took a picture of Steve and the couple.

"You want me to take a picture of you with them too?" the honeymooning wife asked.

"Would you?" Heather showed her how to work the camera then joined Steve again.

After their pictures were taken, the Japanese couple offered to take pictures of the honeymoon couple with Steve and Heather. Then with many bows, arigatos and thank yous, the elderly couple resumed their descent. By that time the crowd had thinned out. Steve introduced Heather to the honeymooners who introduced themselves as Doug and Gina, from Effingham, Illinois. They had been talking for a few minutes when a family of four joined them in the lookout.

The little boy looked to be about Matt's age. He was very thin and pale, and appeared to be bald under his Grizzlies cap. He took one look at Steve, grabbed the ninety-five on his chest in one hand and pulled on his dad's arm with the other.

"It's him, isn't it Daddy?" he whispered. "That's Steve Jeremiah."

Before the boy could ask him the obvious, Steve walked over and knelt down beside him. Heather walked over to talk to the mother.

"Would you mind if my friend took a picture of you with me?" Steve asked humbly.

"You want my picture?" The little boy put his hand on his chest. "Why do you want my picture?"

Steve heard the mother whispering to Heather.

"Because I think that boys who battle leukemia are real heroes," Steve kept the tears from his voice. "Can I pick you up?"

The boy looked up at his dad, who smiled and nodded.

"Sure," he said and held up his arms.

"What's your name?" Steve asked as he carried the boy over to the end of the lookout so Heather and his mom could take pictures of them.

"I'm Eddie and my sister is Melissa," the boy told him. "Daddy is Jim and mom is Heidi. What's your girlfriend's name?"

"She's Heather."

"Are you going to marry her?"

"Eddie!" Heidi scolded him. "That's none of your business."

Steve put his hand up to shield Eddie's ear and whispered something into it. Eddie giggled and grinned.

"Okay," he said.

Steve insisted on pictures with the whole family. Eddie wanted Heather to join them, so Doug took a few pictures before he and Gina headed down the trail. Then Eddie wanted pictures of just him and Heather but he wanted her to sit by him, not hold him.

"I know you're big enough to hold me," he whispered to her, "but that wouldn't be very manly, to be held by a pretty lady. So you can just sit on the bench by me, okay?"

While Heidi was taking pictures, Steve talked quietly with Jim. He found out that they had come up this far but would be going back down after Eddie rested. Though the boy really wanted to reach the summit, he wasn't able to walk any further. In fact, Jim had carried him from the last lookout. Though he had the desire, he didn't have the strength to carry Eddie the rest of the way.

"If you don't mind," Steve said. "I'd like to carry him the rest of the way. It would be a shame for you all to make it this far, only to have to turn around."

"You would do that for Eddie?"

"And more if I could," Steve said.

"It's up to him," Jim told him. "He doesn't like to be weak, especially around strangers."

Steve walked over and sat down on the bench by Eddie, resting his elbows on his knees. "Hey Eddie, can I ask you a favor?"

"Sure, Mr. Jeremiah," Eddie said.

"First, I really would like it if you and Melissa would call me Uncle Steve instead of Mr. Jeremiah," Steve said. "Here in Hawaii, that's how the locals show respect for people older than them. Can you do that?"

"Sure, Uncle Steve," he turned to Heather. "Does that mean I call you Aunt Heather?"

"Real close, buddy," she smiled, "but in Hawaii it's Aunty not just Aunt."

"Okay, Aunty Heather," Eddie grinned broadly.

"But that was the easy favor," Steve said seriously. "I have another, bigger one to ask you."

"Okay," Eddie matched his seriousness.

"Have you ever heard of something called claustrophobia?"

"That sounds serious. What is it?"

"It's when someone gets afraid in tight or small spaces. I have it, especially in tight, dark spaces."

"You get afraid?" Eddie was astounded by that revelation.

"I sure do, Eddie," Steve confessed. "See when I was young like you, some bad things happened to me. I didn't have God or a great daddy like yours to help me, so I got afraid in a way that stayed with me even after I started playing football for the Grizzlies."

Eddie frowned thoughtfully.

"Well, you must be getting better because you made it through that tunnel down there," Eddie observed, pointing at the mountainside in front of them.

"Oh, I've been getting lots better because I worked with counselors," Steve agreed, "but I'm not all better yet. Heather had to help me get though the first tunnel."

Eddie looked to Heather for confirmation and she nodded.

"But," Steve said. "I don't think she can help me the rest of the way."

"Why not?"

"Well, she ...," Steve cleared his throat and looked apologetically at Heather. "Would you mind going over there? This is going to be man talk."

Eddie's little chest puffed up with importance.

"Melissa, you should go too," Eddie said to his big sister. "You and Aunty Heather go over there by Mom while we talk. Dad, you should come here with us men."

After everyone was properly situated, Eddie very seriously invited Steve to continue.

"Even though I'm getting much better controlling the claustrophobia," Steve explained. "I still need someone to help me in places like these tunnels."

"And Aunty Heather can't?"

"Don't tell her, because I don't want to hurt her feelings," Steve said in a low voice, "but she makes me nervous and that makes it really hard to control my fear."

"Why does she make you nervous?" Eddie whispered.

"Because I want to kiss her."

"Why do you want to kiss her?"

"Because I'm in love with her."

"Then why don't you kiss her?"

"Because we're not engaged to be married yet."

"Do you have to do that before you kiss a girl?"

"I think you should if you want to do things the way God wants you to."

"So why don't you engage her so you can kiss her?"

"Because she isn't ready yet."

"Why not?"

"I don't know. She's a woman."

Eddie frowned at the three women sitting on the other side of the lookout. "They're strange, aren't they?"

"Yes they are," Steve agreed. "I don't want Heather to try to help me in the last tunnel because she makes me nervous. But I really want to go all the way up, and I don't want to hurt her feelings. So I want you to help me. You'll be better anyway."

"How will I be better?" Eddie asked.

"Heather had to walk in front of me, but I can have you ride on my back," Steve said very seriously, "and you can talk to me the whole time, right in my ear. You know, tell me stories, sing to me, encourage me. You're a real hero, so you'll help me feel much more courageous. And you won't make me nervous."

"'Cause you don't want to kiss me," Eddie said thoughtfully, "but how will you get back down?"

"I'm hoping you'll help me then too," Steve said.

"What do you think, Dad?" Eddie turned to his father. "Should I help Uncle Steve? I guess that means you all would have to go all the way up too."

"I think we can do that," Jim said thoughtfully. "Mom probably has her second wind by now."

"Okay, Uncle Steve," Eddie turned back to Steve. "I'll help you but once we get to the top, you have to put me down, okay?"

"Deal," Steve stuck out his right hand for Eddie to shake. "Why don't you climb on so we can get this show on the road?"

EDDIE AND STEVE went up the steps first. Eddie took his job very seriously, talking almost non-stop to Steve. Jim and Melissa followed, and Heather and Heidi brought up the rear. Most of the way they had to go single file, so Heidi deliberately dropped back enough to talk to Heather without the others hearing.

"Did Steve tell the truth back there? About the claustrophobia?" Heidi asked.

"If he didn't," Heather told her. "Then he's the finest actor in the world and should be making movies instead of tackles."

"You saw him have an episode?"

"Yes. When he saw the tunnel earlier, he panicked big time."

"How did he get through it?"

"We went back down to that lookout just before the steps," Heather explained. "When he calmed down, he fortified himself with positive thoughts and then followed me through."

"So he's really been working with counselors?" Heidi asked. "He's learning to control his fear?"

"Yes, it appears so."

"How did he know to share all that?"

"I guess God just told him what to say," Heather shrugged. "I know he's done it before, come up with the right words unexpectedly. It's a God thing."

"Well it means a lot to us, what he just shared," Heidi said. "Eddie has been bothered by people knowing that he has this weakness. He doesn't want people thinking he's a wimp. To hear Steve Jeremiah confess that he has weakness …. Well, I don't think you really understand how much that will help Eddie not worry about his own weaknesses. Now, since Steve Jeremiah has asked for his help, he'll learn to let others help him when he needs it."

Heidi wiped her eyes before she continued. "And the counseling confession! I know Jim was touched by that. The doctors recommended counselors to us, but Jim got it in his head that it was not manly to go to counselors. But if Steve Jeremiah sees a counselor, I think we will be too. That's a very special man you have there, Heather. I'd advise you to not let him get away."

"I don't intend to," Heather said, "but I'm also not going to rush God."

"You're both believers?" Heidi asked.

"Yes, we are," Heather answered. "In fact Steve goes to my church when he's in town."

"Is that how you met?"

"No," Heather laughed. "We met over a broken down car."

"He rescued you?"

"No, I rescued him!"

"You did. That's fascinating. Do tell."

So Heather did. Then Heidi told her how she and Jim had met. It was another unique story, since he had rear ended her at a traffic light.

By the time they reached the summit, the women were talking story as if they'd known each other all their lives. That didn't keep them from splitting up and spending some quiet time with their men while they enjoyed the spectacular view.

"You're something special, Steve Jeremiah," Heather walked up beside him where he stood at the rail, staring out toward the Ewa side of the crater.

"I don't think I'm half as special as you are," Steve said, putting his arm around her waist and pulling her close to his side.

"Me? I didn't do anything for Eddie but smile and agree with you," Heather said.

"And that smile was plenty," Steve said, "but I wasn't talking about Eddie. I was talking about me. How did you know to do all that down there when I panicked?"

Heather sighed and rubbed her eyes before she answered.

"PTSD," she barely even whispered. "I dealt with it myself. Still do at times."

"That's not surprising, after what you went though over in Iraq," Steve said.

"What about you?" Heather raised sad eyes to meet his. "Your dad used to lock you in the closet, didn't he? That's why you're claustrophobic."

"We're a sorry couple of heroes, aren't we?" Steve laughed ruefully. "People see the strength and never expect the weaknesses."

"But in our weakness, God is strong," Heather reminded Steve. "He used your weakness to minister to Eddie and his family."

Heather told Steve what Heidi had shared with her. Steve stared out at the deep blue of the Pacific, broken near the shoreline by the white-capped waves rolling over the reef. Hanauma and Koko Head stood far off on his left and the Koolau Mountains curved up behind him, rising above their famous baby sister. God had created all this beauty, the beauty not just of the land called Hawaii, but the beauty of people loving and helping others.

"It never ceases to amaze me how God works," Steve said in awe. "Today was certainly a divine appointment."

After a few minutes of enjoying the view, Steve looked around to see where Eddie was.

"I have a confession," Steve whispered to Heather.

"What's that?"

"The thought of going down that spiral staircase in the tunnel is terrifying."

"Why?" Heather was puzzled. "You seemed to have no problems coming up the stairs."

"That's because it was up," Steve said. "I could see light ahead of me. But going down ...?"

Steve shook his head and frowned his distress.

"Going down, I'll be descending into the dark. And it's tight and twisty and terrifying."

"So you want ...?"

"Please go down first, with Heidi," Steve took her hand in his. "Talk and laugh and let me hear your voice. With Eddie entertaining me from behind and you guiding me from the front, I should be good."

Chapter 19

Steve's plan worked well and the trip back down was uneventful, except when Eddie fell asleep riding on Steve. Worried that he wouldn't hold on well enough when asleep, they stopped at the makai lookout below the last of the steps and Steve transferred him to the front. He carried the sleeping boy easily on his left arm with Eddie's head resting on his shoulder, arms dangling.

At the lookout the cameras came out again. They got a wide variety of pictures with them standing in the narrow twin catwalks. Jim got down on his knees trying to get pictures that made it look like they were suspended over the ocean. Melissa and Heather each got in one of the catwalks by herself and mimicked the Little Mermaid, leaning into the rail, arms out, face to the wind, laughing.

When they started out again, Heather and Melissa went first with Steve behind them, Eddie sleeping peacefully. Jim and Heidi brought up the rear.

They had taken their time on the hike and spent enough time at the summit that it was nearing the noon lull, so they didn't see a lot of upward bound hikers. Melissa and Heather walked side by side as much as possible. Steve picked his way over the uneven terrain much more carefully coming down with his precious cargo, so they often found themselves well ahead of the rest. They stopped and sat to wait on a concrete wall about two thirds of the way down.

Heather directed Melissa's attention to Wilhelmina Rise with its broad, straight road running almost to the summit of the mountain. As Heather pointed, her sleeve pulled up enough for Melissa, who was sitting on her right, to see the scar on her arm.

"Oh! What happened to your arm?" she asked with a ten year old's curiosity and sympathy.

Heather leaned close and whispered, "I got shot."

"Really?" Melissa's eyes were wide. "How?"

"I was a soldier in the war," Heather said.

"You were?"

"Uh huh," Heather nodded.

"Can I look at it?" Melissa asked earnestly.

Heather pulled up her sleeve so the full scar showed. Awed, Melissa traced it with her right index finger.

"Does it hurt?"

"Not now," Heather said, "but it hurt a whole lot when it first happened."

She saw that Steve had passed the last switchback corner with Eddie's parents right behind him. Pulling her sleeve down, she stood up and turned to lift Melissa down from the wall.

"Shall we go?" She wanted to put off Melissa's revelation about her scar for now. Forever if possible.

The girl followed her down the path, making room for a few hikers going up and then hopping forward to walk beside her again. As they rounded the next switchback, Melissa looked up and saw the others coming down. She frowned worriedly.

"Uncle Steve's been carrying Eddie a long time," she expressed her concern. "Is he strong enough? He's not going to drop my brother is he?"

"Honey, if the world turned upside down and tried to shake him off, Uncle Steve would still hold onto Eddie," Heather assured her.

"Oh, okay," Melissa said. She thought for a moment. "It won't will it?"

"What won't?"

"The world. It can't really turn upside down can it?" Melissa's question was much too serious for Heather to laugh. She gave her a one-armed hug as they walked down the trail.

"No honey, it's not," Heather said. "That was hyperbole."

"Hyperbole," Melissa repeated carefully. "What's that?"

"It's exaggerating something to make a strong point."

Melissa thought about that for a while.

"So you came up with something really bad to happen," she finally said, "to show me that there wasn't anything that could happen that would make Uncle Steve drop Eddie."

"That's right," Heather said.

"So exaggeration is okay if it's hyper– .... What was that word?"

"Hyperbole," Heather pronounced carefully.

"Hyperbole," Melissa repeated. "Hyperbole is okay?"

"Yes," Heather knew she had to tread carefully. "Hyperbole is the kind of exaggeration that helps someone understand something that's important. Jesus used it in the bible."

"He did?"

"Yes. Like when he said to not let your left hand know what your right was doing when you gave away money."

"And you can't really do that," Melissa said thoughtfully, "not unless you cut off your left hand."

"That's right, and that would be really bad so we know he didn't mean it literally. Jesus said that to show people what he meant about not doing things so that other people would think you were great."

"So that was exaggeration, but it was hyperbole and it was okay."

"That's right. What's not okay is regular exaggeration which is something we use to get our own way."

"I think I get it," Melissa said thoughtfully.

"So if I said, 'My feet are killing me,'" Heather pointed to a shaded bench next to a maintenance shed. "'Let's sit down here and rest.' That would be …?"

"Exaggeration," Melissa said proudly, "because your feet can't really kill you. You just want me to feel sorry for you so you can get your own way."

"Is it working?" Heather said hopefully.

"Yep," Melissa giggled, walking over and plopping down on the bench. "Because my feet are killing me too."

They giggled together and Heather gave Melissa another hug. "Shall we wait for the others to catch up?"

"I guess we should," Melissa said. "I don't want Mom to start worrying about me. She has enough to worry about with Eddie."

It was only a few minutes before the others approached. Steve was still carrying Eddie, but the boy was beginning to wake up from his nap. When they got to Heather and Melissa's bench, Steve set Eddie down next to his sister then plopped down in the dirt at their feet, knees bent, arms propped on them with hands dangling.

Eddie rubbed his eyes and yawned, then leaned against his sister.

"Are you having fun, turkey?" Melissa put her arm around her brother.

"I fell asleep," Eddie complained.

"You didn't miss much," his dad said as Heidi and he joined them.

"The view was pretty much the same going up as coming down," Heidi said. "How about some water?"

Jim turned so that Heidi could get a couple of water bottles out of his backpack. Heather and Steve dug out their own bottles.

"I wanted to walk after I got done helping Uncle Steve," Eddie complained as he handed his bottle to Melissa.

"You still can, buddy," Heather said. "We're not pau yet."

"We're not done yet," Steve interpreted when he saw Eddie's confused look.

"What did she say?" Eddie frowned at Steve and pointed with his thumb at Heather, sitting next to him on the bench.

"She said 'pau.' That's Hawaiian for done," Steve explained with a small smile, thinking about his own recent education on the way kamaaina talk.

They rested and talked story for a few minutes, then Jim said it was time for his family to hit the road.

"Are you coming too?" Eddie asked Steve.

"No, he isn't," Jim said. "He came here to spend time with Heather and we've been keeping them apart."

"That's okay," Heather said quickly. "We really enjoyed our time with you."

"Yes, we did," Steve drawled, then he gave Eddie a wink and nodded his head toward Heather. "But you should probably go on ahead now."

Eddie looked thoughtfully from Steve to Heather. He looked back at Steve and nodded his head seriously. "Yeah, I guess we better."

"I'd really like to see you again before you go," Steve said. "When are you leaving?"

"We have to be at the airport at nine tomorrow morning," Heidi said.

"Then that won't work," Steve frowned. "I wish we'd met you earlier, but I'll be back on the Mainland soon. You don't perchance live in Illinois, do you?"

"No, Muscatine, Iowa," Jim told him.

"Hey, that's not far from Chicago," Steve said. "Can I come see you when I'm back there?"

"You wanna come see us?" Eddie could barely contain his excitement. "Can he Mom, please?"

"If he wants too, sure," Heidi said. "But you should call first. It's a long drive to come just to find out we're not home."

"Okay. Give me your address and phone number," Steve said.

After Jim and Steve exchanged contact information, Eddie and Melissa both hugged Steve and Heather before running down the path with their parents. They turned quite a few times to wave before they disappeared around the curve.

Steve sighed heavily and looked sideways at Heather.

"I did not know that a seven year old child could get so heavy," he groaned.

Heather's laugh rang out and Steve shook his finger at her.

"Laugh if you will," he said, "but I swear my left bicep has grown after that workout. Look."

Steve stood up and faced Heather with a twinkle in his eyes, flexing both arms. "See, it's bigger isn't it."

"No, it's not," Heather blushed, looking away. "You're just showing off."

"Fat lot of good it does me if you won't look," Steve grumbled. "How does a peacock do it?"

"Do what?" Heather asked warily.

"Keep the peahen from being so bedazzled by his stunning beauty," Steve sighed. "How's he supposed to court her if she's too awed to look at him?"

"I guess he could start with a touch of modesty," Heather suggested wryly.

"Maybe he shows off so much that she gets used to his magnificence," Steve said thoughtfully as some young people strolled up the path, the boys with their shirts off, showing off their smooth youthful bodies.

"Maybe I should take off my shirt, too," Steve whispered as they walked past.

"Don't you dare," Heather whispered furiously. "You're supposed to be the one who behaves."

"I am?" Steve feigned forgetfulness. "Oh yeah, that. I'll behave if you get some food in me. I'm starving after this workout."

"You want me to cook?" Heather asked slyly.

"Heavens no, woman!" Steve's horror was not feigned. "Take me to a restaurant that has some ono grinds. I'll buy."

"Ono grinds it is," Heather said as they started down the path, "but what kine grinds. You want Korean, Vietnamese, Thai, Chinese, Hawaiian, Italian, or a big old American burger?"

Steve decided that pasta was just the thing to restore his depleted strength, so they went to a little Italian restaurant not far from Heather's shop. By the time Steve dropped her off just after two o'clock, Heather knew that there was no way she could stop her traitorous heart from loving Steve, but how were they ever going to make it work?

Chapter 20

*E*arly Friday afternoon, Heather dropped into the customer chair in the reception area. She sighed and tossed her cap on the corner of Malia's desk, stretching her legs out and rubbing the back of her neck with her right hand.

"Tell me we have nothing coming in tomorrow?" she pleaded with Malia.

"Well, I could," Malia smiled apologetically, "but that would be lying."

"Oh no. I was hoping I could call it a week now," Heather groaned.

"It's just two services. I bet Greg would do it," Malia said.

"Yes, he would," Heather said, "if he weren't working at the beach tomorrow. So I'll have to come in."

She reached up and unpinned her hair then started unbuttoning her coveralls.

"I sure would like this job a whole lot better if I didn't have to do it for a living," Heather sighed.

"Once you marry Steve, you won't have to," Malia said slyly.

"Brat!" Heather threw her cap at her cousin and stood quickly. "I'm going home to get my last true friend and take him to the hospital. You, I won't see until Sunday at church. And that will be a day too soon if you ask me."

"I love you too, Heather," Malia sang out as Heather stalked through the door. "Be blessed at the hospital today."

"I always am," Heather replied as the door swung shut behind her. She smiled broadly as she walked the short block to her house. Friday afternoon was one of the highlights of her week. Though it would be hard to top yesterday's trip up Diamond Head with Steve, her weekly visit with Moose to the pediatrics ward at the hospital was always a delight.

Moose knew what time it was too. He greeted her with extra bounce in his joyful assault at the door.

"Yeah, get it all out, you big bear, before I get changed," Heather laughed and put Moose in a gentle headlock. She dropped to her knees and rolled over on her back before she released him, laughing as he pounced on her with his big front paws, trying to lick her face. They wrestled on the floor for several minutes before they both sat back, grinning happily at each other.

"Are you ready for me to get ready?"

Moose barked an emphatic yes.

"Okay, I'll be out in fifteen," Heather said as she scrambled to her feet.

Fourteen minutes later, Heather gave herself a once over in the full-length mirror in her bedroom and smiled in approval. She loved going to see the keiki at the pediatric ward because she always felt so feminine, not an easy feat when you're a six foot tall auto mechanic. She had discovered early on that the children were not intimidated by her height nor were they bothered by her scars or her trade. In fact, they found everything about her a delight, even without Moose. She dressed up for them because she loved to bring light and color into their sad lives.

Today she was wearing a new outfit that Mom had made especially for the keiki. The blouse had a gold silk, scoop-necked, sleeveless undershirt with a pale orange gauze over blouse. The over blouse was layered like overlapping flower petals with small cap shoulders from which fell flower petal sleeves. The blouse barely touched the top of her skirt which was orange, pink, yellow and pale green, swirled together in an apparently random design. It was form fitting from waist to mid thigh where it swirled out in handkerchief panels.

The outfit disguised but didn't hide her scars because many of the children at the hospital had their own scars. When they saw Heather's, they felt much better about their own.

This was also the only time she wore her hair down, except when she danced at church. Today it fell in curls almost to her waist, adorned with a single plumeria tucked behind her right ear. Her outfit was completed by a puka shell necklace with a matching ankle bracelet and a pair of jeweled slippers with three-inch heels. A touch of pikake and jasmine perfume topped it all off.

Heather spun around once, watching the outfit float around her. Oh yeah, the keiki would love this one. She tried not to wonder what Steve would think about it if he ever saw it.

When Heather came out of her room, Moose was sitting at the door waiting. She grabbed her keys, purse and keiki bag. When she opened the door Moose loped straight to the car, waiting for her with plumed tail gently waving.

At the hospital, Moose paced patiently beside her as they got off the elevator and walked to the dayroom. He began to whine eagerly just before Heather heard a familiar deep voice.

"I called Nurse Diane. I told her I wouldn't be in yesterday."

"But why not?" That was Anela. "You always come on Thursday."

Heather stopped just before the door to eavesdrop for a while.

"I had something special to do with a very special friend. So I asked if I could come in today instead. Forgive me?"

"I don't know yet," Anela was obviously still pouting.

"Awe, come off it, Anela." That was little Kimo. "Let's just play."

"Hey, no tickling!"

Heather leaned down and unhooked Moose's leash. She peeked around the corner and saw Steve with keiki hanging on, climbing on, and clinging to him. Smiling softly, she sent Moose in and slipped in behind him.

"Moose! Moose!" The children started squealing.

"Moose?" Steve looked down at the dog who had planted his front paws on Steve's abdomen and was licking Anela's leg. She giggled and climbed higher up Steve's chest. He smelled flowers.

"Moose!" Steve said and turned toward the flowers. The dog pushing on his chest, the children on his legs, arms and back, and the vision before him all conspired against him. Steve began to lose his balance as he turned. He tightened his hold on Anela but couldn't do anything to keep from landing on the other children if he went down. Suddenly a pair of strong, slender arms were pushing him back up, a curly dark head pressing against his shoulders.

"Better run, menehune," Heather was laughing. "I think Goliath is going down."

As the small crowd dispersed, Steve got his feet back under him and turned to Heather.

"No Shepherd will take down this Goliath," Steve growled.

"Wanna bet?" Heather smiled softly, looking at him through a veil of hair as she turned toward the kids.

No, he didn't want to bet.

"Uncle Steve, why's your heart beating so hard?" Anela asked in concern, her little hand pressed to his chest.

"I guess I got scared when I nearly fell with you," Steve lied boldly and Heather laughed.

"Do you know Aunty Heather and Moose?" Kaipo tugged Steve's arm.

"Yes, I do," Steve said. "She's the special friend I was with yesterday."

"Then I guess I forgive you," Anela sighed, "'cause she's lots of fun."

"Thank you," Steve kissed her on the cheek.

"Put me down now," Anela commanded. As soon as she was on the ground, she took off to the couch where all the kids were swarming around Heather and Moose. Jon had dug a dog brush out of Heather's bag and was brushing Moose who panted with a happy smile on his face. Laura was climbing up on Heather's lap with a book.

"This one first," she said.

"Ah! *Green Eggs and Ham*," Heather smiled at the little girl. "How did you know it was my favorite?"

A small hand slipped into Steve's, and he heard a heavy sigh. He looked down at Kimo who stood with drooping shoulders and smiled sadly up at Steve. "I guess I'll stay here with you so you won't be all alone."

"I've got a better idea," Steve said. "How about I go over there with you while Aunty Heather reads to all of us?"

"Okay!" Kimo agreed, pulling Steve over to join Heather.

Steve stretched out on the floor directly in front of Heather, propping up his head on his left arm. He made a great backrest for some of the children as they enjoyed Heather's dramatic reading of the Seuss classic.

Steve enjoyed the view even more. He had known Heather was beautiful, but he hadn't realized how truly feminine she was. He'd only seen her in jeans, capris or shorts with t-shirts or polo shirts and an almost manly blouse for church. The only time he'd seen her hair out of the braid was that brief moment in her grandma's kitchen. He'd never seen her with jewelry or in heels. Even her scent was more feminine today.

After two books, it was beauty time for the girls. They brushed Heather's hair as she braided flowers in theirs. The boys played with Moose, getting him to do their favorite tricks. Steve enjoyed it all, playing when invited, watching when the play swirled around him.

The time passed all too quickly. Nurse Diane came in to tell them that they had fifteen minutes before it was time for the keiki to return to their rooms for the evening. This was obviously a special time with Heather, because three of the children scrambled to her bag and dug out a CD. Anela took it to the stereo in the corner while the rest of the children gathered in a circle.

The first song was "Be Our Guest," from *Beauty and the Beast*. The children danced gleefully, encouraged by Heather and encouraging Steve. He knew he looked more than a little silly, towering above everyone else and yet acting like one of the little boys, but he really didn't care. He wasn't sure when, if ever, he'd had so much fun. But the song soon ended and the next one, "You'll Be In My Heart" from *Tarzan*, started low and sweet.

Heather began to dance with each of the children in turn. She danced a few measures with each child then swung them gently. When she set them back on their feet, she spun into the arms of the next waiting child. She wasn't even through the first chorus and still had four boys to go when the giggling keiki pushed Steve out to be the arms she twirled into.

Heather spun up against Steve as Phil Collins sang about "the way we feel." With her heels on, she was staring right into the hollow of Steve's throat. He slipped his right hand into her left and rested his left hand lightly on her back, just above her right hip. She slowly raised her right hand to his shoulder. He spun her gently as Phil Collins sang that they weren't so different. Their steps became more sure, more perfectly in tune as the song swelled and Steve knew this woman would indeed be in his heart forever.

The children were delighted as Steve and Heather spun and twirled, dipped and swayed to the music. As the song crested, so did the drumming of their hearts. Heather knew that there was no going back for her. She smiled softly and warmly as she slipped out of his arms when the song tapered off with the promise of "always." This show wasn't over.

She spun away and came to rest at the far end of the room. She stepped out of her heels and stood with head bent slightly, right foot forward, arms hanging gracefully, hands curved slightly toward her body.

Steve stood there feeling strangely lost without her in his arms. Small hands tugged on his arm and he looked down.

"Sit down," Anela whispered. "You gotta sit."

Steve gladly sat on the floor, legs stretched out in front of him, leaning back on his arms. Moose trotted over and laid perpendicular to Steve, his head on Steve's left thigh. Three of the kids leaned against Steve's back, Anela snuggled up to his right side. Kimo and Kaipo laid their heads on Moose.

When Mark Harris's "Find Your Wings" began, Heather raised her hands gracefully and her hips began to sway. Through the first verse and chorus she danced a slow hula, hands and arms singing the words in sweet graceful signs while her feet and legs gave a gentle sway to her whole body.

As the second chorus burst forth, so did Heather. Suddenly she wasn't bound by the rules of hula but was soaring upon wings of passion, still graceful, still signing but now free to dream. It was a creative sign dance, but it was more than Steve had seen before. Grace, power and passion flowed with her every move, reaching beyond the expected into greatness.

Steve watched enthralled, not suspecting that the sight of him loving and being loved by the children was equally as enthralling to the dancer. She had been dancing almost all her life, but today she reached higher and flew further than she had ever done before.

As the song soared to its conclusion, Heather gracefully raised both arms, hands stacked and fingers fluttering. She stepped forward, sweeping her left leg behind her, going up onto the toes of her right foot. At the apex of her reach she opened her hands, fingers still fluttering. Steve could almost see the bird released. She continued to watch the flight as she slowly sank down, left knee to the ground, right one up, hands coming to rest on her right knee while still she watched the flight of the bird. As the last note died, her head dropped.

Steve didn't hear the applause, all he heard was the thunder of his own heart. He felt ready to soar knowing that love like that was giving strength to his wings, and the song wasn't even intended for him, didn't even really fit. Giving himself a mental shake, Steve brought his attention back to the children, the ones for whom she had prepared this dance. In their little faces, he saw that she had struck a cord with them too.

The keiki swarmed over Heather for hugs and kisses before returning to their rooms, most of them hugging Steve too before deserting him for Heather. When he was clear of little people, he stood, only then realizing that a small crowd of parents and hospital staff had gathered in the doorway to watch

Heather dance. He had no idea when they had begun to gather, so lost was he in the woman herself.

The crowd dispersed with the keiki. It was very quiet with just the two of them in the room. Steve took a step toward Heather where she stood, still smiling toward the door where the children had disappeared. She put up a hand to stop him before he came any closer.

"This," she said with a sweep of her hand encompassing herself from head to toe, "was not for you. I didn't know you even came here."

"Seems we both left something out of our 'what do I do' litanies," Steve took another step toward her.

"I told you Moose was a therapy dog," Heather took a step back.

"But not what that meant," Steve took another step. "You knew I did volunteer work with keiki."

"But not here in Honolulu at this hospital," Heather took another step back. This wasn't working well. His steps toward her were much larger than her backwards steps. Something dawned on her. "Hey, who's been teaching you? 'Keiki' today, 'grinds' yesterday? Wazzup, brah?"

"Greg," Steve said, taking a step closer. He was close enough to reach out and lightly touch her right arm where he could see the scar through her petal sleeves. Heather shivered and stepped back again. She didn't have much farther to go before she hit the windows.

"He's been over for dinner most nights this week," Steve stopped pursuing Heather and put his hands in his pockets like a good boy. "In fact, as of last night he's moving into one of my spare rooms by the first of May."

"Who is?" Heather asked. Somehow she had lost her train of thought. Steve's polo shirt had horizontal orange, pink and white stripes. Horizontal stripes draw the eye across them, broadening. Steve's torso didn't need to be broadened. She frowned. Of course the shirt was too tight.

"Greg Shepherd. Your brother," Steve said with a soft laugh.

"You should wear aloha shirts more," Heather said. "They're much less distracting."

"You should wear dresses more," Steve said. "They're much more distracting."

"Not likely," Heather laughed.

"Why not?" Steve said. "You're always beautiful, but in this .... In this you're drop-dead gorgeous."

Heather couldn't believe her ears. No one but Dad, Mom and keiki had ever told her she was beautiful. They didn't count because she knew they saw through eyes of love. From the time she was in middle school, she'd just been a freak, the girl who should have been a boy from the way everyone talked. She'd always wanted to be feminine and beautiful but she was so big and tomboyish, not petite and fragile like her moms.

For the first time, a man other than family made her feel petite and feminine. He said she was beautiful. She didn't know whether to laugh or cry.

Steve saw something flash in Heather's eyes before she looked down.

"Has no one ever told you that you're beautiful?" Steve was stunned. It was impossible that this magnificent woman had been so mistreated.

Heather didn't know what to say. If she spoke at all she would cry. She hated to cry, despised women who used tears to manipulate. She shook her head and shrugged slightly. Steve stepped closer and started to raise his hand. She slipped away from his touch and started to gather up her things, to gather up her thoughts and emotions. CD, hair brush, one book, dog brush. Where was the dog?

Over there by Steve. The traitor, just like her brother, always turning her back to Steve.

Her brother? What had Steve said about Greg?

"What did you say about Greg?" she asked.

"You mean that he's been over for dinner?"

"No, the other."

"He's taught me some local lingo?"

"The other other," she gave a frustrated huff. "You know what I mean. He's staying with you?"

"He will be," Steve said, suddenly unsure of his idea.

"Why?" Heather said, taking a step toward him.

"Because I want someone to take care of the place while I'm on the Mainland," Steve refused to step back from her advance, even though a surprising cowardly streak was telling him he might need to flee.

"That's what you told him," Heather jabbed his chest with her right index finger. "You tell me the truth."

Steve kept his hands in his pockets and looked down at Heather, trying to read her mind. Would she approve or think he was intruding? Should he distract her from her present course?

"You smell good," he leaned closer and sniffed. "What is that?"

"Pikake and jasmine," Heather stilled the flutter of her heart. "Don't try to distract me. Answer my question."

"He needs a hand up if he's going to get through bible college in less than seven years," Steve said with a small shrug.

"Oh! Thank you, thank you!" Heather cried, throwing both arms around him.

Steve guessed that meant she approved. He returned her hug, breathing deeply her pikake and jasmine scent, relishing the warmth of her embrace.

Heather suddenly realized what she was doing. She stepped back quickly, blushing furiously. Their embrace had felt so good, so right, but she knew it wasn't wise. So did Steve.

"I need to go," Heather said, even though she knew she had nothing else to do. Maybe rent a movie and pop some microwave popcorn. Maybe slam her hand in the car door a few times. Anything to take her mind off Steve who was quickly consuming her thoughts. Thoughts that belonged to God.

"I guess dinner tonight wouldn't be a smart choice," Steve said ruefully.

"No, it wouldn't," Heather said with a half laugh. "This is a little too fast."

"I wish you weren't right," Steve smiled softly.

"Me too," Heather sighed. "Come on, Moose."

She stepped back and dropped her gaze before she turned to pick up her bag and Moose's leash. She smiled over her shoulder one more time before she walked to the door.

"Heather," Steve called softly. She turned and saw him standing with a big smile, her slippers in his hand.

Chapter 21

Sunday morning Steve tried not to be disappointed when he didn't see Heather before worship started. He knew that he should be more excited about the fact that it was Easter, the celebration of the Resurrection of the Lord, than he was about seeing Heather again but it was hard to keep his attention on anything but her.

"She's here somewhere," he heard Greg say behind him.

"Don't know what you're talking about," Steve said. "I wasn't looking for anyone."

"Sure you weren't," Greg laughed. "You sound as bad as Heather."

"I'm sure you're wrong about that," Steve said wryly. "You weren't kidding when you said she'd be a tough nut to crack."

"I never kid around," Greg said with a straight face.

"Watch for the lightning," Steve held up his hand to stop Luke as he approached.

"What's my brother lying about now?" Luke greeted Steve with their customary handshake and half hug then turned to eyeball Greg.

"Not lying," Steve snorted.

"That's not what I said," Greg denied.

"May as well have," Steve said.

"Boys, can't you behave in church on Easter Sunday?" Gloria scolded as she came to greet them all. "Has anyone seen Heather yet?"

"She was with Nalani earlier," Luke said.

"Told you she was here," Greg told Steve.

"I didn't ask," Steve declared.

"Didn't have to," Greg said smugly.

"Now boys," Gloria took Steve's arm and walked toward the chairs. "If I have to separate you, I will."

"He started it," Steve said.

"Did not," Greg followed them. "He did. He was mooning around for Heather."

"Was not," Steve denied.

"I won't let you two join the Easter egg hunt at Kenji's if you keep this up," Gloria scolded them both, trying to keep a straight face.

"I didn't know we were having an Easter egg hunt!" Steve sounded delighted.

"Don't tell me you've never had an Easter egg hunt," Luke stopped and said in surprise.

"Grandma sometimes got us Easter baskets," Steve shrugged, "but no, we never had an Easter egg hunt."

"That will change today," Gloria patted Steve's arm as they walked toward the chairs. "We'll hide some eggs up in the trees, just for you. I'll have my boys hide them to get them up there high enough for you."

Greg and Luke still stood where they had stopped at Steve's revelation.

"Did the man even have a childhood?" Greg frowned at his brother.

"I thought we had it bad with Mom dying when we were kids," Luke agreed, "but compared to Steve, we had a charmed childhood."

"We had three great parents," Greg said. "He didn't have any. Sometimes life isn't fair."

"Well, he's got us now," Luke said.

"Us! Like I said, life isn't fair," Greg shook his head and sighed.

Luke laughed and punched Greg on his shoulder, then they followed their mom and Steve to the chairs as Nalani and the worship team began to take their places. Before Luke could look around for his younger brothers and his sons, they were slipping into place beside him, slightly out of breath from whatever game they'd been playing before service.

"Hey, does Steve know Heather's dancing this morning?" Luke whispered to Greg.

"Not a clue," Greg replied.

"Has he seen her dance yet?"

"Yeah, he has," Greg laughed softly.

"When was that?" Luke was still whispering even though Mom was giving them stink eye.

"Friday, at the pediatrics ward," Greg whispered. "Ask him about it sometime."

"I think I will!"

Luke was glad Heather was back in church for her own sake but he was also glad because he had missed her dancing with the worship team. She didn't do it every week but when she did, it was powerful.

Steve tried to focus on the worship which was normally one of the highlights of the service for him. He loved music, loved to sing, especially during worship, but Heather was nowhere to be seen and he wanted to see her. No matter how much he chastised himself for not focusing on the service, he couldn't keep from looking for her.

He was beginning to wonder if Luke could have been wrong about seeing her earlier when the pastor announced a special number before the message. Nalani and the worship team came back out and Heather was with them.

Dressed in a flowing black skirt, bright yellow blouse and barefoot, she was obviously going to dance. After Friday's dance, Steve expected her to supercharge the creative sign dance that he had come to know in Hawaii. She didn't disappoint. Between Nalani's beautiful voice and Heather's explosive dance, on this Easter morning no one in the congregation was unmoved by the joy of the Resurrection.

STEVE DID INDEED hunt Easter eggs later that morning. The children worried that he would step on eggs because his feet were so big, so they insisted that he get down at their level. Gloria fussed that he would get grass stains on his khaki pants, but Steve just laughed. By the time the children declared the grass to be egg free, Steve had plenty of grass stains on both his pants and his aloha shirt since he spent much of his time being tickled and tackled by the little ones. He insisted that they help him find the eggs that had been hidden in the trees. They took turns riding on his shoulders, air planing on his hand, or hanging on his back.

Heather watched it all from Uncle Kenji's lanai, arms crossed on the rail, chin on her hands. Luke and Nalani joined her after a little while, standing with their arms around each other and leaning against the rail beside her.

"That man is afraid he won't be a good dad," Heather said offhandedly.

"Steve?" Luke looked down at her in surprise.

"You lie," Nalani declared. "Steve's going to make one great dad."

"I think he knows more now than I did when Jeremy was born," Luke said, "and I'd already been a dad for two years."

"I know you're right," Heather said, "but because of his parents, he doesn't know."

"He missed out on so much in his childhood that he's going to make sure his keiki don't miss out on anything," Nalani said. "If anything, he's going to spoil them, not be abusive."

High-pitched laughter rang out as Steve went down under a swarm of children, begging them not to tickle him.

"Don't worry about him, Shadow," Luke reassured Heather. "He's going to be a godly husband and father."

"I know," Heather sighed heavily. "That's why I can't ask him to take the risk of never having children of his own."

"He loves you, Heather," Nalani said. "He isn't going to need to have children to make his life complete."

"So he thinks now," Heather said, "but what about after he watches you guys have another couple kids and Greg get married and have a half dozen, and then Tim, and then Robert, and we still don't have any. Will I still be enough?"

"You can always adopt," Nalani said.

"But they won't be our own flesh," Heather sighed. "Will that be good enough?"

"What, you think you can't love keiki when they aren't from your own body?" Luke asked incredulously.

Heather stood up and punched him on the arm. "You mean like Mom doesn't love us because our other mom gave birth to us?" She glared. "Get real, jerk. You and Greg of all people know that's not a problem for me. But what about for Steve? Can you honestly say that you know he'll be satisfied with just adopting? Can he say that and know for sure?"

Luke stared at her thoughtfully.

"My advice to you, Shadow, is marry the man," he finally said. "After a year start adopting kids like him. Ones who have never had a birthday party, never had an Easter egg hunt, who were lucky to get socks and a new t-shirt for Christmas. You do that and he'll be more than happy the rest of his life."

"You may be right, Big Man," Heather said thoughtfully, "but how will I know for sure?"

"You don't, honey," Nalani said. "You just trust God."

Heather looked out at Steve, grumbling with her nephews and keiki cousins as Aunty Hannah called them all in to get cleaned up for dinner. She trusted God and she was pretty sure she trusted Steve too. But could she trust herself to know God's will? Why did she continue to hold back when she was already so much in love with Steve? If God would just come down and talk story with her, then she would know exactly what to do! Until he did, she was just going to have to keep at the task before her and hope someday the way of her future would become clearer.

HALF AN HOUR later, Heather, all her brothers, Nalani, and Steve were sitting on the lanai with their lunch plates. Steve had a burning question, so he jumped right in almost before Luke and Nalani even got seated.

"Jeremy said he was supposed to get to go to the water park for his birthday."

"Yeah," Luke grimaced, "but we've had a problem arise. Neither of us is going to be able to get off."

"And no one else can take him?"

"We already asked," Nalani sighed. "Everyone has a conflict with either part or all of the day. The best we can do is an hour out there with Heather late in the morning."

All this was news to Heather! They better have a really good excuse for lying on her like this.

"It's worse to take him out for so short a time than not at all," Luke shrugged, "so it'll have to be another time."

"But this Friday is his birthday," Steve frowned.

"Sorry, we tried," Luke apologized.

Heather started to say something but Greg stepped on her foot, hard. She glared at him and he winked.

"We asked everyone," Nalani looked sad.

"You didn't ask me," Steve said.

"No, we didn't," Luke said thoughtfully, as if it hadn't occurred to him before.

"I didn't think to ask you," Nalani seemed surprised at the idea.

"Would you ... want to?" Luke hesitated to ask.

"I would love to," Steve said.

"Oh, thank you," Nalani gushed. "Germy will be so happy."

Heather frowned. Nalani didn't gush. What were they doing? She listened as they talked details. If she even thought about saying anything, one of her younger brothers would jab, nudge or step on her.

She was ready to burst by the time Steve finally got up to go for seconds on dinner. As soon as he was out of earshot, Heather pounced on her brother and his wife.

"You just played that man!" she accused.

"Like a well-tuned ukulele!" Luke laughed.

"You were magnificent, dear," Nalani kissed him.

"But why?" Heather demanded. "What are you up to?"

"A surprise birthday party, my dear," Nalani said happily.

"It was the best way we could come up with to get him to a party totally unsuspecting," Luke explained.

"So whose idea was this?" Heather asked with a smile.

"The party? Mom's," Luke said. "The subterfuge? Greg's."

"I should have known," Heather laughed. "What's the plan from here?"

"Right now, you and I are going to go help with something," Nalani said.

"But why?" Heather pouted. "I wanna help plan."

"But you're not going to, Shadow," Luke said. "At least not today. I was hoping to get this done without you being aware of it at all."

"Too bad he brought it up with you right here," Nalani shook her head.

"Why? What's wrong with me?" Heather glared at them all.

"Because you can't lie to Steve to save your soul," Greg said.

"Which is going to make you a great wife for him someday, but right now you're so bursting with the news that he's going to know something's up as soon as he comes back," Luke said.

"And you won't be able to come up with a lie," Tim said.

"And you'll blurt out the truth," Nalani laughed.

"So vamoose before he gets back," Greg ordered.

When Steve came back a few minutes later, he was obviously disappointed that Heather was gone. None of her brothers offered any information and Steve let the conversation drift toward sports.

After a few minutes, Tim and Robert decided it was time to raid the Easter baskets for dessert. A short time later, the sound of women and children laughing rose from the yard.

All three men stood to watch Tim running across the yard with an Easter basket tucked under one arm. Heather was in hot pursuit with half the keiki behind her. Nalani and the other half of the children chased Robert and another Easter basket.

The yard wasn't big enough. Tim had to curve back toward the house and Heather anticipated his move. Two steps, a flying tackle and she and Tim were rolling in the grass, candy flying everywhere. They lay there laughing while squealing children ran around picking up the candy.

"Your sister is an incredible woman," Steve said.

"She's a keeper," Luke agreed.

"She's beautiful," Steve stated.

"Can't disagree," Greg smile proudly, watching Heather catch little Brianna as she pounced. She pinned the little girl's arms so she couldn't tickle, then rolled over and smothered her face with kisses.

"So how come she doesn't know?" Steve frowned.

"Excuse me?" Luke said. He and Greg both turned toward Steve.

"How could she not know?" Greg said. "She looks at that face every day in the mirror."

"I wouldn't bet that she does know," Steve said thoughtfully.

"Why do you think that?" Luke looked at him with narrowed eyes.

"At the hospital on Friday, when I told her she was beautiful," Steve said sadly. "She shrugged it off as if it was just a line. Just so you know, it wasn't. It was the honest truth."

"How could she not know she's beautiful?" Greg demanded.

"Mom and Dad have always told her she was," Luke said.

"Did you believe everything your mom and dad ever said about you?" Steve asked.

"No," Greg said thoughtfully. "I think they tend to exaggerate."

"And so does Heather," Luke sighed.

"And all those guys were calling her a freak," Steve said. "You told me that Greg, so I know you know it."

Luke and Greg frowned at each other, wondering how they had missed their sister's growing insecurity.

"My sister ran away when I was only fourteen," Steve said. "So I never really got a chance to do the protective brother thing. I might be wrong but it seems to me that you all should have been defending her against those kind of lies."

"But I always told her not to listen to them," Greg ran a hand through his hair. "I said she was perfect the way she was."

"Did you ever specifically say she was beautiful, smart, talented?" Steve asked.

"In so many words? No," Luke said.

"So the only guys who could actually say something that she would believe, let her down," Steve said. "You were, in your own way, as bad as all those idiots who treated her like a freak."

"Now wait a minute," Greg wasn't ready to accept that.

"No, he's right," Luke admitted. "We never said anything nice about Heather, at least not so she could hear. Just like she normally never said anything nice about us. If we had said she was beautiful, she would have been shocked, but she would have listened. Just like I listened when she told me that not trying was the only thing that could keep me from being a lawyer."

"Just like how I hear her when she tells me how smart I am," Greg shook his head. "She helped me believe in myself when Mom and Dad couldn't."

"Because you always knew she saw the real you, warts and all," Steve said.

"And we were too dumb to see that she needed the same kind of encouragement from us," Luke said. "We let her down."

"And made my job so much harder," Steve shook his head. "Thanks guys."

Chapter 22

*F*riday evening, Heather paced nervously in Luke's living room as six o'clock came and went. Steve and Jeremy were supposed to be back from the water park by six.

"What if Germy convinces him to stop at McDonald's?" Heather said. "He's always begging to go there."

"Steve's not going to stop for dinner," Luke said calmly. "He knows Mom is coming over for Jeremy's birthday dinner."

"Then where are they," Heather fussed.

"Heather, it's only five minutes after," Nalani said. "I'm sure it's just the traffic."

Heather harrumphed and spun to pace back the other way, her hair, skirt and blouse swirling softly around her.

"She acts like someone in love," Robert said slyly.

"Relax, Shadow," Luke said. "He's going to love the party."

"If he even sees that it is a party," Greg said. "As gorgeous as you look in that outfit, I'd suggest you hide in the kitchen for a while."

Heather frowned at him. Greg never complimented her. She looked down at herself. "What's wrong with my outfit?"

"Nothing," Luke said. "You're beautiful."

"Nalani, is my skirt hanging straight? Is something wrong with my hair?" Heather asked in a near panic. Her brothers never complimented her, so there must be something wrong with the way she looked. Something embarrassing. Why was she so nervous? She danced at all the family birthday parties. That's all this was.

"Come on into the bedroom." Nalani took her arm and led her down the hall. "We'll give you a once over without the boys to distract us."

As Nalani and Heather disappeared, Greg looked at Luke and shook his head in disbelief. How had they missed how insecure Heather had grown about her looks? She had a face and a figure that most models would kill for but she had no clue.

"There they are," Matt cried from his lookout point at the front window.

There was a flurry of activity as people who shouldn't be at Luke's house took their places so that they couldn't be seen on Steve's walk up to the front door. Only Luke, Mom and Matt sat on the living room furniture. Robert was pressed up against the wall behind the door, Greg was laying on the floor under the front windows, and Tim and Pete were scrunched into the far corner. Pete's and Nalani's parents, and Pena and Kenji guys were all gathered under the Happy Birthday banner strung over the kitchen archway.

Silence descended quickly. Heather and Nalani were standing in the hallway, Heather peeking out from behind Nalani, when they heard Steve's rumble and Jeremy's childish laugh at the door. Matt stepped up to play his roll perfectly.

"You're late," he grumbled as he swung open the door. "I'm starving, hurry up."

"Sorry buddy," Steve smiled down at Matt as he stepped through the door with Jeremy in his arms. "Traffic was bad coming back into –"

"Surprise!"

Startled, Steve looked up as voices shouted all around him. It took a moment for it to register that the birthday banner said "Steve & Jeremy." He looked down at the boy in his arms. "Did you know about this?"

Jeremy shook his head vigorously, eyes wide in amazement at all the balloons. Steve looked around the room taking in the crowd.

"Wow! This is really a surprise," he grinned. "Thank you all."

"Don't just stand there, Stevie-boy," Pena grumbled. "Get in here so we can eat."

"Yeah, you really are late," Luke laughed, taking Jeremy from Steve and giving him a hug and kiss before setting him on his feet.

"And we really are starving," Greg complained.

Everyone swarmed around to give hugs and birthday wishes to the two birthday boys. Steve didn't reject any hug but he kept looking around the room for the one he wanted most. He had somehow drifted across the room during the greetings. When Greg gave him a quick hug, he finally saw her leaning against the wall by the hallway.

She wore an outfit similar to the one last Friday, but this one was rose and pale pink with black and gold splashes in the skirt. Steve smiled slowly. She smiled back, then pushed off the wall and walked over to pick up Jeremy before turning to give Steve his birthday hug.

"Well, birthday boys," she bounced Jeremy on her hip and looked sideways up at Steve. "Are you ready to eat?"

"Are we going to have cake and ice cream?" Steve asked hopefully.

"Later," Heather laughed. "First you have to eat dinner."

"But it's our birthday," Jeremy whined.

"Yeah it's our birthday," Steve echoed.

"No dinner, no birthday cake," Heather scolded them both gently.

"Then let's pray," Steve reached over and took Heather's hand, stepping back and stretching out his right hand toward whomever happened to take it.

AFTER DINNER, NALANI informed them that there were two games before cake and ice cream. The first was pin the tail on the donkey. Heather's brothers made a big show of hanging the donkey at a five year old's level. Steve went last which gave him plenty of time to decide on payback. When they blindfolded him and spun him around, Steve reached out and grabbed whichever brother he could get, proudly pinning the tale of the donkey to a very large arm.

"I win," he declared as he ripped off the blindfold and saw Greg standing there, a donkey tail hanging from his arm and a surprised look on his face.

"That's a hard one to argue with," Heather giggled.

"Looks to me like he's the only one to actually hit the donkey," Robert agreed.

The next game was a modified hot potato. All the kids, which included everyone from Luke down, sat in a big circle with four beanbags among them. Mom manned the stereo. When the music started, everyone was supposed to bat the beanbags around, trying not to be caught with one when the music stopped.

Steve was the first one out because Heather's brothers immediately pelted him with all four of the beanbags. He couldn't get rid of them all before the music stopped, but he took Greg and Robert with him. After much laughter and complaints of cheating, Suzie finally emerged the victor.

Then it was time for presents. Steve and Jeremy sat on the couch and had to shut their eyes. When they both immediately peeked, Heather and Nalani stood behind them and covered their eyes with their hands.

"Okay, you can look now," Gloria announced. Heather and Nalani moved their hands and the birthday boys saw matching red wagons with wood slat sides stood in front of the birthday boys, both overflowing with presents.

"Twins always get matching presents," Heather said, "as well as individual ones."

"So there are some presents here that you have to open at the same time," Nalani finished. "Mom Shepherd and Matt will help you find those."

They got a pair of radio controlled monster trucks, Play Doh, matching shorts and cartoon-character aloha shirts, and a Veggie Tale video each. When it was time to start on their individual gifts, Steve remembered he'd left Jeremy's present in his trunk. Kenji went out to get it because everyone insisted that Steve had to stay and open his presents.

They took turns. Jeremy got a new glove and Steve got a set of Hawaii golf balls. Jeremy got Duplos and Steve got a *Twins* DVD. Something was wrong with it, so he looked closer then laughed.

"Hey Germy," Steve pointed at the box. Robert had covered the faces with his and Jeremy's. "You're Danny DeVito."

"He's a little small for DeVito," Greg said.

"Nah," Heather smiled dreamily. "He's the right size. The problem is that Schwarzenegger is too small for Steve."

Laughter filled the room while Heather blushed furiously.

"Open another present, would you?" Heather smacked Steve lightly on the shoulder.

Steve obliged, ripping into a flat rectangular package with the same restraint Jeremy showed. Suddenly he howled as if burned, jumping up and back while dropping the shirt box on the floor. He sat on the back of the couch, pointing at the floor in horror.

"Who did it?" he demanded. "Who dared?"

That wasn't too hard to figure out since Robert and Tim were rolling on the floor with laughter while Greg was looking much too innocent. Heather leaned over the couch and peered into the box. She too began to laugh hysterically.

"How can you laugh at such a thing, woman?" Steve demanded.

Mom bent over and picked up a jersey from the box, a purple and white, number seven Berserker jersey, identical to the one in the painting that hung in Steve's bedroom. Everyone laughed as Steve jumped off the couch.

"Don't touch it!" he cried frantically, causing Mom to drop the jersey with a start. Steve picked Gloria up and moved her away from the box where the jersey now lay in a crumpled heap. He nudged the corner of the box with his toe and jumped back. "Someone call an exterminator!"

"Why darlin', look," Heather said through laughter. "Someone gave you an old rag."

"It'll probably work for cleaning toilets," Luke suggested.

Steve shuddered. "Then you keep it. Please, someone get it out of my sight." He threw himself down on the couch very dramatically, one arm over his eyes. He listened for the sound of someone picking up the box.

"Pssst," he peeked up at Heather, still standing behind the couch. "Is it gone yet?"

"Yes dear," she patted his shoulder. "That nasty filthy rag is gone."

Steve sat up and glared at Greg.

"You will pay deeply, very, very deeply, for that one," he promised.

"What did I do?" Greg said innocently.

"Just wait," Steve glared. "One day, when you have forgotten all about the dastardly deed done this day, you will pay."

"Be afraid. Be very afraid," Luke said hoarsely.

"What he said," Steve nodded his head toward Luke.

"Oh hush your fussing," Gloria scolded. "Let's get pau with these presents. There's cake, ice cream and entertainment waiting."

There weren't many presents left, just three each, but they were good ones. Jeremy got a VeggieTales Pirate Ship from Aunty Heather, a battery operated fire truck with sirens, lights and a ladder that raised and extended from Grandma and Grandpa Kawada, and a child-sized set of real drums from Uncle Steve.

"Oh. You shouldn't have," Luke said dryly, to both Steve and his in-laws. "It's too much."

"Just a little something I saw at the toy store," Steve smirked. "It's really nothing."

"No, seriously, you shouldn't have," Luke shook his head in despair. "Finish opening your presents, you jerk."

Steve's last three were from Gloria, Luke and Heather. Gloria's gift was two stunning aloha shirts, very different from the normal patterns.

"They're Christian aloha wear from Salt & Light," she explained. "The feather cape patterns are based on the Hawaiian alii feather cape, showing Jesus as the King of kings, of course."

"So what do the pattern's mean?" Steve asked as he held up the yellow and black pattern.

"That one is 'Only Through Him,'" Gloria explained. "See the wood beams? Look carefully and you'll see that the cape hangs from the cross. The red and yellow one is 'King of kings.' It's a Palm Sunday theme. See the palm branches and the stones for the road?"

"What's that in the palm branches?" Steve looked closer. "Is that thorns? The crown of thorns?"

"Yes. It's incredible isn't it, how the artist used his craft to show his love of the Lord?"

Steve thanked Gloria with a hug. Greg complained that he was holding up the cake and ice cream, so Steve turned to his last two presents. He received another framed photo from Luke. This one was of him sitting on the floor with the keiki and Moose in the pediatrics ward last Friday. It was signed by all the keiki.

"How did you get this?" Steve was delighted but puzzled. "I don't remember any cameras."

"Diane always slips in and takes pictures with my camera whenever she can," Heather said. "You just didn't notice her."

"You probably had your attention focused elsewhere," Greg said.

"Wonder where that could have been?" Tim mused.

"Ignore the punks and open your last one," Heather said.

From the shape of the package and the fact that it was from Heather, Steve wasn't surprised to discover another painting. This one was a whale breaching with the sun setting behind him. It was beautiful and an incredible reminder of a wonderful day. This one would make the trip to the Mainland with him.

"He has two Heather paintings," Greg whined. "I don't even have one."

"Yeah, what's up with that?" Tim grumbled too. "That's not hardly fair."

Steve just smiled and Heather blushed. She was doing a lot of that these days. She really needed to quit.

Steve reached up and covered her hand, dangling on the back of the couch where she was leaning.

"Thank you, I love it," he said quietly. Then to everyone. "Thank you all. This really has been the best birthday ever."

"Well, it isn't over yet!" Gloria said from the archway to the kitchen. She and Nalani had cakes. The lights went out and Nalani led everyone in singing "Happy Birthday" while they carefully carried the cakes to the birthday boys.

"Blow out those candles before my house burns down," Luke ordered.

"Wait!" Jeremy threw up a hand to stop Steve. "Don't forget to make a wish! You gotta make a wish."

"What should I wish for?" Steve asked him. "I've got so much already."

"You could wish for friends," Tim suggested.

"Yeah, but then he'd hang around with them instead of us," Greg complained.

"I know!" Jeremy scrambled up on his knees and started to whisper in Steve's ear. He stopped, frowned up at Heather and pointed to the corner by the front door. "Go over there Aunty Heather. This is his wish not yours."

She complied and Jeremy whispered his suggestion.

"That's a great wish," Steve said in awe. "How do I make it come true?"

"Blow out all your candles at one time," Jeremy said earnestly, "and don't tell anyone what your wish is 'til after it comes true."

"Okay," Steve said. "Are we ready now?"

The candles were already burning very low.

"Yeah, we better hurry." They both took deep breaths and blew hard. Darkness descended on the room, everyone cheered and someone flipped on the overhead lights.

"Yippee, we get our birthday wishes," Jeremy bounced on the couch.

Nalani and Mom took the cakes back into the kitchen to dish up cake and ice cream.

"And now," Luke said, "for the entertainment portion of the evening. Hey, wait a minute. Someone needs to go help Mom because Nalani is on now."

There was a flurry of activity as Hannah and Connie went in to help with the dessert and Tim and Robert rearranged furniture so there was a small stage area in front of the hallway with a backless stool on the right side. Everyone else made sure they were situated to see well. As the aunties passed out the cake and ice cream, Nalani came from the hall with her guitar and perched on the stool while Heather stepped into the open space on her left.

"It is tradition in this family," Nalani explained for those who were new to the ohana. "That a birthday is celebrated with a special song, done by me, and dance, done by the beautiful Miss Shepherd."

"That's me," Heather spread her skirts in a curtsey.

"Since we have two birthday boys, we will do two songs," Nalani said. "After much debate, we selected the ones you are about to hear and see. Just for the record, this time Heather was very difficult to work with for some reason. She had a reason to object to every song, so I finally totally overruled her and made her do these songs."

Enchanted by the dancer, Steve hardly even heard the music. The first was something funny and fast, each verse faster than before. Apparently everyone else knew it because they sang along. Heather's dance picked up the pace with them, amazingly maintaining grace even as the voices became sillier and sillier. Finally, however, she collapsed into a breathless, laughing heap.

The second song was a sweet song about the journey of life and the love that carries us through, the memories that give us strength. Steve was mesmerized by the gentle grace that flowed through Heather, the love that flew from her fingertips and fluttered lightly around him.

Then it was over and everyone was complimenting the women on their performance. A shiver of melancholy slid through Steve as he thought about how soon all this would be behind him as another season of training and football started. But that was not until next month, so he shook off his mood and joined the fun. It helped that Hannah and Gloria both promised him a DVD of the entertainment. This night would sustain him through many hot summer days and cold winter nights in Illinois.

Chapter 23

*T*he next day, Steve invited Heather to go riding. Since she worked half a day on Saturdays he picked her up at noon. After a quick bite to eat at a grocery store lunch counter, they headed across the Pali Highway. They stopped at the Pali Lookout and Heather told Steve the legend of how King Kamehameha had pushed his enemies off the cliffs there in the final battle over Oahu.

"We have no idea how many skeletons could be laying somewhere down there," Heather said with a little shiver.

"Anyone pushed off lately?" Steve asked casually, draping an arm around her shoulders and pulling her into the shelter of his body.

"Not that I've heard of," Heather snuggled up against him, thankful for his size. The wind could get fierce up here. Some people claimed that when the trade winds were strong enough you could jump off the Pali cliffs and blow right back into the parking lot.

"You ever been tempted to push one of your brothers, maybe Greg?"

"Not even Greg," Heather laughed merrily.

"Good, then you won't push me if I tell you that I actually bought all three of the motorcycles we looked at," Steve said with a relieved grin.

"Why did you do that?" Heather pushed away from him and frowned up at him. "You only need one."

"But I wanted all three," Steve sat on the wall and pulled her forward so that she again stood in the shelter of his body.

"Why?" Heather frowned.

"The first one seemed like a good one for someone to learn on."

"Learn what?" Her frown became suspicious.

"Learn to fix it," Steve leaned forward to smooth hair back from her cheek. The wind blew it right back. "Learn to ride."

"Who?" She gave him stink eye.

"You of course," Steve smiled innocently, "and Greg and Luke too if they want. Even Tim and Robert if it's okay with Aunty Gloria."

"I –," Heather opened her mouth to disagree when suddenly she realized she did want to learn. Steve smiled broadly at the surprise in her eyes.

"I have information about the motorcycle safety class at the community college," Steve put his hands on her hips and tugged her closer. "It's the best way to learn. You and Greg can take it this summer."

"And the other motorcycle?" Heather smiled.

"Well, you won't want to always ride behind me," Steve said.

"Wanna bet?" Heather flirted gently.

"Shall we ride now?" Steve leaned his forehead against hers.

"Please," Heather stepped out of the circle of his arms and started down the walk to the parking lot, smiling back over her shoulder at him.

They rode up through Kaneohe and around the North Shore, coming back into town via the H2. Over the next few weeks, they rode many more times, sometimes just short jaunts after Heather was done with work, sometimes long rides out to the Leeward Coast or up to the North Shore.

April ran on swift feet toward May. Greg was gradually moving his things up to Steve's house. Since he spent most evenings that he wasn't working up there, Heather came over more often for dinner but she always called first to make sure Greg was going to be there. Every Sunday was ohana day, usually at Mom's but sometimes at Luke's. Saturdays the guys frequently went surfing in the morning, twice they all went bowling in the afternoon. Steve was surprisingly good, using skill more than power. He told Heather that bowling was one of the few available pastimes in Abilene, Kansas. It was also one of the few Steve's father allowed so he had grown up bowling, learning technique long before he had the power to muscle the pins down.

Steve was gradually being pulled into the harmless high-jinks of Heather's fun-loving brothers. When Greg found a pink sweater for Moose, Steve only objected briefly before helping slip it on the happy dog while Heather was inside helping get dinner ready on Sunday afternoon. He was much better at feigning innocence than Heather's brothers were, so he escaped her wrath. His innocence was made easier by the fact that he didn't know what her brothers did – Heather hated the color pink. Steve also escaped her ire when Luke instigated a pyramid of green bean casserole supplies on her kitchen counter and when Tim and Robert recruited him for a tubful of Jell-O.

"I'm not so sure I should be doing this," Steve said with a worried frown as he and Greg dumped gallons of boiling water into Heather's tub while Tim and Robert stirred the water to dissolve the powder. "I'm supposed to be driving her crazy with love, not frustration."

"Is there a difference?" Greg looked at him in surprise.

"Good point!" Steve grinned.

"Besides," Robert smiled slyly, "you're bonding with her little brothers. She'll love you for that."

"There is that," Greg said with commendable seriousness.

"I'm not sure it will be enough, or the right kind of love," Steve moaned.

"Don't worry," Tim assured him, "she won't suspect you. Yet."

She didn't, but she did begin to suspect him when someone painted pink flowers on her car tires, when a "Heather's Junk Yard" sandwich board sign showed up in her auto repair shop back lot and when she came home one day to find that every food delivery ad in the Yellow Pages had been clipped and posted somewhere in her house. She knew he was involved when she stepped into a water gun ambush one Saturday afternoon when she got to Mom's house.

They had kindly left her a tiny gun and half a dozen water balloons to counterattack against their long-range weapons. When all the ammunition was eventually expended, Heather was totally soaked while the guys were all relatively dry. She flopped down in the grass and when Steve offered her a hand up, she pulled him down next to her.

"Hey, the grass is really wet," Steve complained as he dropped beside her. "My shorts are going to get all wet!"

"Oh! You poor baby," Heather crooned with no sympathy at all. "How deeply have my brothers gotten you involved in their nonsense?"

"What nonsense?"

"The very fact that you have the audacity to say that tells me you're very deeply involved," Heather sighed and shook her head. "The question is, when did it start? Was it my tires, the Jell-O or even further back?"

"Sweetheart," Steve said soothingly. "I don't know what nonsense you're talking about, but I have been bonding with your brothers."

"I wish you wouldn't," Heather moaned. "I think you're worse than all four of them combined."

"Define worse?"

"More ingenious even if not more enthusiastic."

"You don't really think I'm more ingenious about causing trouble than Greg is, do you?" Steve asked with that one eyebrow almost buried in his hair line. Heather loved the way he did that. She reached up and smoothed the hair back from his forehead.

"I think the jury's still out on it, Goliath," she said with a heavy sigh. "I'll have to hang around a little more before I can come in with a verdict."

They were always looking for ways to hang around together, sometimes just the two of them, sometimes with Heather's family. The favorite outing for everyone was the zoo, but Steve and Heather also took Matt and Jeremy to the Children's Discovery Center, went horseback riding with Tim and Robert, and took Mom and Greg to a symphony. One Saturday afternoon on a leisurely ride along the Windward shore, Steve discovered that there was a radio-controlled airfield on Kapaa Quarry Road. The rest of the afternoon they watched the model planes. After the questions he asked, Heather wasn't surprised when Steve bought his own plane.

Unfortunately, the time for him to learn to fly it was already gone. Mother's Day was upon them and Grizzly football camp started immediately thereafter. When Steve left, he wouldn't have time to return to Hawaii before the end of the season. Heather decided to play Scarlet O'Hara and let the worries of another day wait.

ON MOTHER'S DAY morning, Steve found himself alone with Gloria and her grandsons. They expected Nalani to be with the worship team, but Gloria was obviously disappointed when none of her children had joined them by the time worship started.

The mystery was solved when Pastor announced a special number before the message. Nalani stood behind the keyboard and Luke stepped up onto the dance stage behind and to her left.

"As many of you know," Nalani began to introduce their number. "This is a difficult day for the Shepherds. It was a year ago, on Mother's Day last year that Dad Shepherd died."

Steve hadn't known that! He put his arm around Gloria as she wiped away tears from her cheeks.

"We wanted to do a special number," Nalani continued, "to not just honor Mom Shepherd but to honor all the moms of the congregation. We couldn't find anything we all liked, so we wrote a song. We hope it will bless you."

"Most of you know," Luke picked up the explanation, "that we three older Shepherds were blessed with another mother before we got Mom. When I was just eleven, our mother died and her cousin became a wonderful nanny to three rascally motherless waifs. We children fell in love with her immediately and after about a year or so, Dad also fell in love with our nanny."

"Our nanny became our mom," Greg stepped up to the right of Luke, "and Mom never seemed to be a 'stepmom' even while our other mother never became less of a mom just because she was gone. When Mom and Dad added two rug rats to the family, they sealed our family bond. I don't think any of us ever think of each other as halfs. We are wholes, wholly brothers and sister bound together through an awesome woman we all call Mom."

"But not everyone has the fortune to be blessed with one such mother, much less two," Heather was standing opposite Nalani on the floor. "Some mothers don't know how to love because they have never received love. We would dishonor our own mother if we did not honor those mothers too. We pray you will be blessed by our song."

Gloria was crying in earnest before the first note even started. Jeremy climbed up into her lap and snuggled up to hug her. Steve kept his arm around her, as much for his own sake as for hers.

As Nalani sang in a clear, sweet voice, Luke and Greg signed the first verse and chorus. Though they were not as fluid as Heather in their dance, the men still went well beyond the simple signing of a song. With power and grace they added vision to the love in the music that swirled around them.

> A fresh breeze and flowers
> In a land dry and drab
> She brought life to the world
> Through both womb and word
> Kisses and hugs and tears
> Saved in a bottle
> Youth still blushed her cheeks
> When she went home to glory
>
> But Momma wasn't gone
> Nor will she ever go
> In our hearts she lives on
> Though the years slide by

As the chorus faded, Luke and Greg turned toward each other and walked side by side to the back of the stage then toward the outer edges. Tim and Robert stepped up from either side of the stage and took their brothers' original places. All four signed together.

> Gentle laughter, sweet song
> Her voice brought life
> Back to a world that had
> Been dark much too long
> Love multiplied and grew
> Under her loving touch
> With joy new everyday
> She lifts God in glory
>
> Momma's love is strong
> It will never be gone
> In our hearts it remains
> Guiding through the years

Tim and Robert turned as their brothers had and walked to the back of the stage then a few steps away from each other. Luke and Greg both took two steps forward. Heather joined them, front and center of their half circle.

> Laughter stolen in youth
> Love ached to be strong

But darkness and sorrow
She couldn't push away
Still love came through
In the best she knew how
A kiss while they're sleeping
A prayer in the dark

Anchored by her brothers' sign dance, Heather danced the anguish of a love never given the chance to bloom. Their dance combined with the pathos of Nalani's song soaring as a prayer to heaven, and it wrung tears from every eye.

Momma wasn't strong
Her love too soon gone
But her heart wanted more
Than she gave all her years

Momma I love you
I'll cherish you always
Forgiving what was bad
I'll remember the good
The whisper of love
Even in pain
A smile, a kiss
Bringing love once again.

Momma, I love you

Steve sat in stunned silence as the Shepherds quietly walked from the stage. People all around were applauding through tears, but he couldn't move. Something pulled at his chest. Suddenly he felt light-headed. He leaned forward and crossed his arms over his knees, pressing his forehead to his arms.

He felt Aunty Gloria's arms around him and the tears began to fall. Maybe he should have been embarrassed but he only felt release as the last of the bitterness and anger towards his parents fell away like scales from his eyes. In the Shepherds' song and dance, he saw that his parents' lives were somehow lost long before he and Jenni ever became aware of their world. His parents had been what they were because they knew no better. He wept for what could have been, for what was and for the new hope he could see for the future.

HEATHER WAS ASTOUNDED to see the effect their special number had on the congregation. They had prayed a great deal as they worked on it and they had all known that Mom and Steve would be deeply moved. When the applause died down however, they discovered that at least a dozen other people were weeping with great wracking sobs, more than half the rest sobbing earnestly.

Rather than just carrying on with the service as planned, Pastor asked the worship team to return to the stage for musical backup. He encouraged the congregants to pray for those around them, and the elders and ministry leaders moved among them, praying and bringing comfort.

The Shepherds gathered around Steve to pray with him but Heather fought her own tears as she thought of his sad mother, battling depression and abuse, unable to protect her children because she didn't know how to protect herself.

She turned to flee but Greg stood in her way, not allowing her to run from what God was doing here today. As her sobs grew, her brother's hands guided her to a chair next to Steve's. Soon she was clasped in his arms and even as her sobs grew, his began to subside. She who had come to comfort him was being comforted herself.

In the arms of the man she loved, heart and soul, and surrounded by her family, Heather released all her worries and doubts. She didn't know how God would work it out for them but Heather finally fully accepted that she would live out her life with this wonderful man of God.

"DINNER'S STILL AT my house, right?" Steve asked as the family headed toward the parking lot after church.

"You mean supper, yeah?" Greg said. "Luke guys are going to Nalani's parents' house for dinner."

"Yeah, we won't get to your house 'til after five, probably closer to six," Luke said.

"You want us to stop and pick up the furry mutt?" Nalani asked Heather. "Or are you going home to get him now?"

"My dear sister," Heather said haughtily, "for your information, Moose Cupid Thumper is a purebred Golden Retriever. He is not a mutt!" Then she deflated. "But I'm too drained to mess with his mutt-like antics, so yeah, can you guys pick him up?"

"Thank you for sparing us from the brats this afternoon," Greg dropped an arm over Nalani's shoulders. "Please make sure their cousins wear them out before dinner."

Steve and the Shepherd crew, minus Luke guys of course, decided to stop and grab some plate lunches before going to Steve's for a nap. They were all profoundly grateful that the little boys and their energy were elsewhere. Gloria laid down in one of the spare rooms, and Tim and Robert sprawled out on beach towels in the backyard. Steve, Heather and Greg lay on the white rug in the great room, their legs up on the new couch that faced the fireplace.

"So you all really wrote that song?" Steve asked.

"Yep, we did," Greg confirmed.

"Nalani picked most of the right words," Heather said, "but we all contributed the ideas."

"Heather more than us guys," Greg said.

"That's a surprise," Steve said dryly. "You all are so sensitive."

"Hey, I'm working on it," Greg yawned and sighed. "It's weird. I feel drained and filled at the same time."

"That's actually a pretty good way to describe the way I feel too," Heather agreed, fighting her own yawn. "It was an incredible morning."

They lay there for a while, staring up at the ceiling.

"I'm not complaining or anything," Steve finally said, "but why are we laying like this."

"Dad used to lay like this," Heather said sleepily. "He had hurt his back and he said it eased the pain."

"I don't remember a time he didn't do it almost every Sunday afternoon and lots of evenings," Greg said

"I remember when Greg first tried laying like this too," Heather laughed softly. "He had his little bottom pressed up against the couch and his legs straight up along the front of the couch, feet in the air."

"I remember Tim and Robert doing that, not me," Greg growled.

"You were two," Heather giggled sleepily. "You wouldn't remember."

Steve cradled his head in his hands and listened to the siblings' banter. A memory came softly to him. He was laying in the backyard with Mom and Jenni. Their heads were together, legs pointing out like spokes in a wheel. They watched the clouds float by, seeing things in them – a dragon, a horse, a cactus, a boat. It was a good memory. Where had it been all these years?

"I didn't know about your mother," Steve said abruptly.

"Surely you told him Heather," Greg sounded surprised.

"'Don't call me Shirley,'" Heather grumbled sleepily. "Of course I did. I always talk about Mom and Mom."

"But you don't differentiate," Greg said. "It's confusing to me sometimes, and I know you have two. ... Heather?"

Greg rolled his head to the left and smiled lovingly. "She always does this."

"Does what?" Steve yawned with his question.

"Falls asleep right off," Greg muttered, "then sleeps longer than anyone."

Steve drifted slowly toward sleep, thinking about Greg and Heather's first mother. He laughed softly. "You're no better than Heather, Greg."

"Since I don't know what you're talking about, I can't argue with that."

"About differentiating between your mothers."

"I differentiate," Greg grumbled sleepily.

"Do not. Back at KTA in Hilo, you said Aunty Mitsue was your mom's classmate. I had no clue that you literally meant *your* mom, not Tim and Robert's. But that's what you meant, wasn't it?"

"Of course."

"What was her name?"

"Kalea," Greg's love was evident even in his sleepy voice. "She was beautiful. Heather looks just like her but taller."

"What about your dad? What was his name?"

"James."

Steve thought about James and Kalea, wondering what they'd been like. Suddenly he realized he'd probably seen pictures of them over at Aunty Gloria's house but he wasn't into family pictures so he'd never paid attention to them. He thought he remembered one of Luke and Greg, much younger with an older man standing between them. They both looked like him in their own way.

"You and Luke both look like your dad, don't you?"

The only response was gentle breathing. Steve smiled as he too drifted off to sleep, loving the real life of this ohana. Silence reigned over the house.

HEATHER GRADUALLY AWAKENED to a rumbling under her cheek. For a moment she was back in time, her head on Daddy's chest, her feet on one of her brothers.

"It wasn't too bad when she was little." Her sleepy brain wondered who Greg was talking to. "She'd curl up in a ball between us, but then she got bigger and she always ended up sprawling her legs across us."

"And you let her sleep peacefully?" a deep voice said under her ear.

Steve. That's why her pillow was so hard.

"Of course," Greg laughed wickedly.

In a flash, Heather realized she was laying with her head on Steve's chest, staring at his chin, with her feet on Greg's chest. Steve had stubble on his chin. Greg had his hands on her feet.

Oh no! No, no. That wasn't good.

Heather tried to roll over quickly and snatch her feet out of her brother's hands but Steve's arm was in her way, draped over her waist. Greg's hands tightened like a vise on her ankles.

"Don't do it," Heather warned and pleaded at the same time. "I'll tell Mom."

With a wicked grin, Greg drew her feet up to tuck them under his left arm and free his right hand. He was going to do it!

She twisted to look back at Steve, grasping a handful of aloha shirt.

"Don't let him, please!" Heather begged.

"Let him what?"

"Ahhh," Heather squealed and jerked spastically. "Help, help!"

It took a few seconds for it to register with Steve. Heather's feet were obviously extremely ticklish. It took another few seconds to determine if he wanted to be defender or tormentor.

He decided defense was his best option, but Heather was already under attack, twisting under his arm, alternately yelling, "Mom" and "Help!"

As soon as Steve moved his arm from around her, Heather snapped at her brother like a rubber band but her self-defense was hampered because Greg had turned her feet soles up, so her knees were on the ground and she was twisted awkwardly. She couldn't quite get to him.

Steve assessed the situation with the same mental acuity that made him a star defensive end. In the space of a breath, he realized a direct attack wouldn't be quick enough. Greg's grip was too firm. Steve had to either make him fumble or give Heather a position of greater power.

Swiftly rolling to his feet, Steve stepped over Heather. He squatted down and grabbed Greg's feet, pinning them to his chest. Using momentum to his advantage, he stood, spun, twisted Greg and planted both feet, all in one fluid motion. Greg was hanging head down, face out, with his feet pinned to Steve's chest. Heather was no longer twisted. Quickly she slid her body close to her brother, like compressing a spring, then with a mighty heave she threw herself backward. Steve was surprised by the power that rocked his body, but he hung on. Greg couldn't.

"Hold him," Heather howled. She scrambled back toward them and Greg squirmed violently. Steve held on, but barely.

"Stay back," Steve commanded Heather. She froze, then scrambled back as she guessed his intent.

Steve swung his right leg over Greg's torso, turning slightly and falling back, using the couch to break his fall. As he fell, he crossed his right leg over his left, locking his ankles. He bounced off the couch and rolled all the way over so that he was on his back on the rug. Greg's feet were pinned to Steve's chest, his arms under Steve's legs. Heather pounced with glee.

"Not in the house!" Mom scolded from behind the couch.

"Awe Mom!" Heather complained.

"She started it," Greg howled.

"Did not!" Heather flicked Greg's ear and he howled as if burned.

"It's my house!" Steve frowned.

"Steve," Mom warned. "Let him go. You three behave before you break something."

"It's my house," Steve pouted. Gloria frowned at him, hands on her hips.

Steve slowly released Greg and they all three sat cross-legged on the floor, looking up at Mom.

"If you can't play nicely, take it outside," Gloria's lips were twitching and her eyes twinkled but her voice was utterly serious.

"Yes ma'am," they chorused, looking at her with the wide-eyed innocence of five year olds.

It was too much. Gloria fled the room laughing.

They did take it outside, but to fire up the grill and get dinner going rather than to wrestle. When Luke guys arrived, Moose was the first one down.

"You're such a punk," Heather complained when Moose ran to greet everyone but her.

"Grandma used to say that if you want a dog that's happy to see you, get a Doberman," Steve laughed, "if you want one happy to see everyone else, get a Golden!"

"I don't know about the Doberman part," Heather said, "but I know that Moose generally ignores me if there's anyone else to play with."

"But he loves you best, even if he doesn't always show it well," Steve draped one arm over her shoulders and gave her a quick hug.

Heather smiled up at him and his heart began to do funny things. He slid his arm down to her waist and turned slightly toward her. She turned toward him, resting her left hand lightly on his chest. Suddenly Moose's head was pushing between them.

"Now he wants you," Steve groaned and rolled his eyes.

"Sometimes he's a bit overprotective," Heather explained unnecessarily.

"Hey, who's manning the grill?" Luke complained as he walked out onto the patio.

The moment was gone and they were separated by the natural flow of a happy, noisy family. Many times that evening they shared a smile or a tender look. They stole touches when they set the food out, held hands when the family prayed, touched shoulders when they ate.

The weight of their coming separation began to bear down heavily on Steve as the sun sank, unnoticed by the family as they enjoyed each other's company. The last two and a half months had been the best of his life. For the first time in his life, Steve felt like he actually had something to lose in leaving. Sorrow pressed upon him and he slipped away from the family.

Chapter 24

*H*eather missed Steve. She looked around the yard and patio for him but didn't see him, then she saw Moose going up the steps to the second floor lanai. Moose never left the fun unless someone was in need.

Heather stepped back to see the lanai. A large, dark shadow was just starting up the stairs to the upper lanai. Moose had to be following him because there was no other candidate up there. Heather followed too.

When she emerged on the upper lanai, Steve was sitting on the floor in the front corner. His back was against the makai rail, his head tilted sideway against the other rail, watching the family in the yard below. His right leg was stretched out in front of him, his left slightly bent, left arm supported on his knee. Moose lay with his head in Steve's lap, Steve's right hand idly stroking his silky ears.

Moose's tail thumped as Heather walked up and sat down, next to and facing Steve, knees up, arms around her knees. Steve didn't look her way. Heather and Moose waited quietly for Steve to be ready to share.

"I love football," Steve finally said. "For twenty years now, I've practically lived for the start of training, eagerly anticipated the beginning of the season. ... For the first time in my life, I don't want to play football."

Heather breathed deeply, struggling against the pain that stabbed her heart. She prayed for wisdom. "That's not exactly true, is it?"

Steve frowned and looked at her. "What do you mean?"

"It isn't really that you don't want to play football," Heather pulled her knees a little closer and laid her left cheek on them, looking sideway at Steve. "It's that you don't want to leave here. If football came here to you, you would play happily."

"You're right," Steve sighed heavily and leaned his head back against the rail. "Of course you're right."

After a long pause, Heather asked what she had been afraid to ask before. "When do you go?"

"Pete's dad is taking us to the airport at seven tomorrow morning," Steve said with a catch in his voice.

"So soon?" Heather's voice was barely a whisper but the anguish came through loud and clear. "Why didn't you say so earlier?"

"Once I said something, it became real," Steve fought the tears.

A long, black void opened up before Heather. She buried her face in her knees and tried to weep quietly. Moose whined. Suddenly Steve was pulling her into his lap. He cradled her against his chest with his left arm and stroked her hair as his tears fell with hers.

Finally their tears tapered off. Steve pressed a kiss to Heather's forehead. Moose whined again and sat up, pawing at Heather's lap with one of his big paws.

"Yes, we'll behave, Moose," Heather promised with a small laugh. Moose put his paw down with the other but stayed sitting where he was, pushed up against Steve, watching them both.

"I love you, Heather Shepherd," Steve whispered against her hair. "I would walk away from football today if it meant I would never have to leave you."

"I love you too, Steve Jeremiah," Heather smiled up at him and gently wiped tears from his cheeks, "but you need to go play football."

"Why?" he challenged her.

"Because it's your calling at this time in your life," Heather said patiently.

"Maybe my new calling is to love you," Steve said.

Heather again prayed for the right words. "Do you love football more than you love God?"

"No, never. I would leave it in a heartbeat if I thought it was what God wanted me to do."

"Do you think he does?"

"I'm sure he wants me to love you," Steve said stubbornly.

"You want to know how you can love me?" Heather laid her head back on his shoulder, absently playing with the buttons on his shirt.

"How?"

"Play the best football you've ever played."

"I don't know that I can."

"I'm sure you can."

"How are you so sure?"

"It's simple logic," Heather reached out to pet Moose, her cheek still pressed to Steve's shoulder. "You played great football when you had God to love more than it. Now that you have God and me, you should be even greater."

"That's simple logic?" Steve's chest rumbled with laughter. "I don't see it."

"Okay, it's like this," Heather explained carefully. "You love football but you don't play it for its own sake. You play it because you know God is glorified by what you do, right?"

"Right."

"So now you get to add to that the greater love you have for me than for football," Heather said. "You now get to play first for the glory you bring God, then for the joy I get from watching you play and glorify God, and only then for football. You'll be the best you've ever been! MVP of the Championship Game!"

"Strangely enough, I actually see your logic," Steve smiled sadly, "but that's not making it any easier to leave you."

"Then know you're going for my sake," Heather said quietly.

"What?"

Heather sat up and turned to face Steve, still sitting on his lap. Moose whined again, putting his front paws between them and laying his head on his paws. They both absentmindedly petted him.

"I need you to go because I'm not where you are yet," Heather said. "I'm too tempted to let you stay and become a permanent part of my life."

"See, that doesn't seem like a bad thing to me," Steve looked at her with hopeful eyes.

"But I know, and you do to, that God doesn't want that for us," Heather said earnestly. "You have a few more years of football to play. It's me who has to leave my life for yours. I'm not ready."

At her confession, Steve closed his eyes and dropped his head. She stroked his hair back from his brow then raised his head with a gentle touch to his chin.

"But I will be," she promised. "It's just a matter of time. I need some distance to discover that I miss you more than I love my life."

She kissed her fingers and pressed them to his lips.

"This time next year," she said huskily. "I don't think you'll be going off to the Mainland by yourself."

Steve wrapped his hand around hers, pressing a kiss to her fingers.

"So you might want to learn to golf next spring?" he whispered.

"I think the probability is very high," she whispered back.

Moose sat up and barked.

"I think Moose thinks we should go back downstairs so that I can say goodbye to everyone," Steve laughed ruefully.

"I think you're both right," Heather stood and offered him her hand.

THE GOOD-BYES WERE hard. Greg was the only one who had known how soon Steve was leaving. Aunty Gloria and Nalani scolded, protested, cried and hugged Steve. Matt hugged him and cried, and Jeremy insisted that Uncle Steve hold him. Robert and Tim feigned nonchalance, opting for asking him about what training camp was like. They were all disappointed to hear that Steve wouldn't be back until the season was over. There wasn't enough time to make the trip and recover from jetlag before playing again. The family promised to try to attend some of his games, especially the ones on the west coast.

Heather stepped back to give Steve this time with the family. She sat on the picnic table under the lanai, fighting the tears. Greg sat down beside her and wrapped his arm around her. She leaned against him, relishing his comfort.

"You okay, Boss?" he asked quietly.

"I will be, I think," she said.

Luke strolled over to join them. "Howzit, Shadow?"

Heather shrugged a little and began to cry. Luke sat down on her other side and took her hand in his. Sitting between her brothers, surrounded by their love, Heather drew strength for the season ahead.

Steve looked at them over the heads of the others. Luke and Greg both nodded to him. He nodded back, eyes sad but not worried. They would be rocks for Heather in this time, just as they had always been.

The rest of the evening passed much too quickly for Heather and Steve. They would have gladly stayed up all night talking since Steve had a long flight during which he could sleep the next day and Heather could go to work whenever she wanted because she was her own boss. But Greg had school and work tomorrow and he wouldn't go to bed until Heather left, nor did they want him to, even with Moose still around.

Just before eleven, Steve finally walked Heather and Moose out to her car. Greg didn't follow but they knew he was watching at the front window.

Heather opened the back door on the passenger side for Moose. After rolling the window down enough for his nose to stick out, she closed the door. Steve leaned against the front door and opened his arms for her. She stepped into his embrace.

"Will you come visit me this summer?" Steve asked. "We do have most of the weekends off."

"As much as I would like to say yes, I don't think I will," Heather sighed. "I'm certainly not going alone and everyone else has plans for the summer already or they need to work."

"Come to a game then, after the season starts," Steve suggested.

"If you want the honest truth, dear," Heather said softly. "I'm not at all sure that I'm going to be able to watch you play."

"What do you mean?" Steve asked.

"It's one thing to watch strangers whom I admire get battered around on the playing field," Heather said. "It's another to watch someone I love."

"Woman," Steve puffed up his chest. "I don't get battered, I do the battering."

"And you do it magnificently," Heather purred, "but sometimes other teams cheat. I don't know how I'm going to react the next time someone hits you like that creep did in the Championship Game."

"I guess I see your point, but I sure would love to know that you're in the stands," Steve sighed.

"Someday I'm sure I will be, but I'm not going to give you any promises about when that will be," Heather slid her arms around Steve's waist and laid her cheek on his chest. "I should go now."

"I want to kiss you," Steve whispered hoarsely.

"Oh that will make the parting so much easier," Heather said with sweet sarcasm.

"I know you're right," Steve tilted her chin up so their eyes met, "but when this season is over ...."

Steve suddenly slid his right arm under Heather's knees while still cradling her shoulders in his left arm, lifting her easily and holding her against his chest. Heather gasped with surprise and threw her arms around his neck.

"Put me down! I'm too big."

"Big? You're small and light to me," Steve laughed with delight. He walked easily around the car to the driver's door.

"Greg's watching, you know," Heather blushed furiously, her face pressed against his chest.

"So is Moose," Steve chuckled, nodding toward the back door of the car. Sure enough, Moose's big nose was pressed against the window.

Steve set Heather on her feet and opened her door. He leaned on the door while she rolled the window down then he shut it for her and squatted down next to the open window, arms crossed on the sill.

"I'll call you tomorrow," Steve said.

"I'll answer or call you back," Heather replied.

"Email me?"

"We can even get someone to help us figure out how to chat with those camera things," Heather suggested.

"Oh God, I don't want to go!" Steve groaned out a fervent prayer, dropping his head to the side of the car. "Not my will, but yours."

He took a deep breath, leaned into the car to give her a gentle kiss on the cheek, then stood quickly. He shoved his hands into his pockets and stepped back from the car. Unable to even say goodbye, he simply watched her drive away.

Long after her car disappeared, he stood there staring into the night.

Chapter 25

*H*eather was moping over her first cup of coffee when her cell phone rang. She almost fumbled the phone in her rush to answer it.

"Hey Beautiful!"

"Hi Goliath!"

"How'd you sleep last night?"

"Sleep? What's that?"

"Yeah, me too."

"It'll get better."

"I guess," Steve sighed. "When?"

"You haven't even left Honolulu yet," Heather laughed. "Give it at least until you land in Chicago."

"Okay, but if it isn't better by then I'm calling you again."

"You do that!"

"So, what're you doing?"

"I'm enjoying my coffee. How about you?"

"We just cleared the security checkpoint. We're almost to the gate now."

"How long until you board?"

"About an hour, I guess."

"I think I'm going to need more minutes," Heather said.

"Excuse me?"

"It just occurred to me that my plan doesn't have enough minutes."

"What do you have?"

"Three hundred a month."

"Good grief woman, that's only five hours!"

"I get free nights and weekends," she suggested helpfully.

"Get a new plan," Steve insisted.

"But I've never used all three hundred minutes before."

"I bet you do this month and it's already almost half over. ... Hey, I can get another phone on my plan for you! That way you can have a phone just for me."

"And carry around two phones? I don't think so. I can upgrade my plan."

"I'd be happy to get you a phone or anything else you need," Steve said. "You've given me so much and I've given you nothing."

"What have I given you?" Heather asked.

"Two gorgeous paintings. Your family."

"I didn't give you my family. I just shared it."

"Same, same. Hey, when's your birthday?"

"Why?"

"Silly question. Why do you think I want to know when it is?"

"Maybe I won't tell you."

"That's okay, I'll call Greg."

"He won't tell you," Heather giggled.

"Why not?"

"You'll find out some day."

"Then I'll call your mom or Luke."

"And use your minutes on them instead of me?"

"I have unlimited calling."

"Of course," Heather said wryly.

"Of course. So what're you going to do today?"

They talked until Steve was ordered to shut off his phone by the flight attendant. It was a long day until he called from Minneapolis where he changed planes before flying into O'Hare.

And so their days went. Heather was soon glad that she'd not just gotten a new plan with unlimited minutes but a phone with hands-free capability too. They also set up a web camera at Mom's house and on Sundays the whole family talked to Steve.

By the time June rolled around, they had slipped into a comfortable routine of morning calls from Heather which caught Steve at lunch and generated much harassment from the other guys on the team. In his evening, Steve would call Heather, catching her in the middle of the afternoon or early evening.

The summer passed slowly. Steve told her stories about the team. Heather told him that Luke and Nalani were having a little girl and Luke was utterly delighted. They had named her Naomi Rachel. Nalani glowed with health and according to the ultrasounds, Naomi Rachel was developing perfectly. Steve asked Heather what kind of toys a baby girl would like.

"Speaking of toys," Heather said, "you never did tell me what you wouldn't let Pete talk about that night he picked us up from the airport."

"It's really not that big a deal," Steve sighed. "I just don't like to talk about it very much because it's from that dark place in my life."

"I don't understand."

"You know why I have the toys, don't you?"

"Because you never had a childhood," Heather sadly. "I guess it's making up for lost time."

"Yeah. When we did get toys, Dad always destroyed them or threw them away within a few days. There's something therapeutic for me when I play with the keiki."

"So what's the part you didn't want Pete to talk about?"

"The dolls."

"Dolls?"

"For Jenni," Steve's voice was thick with emotion. "I know she's coming back sometime and I get dolls for her – baby dolls, Barbie dolls, china dolls, rag dolls."

"You'll find her someday," Heather promised, "and all those dolls will show her that you never stopped loving her or missing her."

"Jenni's going to love you," Steve said softly. "You're a very special woman."

JUNE SLIPPED TOWARD July. They talked about everything and nothing. Heather told Steve how much the family missed him and he told her how much he was enjoying the DVDs he'd received from the aunties. He told her he hadn't realized how many times the movie cameras had been rolling while they were having fun, and she assured him that it was more likely they were on than not. Heather told stories about being a missionary kid in Africa and Steve talked about growing up on the wrong side of the tracks in Abilene, Kansas.

"Seriously, I literally grew up on the wrong side of the tracks," Steve said.

"That's just a figure of speech for a part of town where there's lots of poor people or high crime," Heather said in disbelief. "There's no 'literal' to the 'wrong side of the tracks' anymore."

"So says the big city girl who has no knowledge of trains and small towns in the Midwest," Steve laughed. "In Abilene there are three sets of tracks between the town and Southeast Sixth Street where I grew up. Two of them are still in daily use, the other is used for the excursion train during the summer. It was always a gamble when you should leave the house to get where you were going because you never knew when a very long freight train would come through. More than once I was late for work because I got caught by a train."

"There were no alternate routes? No bridges that went over or under the tracks?"

"In Abilene, Kansas?" Steve laughed wryly. "Oh sweetheart, you really don't understand small town America. I'll have to take you there someday."

They also talked about the places they'd traveled to, childhood pets, summer vacations and the trouble Heather had gotten into as a girl. Often they couldn't remember what they'd talked about afterward, but they remembered the way love grew through their conversations.

Heather didn't tell Steve how lonely she was doing what she'd always done, how much she missed him. She didn't tell him how many evenings she had dinner with Greg, just to be at Steve's house, but she did tell him about their adventurous weekends taking the motorcycle safety class at the community college. She didn't tell Steve how many times she stood at his bedroom door, wanting to see his inner sanctum and feel closer to him but respecting his privacy too much to invade, but she did tell him how much she was learning about motorcycle mechanics.

Steve told her that sailing on Lake Michigan was nothing compared to the Pacific. He told her how much he missed learning to surf, riding with her two-up around the island and playing with the keiki. Steve told Heather about the night he and Pete took the rookie defensive players to a sushi bar in downtown Chicago. He told her how much the other players' children made him miss Matt, Jeremy and the keiki cousins. Steve told her how much he ached after some of their practices. He told her about the golf courses around Chicago, his visit with Eddie's family in Muscatine and the impressive view from the Sears Tower.

"You actually rode that elevator?" Heather was astonished.

"After our jaunt up Diamond Head, I figured that elevator would be the next step," Steve said proudly.

"Who went with you?"

"Why did someone have to go with me?"

"This is me you're talking to, Goliath," Heather laughed. "I know that without someone to ... encourage you, you wouldn't have done anything other than watch the elevator doors open and shut."

"You're right," Steve sighed, "I did get on the elevator and ride all the way up, but if it hadn't been so far, I would have walked back down. Let's just say that Pete's ... encouragement isn't as encouraging as yours."

Heather told Steve about interesting jobs at the shop and Moose's funny antics, but she didn't tell him that she would sit on the swing on his lanai and cry as she watched the sunset. She told him about Matt and Jeremy's latest escapades, but she didn't tell him that when the preseason started she banished even Moose from the house, refusing to watch with anyone else. She told him about Greg's letter from the bible college informing him that he had gotten a full scholarship, including textbooks

"Do you know anything about that?" Heather asked. "Did you give money to the bible college so Greg would get a scholarship?"

Silence was her only answer.

"See, the fact that you won't answer my direct question tells me you *did* give money to the bible college."

"But maybe I didn't answer because I *didn't* give money and I don't want to disappoint you."

"You wouldn't be that devious, would you?" Again, silence answered her question. "That's not right! Based on my earlier logic, that means you *would* be that devious. But based on your reply, you *couldn't* be that devious. I'm confused!"

"So am I, Heather! So am I. How about we change the subject? What did you think about the game?"

"We already talked about the game."

"I was magnificent, wasn't I?"

"That's what the commentators said, but you know what I think about commentators!"

"From previous conversations I recall something about fools and brainless."

"So, do you think I would ever confess to agreeing with them?"

"Probably not!" Steve's rich chuckle warmed Heather's heart enough to carry her through to their next call.

Steve told Heather how his claustrophobia developed after his father had discovered him hiding in the closet one day and locked him in, starting a pattern that continued until he died. He told Heather how much he missed Jenni and he told her about the night that Jenni left.

"I was sound asleep," Steve's voice was thick with emotion. "If I had known what she was doing, I would have woken up and gone with her, but I didn't know."

"You would be a different man today if you had," Heather reminded him gently.

"But I'd still have my sister," Steve sighed heavily. "Instead I have her softball."

"It's still safe on the mantle," Heather said. "You told me that you were leaving it because this is home now, but you haven't told me why you have it."

"The night she left," Steve said after a long pause. "She laid the softball on my pillow, next to my head. She whispered, 'Hey brat, take care of my ball until I get back, okay?' I was barely awake, so all I did was whisper, 'Okay, I love you.' Then she was gone and I haven't seen her or heard from her since."

"You've looked for her, haven't you?" Heather's question was more of a statement. She knew him well.

"Ever since my first year in the League when I could afford to hire a private detective."

"What have you found?"

"She was in Denver two years after she left. She was arrested for prostitution," Steve said sadly. "The following year she was arrested in Houston for prostitution and drug use. San Francisco two years after that, same thing. But nothing after that. I don't know if she got smarter about not getting caught, changed her lifestyle or died."

"I don't think she died Steve."

"Why not?"

"I think it's easier to hide when you're alive than when you're dead."

"I don't follow your logic."

"If she was arrested as Jennifer Jeremiah in Denver then her fingerprints are on file, yes?"

"Yes," Steve caught her drift. "Which means that if she were dead, the morgue would have identified her by her fingerprints."

"And your detective would have easily found record of her death."

"As long as she had identifiable fingerprints," Steve sighed.

"Don't borrow trouble, Steve," Heather said. "That probably happens a lot more in the movies and TV than it does in real life."

"I hope so."

"So why a softball?" Heather decided to get Steve back to happier memories. "Did Jenni play?"

"Oh yeah," Steve said proudly. "She was incredible. She was shortstop and nothing got past her. And she could hit! If I could have hit a ball like that, I would be playing baseball instead of football."

"Baseball is so boring most of the time," Heather complained. "I like football much better."

"I'm glad you do," Steve laughed softly. "It made it so much easier to catch you."

"Oh really," Heather said sassily. "You think you've caught me?"

Steve sighed. "I know I'd like to catch you up in my arms again."

"Patience young grasshopper," Heather said sagely.

As always their conversation wandered illogically and erratically until it was time for Steve to call it a night. They talked about movies, books and Greg's most recent escapades.

Heather called Steve when Naomi Rachel was born on August twentieth. She emailed him dozens of pictures. Some of them with Aunty Heather were quickly printed and framed.

Steve expressed his frustration with the Grizzly offense. She expressed hers because Tim's and Robert's coaches weren't letting them play until the end of the fourth quarter.

Then it was Labor Day. Heather was missing Steve more because Greg was already deep into studying for his classes at bible college. He was carrying twelve hours because he didn't have to work as much since he didn't pay rent and he had the scholarship.

"So you never told me, *do* you know anything about that?"

"About what?" Steve feigned ignorance.

"About Greg getting the scholarship," Heather asked even though she was certain she knew the answer. "Did you have something to do with that Steve?"

"Me do such a thing?" Steve said innocently. "Inconceivable."

Heather laughed. Steve must want to parody Vizzini in *The Princess Bride*. This should be fun!

"That word doesn't mean what you're pretending to want me to believe it means," Heather said, happy to parody Inigo Montoya's doubts.

"Not fair Beautiful," Steve grumbled. "I'm supposed to be the one with the dizzying intellect. I'm not supposed to be dizzy from trying to follow yours."

"Sorry Goliath," Heather said contritely. "Carry on, oh most dizzying intellect."

"Clearly," Steve said with great self-importance. "If I had done such a thing, and I'm not saying I did, only supposing a what if. *If* I had done such a thing I should have told you right off to garner your undying gratitude."

"You have a point."

"Unless I did such a thing but I didn't want you to know because I wanted you to fall in love with me not for my incredible generosity but for my stunning good looks and sweet nature."

"That makes sense," Heather giggled.

"On the other hand," Steve sighed. "If I had not done it and you asked if I had, the shame of not doing it would have been too great to confess that it wasn't me."

"That must be it."

"Perchance however," Steve said craftily. "I have done it and yet I merely wish for my left hand to not know what my right hand is doing."

"I see," Heather pondered.

"In which case," Steve said slyly. "If the two perchance would become one ...?"

"You mean your left hand and your right hand become one hand?" Heather asked with credible puzzlement.

"Of course not, woman! Don't play dense with me."

"Oh! You mean if I were to become your wife ...."

"Then your right hand would be my right hand."

"That sounds like blackmail," Heather laughed.

"More like bribery," Steve confessed cheerfully.

"So if I marry you, you'll tell me the truth," Heather said shrewdly.

"I didn't say that," Steve said quickly. "You may have deduced that, and I'm not saying you deduced it rightly, but I *did not* say that!"

"Ah, you are a sly one."

"Remember the third rule of engagement," Steve said much too seriously.

"What's that?"

"Never get involved with a Kansan in a food fight."

Silence for a moment, then Heather's laugh pealed out. "What does that have to do with anything?"

"I don't know. It just came to me with sudden clarity. It was fated that I should say it."

"You're crazy!"

"Crazy in love with you, Beautiful, and your insane family too."

"The feeling's mutual, all the way around."

FINALLY IT WAS the start of the regular season. Heather watched the game alone again, well aware that this would be the most tense game she had ever seen. Unlike preseason when all the rookies were tested and the seasoned players often warmed the bench, Steve would be out there for almost every defensive down. The camera would see him often. The commentators would assess his play. She had seen it all many times before but this was going to be different. Steve was now her man. She had no idea how she was going to deal with it.

Steve was magnificent and that wasn't just her opinion. Nothing got past him, either on the ground or through the air. He sacked the quarterback, caused a fumble and even blocked a field goal. The commentators said that if the Grizzlies had won the game, Steve would have been the most valuable player.

The game was decided by a failed field goal attempt in the final seconds of the game. The camera picked up Steve as he slumped in despair when the ball bounced off the uprights and back toward the field. Heather knelt before the television, kissed her fingers and pressed them on Steve's image on the screen. She ached for him knowing that he would spend the evening alone, reliving the game, wondering what he could have done differently.

"Next year, love. Next year, I'm going to be there for you," Heather promised.

She paced her living room for almost two hours waiting for his call.

"Hi Beautiful," he sounded tired.

"Steve," Heather realized she didn't know what to say. "I'm sorry" was so trite!

"You watched the game?"

"Yes."

He sighed heavily.

"You were incredible."

"We lost!"

"I wasn't talking about the team, silly," Heather couldn't help but giggle. "I was talking about *you*!"

"You think so?" Steve sounded doubtful.

"I know so," Heather said firmly, "and all America knows it too!"

Steve laughed and Heather's heart soared.

"I love you so much," his voice was like a soft caress.

"I love you too."

"So what's the verdict?"

"Verdict? About what?"

"You coming to the games."

"I think it's a very high probability," Heather said happily, "but not until after Tim and Robert are done with their season. I don't want to miss even one of their games this year."

"When will that be?" Steve stifled a groan.

"They've already lost their first three," Heather sighed. "If they don't win soon, their season will be over the second week in October."

"Well I can't hope they lose!" Steve said. "So what if they win?"

"Post season goes all the way to the week before Thanksgiving."

"That long!"

"It's only a little over two months."

"And if we don't win some, it's going to be a very long two months."

"You do realize that I'm not going alone to the Mainland," Heather said.

"A wise decision. I tell you what," Steve suggested. "I'm going to have five tickets for you every game starting in October. If you make it, I'll see you after, okay?"

"You aren't going to sit us up in some box somewhere, are you?"

"Where do you want to be?"

"At the fifty yard line, as close to the field as possible," Heather said.

"Done!"

THE NEXT TWO games were agonizing. Steve and the defense were inspired, but the offense couldn't get anything together. They lost their second game by a discouraging margin. The third game, the Grizzlies first home game, followed suit right up to the fourth quarter.

In the opening play of the fourth quarter, Steve tipped a pass that spun right into the hands of a defensive lineman who carried it down to the eleven yard line. It took three downs for the quarterback to connect with a wide receiver in the end zone. With most of the fourth quarter left, the Grizzlies were down by twelve.

The defense was practically perfect when they went back out on the field. The Mustangs lost six yards before they punted on the fourth down. They had barely used a minute on the clock because Steve pushed the running back out of bounds on the first down and Pete batted down the ball for an incomplete pass on the second. The third down ended with a bone jarring sack, much like the one in Heather's painting.

After the punt, the offense took the field and put up a titanic battle. The Grizzlies marched down the field for seven but they used up too much of the clock doing it. The Mustangs ran the kick up to the thirty-five yard line. They had a little over five minutes left on the clock.

The Grizzly defense was good, but the offense took the yards three and four at a time. The Grizzlies had to use their timeouts while the Mustangs burned up two minutes. They had crossed the fifty yard line and were bearing down on the Mustang's forty. Steve was only looking to give the ball back to his offense with time left on the clock when he charged the quarterback.

It was one of those perfect moments. He saw the quarterback's arm moving, quickly calculated the trajectory and launched. He got enough of a hand on the ball that it was his! He bobbled it a little going down but by the time he hit the turf, the ball was tucked securely. He kept his momentum going, rolled onto his feet and sailed into the end zone with no flags anywhere on the field.

Heather erupted from the couch, dancing wildly, arms waving, shouting joyfully. Moose, who had finally been allowed to watch with her, barked happily at Heather, bouncing like a puppy.

The game wasn't over yet. After the extra point, the defense was back out on the field to preserve their two point lead. The Mustangs had two timeouts left and the ball on the twenty-nine yard line. It was going to be a long two minutes.

The Mustang quarterback connected with a sweet pass to the wide receiver on the right side of the field, well away from Steve. They picked up fifteen yards, but then Pete stuffed the ball back down the running back's throat and the Mustangs were at second and thirteen.

And so it went, the Mustangs inching ever closer to field goal range, managing the clock shrewdly. Steve's frustration was mounting, especially since the Mustangs were keeping the action well away from him. Heather was sitting on her floor with her back to the couch, left arm around Moose, chewing on the knuckle of her right index finger.

Second down, twenty-two seconds left on the clock. One time out left. Three yards to comfortable range for the Mustangs' kicker.

Heather saw it and screamed, "He's coming your way!"

Steve saw it with utter clarity, knew exactly where to intercept the running back. He hit him low and hard, using his greater height to lift the Mustang well off his feet, Steve's right shoulder getting under the arm that tucked the ball into the running back's side.

Steve sensed more than saw the ball pop free as they were still falling toward the ground. The running back hit the ground hard but Steve was scrambling for the ball even before he had the ground beneath him. He saw too many legs converging on him before he smothered the ball and was in turn smothered.

Heather remained breathless for long seconds, then Steve suddenly scrambled free of the pack, the ball tucked firmly in his arms.

The stadium erupted with joyous screams and Heather screamed with them. Moose barked at Heather and she gleefully tackled him, rolling on the floor laughing and kissing him. She didn't even bother to watch the Grizzly offense take the field to kneel the ball for one last down while the last eight seconds of the game ticked off.

When the reporter snagged the game MVP for a quick interview, Heather flopped dreamily onto the couch and stared at the big man with his adorable grin.

"Steve Jeremiah, you were on fire today," the reporter said.

There was no question there, Heather thought lazily as she gazed at Steve on the television. Steve smiled and raised his eyebrow, asking for a question if the man wanted an interview. Heather giggled.

"Uh, what's your inspiration?"

"God is always my inspiration," Steve said.

"How'd it feel out there, intercepting that pass and causing the game winning fumble?"

"The game was won inch by inch by the whole team," Steve shook his head. "I did my part and everyone else did theirs."

"But you –"

Steve looked over his shoulder and nodded to someone. He dropped a big hand on the reporter's shoulder.

"Sorry brah, gotta go," he said. He smiled at the camera and flashed a shaka before turning and jogging off screen.

"That was for me," Heather sighed dreamily and flopped over onto her back, snuggling into the softness of her couch.

"Moose, how do you feel about living in Illinois?"

Suddenly Heather realized that she tasted blood, then she became aware of pain in her right hand. She had bitten her knuckle hard enough to draw blood! No more games by herself. She needed a brother to beat on.

Chapter 26

Steve had never been more excited to land in Honolulu. The Grizzlies' bye week had come early enough for him to see Tim and Robert play and he wasn't missing the opportunity. Greg was the only one who knew he was coming. For everyone else it would be a surprise.

He hadn't been able to get a flight early enough to do anything except jump in the car when Greg pulled up then rush over to the game. Steve called Greg as soon as he got into the terminal.

"You gotta get bags?" Greg asked.

"Nope," Steve said. "Just get your sorry self over here."

"Oh, I will," Greg agreed. "Everyone's mad enough as it is."

"Why's that?"

"I'm missing the first quarter of Robert's JV game is why!"

"Then shut up and get off the phone so you can drive."

As Steve walked through the terminal doors, he saw his BMW convertible pulling up to the curb. Greg popped the trunk.

"You wanna drive?" he called as Steve walked up and threw his carry-on bag in the trunk.

"Nope," Steve slammed the trunk. He didn't bother to open the door, just stepped over it and dropped into the seat, reaching for the safety belt. "You just get us there quickly and in one piece."

"Will do boss man," Greg shifted the car into gear and pulled away from the curb.

"Sweet ride you got," Steve grinned.

"Yeah, I got this friend who has more money than brains," Greg grinned back. "He lets me drive it sometimes."

Steve leaned over and looked at the odometer. He frowned.

"You aren't using it much," he complained. "Is this the first time since I left?"

"Yeah," Greg replied with a shrug.

"Man, you gotta use it," Steve said. "Ask your sister. She's already given me scoldings about letting a high performance machine sit for so long. If she has to fix it before I can drive it after the season, she'll have both our hides!"

"It's hard man," Greg sighed, "being ... ya know."

"I know, brah. Believe me, I know," Steve said, "but look at it this way, you drive Luke's car sometimes, yeah?"

"Yeah."

"And Heather's?"

"Yeah."

"So drive mine," Steve said. "Seriously, I need you to."

Greg just grunted. He grabbed a t-shirt from between the seats and threw it at Steve. "Here, wear this."

"They came in!" Steve held up the shirt and admired Tim's football picture on the back before slipping out of his other shirt with a grin.

"This is great," Steve smoothed his hands over his chest, "but I can't see Tim's picture."

"Yeah, but everyone behind you will see it," Greg grinned.

"Will there be many people behind us?"

"Third row up on the fifty yard line, that's where we always sit," Greg grinned. "Everyone will see you."

"Even with all the big Samoans there?" Steve laughed.

"Yeah brah, even with them."

They neared the Middle Street merge and Steve groaned when he saw the traffic. "Oh man, this is going to take forever."

"Relax brah," Greg laughed. "We'll take the Likelike ramp, swing through Liliha and around the Punchbowl. They're playing in the Roosevelt Stadium tonight. It won't take long."

"They're playing Roosevelt?"

"No. They're just playing at the Roosevelt Stadium."

"If they aren't playing against Roosevelt, then why are they playing in their stadium?"

"I keep forgettin' you don' know not'ing 'bout Hawaii," Greg sighed. "What did you and Pete do the last five years? Stay home and pout 'cause you blew your season?"

"Pretty much," Steve shook his head with a wry grin. "Besides, I've never been here during football season before."

"That's true. So here's some local football education. Quite a few of the high schools don't have their own stadium. We're one of those schools. We play home games mostly at Roosevelt, but also at Castle or Aloha Stadium."

"That must be pretty cool for high school boys."

"It sent me over the moon the first time," Greg grinned at the memory. "I wanted so bad to play there with the Warriors."

"What happened?"

"Reality," Greg said sadly. Steve waited for more. Heather had said Greg had been good but no one had ever told him why Greg hadn't gone on to play college football. Heather had mentioned that he wasn't a very good student, but it didn't take more than a C average to get a football scholarship to most colleges.

Greg didn't offer more information. He was glowering at the merging car that was blocking his escape off the H1 onto the Likelike ramp. Steve figured it was a dead subject. He sighed in frustration. Why did everyone have to be so closed-mouthed about their past while his was an open book? One of these days, he was going to make Greg talk but right now he wanted him to drive. They had a football game to watch.

"Are we there yet?" Steve whined.

"Not yet Stevie-boy," Greg grinned, "but it won't be long."

Greg was wrong. It took a long time, then Greg took his time parking. Steve heard the crowd roar and a whistle blow.

"Hurry, the game already started," Steve insisted.

"I told you it did," Greg laughed. "Why you so excited about a JV game?"

"I just love high school football so much," Steve said wryly.

When they got to the ticket window, Steve discovered that he didn't have anything smaller than a fifty.

"I can't change that," the woman complained.

"Then give me as many as it will get me." Steve was very impatient.

The woman gave him eight tickets and two dollars in change. Greg had his season pass, so Steve only took one ticket and handed the strip to the man behind him.

"Here, take one and pass it back," Steve was frustrated with the delay so he answered the man's thanks with a quick shaka as he stepped to the gate.

EVERYONE BUT NALANI and Naomi were at the game. By the time the second quarter started, Luke was definitely upset with Greg. He knew more than any of the others what it meant to a teenaged boy to have his whole family at the game rooting for him. Where was he? Luke frowned, looking down the track for his brother. He found more than he expected.

"Greg's here," he turned to Heather with a huge grin.

"It's about time," she took the water bottle back from Jeremy and capped it as she looked up at her big brother. "What? Greg's not that exciting."

"No, Greg isn't." Something about the way Luke dragged out Greg's name drew her attention to the people entering the stadium via the track around the field. With a squeal of delight, Heather was out of her seat and flying down the ramp.

The whistle blew on the field and Steve glanced over to see the action. Greg nudged him just in time for him to keep from being bowled over by the human dynamo bearing down on him. Steve caught Heather and she threw her arms around his neck, hugging him tight.

"You're here!" Heather exclaimed in delight as he set her back on her feet.

"It's bye week," Steve shrugged. "I couldn't think of anything better to do than catch some high school football."

"So you flew to Honolulu because there was nothing going on back on the Mainland?" Heather laughed as Steve grinned and shrugged again. She turned to her brother and punched him in the arm. "That's for not telling me he was coming. Now let's go enjoy the game."

Heather tucked her hands around their elbows and sailed down the track, happier than she had been for many months.

Steve enjoyed the rest of the first half but something was missing. He finally asked. "Where's Robert?"

Robert's older siblings looked at each other, shook their heads and shrugged. Heather had told him the coach wasn't playing Tim and Robert but he'd hoped the man had wised up since then.

"He should be playing," Steve frowned. "He's at least as good as the other boys out there, better than most."

"Don't tell us," Luke grumbled. "Tell the coach."

"Maybe I will," Steve muttered thoughtfully.

When the half ended, the Dolphins were down by six. Steve watched as the team gathered by the trees at the mauka end of the field. The Honu went makai. Obviously they were not using locker rooms for halftime.

"I'll be back," Steve said to Heather.

"What are you going to do?" Heather suspected he was up to something but she couldn't guess what.

"Don't worry, Beautiful," Steve squeezed her hand. "I promise not to get into trouble."

Heather watched Steve walk with a purpose down to the track and toward the mountain end of the field. When he passed the scoreboard, he walked off the track and stood about twenty feet from the cluster of boys with their coach. He crossed his arms and just watched.

Luke began to chuckle.

"Wouldn't I love to be a bug down there about now?" Greg snickered.

"Why? What's Steve doing?" Mom asked.

THE COACH DIDN'T know anything was amiss at first. As usual he was lecturing the boys about the first half but he soon realized that he was losing their attention. They kept looking at something behind him and to his left.

He didn't want to look, so he growled at the nearest boy. "Mana, what's your problem? You wanna play football the second half, you better listen up."

"Sorry Coach," Mana said, "but that guy over there looks like a football player. I just can't remember who."

"You all look like football players to me," the coach growled. "Get your head where it belongs, boy."

"But Coach," the center said, "that looks like Jeremiah, from the Grizzlies."

"Yeah," a couple of the other boys agreed with him.

"No Grizzly is going to be at our football game. They play football in the fall just like we do," the coach disagreed.

"Isn't it their bye week this week?" the kicker asked.

The coach couldn't resist any longer. He threw a look over his shoulder. It was Steve Jeremiah from the Grizzlies. He'd heard rumors that Jeremiah was living in Honolulu in the offseason.

"Is he here for one of you guys?" the coach asked.

Robert slowly raised his hand. "That would probably be me, Coach."

"You!" The coach was surprised. "You know Steve Jeremiah, Robert?"

"Yeah. He's kinda dating my sister."

"Since when?" the coach challenged.

"Since about March," Robert wasn't sure if he was supposed to be embarrassed or proud.

The coach looked thoughtfully at him for a long moment then he inclined his head slightly toward Jeremiah.

"Get over there and find out what he wants. Get rid of him so you guys can get your attention back on the game."

Robert scrambled to his feet and trotted over to Steve who didn't bother to hide his grin. They greeted each other with a handshake and one-armed hug. Steve was surprised to see that Robert had grown at least a couple inches. He was probably as tall as Greg. He'd probably end up being taller than all his brothers.

"Hey brah," Robert laughed. "I didn't expect to see you here tonight."

"It's bye week, you know," Steve laughed too. "I didn't have anything better to do than catch some Dolphin football."

"We have a real good-looking cheering section," Robert said slyly.

"Yeah, I noticed," Steve turned to look over his shoulder at Heather and the family. "Besides, I wanted to see the new niece before she gets too old."

"Why you come down here on the field?"

"I was just wondering if Coach had said anything about you playing the next half."

"He hasn't yet," Robert grinned up at Steve.

"Well I sure hope you get some playing time, Tim too," Steve said. "I'd hate to have come all this way for nothing."

"Yeah well, maybe you can find something to keep the weekend from being a total loss," Robert said slyly.

"Get back with the team, you smart aleck," Steve laughed, "and don't blow your chance."

Steve watched Robert run back to the team, waiting until the coach turned and made brief eye contact, then he turned and walked back to the stands. When he sat back down by Heather, she nudged him with her shoulder.

"You like to fix things, don't you?"

"When things can be fixed, why not?" Steve smiled.

"How do you know what to fix and what to let go?"

"Well in some cases all you need to figure out is whether they're looking for a hand out or a hand up. I don't mind giving a hand up when it's in my power to do so."

"You're not half bad, Steve Jeremiah," Heather laid her head on his shoulder and sighed.

"Hey, this is football," Greg complained. "None of that mushy stuff!"

"Yeah," Matt sighed sadly. "I thought I wouldn't get embarassed since Mom stayed home."

"It's been a great season so far, hasn't it bud?" Greg asked with a sad sigh.

"I thought the Dolphins haven't won yet." Steve looked down at Heather.

"They haven't," Greg acknowledged, "but without Nalani here, we've been able to watch like men should."

"Yeah, with no mushy stuff," Matt rolled his eyes and leaned against his uncle with a heavy sigh.

Playful banter swirled around until the start of the second half. The Dolphins received the ball and Steve wasn't surprised to see the offense giving a little more than they had before. When they finally scored on a fifteen yard run, the crowd rose with a cheer.

Heather was as loud in her cheers as anyone else and Steve grinned down at her. Greg caught his look and laughed.

"You ain't seen nothin' yet," he promised with a shout over Heather's head. She elbowed him in the gut and he just laughed. Steve laughed too. It was good to be home.

The Dolphins kicked the ball and the defense took their stand at the thirty yard line. Robert played safety and he was on fire. He took down every receiver who caught a ball on his side of the field, broke up two catches and came perilously close to a pass interference call.

Heather was on her feet with every good play, cheering her approval. It was halfway through the fourth quarter when it dawned on Steve that she was trying to behave. It was the flag that gave her away.

Right in front of them, an offensive player held Robert who was in great position to take down the Honu running back, except for the hold. Heather surged to her feet even as the ref reached for his flag.

"Holding! Holding!" She raged as the running back high-stepped into the end zone. "That better be a holding flag! You better bring it back 'cause that was holding!"

She wasn't the only fan complaining about the hold but she was definitely the most adorable. When the ref picked up his flag and announced his agreement with her assessment, Heather crossed her arms and plopped back down in her seat.

"Yeah, you better call it that way," she said. She began to blush as she realized Steve was grinning like a fool. He leaned in front of her to talk to Greg and Luke.

"Is she always like this?"

"Nah," Greg laughed. "She's behaving because you're here."

"You should see her when she really lets loose," Luke agreed.

Heather shouldered Greg hard enough to get Luke too.

"Shut up and watch the game," she commanded.

"It just gets better and better," Steve murmured as he sat back beside her.

Chapter 27

*A*fter five losses to start the season, the JV finally won their first game in a well-fought contest. The Dolphin fans were excited and when the band arrived in the intermission before the varsity game, they got even more pumped up. Steve had almost forgotten the special energy and enthusiasm of a high school game. He enjoyed himself more than he had in a long time.

The varsity Dolphins lost the toss and had to kick the ball. The defense was good but after six minutes of play, the Honu's running back slipped into the end zone through a hole that Heather disgustingly declared was big enough for a Mac truck.

Tim was a wide receiver and his family was excited but not surprised that he trotted out when the offense took the field. Heather was infuriated when the quarterback threw an interception into double coverage rather than throwing to Tim who was wide open. Apparently the coach was too.

The offense had another four minutes to correct their mistake. Fortunately it only cost them a field goal. They went into the second quarter down by ten but with the ball in Dolphin territory. Heather was grumbling that it didn't do a whole lot of good to put Tim in if they weren't going to let him touch the ball. Steve agreed, but he thought it was probably just because the quarterback wasn't comfortable with Tim as a receiver.

All that changed on the first play of the second quarter. Under pressure, the quarterback threw the ball up in the general direction of Tim who was unfortunately in double coverage. Heather saw the danger as soon as Steve and her brothers did. They all jumped to their feet, Heather with both hands to her head and a grimace on her face.

"No, no, no!" She cringed to see Tim in such pressure on his first real chance to prove himself. Then he came back toward the ball, jumping above the defenders with his greater height and reach, snatching the ball out of the air. He came back down on the balls of both feet, spun around, juked the safety and took off toward the end zone.

"Yes, yes, yes! Go, go, go!" Heather jumped up and down.

"Go Tim, go!" Luke roared behind her.

"Touchdown, Dolphins," Steve threw both arms up in the air then picked up Heather and spun her around.

"That's my boy," Greg was pointing with both hands at the back of his t-shirt as he strutted back and forth. "Oh yeah, that's my brother."

Gloria was standing with both hands to her cheeks, laughing. Suddenly she jumped up on the wide ledge that served for both step and seating. She grabbed Steve's head and pulled it down for a big kiss.

As they all settled down to watch the extra point, they heard someone behind them complaining. "Where's that kid been all year?"

"If he'd been playing earlier, we might have already won a game," someone else responded.

Steve knew it took a team to win games, not just star players, but he couldn't help agreeing with the assessment. A coach who missed that kind of talent probably was missing something vital for his team.

That became more obvious as the game progressed. Tim caught everything that came his way but not much did. When he wasn't called on to be a receiver, Tim got into the play anywhere he saw the need. He threw blocks for the running backs and tackled the defender coming back with the ball when the quarterback threw a pass with no Dolphin receiver anywhere in the vicinity.

Even though the offense couldn't get anything going, the defense kept the game close. The game was still ten to seven when the Dolphins got the ball on the twenty-one yard line five minutes into the fourth quarter.

They took the ball thirty yards with three first downs and a third down conversion, much to the pleasure of the fans. Then, on second down from the Dolphin forty yard line, the quarterback connected with Tim on a beautifully executed double reverse flea flicker. Tim blasted the last five yards into the end zone. The crowd surged to their feet with a roar of approval.

With only thirty seconds on the clock after they scored, the Dolphins hung on for the win, their first all season. The Shepherds collapsed back onto the seats with joyful laughter. A number of people stopped and congratulated them on Tim's performance. Some of them eyed Steve strangely but no one even asked if he was who they suspected. Steve was glad because this night was about Robert and Tim who, given the chance, proved themselves to be more than able.

The crowd cleared out slowly. Rather than joining the traffic jam, Steve and the Shepherds sat in the bleachers for a while. Gloria wouldn't need to pick up the boys from the high school for at least an hour since after their games they always ate a dinner provided by some of the parents.

"What's on the agenda for tomorrow?" Steve asked.

"You wanna surf?" Greg asked.

"Not during the season," Steve shook his head regretfully. "Nothing even remotely dangerous, other than football itself, of course."

"Why not?"

"Part of my contract with God, I guess you could say. When I'm being a Grizzly, I make sure I don't intentionally do anything that could jeopardize my ability to play."

"That's wise," Gloria said. "So how about just a family day? When are you going back?"

"I have a red-eye Sunday evening," Steve said.

"Then how about we call Kenji and Pena guys and do the ohana thing tomorrow?" Gloria suggested.

"Let me see if Nalani feels up to it at our house," Luke said. "That way we don't have to take Naomi out."

"Sunday we can do regular ohana day at my house after church," Steve suggested, "but right now, Greg needs to take me home. I'm still on Chicago time and it's almost four in the morning there. He's probably going to have to carry me into the house as it is. I'm exhausted."

They all stood and started toward the gate.

"First, of course," Steve said, putting his arm around Heather. "I need to walk this gorgeous woman to her car."

Fortunately, Heather wasn't parked far from Steve and Greg. Steve leaned against the passenger side of the car and gathered Heather into his arms.

"It's been a wonderful evening," Steve sighed, "but I'm so tired I could fall asleep standing here."

"I'm glad you came," Heather said.

"So am I," Steve chuckled. "You really are a football fan, aren't you?"

Heather blushed and ducked her head against his chest.

"Hey, no shame sistah," Steve said softly. "I love that you love the game. And you understand it too! That's so cool."

"Not everyone thinks so," Heather wrinkled her nose.

"Everyone who counts does," Steve assured her with a huge yawn. "We know you live life honestly, no holds barred. No half-stepping for you."

"You," Heather said, tapping his chest with her finger, "need to let my brother take you home now. I'll see you in the morning."

"Come for breakfast?"

"Are you cooking or is Greg?"

"Me, of course."

"Then it's a deal."

Steve gently kissed Heather's forehead and opened her car door. He watched her drive away before walking slowly to his car.

Greg drove again even though he didn't like driving Steve's car, especially with him in it. Rather than whipping a u-turn as he would have done in his car, Greg went down Auwaiolimu and turned right on Nehoa which quickly turned into Prospect.

"Hey brah, thanks for what you did for Tim and Robert tonight," Greg said as they passed the middle school on the side of the Punchbowl. "It means a lot to me."

"I don't understand why the coach wasn't playing them," Steve said tiredly. "They're obviously good. He had to know that."

"Sometimes being good isn't good enough," Greg said with a heavy sigh. "It was probably my fault."

"Yours! How so?"

"Coaches in Hawaii have long memories. I was pretty good when I was in high school but I couldn't maintain my academic eligibility my junior and senior years. Coach couldn't depend on me. Family connections mean a lot in Hawaii. Coach is apparently afraid to depend on Tim and Robert because they're my brothers. Too bad he couldn't remember Luke was dependable, but then again he says he wasn't as good as I was."

"I don't like it but I understand. I saw it in Kansas too. Guys who should have played didn't and guys who shouldn't have played did, just because of family connections."

Steve wanted to ask why Greg, who was extremely intelligent, couldn't maintain his academic eligibility, but he was just too tired. Greg didn't have to carry him into the house but he did have to wake him up and keep his sleepy brain on track or he wouldn't have even found the door to the house.

THE WEEKEND WAS a peaceful time for Steve. Lots of laughter and fun punctuated quiet, restful moments of companionship with the family and sweet stolen moments with Heather. They continued to creep closer and closer to the time when their commitment would be made and their lives would begin to irrevocably change. Love had already forever changed who they were inside but their lives were still more inclined to what they had been apart than what they could become together.

The more time he spent with Heather, the more Steve was sure that he wanted to make the commitment to marriage, to change his life and make her an important part of it. However, he also grew acutely aware of what Heather would be sacrificing to make that commitment. As he watched her with her big, boisterous, loving family, he ached to think of her alone in Chicago without them. Was it right for him to ask her to give up all this, even if it might only be for a few years?

On the other hand, how could he not ask her? She was so deeply entrenched in his heart that he couldn't imagine himself in Chicago next year without her. It was hard enough to go back from this trip.

On Sunday evening, Heather and Moose took him to the airport. Steve waited until then to ask a crucial question. "Since the Dolphins aren't going to the playoffs, will you be coming to the game in Chicago in three weeks?"

"I don't know," Heather smiled. "We're considering it."

"What's to consider?" Steve complained.

"Time off. Who can go," Heather quickly decided not to reveal too much. "We do have lives you know."

"Ah yes. School, work, babies, and dogs," Steve sighed. "Sometimes I forget that some people actually have real lives. Not everyone's life revolves around football."

"Nope," Heather laughed. "Mere mortals squeeze it into their lives, while the titans make it their lives."

"It's not my life, Heather," Steve said seriously. "It hasn't been for a long time. I'm willing to walk away from it."

"But you aren't going to, Steve," Heather said as she took the airport ramp off the H1 freeway. "It's God's will for your life. You make a difference in many people's lives."

"Why don't I see it?" Steve frowned.

"You plant seeds that others water," Heather said gently. "Besides, you have seen it, in Tim and Robert."

"They just needed a chance is all," Steve shrugged.

"I'm not talking about just Friday night," Heather said. "I'm talking about the prayer breakfast and that little thing last spring."

"Oh that!" Steve sounded surprised.

"Yes, that," Heather pulled over to the curb and turned off the car. She walked around the car, stepping up on the sidewalk with Steve after he closed the trunk.

Slipping her arms around his waist, Heather hugged him tight before stepping back and softly stroking his cheek.

"You keep playing and I'll keep praying. In God's time, I'll be ready to follow you," she smiled sassily. "'To infinity and beyond!'"

Steve laughed and leaned over to give her a quick kiss on the cheek.

"I'll be happy with a simple golf course," he whispered.

Then he was walking into the terminal, turning to wave before ducking through the doors.

Chapter 28

*W*hen Steve called on Wednesday evening, Heather was ready with a scolding. She barely gave him time for his customary greeting.

"Hi Beautiful."

"I got a strange phone call today."

"You did?" Steve sounded wary.

"A local travel agent thinks she has an expense account for me."

"Oh that," Steve gave a relieved sigh. "I imagine she does. I asked my accountant to set it up."

"Your accountant?"

"You didn't think I handled all that money by myself, did you?"

Heather was silent.

"You know I get paid an obscene amount of money to play football."

Still no reply.

"We talked about this the first day we met, remember?"

The silence stretched on as Heather struggled to grasp the full impact of what she'd only been vaguely aware of before.

"You were the one who brought it up. Millions of dollars every year."

Still nothing but a puzzled silence.

"The car, the house, the motorcycles," Steve said. "You know I have money."

"Have money, yes." The dam finally burst. "But ... but not that! ... Not millions. You're such a regular guy. Well, not regular regular because you're so huge and strong and built. But you're normal. You're funny and smart and you like my family." Heather knew Steve was laughing at her but she couldn't seem to stop the flood. "And you wrestle with my brothers and play with Moose and you're an orphan and you're claustrophobic and ... and –"

"None of which keeps me from being obscenely wealthy," Steve was finally able to break into her flood of words. "Or from being as obtuse as any other man. I was halfway to Chicago when it dawned on me that you all couldn't afford the flight and the hotel to come to the games."

"So you fixed it."

"No Heather," Steve knew what she was thinking. "This is neither a hand up nor a hand out. This is a plea from me. ... Every week I'm surrounded by thousands of fans but I'm lonely. I go back to my home or hotel room, alone. ... It wasn't so bad before ... before you and your family came into my life."

Steve didn't want to cry but when he heard Heather's ragged breathing, the tears began to fall. He leaned his forehead against the cool glass of the lanai doors in his Chicago penthouse.

"Now I feel the loneliness like I haven't since Jenni left," Steve sighed. "It would mean so much to me to have you all up there watching me, like you watch Robert and Tim."

There was a long silence.

"I'll see what we can do," Heather said grumpily, "but don't you start thinking you're going to be getting your way all the time."

Steve smiled out at the Chicago skyline, imagining Heather's sassy look as she lightened the mood.

"Next time," she sniffed loudly, "you better come up with something much better than the poor little rich boy routine!"

Steve laughed.

"I'm serious," Heather scolded. "Robert Downey, Jr. does it much better in *Iron Man*."

"Oh Heather, my love," Steve laughed. "What would I do without you?"

THE GRIZZLIES NEXT game was a Sunday evening home game. Since Heather was no longer secluding herself to watch the games, the whole family gathered with Greg to watch the game on the big screen TV in the family room at Steve's house.

It was Grizzly ball from the opening kick. They won the toss and elected to receive. The Berserkers couldn't stop the Grizzly kick returner and they were up by seven. They never looked back.

Grizzly offense scored on every possession in the first quarter, and they had plenty. The defense totally shut down the Berserker's offense, allowing them only seven passing yards and a negative fifteen yards rushing, with no first downs. The quarterback was sacked three times, fumbled twice and had three incomplete passes. Almost every time Steve was right there.

During the halftime show the commentators discussed Steve's performance when they reported on the game.

"Jeremiah is *hot* tonight!"

"He is *brutalizing* that quarterback."

"He's been hot all season. What's with the man?"

"Maybe he's finally found a woman."

"Bet she's holding out for a ring and he's taking out his frustration on the field."

"Yeah, but what ring is she holding out for, a diamond or a championship ring?"

Heather stared in stunned silence at the television screen.

"Chill Heather," Luke patted her knee. "They're idiots, you know that."

"They're just trying too hard to be funny," Greg said as he leaned over the couch above her. "Don't let them get to you."

Heather stood slowly and planted her fists on her hips.

"We'll see," she shook her head at the television then turned to her family. "Who's up for some live football next Sunday?"

"Me!" Mom's hand shot up in the air.

"Our last game is Friday night," Tim looked at Robert. "It's a short flight to L.A."

"All my classes are Tuesday through Thursday," Greg grinned. "Just get me home before bedtime on Monday."

FIRST THING MONDAY morning Heather called Steve's travel agent and got everything arranged. Fortunately the agent even knew whom to contact to make sure they got their tickets when they arrived in Los Angeles.

Everyone agreed that they wouldn't tell Steve they were coming. They wanted to surprise him just as he had surprised them during the bye week. They flew in on Saturday morning, spent a leisurely day catching some sights and went to church in the evening since the game was on Sunday morning.

None of them had ever been to a professional game before, just the Superstar Game which was more of an exhibition than a game. Even then they had sat in the nose-bleed section. This time their seats were close to the action, the third row up, just to the right of the fifty yard line on the Grizzly side of the field.

When the Grizzlies trotted out onto the field, Heather felt a surge of pride seeing Steve at the front as one of the defensive captains. Even among all these big men, he was huge. Mom, Tim and Robert were as excited to see him as Heather was, but Greg was playing it cool. He even reminded Heather that Pete was out there too, right next to Steve. Somehow she had missed him.

Heather was disappointed when the Grizzlies won the toss because of course they elected to receive. It was a very long five minutes and thirty-six seconds before Steve jogged onto the field after the rushing touchdown. Heather felt chicken skin rise from the top of her head all the way down to her toes. This was so much better than even a big screen TV.

The Shepherds thundered and roared with the rest of the Grizzly fans as they watched the two teams battle up and down the field. The Wolves took almost eight minutes to answer the Grizzlies seven with a field goal. They paid dearly for every inch, especially when they tried going up the left side past Steve. The wide receiver caught his five yard pass but was immediately pounded into the turf. The running back gained mere inches if that. Balls were batted down. Going up the left side, the Wolves gained less than five yards in their fifty yard push to get into kicking range.

The Grizzlies got the ball back with two minutes left in the quarter. They drove down the field and put up their own field goal in the opening minute of the second quarter. That was the last score of the first half as the rest of the second quarter belonged to the defensive squads. The Grizzlies went into halftime up by seven.

The Shepherds decided to complete their first professional game experience by buying overpriced hotdogs, nachos and soda. They barely made it back to their seats before the teams returned to the field. They settled in to enjoy the second half of the game, groaning and cheering as the Grizzly defense gave up yards then took them back.

Then it happened. Two minutes and seventeen seconds into the third quarter the referee threw a flag, on Steve, right in front of Heather.

"Face mask! Are you crazy?" Heather raged to her feet. "That was no face mask. You need an eye exam ref!"

Laughing and blushing, Gloria tried to pull Heather down but it was too late. The ref ignored her, but Steve suddenly stopped and turned.

Heather was easy to spot, standing with her three big little brothers, all in number ninety-five jerseys. They could see Steve grin as he trotted backwards a few steps before turning to run to the defensive huddle.

The referee's call stood even though the Jumbotron showed that Heather was right, it wasn't a legitimate face mask penalty. At the worst it was inadvertent, but even that was iffy. Still, the Wolves got the fifteen yards. Then Steve took it back, with change, just two plays later.

It was a beautiful, brutal hit, one that shook the rafters. The running back fell toward the turf and Steve reached in and stripped the ball from him. After two stumbling steps while he got control of the ball, Steve tucked it and ran all the way to the end zone for the score. Then he trotted along the Grizzly line, back toward the Shepherds. With a graceful leap, he gently tossed the ball to Heather. Landing lightly on his feet, Steve pulled his helmet off then grinned and winked before trotting back to the bench.

A clever camera crew caught the sideline action and suddenly Heather realized that she and her brothers were up on the Jumbotron. She blushed and sat down quickly, hugging the football.

"Dang," Greg groaned. "I finally get on TV and I can't even say, 'Hi, Mom,' 'cause she's sitting right next to me! That just ain't fair."

That turned out to be the play of the game. When the Grizzlies held on to win by fourteen, Steve was once again named MVP. Later, Luke and Nalani told them that after the game the commentators took pleasure in showing the sideline handoff whenever they showed the play that preceded it.

The Shepherds watched the post game activities on the field, debating what they should do, how they would hook up with Steve after the game. Finally the man himself broke away from the people around him and loped over.

Steve had taken off his pads and jersey. His hair and sleeveless midriff-length t-shirt were soaked with sweat and his bare arms glistened. He was adorable and Heather's heart beat triple time.

"Where are you all staying?" Steve asked Heather with a gorgeous smile. Greg answered for her.

"That's the same hotel we're in," Steve was surprised. "What's your room number? I'll call when I get back in."

He blew a kiss to Heather and then ran off to the locker room.

Heather sighed theatrically then sank back into her seat.

"I think I'm in love," she sighed.

"Wow! I didn't see that coming," Greg feigned shock.

"Like a bolt out of the blue," Robert chortled.

"Yes, what surprise," Gloria laughed.

"Et tu, Brute," Heather pressed her hand over her heart and rolled her eyes in grief at her mom.

They all laughed as they gathered up their things and left to find the ride that their travel agent had arranged. None of them noticed the figure standing in the shadows.

Chapter 29

Steve met them in Heather's brothers' room about two hours later. He expressed his delight with their surprise but scolded them for not letting him spend Saturday evening with them. When Pete stopped in to say "aloha" before the team took off, the Shepherds discovered that the team usually went back to Chicago the same day as the game but Steve had changed his flight time to early in the morning. They had the whole evening together.

They had dinner in a restaurant downstairs, a Mexican one with an atmosphere much more suited to their boisterousness than the French one. Tim decided to try the "authentic" Mexican hot sauce and everyone laughed uncontrollably over his extreme distress, unquenched by water. Greg requested a love song from the mariachi band. When they obliged, Heather's brothers joined them in a horrid off-key howl that had Steve breathless with laughter. They declared victory in the romantic music department since Steve "swooned" over their sister. The band decided to agree and they invited the gringos to join them in another number, then another. Soon everyone was singing and new customers were lining up to see what the fun was all about.

It was nearing ten o'clock when Steve finally asked Heather if she'd like to take a stroll.

"Where do we stroll at night in this part of L.A.?" Heather asked.

"Right here in the hotel," Steve said. "They have a little mall where we can window shop. Some stores might even still be open."

"Window shopping with a guy?" Heather frowned. "Can that happen?"

"It can when the guy is crazy in love and wants any excuse to prolong the evening," Steve drawled.

"Well then, okay," Heather agreed a little breathlessly.

Steve tucked her hand in the crook of his arm and they strolled out of the restaurant, taking a left as they went out the door. Sure enough, next to the restaurant was a clothing store that Heather hadn't noticed earlier. In the window stood a stunning silk and lace long black dress with jeweled butterflies cavorting over it.

"That dress would be gorgeous on you," Steve smiled down at her.

"I don't know. I think it's a little ostentatious," Heather wrinkled up her nose at him. She pointed to another dress hanging behind it. "That one would probably be better."

"You're right," Steve said, still looking at Heather.

"How would you know?" Heather laughed and pushed him lightly with her shoulder. "You didn't even look at it."

"Don't have to," Steve said smugly. "If it's on you, it's going to look gorgeous. You make coveralls look gorgeous."

"Do not!" Heather denied.

Steve just smiled. Heather tossed her head and pulled him away from the window. "Come. There are more windows to shop."

They strolled along for a few minutes, turning left again at the end of the hall to look at more shops. They stopped in front of a toy store and Heather started laughing. At Steve's questioning look, she pointed back to the end of the hall where her mother and brothers stood, window shopping also.

"I feel like I'm in a movie, but I can't remember which one!"

"Wasn't there a scene like this in *Fiddler on the Roof*?" Steve laughed too.

"Maybe. I can't remember right now," she leaned toward him a little and sighed. "I don't seem to be thinking too clearly."

Greg coughed loudly.

"Which means it's a good thing we have chaperones," Steve smiled softly as he stroked some stray wisps of hair off her cheek. "Because my brain's a little mushy too."

"Someone call a fire truck," Robert said loudly.

"Yeah, somethin' is *s-mokin'* down there," Tim sounded just like Jim Carrey in *The Mask*.

"Your family is pretty special," Steve said.

"If you mean like special circumstances in a homicide, I guess you're right," Heather rolled her eyes.

Steve laughed and turned her away from her brothers. "Let's walk."

They walked all the way around the hotel mall, taking their time. Somewhere along the line, Mom slipped away but Greg, Tim and Robert remained in their shadow.

It took them almost an hour to circle the tiny mall. As they approached the front hall, Steve sighed. "As much as I would like this evening together to go on, wisdom warns me that I need to sleep. It was a long day and I'm tired."

"It was a wonderful day," Heather smiled. They walked to the elevators. "I'm glad we came."

"Me too," Steve said. "Are you coming to Chicago next week?"

"I sure hope so," Heather sighed.

The elevator dinged, the doors opened, and suddenly they were swept into the elevator by Heather's brothers.

"That was certainly an educational experience," Robert sighed loudly as he punched the button for their floor.

Steve reached over and pressed the one for two floors up.

"One should always get a good education," he said dryly, then he smiled down at Heather. "I'll hand you over to the three stooges now rather than walking you to your door. I'll see you next week, hopefully with better looking company!"

"Musketeers," Greg said. "We're the musketeers, not the stooges. And the company can't get any better looking than what's right here in the elevator with you guys."

"Whatever," Steve said without taking his eyes off Heather. "If you can, come early and bring the stooges to my place for dinner Saturday night."

"Sounds like a plan," Heather smiled as the elevator dinged again and the doors whispered open.

"Musketeers," Tim and Robert said emphatically.

"Whatever," Steve said as he leaned against the back wall and blew a kiss to Heather before the doors closed again.

THE NEXT MORNING, Mom was in the shower and Heather was dressed and already packing when the room phone rang. Curious about why her brothers would call her when they could just knock on the connecting door, she picked up the phone and said a cheerful hello. For a moment there was no response on the other end.

"H-hello." It was a woman's voice. "I ... you don't know me. ... I'm sorry ... to bother you. ... Um, I wondered if I could meet you. ... Oh, I'm sorry. My name is Jenni."

"Steve's Jenni?" Heather whispered as she sat down on the bed.

"He told you about me?" Jenni was surprised.

"Oh yes, Jenni. He sure has."

"Can you come down and talk?"

"Are you downstairs now?"

"Yes."

"I'll be right down. I'll meet you in the café."

"Um, Heather. It is Heather, right? Please don't tell anyone who you're meeting."

"Why not?"

"Let me explain when you come down."

"Okay. I'll be right there."

Heather hung up the phone and grabbed her purse and room key. She banged on the bathroom door and called out to her mom that she was going downstairs for a while. Just in case Mom hadn't heard, she also knocked on her brothers' door. All Greg wanted to know was whether she planned to leave the hotel or not. They told her to enjoy her breakfast in the coffee shop, but they were ordering room service.

It wasn't hard to spot Jenni when she got down to the café, she was the only woman around who could look Heather in the eye when standing. She also had Steve's blue, blue eyes and dark hair.

"This is really awkward," Jenni rubbed her temples with both hands. "I feel like a stalker or something, but I didn't intend for this to happen."

Heather looked startled and Jenni gave a small laugh. "Let me start over. I went to the game yesterday because I wanted to see my brother play. I saved up for a long time to get a good seat where I could actually see him. I had no idea he was involved with someone or that you would be there, but I guess God was orchestrating things."

The waitress approached and Heather ordered hazelnut coffee. Jenni asked for a refill on her regular coffee.

"I noticed you all right off," Jenni continued her story after the waitress left. "It was hard not to, as big as you all are and all in Jeremiah jerseys." She laughed a little. "When you went off about that flag, you stole the words right out of my mouth! I was intrigued. Then when Steve came back and gave you the ball, I was stunned. I don't really even know much about the rest of the game because I was watching you and your family."

Jenni blinked back tears. The waitress approached with the coffee and she waited to continue.

"I'm so happy for Steve, that he's finally found a real family," Jenni smiled sadly. "I guess you know that ours was ... shall we say pretty bad?"

"Your childhood was horrendous," Heather said flatly, covering Jenni's trembling hand with her own. "No one should ever have to live like that."

"Yesterday," Jenni wiped away tears. "I didn't intend to make any contact with anyone, just watch Steve like I used to do when he was younger but I couldn't leave the stadium until he did, knowing as I do that I might never get that close to him again. I was still watching when he came over, asked where you were staying then asked for the room number."

"And you struggled with yourself all night, trying to decide if you were supposed to use the information or not," Heather smiled.

"Exactly. I finally decide that if Steve was still here, I wouldn't do anything with it. So I called the hotel and asked to be connected with his room. They said he'd already checked out, so I knew I had to come and try to meet you."

"Why don't you want to see Steve?" Heather asked. "He loves you so much. He's been looking for you for years."

"I know he loves me," Jenni blinked back tears, "but he doesn't need me in his life."

"Why do you think that?"

"Do you ...? Does he ...?" Jenni bit her lip. "Did he figure out why I left?"

Heather nodded with tears in her eyes. Jenni ducked her head. "Then you know why he doesn't need me in his life."

"No, I don't," Heather said firmly. "You own no shame for what happened to you."

"But I do for what I did after," Jenni began to cry, trying to hide her tears behind her hand.

Heather made a quick decision. Pulling her phone out of her purse, she called her mom. While it was ringing Heather reached out to Jenni, helping her to her feet. The waitress headed their way. Heather waved her room card at her and told her to put their coffees on her room tab.

"Mom," Heather said without preamble. "I need the room to myself for awhile."

"Why?"

"Not now, please Mom," Heather said. "I'll explain later if I can. Please go have breakfast with the guys. I'll meet you there when I'm pau."

"Okay, but this isn't –?"

"No Mom. Steve's already gone. This is nothing you would object to if I were free to tell you what it was about."

"Okay honey. I'll have breakfast with the boys. Do I tell them you sent me?"

"No! Please don't."

"Okay. I love you, Heather."

"I love you too, Mom." By this time they had reached the elevators.

"In case you didn't figure it out," Heather told Jenni. "We're going up to my room to talk in private."

"Thank you," Jenni said. "But you don't –"

"Oh yes I do," Heather said. "I fully expect to be your sister-in-law sometime in the hopefully not too distant future so I most certainly do!"

"Steve's a lucky man," Jenni said as they stepped into the elevator.

"Oh we'll have our ups and downs," Heather smiled, "but I think we're both blessed."

"So you're a Christian," Jenni observed more than asked.

"Since I was a little tyke," Heather smiled softly. "Steve is too."

"I know," Jenni smiled too. "I know a lot about Steve. It's not too hard to follow what's going on in his life."

"No it isn't," Heather agreed. "What about you? Are you a Christian?"

"Not much of one yet," Jenni said. "I got saved in a shelter about six months ago but I don't really know what I'm doing yet."

"That's simple to fix," Heather grinned broadly as the elevator doors opened for them. "Not easy, but simple."

Heather stepped into the room first to make sure that Mom had already gone to her brothers' room. When she heard Mom's voice next door, she motioned Jenni into the room. Heather started coffee in the room's coffee pot then she sat cross-legged in the middle of the double bed and patted the bed in front of her.

"Come sit and let's talk."

Jenni kicked off her shoes and climbed slowly onto the bed, mirroring Heather's pose.

"I'm going to tell you what I know and make some guesses about what I don't," Heather told Jenni. "You can agree with me, correct me, or interrupt me at anytime, okay?"

Jenni nodded.

"The reason I'm going to do this," Heather kept her voice gentle. "Is because sometimes you want to share things but it's hard. So I'm going to help you as much as I can, okay?"

Jenni nodded again.

"First, you ran away not just because of what your father was doing to you," Heather's voice was like a whisper on a breeze, gently comforting, "but also because you began to fear for Steve's life, didn't you?"

Jenni looked a little surprised but nodded.

"I also have a brother two years younger than me," Heather explained softly. "I remember realizing he was growing into a man. I know what he would have done if we had been in a situation like you and Steve were in. I would have tried to protect him too."

Tears welled in Jenni's eyes.

"You knew that Steve was growing up, that he was becoming more aware, more angry at your father," Heather felt like weeping for both Steve and Jenni. "You were afraid he would end up getting hurt defending you, so you ran away."

"Yes," Jenni whispered.

"But it didn't get better for you when you ran away," Heather felt tears slipping down her cheeks. "You ended up selling your body just to survive."

Again the nod

"Drugs."

Another affirmative.

"Abortion?"

This time Jenni just drew her knees up and buried her face in them.

"And you ended up in an abusive relationship?"

Heather scooted closer to Jenni and stroked her hair.

"Jenni, all this is so familiar to God," she whispered. "Thousands upon thousands of times he's wept with little girls just like you, his heart breaking as he watched the devil try to destroy what he loves. He was weeping and waiting for you to turn to him for safety instead of to all the things the devil tempts you with while you listen to his lies."

Heather continued to stroke Jenni's hair. "When you turned to God, he wiped it all clean. To him, you're as perfect as my beautiful baby niece. Don't you let the devil tell you differently."

Heather sighed. "Now you have to help me. For the life of me, I can't figure out why you wouldn't want to see Steve. He loves you very much. He's never quit looking for you."

"How could he still love me?" Jenni asked with her head still on her knees.

"Because he's a true man of God," Heather said. "Wait a minute. I have something to show you."

Jenni raised her head and watched curiously as Heather rolled to the head of her bed and grabbed the digital camera on the night stand.

"I brought this silly thing for a reason," she muttered as she began pushing buttons on the camera. "Even if I left it sitting in the room the whole time. Ah, here it is."

She handed Jenni the camera so she could see the picture in the preview window.

"Okay," Jenni said doubtfully. "You two make a great-looking couple."

"No silly! Look there, to the right," Heather pointed at the picture again. It was a picture of her and Steve taken at his house two weeks ago in front of the fireplace upstairs, the mantle behind them.

"Is that ... my softball?" Jenni said in amazement. "He kept it all these years?"

"Yes, that's your softball," Heather said. "You snuck into his room the night you left. He was half asleep when you kissed him. You said, 'Hey brat, take care of my ball till I get back, okay?' Steve said, 'Okay. I love you.' You said, 'I love you too,' then you disappeared out of his life."

"He remembers that?" Jenni felt fresh tears falling again. "But he was asleep."

"Not too asleep," Heather smiled. "He kept that ball all those years. It's one thing he never lost."

Heather laughed softly and blushed a little.

"It's still in Honolulu," she said softly. "Last season, before we met, he took it back to Chicago when he left Hawaii but this year he left it."

Heather smiled through softly falling tears. "He said, 'This is home now. You're my heart and this is my home. Jenni belongs with my heart in my home. Watch over her for me, will you please?'"

"He said that? Really?" Jenni was incredulous.

"Yes. That's why you have to go see him," Heather said earnestly. "He loves you and misses you. Not having you is the dark place in his life."

"I can't do that to him," Jenni whispered vehemently, jumping to her feet and pacing the room. "Don't you see that they'll have a field day with it?"

"What do you mean?"

"Here he is at the top of his game, better than he's ever been before, in love and about to be married and the sister shows up with her track marks, two illegitimate brats in tow, haunted by her abusive ex-boyfriend. They'll eat him alive."

"You have children!" Heather latched onto the wonder of it. "Steve has ...?"

"Nieces," Jenni sunk back down onto the bed. "Karasi is eight and Anastacia is four."

"Steve has nieces," Heather laughed. "He'll be so excited. Do you have pictures?"

"Yes," Jenni dove into her purse, pulling out a small photo album. She stopped suddenly without opening it. "I'm a good mother, I promise."

She clutched the album to her chest, begging with her eyes for Heather to understand.

"I was off the drugs even before I knew I was pregnant with Kara," she said earnestly. "I quit prostitution completely as soon as I knew I was pregnant. I didn't want another abortion. I wanted to be a mother. I ran away again but this time I ran to a shelter. They helped me find a job, keep the baby."

She began to cry again.

"When Kara was two, I met Bill. He seemed so sweet and we lived together for just over a year. When I got pregnant with Ana, I thought we'd get married. I got beat instead." She wiped tears away furiously. "I left that night with Kara, pressed charges against him and I never looked back. I got help from another shelter, got back on my feet."

Jenni hung her head in shame.

"Then I did it again, walked into a relationship with another man like my father," her lips began to tremble. "I let Mason beat me for almost a year because I had decided that's just the way things are. Then one night he looked at Kara and it was like seeing my father look at me."

She hugged the album close.

"I waited until he fell asleep that night," she whispered. "I packed some things and we left. He's found me twice and I left again, both times. I'll do it as many times as it takes because he's not going to ever touch my baby."

"Steve will help you," Heather said. "I know he wants to."

"No! You can't tell him," Jenni said. "I'm not ready. Please say you won't tell him. Let me tell him in my time."

"Okay, but there are a couple of conditions," Heather said.

"What are they?" Jenni asked warily.

"Move to Chicago," Heather said. "Be close to him so that the next time you feel like running, you can run to him."

"I would love to, but how can I do that? I don't have enough money to go halfway across the country."

"I'll help you," Heather smiled. "I'll give you a hand up."

"Why should –?"

"Like I told you before, Jenni, I intend to be your sister-in-law sometime in the spring. You're family, and family helps each other out."

"If we can work it out, okay," Jenni agreed. "It'll be much harder for Mason to find me there anyway. ... What's your other condition?"

"You have to see him before February when he goes back to Honolulu," Heather said firmly.

"Why?"

"Because I'm a horrible liar, especially around Steve," Heather sighed dreamily. "It won't take but a day or two until he knows I have a secret and I'll end up blurting it out."

Jenni began to giggle. "That's a terrible problem for a woman in love to have."

"Tell me about it," Heather rolled her eyes. "Now, let's look at those pictures."

Chapter 30

*H*eather quickly found out that Steve wasn't the biggest challenge she was going to have in keeping Jenni's secret, her family was. While they were still at LAX, she casually announced that she was going to stay the next week in Chicago since the Grizzlies had back-to-back home games. Mom and Greg both exploded while Tim and Robert frowned in disapproval.

"I'm not going to stay with Steve," Heather said haughtily, "so chill."

"You aren't even going to tempt yourself with it," Mom scolded her. "You're going to fly back to Honolulu and return the following week, like you know you should."

"No I shouldn't," Heather said. "I have something that I need to do so I'm staying."

"Then I'll stay with you," Mom said, "and Greg can stay with the boys at the house."

That was tempting but Mom wasn't part of the plan with Jenni. She'd insisted no one but Heather could know. Besides, Mom couldn't keep a secret any better than Heather could.

"No Mom," Heather said firmly. "You will not. I can take care of myself. I'll stay in Chicago for one week, by myself."

"Over my dead body," Greg glared at her.

"Don't tempt me, punk," Heather glared back.

She was temporarily saved from further argument when they had to board the plane but unfortunately Greg was seated next to her on the aisle. She was trapped in her window seat. He waited until they were airborne before he resumed the subject.

"Don't do this Heather," Greg pleaded. "It doesn't make sense."

"It makes perfect sense to me," Heather said. "I'm doing it, so drop it."

"You've been my best friend all my life," Greg said sadly. "I've never been ashamed of anything you did. You've always been the epitome of womanhood to me. This ... this hurts."

"Can't you just trust me that I am not going to be with Steve?" Heather whispered.

"Can't you just trust me enough to tell me what you are going to be doing?" Greg whispered back.

"You punk," Heather started crying. "I hate it when you do this to me!"

Greg just sat there, waiting. His eyebrows twitched once. Other than that he sat like a rock.

Greg was excellent at keeping secrets. He would definitely be a help in Chicago. "Okay, but you can't tell anyone else."

Another twitch, then the rock. "Okay Luke too, but no one else. That's it. The three amigos, okay?"

"Okay."

So Heather and her brothers went to Chicago for a week. They of course couldn't keep their true purpose from Nalani from whom Luke couldn't keep a secret if he wanted to. She was in favor of the mission, except for keeping it a secret from Steve, and she helped them with internet searches for information.

The Shepherds left Honolulu on Thursday evening after Greg's last class. Greg got excused from his classes the next week when he explained that he had a family emergency. They didn't tell Steve how early they were arriving because they wanted to use Friday and Saturday to go apartment hunting. Jenni and the girls were driving over from California, arriving late Monday morning and the Shepherds wanted to narrow the field of possibilities for them. By Saturday evening when they showed up at Steve's for dinner, they had already lined up three potential apartments for Jenni to live in. Since they were trying to keep her in Steve's neighborhood, it was obvious that the rent was going to be more expensive than Jenni could afford. They decided they would use a simple subterfuge. They would put the lease in Luke's name, telling Jenni that it would be harder for Mason to find her that way. Together they would pay the difference without Jenni ever knowing.

The Grizzlies won their Sunday afternoon game by a comfortable margin. Rather than letting Steve fix dinner after he played so hard, Heather and her brothers insisted that they have dinner at a restaurant in their hotel. Since Pete was a permanent fixture in Steve's life especially here in Chicago where he lived right across the hall, he joined them. Steve was upset because they were staying at the hotel.

"I still don't know why you don't just stay at my place," Steve grumbled as they took their seats around the table. "I have plenty room."

"Heather is not staying in your apartment regardless of how many of her brothers are here," Luke said with finality, snapping open his menu and carefully perusing it to show that the conversation was over.

"It's a penthouse," Steve complained, not wanting to let the subject die.

"Like that makes a difference," Greg snorted in disbelief. "You're pathetic."

Steve couldn't win the argument because the Shepherds were concerned not only with avoiding temptation but also with keeping Jenni's secret. It would be virtually impossible if they were staying in Steve's penthouse.

On Monday morning when Jenni called to say they'd arrived, Heather and Luke went down to meet them since Greg was still getting ready. He had overslept because neither of his siblings wanted to wake him. They knew he worked too hard with his two part-time jobs and his full schedule at school. He often didn't get enough sleep anymore so he was using his mini-vaction to make up some lost sleep.

Jenni frowned at Heather when she saw that Luke was with her. He looked way too much like Greg, whom Jenni had seen in Los Angeles, to be anyone other than Heather's brother. Luke squatted down to talk to her daughters and Jenni grabbed Heather's arm, dragging her off to the side.

"You promised it was just us," Jenni hissed. "You lied to me."

"Don't get all huhu about my lie, Jenni," Heather said dryly. "You're asking me to lie to the man I love, so at least give me the decency of hearing me out before you jump all over me."

"It better be good," Jenni glared.

"Or what, you'll run away again?" Heather glared back. "I don't think so Jenni. I think you're done running."

"I think," Jenni said with a slow, sly smile, "my little brother is getting into more trouble than he knows."

"I don't know what you're talking about," Heather said with admirable sincerity. "I had to tell my brothers because I realized that you and I couldn't do this by ourselves. Two women and two keiki in a town that none of us knows? Luke and Greg have already helped tremendously. We have three apartments for you to look at this afternoon. They're all empty which means you'll probably get to move in this week once you pick the one you want. My brothers will provide plenty of muscle to help with that. They'll help with the girls too. And they're both great at keeping a secret. As I told you before, I'm not. They'll cover for you and keep me from blowing it."

"He seems nice enough," Jenni looked over at Luke and the girls. Ana was already holding out her arms for him to carry her. "Do they know about ... what I ...?"

"They don't know anything about your past that Steve doesn't already know," Heather assured her, "and Luke probably not even that much. He's not gotten as close to Steve as Greg has."

"Okay, but if they tell, I'm going to be angry," Jenni suddenly grinned and quoted slyly. "'And you won't like me when I'm angry.'"

"I'll bet I won't," Heather laughed. "Somehow I can see you turning all green and Incredible Hulkish, but not ugly. Don't worry. Your secret is safer with my brothers than it is with me!"

They all went up to the suite where Greg was finally ready to face the day. Kara and Ana were delightful and they quickly fell in love with Uncle Luke and Uncle Greg while they shyly adored Aunty Heather. All three Shepherds fervently pleaded with Jenni to let Steve know about the girls but she adamantly insisted that it was one more thing he didn't need at this particular time.

Steve and Pete had practice that day so the Shepherds spent the afternoon with Jenni looking at apartments. They made sure that they included sufficient sightseeing events to have things to talk about when they went to Steve's house that evening.

On Tuesday the Grizzlies didn't practice. It wasn't hard to convince Steve that he should hang out with Heather while the brothers did their own thing, with Jenni and the girls of course. Luke's and Greg's day included seeing the landlord of the apartment Jenni wanted and signing the lease. The landlord gave them the keys immediately so they searched through thrift shops and discount stores to help Jenni start furnishing her new apartment.

Pete was a bit of a problem since he wanted to spend time with Greg and Luke and he couldn't be distracted by hanging out with Heather. Fortunately he still wanted to do his normal Tuesday volunteer work, so they arranged to meet him in the late afternoon. The two groups met up for dinner at a Chicago pizza place because Greg had heard that there was supposed to be something special about Chicago-style pizza. Steve and Heather had gone up Sears Tower and visited museums and art galleries in its vicinity so that evening Heather found lots of stories to share with her brothers so Steve never did get the chance to ask what they'd done all day.

On Wednesday, Jenni and the girls moved from the hotel to their new home. It was a nice little tenth floor apartment with a big, secure playground in the back, just one block from a highly respected grade school and a five minute walk from Jenni's unsuspecting brother. The Shepherds helped her get furniture and line up day care for Ana. Fortunately, Jenni didn't have to find a job since she was working for a national department store that was more than happy to transfer her, at her expense, to a Chicago store. Heather and her brothers also helped her find churches in her area.

Thursday and Friday all six of them did some serious sightseeing since there wasn't much left to do to get Jenni moved in. She only had a few boxes to unpack and there weren't that many purchases to put in place. By Friday evening, the apartment had beds and dressers for Jenni and her daughters, a dining room table, a couch and two armchairs. The washer and dryer had come with the apartment along with all the major kitchen appliances. Jenni had enough dishes, bedding and towels. Heather and her brothers even made sure that they had a few of the things that make a residence become a home, like framed pictures of Steve for the walls, some knickknacks for the girls' room and scented bubble bath for Jenni.

The Shepherds said goodbye to Jenni and the girls early Saturday afternoon. They were spending the evening with Steve and Pete who had Saturday practice for half a day. After the game on Sunday morning, they were taking a late afternoon flight to Honolulu.

Once again they all begged Jenni to tell Steve. Once again she demurred, but she did promise them to pray about it. They promised to see her when they were in town for the home games.

Sunday's game started well. After four straight wins, the Grizzly fans were cautiously optimistic about their offense and extremely excited about their defense. The defense didn't disappoint but the offense did. Pete and Steve scored the only Grizzly points of the game. Pete got a touchdown off an interception and together they sacked the quarterback in the end zone for a safety. Unfortunately their nine points were not enough to beat the Sharks' touchdown and field goal.

"This is the week I need consoling," Steve moaned when they stopped at Cracker Barrel on the way to the airport, "and you have to leave. Can't you stay, just till Wednesday?"

"No can do Goliath," Heather smiled. "Moose has a big day on Wednesday. He has his first career day."

"Well good for him," Steve pouted. "Give him the directions and let him go by himself."

"Petulant when we lose, are we?" Luke said.

"It's your own fault, ya know," Greg said.

"Mine! How's that?" Steve was surprised.

"You should have won MVP last week," Greg said confidently.

"What?" Steve fought a laugh. He didn't want to laugh. "How do you figure that?"

"It's simple logic you know," Heather said innocently. "Even I get it."

"Not Shepherd logic, please!" Steve dropped his head in both hands and groaned. "Please, please, do not attempt to explain your simple logic."

"Please do Greg," Luke said. "Steve, don't listen."

"It's like this," Heather started the explanation. "The first two games of the season, Steve would have won MVP if the Grizzlies had won, right?"

"Right," Greg said smugly, "and the next three games he did win MVP, 'cause the Grizzlies won."

"So then the Grizzlies won but Steve didn't get MVP," Heather said.

"Ah! So that means," Luke finished, "that they can't win again until Steve would have gotten MVP if they did win."

"Simple logic," Heather said with a smile.

Steve stared at them all for a long moment, trying very hard not to smile.

"You mock my pain." He slumped back and sniffed sadly, rubbing a finger across his cheek as if wiping at tears. "You're heartless, every one of you."

Greg suddenly threw himself to his right, plastering his ear to Luke's chest. He listened for a few seconds then sat up again.

"Nope, you're wrong," Greg informed Steve. "He has a heart! I heard it."

Heather flopped her head over onto Greg's chest. "Yep, I hear it." She sat back up and smiled at Steve. "Greg has a heart too."

Steve looked at Heather for a moment, then he looked at Greg and Luke. He looked back at Heather and his left eyebrow began to rise. When he started to straighten up with a sly smile on his face, her brothers deduced his intent.

"She has a heart," Luke reached over and grasped Steve's shoulder.

"Trust me! It beats true," Greg pulled Heather's chair next to his and wrapped an arm around her.

"I'll trust you, for now," Steve laughed, "but when we go golfing ...."

"Then it will beat only for you, Goliath," Heather smiled sweetly.

"What's this about golf?" Luke asked. Steve and Greg laughed and Heather blushed. Luke laid both arms on the table and leaned toward his sister. "Oh this I gotta hear. Fess up, Shadow."

She didn't but Greg did, with embellishments. The laughter and high-jinks continued and Steve felt peace settle over his heart again.

He must have missed some subtle sign because Heather's brothers suddenly stood at the same time.

"I want to go look in the gift shop, see if I can find something for Nalani and the kids," Luke said much too casually.

"Yeah, we've been gone so long, we better go back bearing gifts," Greg agreed.

"I'll take care of this," Luke picked up the bill before Steve could get it. "You two kids enjoy some more coffee."

"And try to behave," Greg suggested.

"That was weird," Steve said. "Your brothers just willingly left us alone."

"It was planned. It's okay since we're in public," Heather said. "I found something for you and they don't like to watch the mushy stuff."

"Mushy with you sounds good to me," Steve smiled warmly and scooted his chair closer to Heather's.

"When I was walking around window shopping on Saturday morning with ... the guys," Heather hesitated over the tiny lie. She should have worded that differently, left out her companion altogether. "I saw this. It isn't unique or anything but I think it's perfect for us."

She smiled shyly as she opened the box that she had taken from her bag. Steve saw the necklaces with the twin charms, half circles with jagged inside edges that fit perfectly together like pieces of a puzzle.

"The Mizpah," Steve said. "'The Lord watch between me and thee ....'"

"'While we are parted one from the other,'" Heather finished. She took the left side charm which had a thicker sturdier chain.

"Greg said you would probably be able to wear it even when you play," Heather said as she fastened it around his neck. The charm rested just below the hollow of his throat. "It's not a prayer for protection like some people think. It's a statement that God is a witness to our commitment to each other, that neither of us will break it because it's made before him."

Steve carefully removed the other charm with its delicate chain. His hands felt clumsy as he worked the small clasp. Heather lifted her hair as Steve slipped his arms around her neck, fumbling with the clasp a little before he got it hooked. It lay on her breastbone, just a little lower than Steve's charm.

"A witness to our relationship," Steve leaned his forehead against hers. "God is the witness to our love."

Heather touched the charm on Steve's chest. "While we are parted, don't forget my promise. In my heart, only God will ever be before you."

Steve sat with his forehead resting against Heather's, overwhelmed by her love. He thanked God for her and for her crazy family, thanked him that he had brought them into his life. He could no longer remember what life had been like before them, could not imagine what it would be like without them.

Chapter 31

*W*ednesday dawned one of those incredible days that you only get in Hawaii. The sky was a perfect blue with just a few mauka clouds snug against the mountains. The humidity was somewhere around forty percent, the trade winds were just a gentle whisper and the sun stroked the skin just enough to keep the breeze from chilling.

Heather and Moose both had a bounce in their step as they climbed out of the car at the school. Heather had been happy to say yes when Mr. Nakashima, who had now taught algebra to all the Shepherds, called and asked her to bring Moose as part of career day. Had she known how beautiful the day was going to be she might have declined and hit the beach instead. She still could, but some students over by the cafeteria had already spotted her and Moose.

Since she was a few minutes early, Heather and Moose strolled over to talk story with the students. With her back to the parking lot she didn't suspect anything was wrong until suddenly Moose growled with a low warning.

Surprised, Heather looked down. Moose never growled.

"Wazzup Moose?"

Moose growled again and turned toward the parking lot, so Heather looked that way too. She saw a kid in a trench coat coming out of the parking lot and walking toward the school. Every alarm bell in her head went off. People don't wear trench coats in Hawaii.

"Down. Get down," Heather said to the students around her.

"Why –?"

"Just do it, and call 911," Heather snapped as the kid in the trench coat suddenly pointed a gun at the security officer. He wavered a moment then he fired, twice.

Facts flashed through Heathers mind in the space of a breath.

The kid didn't know how to shoot.

The kid wanted to hurt someone.

Her brothers were somewhere in the school.

Even if one of the students had called the cops, they were probably five minutes away.

The kid almost certainly had more weapons in his trench coat.

You can do a lot of damage in five minutes with any kind of weapon.

Moose was a trained therapy dog, not Schutzhund trained. He was in more danger than she was.

The security guard was already down and someone else was going to get hurt too.

She could either seize control now or watch the carnage.

She knew she could take a bullet from that little peashooter and live to tell about it, as long as he fired before she got too close.

And he might miss her.

Thank God he had a thirty-eight instead of a Glock.

If she got shot, it was going to be a long time before she saw Steve.

Before the kid with the gun had taken another step, she had processed the facts and sketched out a plan.

"Down Moose. Stay." Heather snapped out the command.

"Hey kid!" she shouted, striding purposefully toward the gunman.

"Stay back," he shouted, waving the gun. "I'll shoot."

"I know you will," Heather said angrily, "but I won't let you shoot just anyone. Shoot me."

Heather threw up both her arms in a threatening gesture. Shocked and puzzled, the kid pointed the gun at her and hesitated. She kept coming toward him, but at an angle away from the cafeteria. Twenty feet now.

"You ain't got the guts to shoot anyone," Heather snapped angrily. *Lord, please let him shoot now or forever hold his piece.* The kid couldn't fire both accurately and quickly. She'd seen that when he shot the security officer. He'd be lucky if he hit her at all. His second shot would be wide and she would have a couple of seconds before he could get the gun and himself under control for a more accurate shot. She knew she could cover a lot of distance in two seconds.

"You're going down kid," she warned loudly, still moving toward him but at an angle that allowed her to keep enough distance until the students in front of the cafeteria were no longer in his line of fire.

"No!" he screamed at her.

Up in his history classroom, Tim had rushed to the window with the teacher and all the other students as soon as they heard the gunshots. He saw Heather walking toward the kid with the gun. He saw the gun pointed at Heather.

"Heather!" Tim screamed out the window just as the kid below pulled the trigger.

Heather flinched and then ran at the kid, hard and fast, remotely aware that her left shoulder was in agony. She heard the second shot. She hit the kid with a tackle that would have made Steve proud, low and hard, lifting him up off his feet entirely then slamming him back down to the ground. She punched him hard across the jaw then stepped on his gun hand, wrenching the gun away. She stood over the kid with the gun pointed at his breastbone.

Tim didn't see any of it because he was tearing out of the room and down the stairs before the echo of his scream bounced back to the building. Down in the parking lot the girl working on a video project for her multimedia class did see it all, as did a half dozen students by the cafeteria who caught it all with their smart phones.

They saw and recorded it all including when Tim ran out of the building followed by half of his class with the teacher screaming at him to get down. They saw Robert run up from the field where his gym class had been playing soccer, his teacher likewise yelling at him.

"Stay back," Heather shouted at her brothers. "I don't know how long he's going to be out. He's got other weapons in his coat. He might get to them before I can put him down again."

She spotted the teacher behind Robert. "Check on the security guy, back over there. I think he got hit with the first shot."

Then she saw Tim's teacher too. "You. Come here and start taking these weapons from him."

He hesitated.

"Come on, man," she cried. "I'm not in the mood to see a kid shot today, and I don't know how much longer I'm going to be able to hold out. Or how hard I can hit if he comes to."

Suddenly everyone realized that Heather was bleeding heavily from her left shoulder.

Tim turned pale and Heather winked at him. "Mom's going to be so ticked off at me. I'll never get the blood out of this blouse and she made it for me."

The kid on the ground groaned. The teacher flinched back from where he had already gingerly pulled two handguns and a knife from his trench coat.

"Where are the cops?" Heather cried, looking up toward King Street where she could hear sirens coming from the station.

The kid groaned again. Heather gave a frustrated moan, switched the gun to her left hand with a cry of pain, dropped her right knee to the middle of the kid's chest and punched him again, hard. Then she quickly snatched the gun back into her right hand. She didn't rise to her feet again.

The sirens were closer.

"Moose, come," she called loudly, not wanting her dog left under the table until one of her brothers thought to release him.

Moose galloped over as someone yelled, "Drop the gun, now!"

"No, no, it's not her," students were screaming. "It was him, on the ground, in the trench coat."

"Ah, the cavalry has arrived," Heather tossed the gun to her right, toward the teacher who had started to disarm the kid. She looked at Moose.

"You're definitely getting Schutzhund trained. Next week." She fainted.

Tim and Robert both jumped forward to catch her. Tim slid under her before she hit the ground. He gently turned her over, rolling her off the kid in the trench coat. Robert pulled off his t-shirt and used it to try to stem the flow of blood from Heather's shoulder. Tim did likewise, pressing his shirt to her back.

Heather's eyes blinked open.

"Don't look so scared, punk, I'm not dying today," Heather smiled shakily at Robert.

"You're in so much trouble," Tim said above her.

Heather looked up and groaned in pain.

"Not half as much as you are." She grinned through her pain. "You're cutting class and I'm telling Mom."

None of them noticed when the news cameras showed up even before the ambulance. They had no idea that by the time the ambulance took Heather off to the hospital, the story was going out over the airwaves. Because it was all over before the camera crews got there, the only footage the news channels had at the start of their coverage were the shots of Heather with her brothers, laying mere feet from the gunman who was being disarmed and cuffed by the police.

THE MAJOR NEWS networks all picked up the footage immediately, importantly telling everyone the bare facts that they had. They played the same footage over and over again. A camera man from the sports network saw it, and it caught his attention. After the third time watching it, he realized where he had seen the woman and boys before. He pulled up his footage from the Grizzly-Wolves game and took it to the producer. Within minutes, the sports network was breaking a huge story – the hero of the school shooting in Hawaii was Steve Jeremiah's love interest.

One of the Grizzlies' assistant coaches had the sports news channel on while he was working in the office. He immediately ran out to get the coach.

"Jeremiah!" Coach called out, then pointed with a toss of his head toward the locker room. "You too Kalaau."

"Not gonna be worth a sieve on a sinking ship," Coach muttered to the assistant coach as he stomped off toward the office. "Get 'em both tickets to Honolulu as soon as you can get 'em outta here. Get 'em back here tomorrow. He'll need to see for himself the girl ain't dying if he's gonna be worth a darn in Monday's game."

As soon as Steve and Pete got into his office, Coach turned on his television. Sure enough, the sports network was still running that darn footage.

Steve paled and sank into a chair. Pete stood behind him, knuckles white on the back of the chair. As soon as the footage was done, the coach snapped off the television.

"Now you know what I know," he sat back and frowned. "Call me as soon as you get to Honolulu and know she's gonna be okay."

"Excuse me?" Pete said.

"He's not gonna be worth a razor to a bald man if he doesn't see with his own eyes," Coach said, "but he ain't gonna get himself down there either. You're a friend of both of 'em, so you go too. Just make sure you're both back by practice Friday. ... Go on, get outta here. Make sure you stop and get the flight info from Fredericks. In fact, he'll give you a ride to the airport too."

As soon as he was alone, Coach picked up his phone and called the producer at the sports network. He was furious about what they had just done to Steve and he was going to let them know that they would pay for it, pay dearly.

WHILE STEVE AND Pete were rushing off to the airport, further east in Washington, D.C., the Senate Majority Leader was about to call for a vote on a bill that he had long delayed because he wanted to make sure it would be defeated. Suddenly an aide came rushing into the chamber and whispered to him. The senator called a brief recess and followed the aide out.

"You better be right about this," he snapped angrily. "I'll have your hide if you aren't."

"Oh I am, you'll see," the aide said. "I only caught it because I recognized her when I saw her on the TV during the game that Sunday. I compared the pictures of her and she was a dead ringer, so I did some digging. It's her all right. She's been dating Steve Jeremiah of the Grizzlies."

"Which really doesn't mean a darn to me," the senator snapped. "What's this about a school shooting?"

"It's all over the sports networks already and I suspect the major news networks are going to be picking up this angle at any time," the aide said. "They already had the school shooting. It was the sports network who identified her. It's just a matter of time until the other networks catch onto the news that Steve Jeremiah's girlfriend is the one who foiled the shooting in Honolulu."

They rushed into the senator's office and saw the staff gathered around the television.

"Is he right?" the senator asked his senior aide.

"Yes sir, he is," the senior aide replied. "It's on all the major news networks now too. They haven't given her name yet, but see for yourself."

The aide handed him a file. He looked at the picture, looked at the woman on the screen then back at the picture. He swore, long and colorfully.

"What do we know about the shooting?"

"The security guard was apparently winged with the first shots," the senior aide reported. "Then she somehow disarmed the shooter, even after she was hit. This one shot ... here, shows there were about thirty kids outside whom she protected, to say nothing of how many kids were in the buildings."

"What kind of weapons are we talking about?" Maybe it wasn't that big a deal, just a couple of rounds from a BB gun or something.

"See his trench coat?" The aid pointed to the television again. "Here you can clearly see four handguns and a knife. There might be more in the trench coat."

"How am I supposed to vote no on a Medal of Honor for someone who not only saved lives in Iraq but also just stopped a school shooting in Hawaii? Will someone tell me that?"

Frustrated, he stormed back to the Senate chambers. He hated this war and he wanted no living hero wandering around the countryside, stirring up support with her courage and strength. It was bad enough having dead heroes but he couldn't be one who voted no on this Medal now. His only hope was that no one else had discovered it yet and he could vote yes, but the total vote would still be a rejection.

His hopes were thwarted. Savvy senators wondered what had caused him to stomp out of the chambers just before that particular vote and they had scrambled their aides to figure it out. By the time he returned to the floor, presented the bill and called for the vote, the news had already swept through the Senate. By a comfortable margin, Sergeant Heather Nohealani Shepherd became the first living recipient of the Medal of Honor in the Iraqi War and the first woman since Mary Walker in 1865.

Chapter 32

*B*y the time Steve and Pete landed in Honolulu, Steve was in a frenzy of fear. They hadn't been able to get in touch with any of the Shepherds before leaving O'Hare. When they'd changed planes in Minneapolis all Greg could tell them was that Heather was in surgery.

Pete's dad was waiting for them in the cell phone waiting area, so Pete called him while Steve tried calling Greg. No answer. He tried calling the other Shepherds, getting no answer there either.

Steve was trying to convince himself that it didn't mean anything other than that they were all at the hospital with its poor reception and no cell phone areas but he wasn't very convincing.

Pete's dad didn't help. Last word he'd received, Heather had gotten out of surgery and was in ICU but still unconscious. He didn't know if it was from anesthesia or injury.

With no check on his fear, no words of true comfort and reassurance, Steve's fear that he would lose her crescendoed. Just like Jenni, Mom and Grandma, Heather was leaving him. This leaving battered him like no other ever had. Something in him broke and he allowed fear to consume him.

Suddenly his phone rang. Greg. He sounded much too cheerful.

They had missed Steve's calls because Heather was awake, but barely. They were moving her into a private room out of ICU. Steve got the room number and sat staring out the window, wondering where the joy was. Heather would live. Funny, for the first time since he was thirteen, laying on the floor, crying out to God while his father tried to beat the life out of him, he wasn't sure if he wanted to live. He felt hollow, empty.

As Steve approached Heather's room, he was surprised to hear laughter. Why was he surprised? This was a family who looked death and defeat in the face and laughed.

He ducked through the door and saw her. She was laying on the bed, almost flat. Her left shoulder was swathed in bandages, her hospital gown awkwardly tied under it. Her hair was a mess, sweat-soaked, three-quarters out of her braid. Her face was pale, dark shadows under her eyes.

She was laughing at something Luke had just said.

A flicker of love and joy pushed at the fear. She lived life with an exuberance that challenged others, himself included. She was a gift from God.

The fear pushed back. No holds barred. Heather screamed her defiance at injustice, just like she raged at the referees. She threw caution to the wind when she saw the need, like she had in the desert, at the school. She lived life as she wanted, regardless of limitations, grudgingly stopping only when pain intruded. Even then she pushed back.

Two choices battled inside him. He could fall to his knees and cry out his pain and fear, begging God for strength, or he could stand and rage at the pain, push at the fear.

He stood.

Standing at the head of Heather's bed, Luke saw the emotions flicker across Steve's face, saw the pain settle into his eyes. He motioned with his head and Greg quietly suggested to his little brothers and Pete that they step out into the hall.

Gloria remained seated at her daughter's left side. Luke still stood on Heather's right, holding her uninjured hand. They watched Steve with wary eyes, seeing the pain and fear clearly etched on his face.

Heather's eyes were clouded with her own pain.

"Steve." A smile twitched at her lips before the pain stole it in a grimace. "You should be at practice."

You should be holding her, kissing her, a small voice whispered from somewhere deep within.

You would be at practice, if she didn't need to be a hero, this voice was louder, more insistent.

"You didn't need to come all this way."

Yes, you did. You need her. You need to see and feel for yourself that she's alive. Go to her, hold her hand. Love her.

No, you shouldn't have come. How many times will her need to be a hero disrupt your life? The angry voice shouted down the voice of love, of reason.

"You should have called," she grimaced in pain again. The hand holding Luke's tightened to white knuckles.

Called! The small voice was silenced. The angry voice raged. *So she could lie about her danger, her pain, and you wouldn't know any different? So she could shut you up and shut you out?*

"Why?" Steve said hoarsely. "So you could lie to me too?"

Heather gasped with surprise and pain.

"What did you do, tell them your pain was a six, a seven?"

Something flickered in her eyes before she looked away.

"Why don't you tell them that it's off the chart?"

"Steve," Luke spoke quietly, trying to sooth him.

"You don't confess your pain because that would be weak and Heather Shepherd is big and strong." Something in Steve said he was going too far, he needed to back off, calm down. He squashed it. "You have to be as good as your brothers or even better. You don't want to be weak or vulnerable because that would make you just a woman, not a hero."

"Did you come all this way just to insult me?" Heather snarled weakly.

"I came," Steve said barely above a whisper, "because I was afraid and I thought you might need me ... since you claim to love me."

Steve looked at Gloria sitting protectively beside Heather, Luke standing as a strong shield. He saw how her hand gripped Luke's and drew strength to push down the pain and stare defiantly at him.

He suddenly saw she wasn't wearing her Mizpah.

"But you don't need me. Your life was perfect before I came along," Steve ran his hands through his hair, closing his eyes against the grief that swamped his soul. "Why did I come? I should have stayed in Chicago, where I belong."

Steve turned toward the door without looking up. He heard Heather's gasp of pain but he didn't turn to see that she had jerked her hand from Luke's and reached toward him, only to fall back in a faint as the resulting pain snatched all the oxygen from her brain.

Steve walked into the hall and saw Greg, glaring with arms crossed over his chest.

"That was well done," Greg growled sarcastically.

Steve just stared at him with empty eyes.

"That was harsh, brah," Pete said quietly. "You're letting the fear talk."

Steve just stared coldly at them. Then he turned and walked down the hall. When Robert reached out to stop him, he just jerked his arm away and kept walking.

He walked down to the elevators but he didn't want to stand there and wait, nor did he really want to ride in the confines of the small box. He passed the elevator and entered the stairwell, his heart growing heavier with each descending floor. He walked out of the hospital and into the night.

IT WAS RAINING of course. It wasn't a gentle mauka shower, drifting in off the mountains, but an all-out downpour that would flood the low-laying areas if the tide was in. By the time he walked out to Punchbowl Street, Steve was soaked to the skin.

He didn't care. If there was any justice in the world, he would catch his death of cold just like Grandma used to warn when he played in the rain.

Standing on the sidewalk, Steve realized he didn't have his car. No matter, he knew where home was. He started up Punchbowl, toward the landmark that gave the street its name. He couldn't see it in the darkness of the night but he knew the small volcano was there, brooding quietly over the city, sheltering the bones of brave veterans in the inverted curve of its crest.

He crossed the street at Vineyard and trudged down the road, hands in his pockets, shoulders hunched against the rain.

Steve laughed bitterly at the irony that he couldn't miss. At six foot eight and two-hundred fifty pounds, he really hadn't thought there was any woman who could take him down but just like she'd promised, Heather had. He had known she was a woman to stand beside a man but he hadn't expected her to overshadow, overpower him.

As he crossed Queen Emma then trudged across Vineyard to the mauka side, Steve wondered if he was so different from the boys who had called Heather a freak, the men who hadn't been able to stand beside her. Was he also too small a man for Heather? Or was he simply afraid? He thought about Jenni, how he'd cried when he realized she wasn't coming back. He remembered the beatings he'd taken, both for those tears and for his father's uncontrollable rage over her going.

Steve remembered the relief and guilt he had felt when his father died, remembered the gentle pastor who had helped him banish his guilt. But his heart, wavering between being a little boy and being a man, couldn't understand why Jenni didn't come home, why Mom didn't come back from her dark place when it was finally safe.

As he crossed Nuuanu and continued down Vineyard, Steve realized that his heart still didn't understand. Why wouldn't they be safe? Mom, Jenni, and now Heather, living just beyond his reach, not letting him keep them safe, be their strength and shelter. He hadn't been enough for Mom and Jenni and he wouldn't be enough for Heather either.

His tears mixed with the rain as he approached Aala Street. Suddenly his BMW was in the crosswalk in front of him. He opened the door and climbed in.

Greg said nothing as he drove the short block to School Street. After he turned right on Liliha, he broke the silence.

"She scares me," Greg said quietly. "She always has. Some of what you said back there .... You know her, you really do."

Steve just sat there, staring out the window.

"But it wasn't the time or the place," Greg said angrily. "Our brothers were at that school. Do you have any idea what it would have done to her, if she had done nothing to stop him, if she'd stayed safe and he had killed Tim or Robert?'

Greg took a deep shuddering breath. Steve sat there, trying to push back the new pain that threatened him.

"She would have gone to a place far, far away."

Steve trembled. He knew about those far away places, knew about living with someone who stayed there.

"So she's laying there, fighting her pain and her fear of what might have been and you come in and throw another ball in the court. Guilt." Greg sighed again, carefully taking the many twists and turns in the road to Steve's home. "She hasn't quit crying since you left. She looks so strong but she needs you. She loves you."

"I'm not strong enough for her," Steve said.

"You don't need to be strong enough, you just need to be there and let God be strong for you," Greg urged. "You just need to love her."

"What do you know?" Steve couldn't control the urge to lash out, to hurt someone. "You've been in love how many times? Talk to me when you really know something!"

"I love you like a brother, Steve," Greg said with narrowed eyes as he finally pulled into the garage. "I'm going to forgive you for that because I know it's just fear and pain talking. But, brah, don't let it run your life. Give it to God before it takes root and poisons everything."

Steve sat in the car for a long time after Greg went into the house. Sometime after midnight, he finally leveraged himself out of the car and trudged wearily downstairs, barely getting out of his wet clothes before falling across the bed in exhaustion.

Chapter 33

*I*t was a full week before Heather got to go home. The doctors were more worried about her attitude than they were about the injury itself. She was distressed by more than the trouble with Steve. When she heard about the investigation into the school shooting, she was shocked to find out that the boy was almost family. Neil Pittman had been a good friend of Robert's when they were in grade school and he had played at their house often. Heather barely remembered him because she was gone from home before Robert and Neil started second grade but Mom, Greg and Tim all remembered him.

When Robert had started football in middle school, the boys had begun to drift apart. Then Neil's parents divorced and he moved with his mother into public housing. He was almost a stereotypical school shooter. A loner, picked on by bullies, somewhat of a geek with no real support system to help him deal with the stresses of life. Unlike most other school shooters, he would live to receive counseling and rebuild his life. For that Heather was very grateful, especially with the family connection. What really bothered her was how close she'd come to losing her baby brother.

Pittman had made a list of nineteen students and three teachers. The students included football and basketball players, honors students and three friends from grade school, all of whom Neil felt had rejected him. Robert was on the list. Pittman's intent had been to kill as many as he could before taking his own life. He had carried enough firepower to do that and then some. The fact that no one died in what could have been a major tragedy made Heather a major hero. When the news came about the Medal of Honor, it only reinforced the intense local fame Heather had already garnered.

The doctors felt pressure to make sure that she recovered fully and quickly, but Heather was barely cooperating. For the first time in her life, Heather didn't lie about her pain. She allowed the doctors to pump her full of painkillers, hoping they would dull the pain in her heart that overshadowed the pain in her shoulder.

Her heart was fracturing into a million little pieces. Steve hadn't come to see her before he went back to Chicago in the early afternoon the day after the shooting. He hadn't answered the phone when she'd called him the day after that, hadn't responded to the voice mail she'd left.

"I'm so sorry," she had said. "I never thought .... I didn't know .... Please forgive me. ... Please call so we can talk."

He didn't call nor did he answer her calls the next day, or the next.

From all outward appearances, nothing was bothering Steve Jeremiah. He was still tearing up the offense, punishing quarterbacks and schooling young running backs. On Monday night, he won MVP again when the Grizzlies dominated the Dragons.

By midweek, the doctors had started to wean Heather off the pain meds and she was able to wear a sling most of the day, so on Thursday she went home. Mom picked her up and they left with a whole slew of medical instructions. She took none of her flowers, not even the bouquet from the President. The one she wanted wasn't there, so she sent the rest of them to be disbursed throughout the hospital.

Mom took her home, made sure she ate some soup then left to fix dinner for Tim and Robert, promising that someone would be by later in the evening to check on her. That someone was Greg. He sat and watched television with her that night and quite a few more. He was waiting for her to be ready to live again. He'd wait a long time.

Heather refused to watch the Grizzly game on Sunday. Greg told her about it, assuring her that their loss was not Steve's fault. He sacked the quarterback three times and allowed only negative yardage up the left side of the field. Heather pretended that she didn't care.

HEATHER'S DAYS SLIPPED into the mind-numbing pattern of sleeping and watching television. Mom came over every day to check on her and make her eat some lunch. Greg came over to watch and wait every evening. When he had to work, he came over before or after, sometimes both.

The weeks slipped away. On Sundays, Heather watched some stupid reality show. Anything was better than a Grizzly game. Greg told her about the games, how good Steve was but how something was missing. He told her how sad Steve looked when they lost again. She told herself she didn't care.

Greg was frustrated about Heather. She wasn't using the sling for her arm much anymore but he was beginning to think she needed one for her heart. He didn't know what to do for her. He needed a woman's advice, but what woman? During his quiet time with God on the Thursday before Thanksgiving, he asked for a woman who could help him reach his sister.

When he got to his Christian Doctrine class, Greg sat in his usual place in the back of the room. What wasn't usual was that he had no company at the two-seater table. Five minutes into the class, the door opened and someone breezed in late, sitting down in the seat closest to the door, right next to him.

He looked over and saw Beth Harrison, a quiet little mouse of a thing who usually sat toward the front. They had both started bible college last fall but he'd never gotten to have a real conversation with her. Not that he hadn't tried, but she was rather standoffish.

"Hey, you're a girl," he whispered.

Beth looked startled.

"Did you just notice?" she whispered back.

"No, no, no, I noticed that right off, the first time we met," Greg tried to get things back on the right foot, "but I was just praying for a girl this morning."

Now she looked a little scared. That so did not come out right.

"Oh God, I sound like an idiot. I could use a little help here," Greg muttered to the ceiling, then he leaned over toward Beth. "I need some advice. From a girl. That's what I was praying about a girl for."

"Ah, you have girl trouble," Beth whispered wisely.

"No, not girl trouble," Greg whispered back. "It's my sister."

"Oh?" Beth's lips twitched as she faced forward, pretending that she was paying attention to the professor. "She's not a girl?"

"Grrr," Greg grabbed his head in both hands. "I'll talk to you on the break if I can get my brain in gear!"

As soon as the professor announced the break almost an hour later, Greg turned to Beth. "I've been sitting here wondering if I sounded half as stupid as I think I did."

"Oh, probably not," Beth soothed him.

"Good," Greg said with a sigh.

"You were probably twice as stupid as you thought," Beth smiled sympathetically, patted his hand and walked out of the room.

Greg stared after her for a moment then laughed. He jumped up and followed her down the hall to the snack machines.

"You're funny," Greg said. "How come I never noticed you were funny?"

"Funny?" Beth looked at him with a cool smile and a raised eyebrow. "I don't remember trying to be funny."

"Oh good, a woman who's funny without even trying," Greg leaned against the side of the soda machine. "But seriously, I do need some advice."

"Is this advice something like what color blouse to get her for Christmas?" Beth asked as she got a diet soda.

"Nah, nothing like that, just how to get her out of a funk," Greg fell into step beside her as she walked back to the classroom.

"Ah, something simple," Beth said with a soft snort.

"Yeah," Greg agreed, then he shuddered. "Much easier than Christmas shopping."

"Well since it's so simple," Beth shook her head, "let's talk after class instead of during break. I don't do simple as well as I do complicated."

"Okay, it's a date," Greg grinned down at her. Now she raised both eyebrows. "I don't mean, a date date, ... not that I wouldn't want to 'cause you're kinda ..., but um, just girl talk, ... uh, I mean, ... I'll shut up now."

Greg dropped into his chair with a deep sigh, knowing that he was turning a deep, dusky red. Beth laughed, clear and sweet.

When class was finally dismissed, Greg waited for Beth to get her things then they walked together out to the lounge.

"Shall we talk here?" Beth asked.

Greg looked around, thinking about how public it was. "Did you already have plans for lunch?"

"No," Beth said a little hesitantly.

"This'll do if you want," Greg assured her. "It's just that my sister is a bit of a public figure and I'd really prefer not to have someone overhear our conversation."

"So what do you propose?"

"Let's run through a drive thru and get lunch, then go to the park and talk while we eat."

"When you say run through, you mean ...?"

"I get in the driver's seat. You get in the passenger seat. I make the car go by turning on the engine, pressing the gas pedal and turning the steering wheel," Greg explained carefully. "We can call it a date if you'd like?"

"No, no," Beth's laugh sounded a little relieved. "It's just that my car isn't ... ready for a passenger. If you were on a bike or something ...."

Greg led the way through the parking lot. When he pressed the unlock button on the remote and Steve's BMW convertible beeped happily at him, Beth stopped.

"That's your car?" she said in disbelief.

"Uh no. That's part of my sister's problem," Greg said.

"A BMW convertible is a problem?" Beth said. "I've gotta get me some of that kind of problems!"

Greg laughed and opened the passenger door for her. As they drove to the fast food place, he asked if she knew about the school shooting.

"Of course I do, who in Honolulu doesn't?" Beth said in surprise as she realized that she didn't know Greg's last name. They rarely used last names at the school. She must have never heard that he was a Shepherd. "That was your sister? How come I didn't hear that part before?"

Greg just shrugged. "I guess it never came up."

"But we prayed for her and her family in chapel! How come you didn't say anything then?" Greg just shrugged. Beth looked at him curiously. She thought about all the things she knew, what she'd read and heard about in the news.

"So," she said, "this is about her and that football player?"

"Bingo."

"What's the problem?"

"They're kind of ... broke up right now."

Beth waited to continue the conversation until they had gotten their food from the drive thru.

"How'd they break up?"

"That first day, right after she got out of ICU and moved into a room," Greg said. "He was scared and stupid. Actually, I guess he still is."

"Why do you say that?"

"He said some things that were true but hurtful. Things about my sister's ... approach to life."

"I can imagine," Beth said dryly. When Greg looked at her with a puzzled frown, she quickly amended her statement. "It's got to be hard on a guy to have the woman he loves be a hero."

"That's pretty much the deal but it's more complicated."

"It always is," Beth said. "So they broke up?"

"Yeah. Even though she tried to call him, he won't talk to her," Greg parked the car and climbed out, walking around to open the door for Beth.

"Is she still trying to call him?"

"Nah, I think she quit after the first week."

They paused to pray for their food.

"So now she's moping around the house? Doesn't eat? Sleeps all the time?"

"You know!" Greg was surprised. "See, I knew I needed a girl."

Beth laughed and Greg knew he was blushing again.

"I mean, I don't really need a girl," he tried a fix. "I just needed you ...."

Greg suddenly stopped and looked up at the sky.

"God, I hope you're finding this funny," he yelled up at the heavens. "I'm not! I'll take my brain back any time now."

He waited expectantly for a moment then looked at Beth with a shrug and a sigh. "Oh well, it was worth the effort."

"What you need," Beth said carefully, "is to figure out how your sister's routines have changed and start slipping her back into them as much as possible. She's lost something very valuable to her, try to help her not lose too much."

Greg stared at Beth in surprise. Why hadn't he thought of that?

"Wow, I'm surprised. You really are smart," Greg said. "I never would have guessed. Try wait, I didn't think you were dumb, I just thought you were .... Never mind. I'll shut up now."

He took a big bite of his burger. "Umm, this is sooo good!"

Beth threw her head back and laughed.

GREG TOOK MOOSE back home that night. Heather couldn't deny that Moose's adoration and controlled exuberance brought a little sunshine back into her life. She smiled a real smile for the first time in a month. Greg reached for a laugh too. Carefully avoiding the topic of their conversation, he entertained Heather with the story of his misadventures in talking with Beth. Hearing her laugh again made sharing his embarrassment well worth it.

Sunday there was no Grizzly game for Heather to avoid because they didn't play until Thursday, a rare Thanksgiving Day game against the Leopards. Greg decided to skip church to be with Heather, hoping he could get her back into her old routine of enjoying football by watching another game in their division. She declined football but she did gladly take a walk with him and Moose, the first one she'd gone on since before the shooting.

She seemed a little more like the real Heather as they walked and talked and he threw sticks for Moose. Greg silently thanked God for Beth, wondering if he could get his foot out of his mouth long enough to ask her for a real date.

Chapter 34

*J*enni had worked the last three Sundays, so she hadn't been able to take the girls to church yet. This Sunday she had off because she was working the entire Thanksgiving weekend. She was looking forward to trying out the church that the Shepherds had listed as their number one suggestion.

She carefully inspected the girls and herself before leaving for the short two block walk to the church. She was glad that the weather was perfect for walking because she was worried about the car. It wasn't running well since they'd gotten here from California and it was going to be a couple of months before she was able to save up enough to get it fixed.

She sat with the girls about four rows up from the back. When everyone stood for a hymn she couldn't help but notice the big guy three rows in front of her. He was almost as big as her brother and he looked vaguely familiar. She tried to figure out why.

When the message started Jenni forgot all about the big man. The pastor was talking about being thankful even in the bad things that happen in life. She was intrigued because she had certainly had enough bad things in her life but she had never seen any need to be thankful in them.

The pastor clarified the difference between being thankful *in* and being thankful *for*, and Jenni began to understand. You could be thankful to God "in" anything because God was bigger than anything you faced and you could be thankful to God "for" all the good things he gives. Being thankful "in" was based on the goodness of God himself, which never changes. Being thankful "for" was based on receiving things from God.

"It's much too easy to focus so much on the things to be thankful *for*, all the good things that God gives us, that we forget about being thankful *in* everything," the pastor said. "God is always good. It's an integral part of his character. He can never be anything but good. Anything that he allows us to go through is going to be used for good. It may be horrible if we look at it by itself, but Paul promised us in Romans 8:28 that God works all things for the good of those who love him. That's *all things*, even things that are too horrible for you to think about or talk about. If you love God, truly love him not just give him lip service, you'll discover that God has worked even those bad things for your good.

"What is it that you think you can't be thankful *in*? Did you ever stop to realize that on that first Good Friday, no one found anything to be thankful *in*? The disciples were firmly convinced that Jesus was the Messiah whom the Israelites had long awaited, but he was brutally killed. Most of us today cannot begin to understand how devastating Jesus' crucifixion was for his followers because we don't understand the religion and culture that Jesus lived in. Imagine for a moment that someone comes along with the ability and charisma to resolve all the conflicts in the Middle East, to end the war over there forever. Imagine that even as our soldiers begin to hope that they'll be home for good, our own government, in conjunction with the Iraqi government publicly and brutally murders him. That's kind of the way Jesus' believers felt on that first Good Friday – hopeless and betrayed.

"But God had a plan that no one could see. No one but Jesus.

"For two nights, Jesus' disciples tossed and turned on their beds, trying to figure out what had gone wrong. They had no hope because there was nothing to hope in anymore. Then the Son rose on Sunday morning and they discovered a hope that far exceeded the expectations they'd had before the crucifixion.

"Look again at whatever it is that you can't be thankful *in*, then look some more. Keep on looking and one day, I promise you, you will find something you can be thankful *for* that can be tied back to that thing you couldn't be thankful *in*. Maybe it'll be a friend whom you can help through a difficult time because you've already been there. Maybe it'll be a job that you find because you met someone during what you saw as a disaster. I don't know what it is, but I guarantee that God is faithful and he is going to work *everything* for your good."

Jenni looked down at the little girls beside her and fully understood what the pastor meant. She had two beautiful daughters who came out of things that weren't anything to be thankful for. She thanked God for her daughters as she gathered up their things to go after the final hymn.

As she stood, she saw the big man walking down the aisle. He made eye contact with her and suddenly froze. Now that she saw his face, she recognized him. He was Pete Kalaau, Steve's best friend and teammate, and he knew her.

"Jenni?" Pete whispered and stepped closer. He was certain he knew who she was because he'd seen her picture many times. It hung in the living room of Steve's penthouse. She was older now and even more beautiful than she had been at fifteen. "You're really Jenni Jeremiah?"

She ducked her head with an embarrassed nod.

"Mommy, who's he?" Ana tugged on her arm.

"This is Pete Kalaau, your uncle's friend," Jenni knelt beside Ana and straightened her coat.

"Do you go to this church?" Ana asked brightly.

"Whenever I'm in town," Pete nodded.

"Does my uncle come here too?"

"Usually, yes," Pete sounded sad and Jenni looked sharply at him.

"We should come here too Mommy?" Ana announced. "Don't you think so Kara?"

"I like this church," Kara agreed.

"So do I," Jenni said absently, still looking at Pete. "Go on back to where we saw the cookies but don't leave that area, okay?"

"Okay Mom. I'll watch Ana," Kara said importantly, taking her little sister's hand as she walked down the aisle.

"What's wrong with my brother?" Jenni stepped close to Pete and laid her hand on his sleeve. "Why is he not in church?"

"You can't guess?" Pete said, looking from the girls to her, still stunned that she would just suddenly be there like that and with two little girls.

"Guess what?"

"Don't you watch the news?" Pete finally focused his attention solely on Jenni.

"No I don't," she huffed in exasperation. "I just moved here and I don't have a television yet."

"You didn't hear about the shooting?"

"Steve got shot?" Jenni felt faint. Pete reached out to grab her by the arms, quickly correcting her misunderstanding.

"No, not him, his girlfriend." Oh, this wasn't better. She went even whiter and swayed.

"Heather?" she asked with an anguished whisper.

"You know Heather?" Pete was shocked at her nod. "We need to talk, but not here. Let's go to the McDonald's on the corner. They have a place for the girls to play."

"Is she ...?" Jenni grabbed Pete's arms.

"She's not dead, but their relationship is going to be soon if your hardheaded brother doesn't come to his senses."

Jenni allowed Pete to turn her toward the door. They retrieved the girls and walked the half block to the McDonald's where Pete had her sit while he went and got the food. She let the girls go ahead and play before they ate, so when Pete came back they were free to talk.

"I remember someone said something about a school shooting in Hawaii a few weeks back," Jenni jumped right in. "Was that Heather?"

Pete nodded, taking a bite of his burger.

"But she's okay now?" Jenni asked.

"She's healing physically but from what her brother says her heart isn't doing so well," Pete said.

"What's Steve's problem?" When Jenni frowned, Pete noticed that she looked just like her brother.

"Frankly, he's afraid." Pete shook his head in disgust.

"Afraid of what?"

"That she'll leave him alone, just like …." Pete looked down at his food, suddenly remembering to whom he was talking.

"Just like I did," Jenni whispered hoarsely. "That's stupid, she loves him. She's crazy about him. She bought him the Mizpah. She promised with God as her witness."

"How do you know about that?" Pete asked sharply. "I didn't even know about it until just the other day."

"Never mind how I know anything right now," Jenni said impatiently. "Tell me about Steve. Why is he afraid of Heather leaving him?"

"Leaving by dying," Pete said. "Closest I can understand it that after your father died, when you didn't come back and when your mom didn't get better Steve saw both of those as a failure on his part. He couldn't make it safe enough for you to come back to him. When Heather got shot, he saw he couldn't keep her safe either so fear tells him it's only a matter of time before she leaves him."

"So he's leaving first this time?" Jenni frowned. "I need to make a call, do you mind?"

Pete shook his head and she pulled out her cell phone.

"Heather? ... This is Jenni."

Pete frowned. He was missing a whole lot of information.

"I JUST HEARD or I would have called earlier."

Heather looked around for a bench to sit on, very glad they had walked to the park instead of just wandering around Kaimuki.

"I'm surprised you didn't hear. It's been all over the news and even the sports channel."

"I haven't watched the news. We didn't get a television when we moved."

"I'm sorry. I didn't even think about that."

"It's not that big a deal. I didn't call to talk about that. I want to know how you're doing."

"Honestly, Jenni," Heather sighed and watched Greg and Moose romping in the grass. "I don't know."

"Has he called you?"

"No."

Jenni scowled. "Did you call him?"

"I did at first but I stopped when he never answered."

"Do you still love him?"

A long pause. "I don't really know anymore, Jenni. I know I still hurt but I don't know if there's any love left."

"Hang in there Heather. I promise, in the long run he really is worth it."

"If you really believe that," Heather whispered, "then why do you live right around the corner from him and he doesn't even know it?"

"Touché," Jenni said softly, pressing the heel of her left hand to her forehead.

"Jenni, I need to go right now," Heather said, "but please, please do call me again. Later today, tomorrow, whenever. I really do want to talk to you."

"I will, Heather. Bye for now."

Jenni snapped her phone shut and slumped sideways in her chair, her back to the wall. When she looked up at Pete, there was fire and determination in her eyes.

"You know if anything happens to his nieces, my brother will kill you, yes?" She surprised Pete with that one. He nodded warily.

"Good, because I need someone to watch them while I have a chat with the pigheaded jerk and you're the only candidate."

"No problem. When they're done playing and eating, we'll go back to my place. It won't be hard to find. I live right across the hall from Steve."

Jenni walked over to tell the girls that she was going to see Uncle Steve, so Pete was going to watch them. When she pointed out the building just down the street, they were okay with her going. Before she was out the door, they were playing happily again.

STEVE STARED GLUMLY out at the Chicago skyline, almost wishing he'd gone to church with Pete. They'd be sitting in a restaurant somewhere talking about the upcoming Leopards' game and he wouldn't be sitting here trying not to think about Heather. But God felt so distant from him and it seemed hypocritical to go to church and pretend he didn't. Steve was beginning to understand how Heather had felt all those months she hadn't gone to church. He wondered if she was going to church now or if she too felt the distance from God.

She wouldn't be dancing yet, he was sure of that. Would she ever dance with the same dove-like grace again? Would her hands ever again send the eye soaring heavenward, watching the flight of the bird set free to dream?

He didn't care. He didn't want to think about Heather Shepherd.

Unfortunately he couldn't think of anything else he did want to think about.

Ah, saved by the bell, Steve hoped it was Pete who was ringing his doorbell.

It was a bundle of fury and she poked him in the chest, hard.

"Where's my ball, brat?" she growled. "You promised you'd take care of my ball."

"Jenni?" Steve was stunned, falling back from her onslaught.

"I gave you my ball to watch and you kept it for sixteen years," Jenni kept poking him in the chest, pushing him further into his living room. The door swung shut behind her.

"And you found a home for it, for you, for me," she kept poking him, "and now you want to walk away. Well, I'm not going to let you." This time when she poked him, Steve caught her hand and pressed it to his chest, wrapping his other arm around her in a fierce hug.

"Jenni!" he said, then he began to cry. "Jenni, you're alive. You're here."

The sobs came from deep within, shuddering his very foundation. Jenni's tears fell with his as she wrapped her arms around him and they wept together.

When their tears subsided, Steve pulled her down to sit on the floor, cross-legged, knees touching, like they had so many times before.

"Where have you been, Jenni?" Steve asked. "I've looked all over for you."

"I know. I'm sorry, so sorry," Jenni stroked her brother's cheek. "I didn't know our father died, not until after you began to make the news. I would have come home had I known."

"Why didn't you come to me then, when you knew he was gone?"

"Because I was ashamed of what I'd become," Jenni dropped her head.

"Hey, no shame," Steve lifted her chin. "No shame for the past. Just look toward the future, to what God can do now."

"You kinda sound like Heather," Jenni sniffed.

"You know Heather?" Steve was shocked.

"That's the second time today I've gotten that reaction," Jenni laughed. "Pete couldn't believe it either."

"You know Pete too?" Steve frowned. "How many other people did you meet before coming to me?"

"Hey, Pete's your own fault, brat," Jenni raised her chin haughtily. "If you had gone to church this morning you would have seen us before Pete, since you're taller than he is."

"You were in church?" Steve said with a grin. "Does that mean ...?"

"Yes little brother," Jenni leaned forward to whisper. "I'm a Christian too now."

"That's great," Steve whispered back, bumping foreheads with her. Something else in what she said had him curious. "Who's the 'us' part of you who were in church this morning?"

"My girls," she whispered still. "Kara and Ana. Why are we whispering?"

"You have daughters?" Steve sat up straight, not whispering any more. "That means I have nieces? Where are they?" Steve looked around as if maybe they had slipped in without him noticing. "How old are they? What do they look like?"

"Not so fast, mister," Jenni frowned. "I came to knock some sense into you."

She suddenly pushed him hard and he fell over backward. She pounced on him, pinning one arm to his body with her knees straddling him, very glad she'd worn slacks to church today. She grabbed his other hand in both of hers, holding the wrist with her right hand, her left hand squeezing his pinkie finger together and bending it backward.

"Dang, Jenni!" Steve roared. "I didn't do anything. What're you pickin' on me for?"

He sounded so much like he did when they were kids, only bigger and louder, that Jenni began to giggle. She couldn't help herself.

Steve took advantage of her laughter, snatching his vulnerable hand away from hers and rolling over to pin her. Somehow she took control of the roll and he was the one facedown in the carpet, arm twisted behind him.

"Dang, Jenni! Someday I'm going to figure out how you do that and, so help me God, you will never pin me again!"

"Don't bet on it, brat," Jenni slapped his shoulder. "I'm the big sister. Besides, I've been learning self-defense. Cry uncle?"

"No! Never!" She pushed his arm up higher. "Woman, I play professional football. Don't dislocate my arm!"

"Cry uncle!"

"Okay! Uncle, uncle!" Steve laughed into the carpet as Jenni rolled off him and flopped down on her back.

"It's good to have you back, Sis," Steve rolled up on his left side and looked down at Jenni.

"It's really good to be back," Jenni smiled up at him, "but we really do need to talk because you really do need some sense knocked into you."

"I don't wanna talk," Steve flopped over onto his back and they were laying head to shoulder. "I wanna play with my nieces and my sister."

"Then you better listen good or you won't see them."

"Are you blackmailing me?"

"Bribing would probably be a better term."

Steve sighed. "Heather."

"Yes, Heather."

"How did you meet her?"

"After the game in L.A.," Jenni said with a smile in her voice. "She helped me move here."

"When?"

"The week she stayed here in Chicago with Luke and Greg."

"So you know Luke and Greg too," Steve wasn't sure how he was supposed to feel about all this.

"Relax, brat," Jenni laughed. "I haven't met any of the others but I sure have heard about them."

"Heather didn't tell me." Steve was hurt.

"She begged me to, said it wasn't fair to you."

"It wasn't."

"I know," Jenni sighed, "but I'm still trying to figure out this whole Christian thing. I only got saved about half a year ago."

"You didn't trust me?" Steve sounded desolate.

"I didn't want to be a burden."

"But I was already burdened by your loss."

"Okay, I didn't say I was being logical," Jenni huffed. "Don't be getting hypocritical on me."

"Excuse me?" Steve angrily rolled up on his elbow.

"Oh yeah," Jenni rolled up too, just as angry. Angrier. She shook her finger in his face. "It's not logical that I didn't want to burden you by relieving a burden that you carried for fifteen years but it is logical that you would be afraid you'd lose Heather so you dump her first? Get real, you jerk."

Steve stared at her, stunned.

"Yeah, sounds kind of dumb, doesn't it, when I put it that way?" Jenni said. "But it is dumb. Why would you willingly give up one minute of one day with that gorgeous, funny, lovable, big-hearted woman who can stand toe-to-toe with you and not let you get away with anything? She defends you, corrects you, supports you, encourages you, loves you and you'll let her get away because you're afraid that sometime down the road she's going to die and leave you alone? How stupid is that?"

Steve rose to his feet and walked over to the windows, to that same spot where not so long ago he had stood and told Heather how lonely he was. Jenni followed, standing beside him with her back to the window.

"Steve, it isn't your responsibility to keep Heather safe," Jenni said earnestly. "It wasn't your responsibility to keep me safe or Mom safe. It's our responsibility, yours too, to find our safety in God and let him redeem everything we live through. There are no guarantees in life, except that God will be glorified. Accept the blessings he's given you. Enjoy them while you have them. Be thankful for Heather and love her with all you have for every day you're given, even if it's just one more day."

Steve looked down at his sister, overwhelmed with love for her, deeply thankful to have her back in his life.

"I thought you said you were new at this Christian thing," he said.

"Oh I am, trust me," Jenni laughed. "That just happens to be one of the things I needed to learn right off. I've got a long way to go."

Steve turned sideways and leaned against the window facing Jenni. "I'm afraid I really messed up with Heather."

"I know you really messed up with Heather," Jenni said. "I talked to her earlier today."

"So what do I do to win her back?"

"You do what guys do best," Jenni grinned. "You be such a pest that she says yes just so you'll quit embarrassing her!"

"'Sacrifice myself on the altar of dignity,'" Steve grinned, quoting from one of Heather's favorite movies.

"I think you have it, old chap," Jenni grinned back.

Steve held out his phone with a plaintive sigh. "Would you dial my phone? I think my arm's broke."

Jenni growled at him and pushed him with both hands. He stood like a rock, laughing at her, then he wrapped both arms around her, lifting her up in a crushing bear hug. "It's good to have you back, Jenni."

Jenni went across the hall to get Pete and the girls. Steve sighed as he looked at the phone in his hand. *May as well do this,* he thought. *It's not going to take that long anyway.*

Of course she didn't answer the phone so he left a voice mail.

"I'm a fool, Heather. Jenni's here and she helped me see that. Thank you for helping Jenni. Please forgive me for being so cruel to you. I have no excuse, only regrets and repentance. I'll call again."

Chapter 35

*H*eather glared at her phone as it showed Steve's name once again. Greg reached for it and she quickly sat on it. She refused to get up and he couldn't very well wrestle it away from her knowing that her arm was still tender. She kept the phone safe from him the rest of Sunday afternoon. When Greg finally left after dinner, she listened to the three voice mails she now had from Steve.

Yes, he had been cruel. She deleted the first.

"I wish you would answer your phone. Maybe I'll get lucky enough that one of your brothers will answer for me and put me on speaker phone. There isn't enough time in voice mail to tell you how sorry I am, how much I miss you, how much I know I messed up, how much I wish I could fix –"

Heather deleted it with a frown, refusing to be touched by the loneliness in his voice.

"Hi sweetheart, it's me again. I don't want you to get jealous that I have a couple of gorgeous women on my arm, but they so wanted to say hi to you. Say hi to Aunty Heather girls."

"Hi Aunty Heather, I love you." That was Kara.

"Aunty Heather, did you know Uncle Steve has really big arms?" Ana giggled.

"I wish you were here Aunty Heather, and Uncle Greg and Uncle Luke too," Kara said. "When you coming back to visit us again?"

"We love you Aunty Heather," Ana sang out happily.

"Heather, I'm sorry. Please forgive me. I love –"

Drat the man, he knew she wouldn't be able to just delete this one. She turned off the phone and dropped it on the counter, stalking off to bed.

When she turned the phone on the next morning, she had more voice mails. She looked at her missed call log. She had missed more from Steve, eight total now. That meant he had called five more times.

He could keep calling. She wasn't answering. She wasn't going to listen to any of his voice mails again either. The man had won her heart then broke it. He had made a vow with God as his witness and walked away. She was done with him, forever.

On Wednesday, Mom came over and challenged that thinking in a way she would never have guessed.

It all started normally enough. Gloria breezed right on in, calling a hello as she came in without bothering to ask if she was welcome. She usually was of course, but that was beside the point. Heather was grumpy and she didn't want company right now.

"I'm fine Mom, thanks for asking," she growled from the couch. "I don't need anything right now so you can go home."

"Monku, monku, monku! Aren't we grumpy today?" Mom said.

"You don't sound grumpy to me," Heather complained, "but I am, so why don't you just go home and leave me to my bad mood."

"What're you huhu about?" Gloria walked in and sat on the couch just as Heather's phone buzzed again.

"That!" She glared at the phone. He wouldn't quit calling.

Gloria picked up the phone.

"It's Steve!" Mom sounded delighted. Before Heather could stop her, she'd flipped open the phone.

"Steve!" Mom was way too happy.

"Aunty Gloria?"

"Yes dear, just a minute, let me put you on speaker phone." Heather shook her head vigorously but Mom just ignored her.

"Thank you Aunty Gloria," Steve's deep voice suddenly flooded Heather's living room. She would not get chicken skin!

"I think it's time for you to stop this Aunty Gloria nonsense." Heather jumped to her feet and made a very emphatic cutting motion at her mom.

"Excuse me?" Steve sounded puzzled and maybe even a little scared.

"Yes son, you should call me Mom, if you don't mind."

"Mind? Me?" Steve was delighted. Heather grabbed Moose's leash and stormed out of the back door, grabbing the key for the gate on her way out. She desperately needed to get away from that voice.

"Oh my," Gloria said with concerned amusement.

"She left, didn't she?"

"Don't worry, son, she'll come around."

"Do you really think so?"

"You just let me have a go at her."

"I messed up big time, Mom," Steve sighed heavily. "I wish I could go back and change things."

"Oh son, you weren't the only one who messed up that day. Heather just hasn't seen it yet."

"What are you talking about, Mom?"

"Luke and I both did you wrong," Gloria sighed sadly.

"How?"

"We should have given you the places we held, but we saw your fear and anger and we wanted to protect her."

"But she needed protecting from me," Steve was ashamed to admit it. "You heard what I said to her."

"Yes, and almost everything you said needed to be said," Mom admitted, "just not in that way."

"But –"

"No, it needed to be said, Steve. If Luke had given you her hand to hold, if I had let you stand guard beside her, you would have cried out your fears instead of raging them, but we stole your place. Will you forgive me, please?"

"Yes, of course," Steve said after a long pause. "I love you, Mom."

"I love you too, son."

"I have to go now. I didn't really expect to get to do anything more than leave a message again. We're already in Detroit and practicing for the game tomorrow."

"I'm curious. How many messages have you left for Heather?"

"I don't know, twenty or thirty maybe."

"Oh my. When did you start calling?"

"Sunday, early afternoon my time, probably about ten in the morning there."

"Oh my, oh my," Mom laughed. "You want a suggestion?"

"Most definitely."

"Back off a tiny bit on the calls and find some other ways to woo her too."

"You mean like flowers? She should already have some."

"Oh! I see them!" Mom spotted a gorgeous bouquet of roses stuck in the corner of the kitchen counter. "Think out of the box too, son. Some trick plays might just be the thing."

"How about a quarterback sneak?"

"Now you're thinking."

"I love you, Mom!"

"I love you too, Steve!"

WHEN HEATHER WANDERED back into the house with Moose twenty minutes later, those blasted flowers were sitting right in the middle of her coffee table.

"Why are those there?" Heather grumbled, flopping down on the couch then wincing when she realized her shoulder wasn't well enough to flop yet.

"Serves you right," Mom said without sympathy.

"I love you too, Mom," Heather rolled her eyes.

"Did you read the card?"

"It isn't a card, Mom," Heather sighed. "It's a novel."

"It's beautiful and so are the flowers."

"I don't care," Heather knew she was pouting but she didn't really care about that either. How long was it going to take the man to get the message that she didn't love him anymore?

"You should care," Gloria scolded gently. "Steve loves you very much."

"It doesn't matter, Mom," Heather said. "I don't love him anymore."

"Oh bull," Gloria said firmly.

"Excuse me?" Heather was more than a little angry. "I think I have the right to decide whom I love and don't love."

"You sure do, but since you've decided to love Steve, why deny it?"

"Are you crazy?" Heather eased her shoulder carefully as she shifted her position so she could put her feet up on the coffee table. "The man ripped my heart out, stomped all over it, then left it to shrivel up and die."

"Seems like Steve's heart got ripped up a bit in the process too."

"Well I tried," Heather didn't want to have this conversation. "He wanted no part of it. Now he wants to try and I want no part of it."

"How many times did you call him?"

"I don't know, five or six."

"How many messages did you leave?"

"One."

"Do you know how many times he's called in the last seventy-two hours?"

Heather didn't say anything, she just glared at her mother.

"I checked. He called thirty-two times. Do you know how many messages he left?"

"Probably every time."

"I'm guessing all but the one I answered."

"So what's your point, Mom? Steve loves me more than I love him. I already knew that because I don't love him anymore."

"Now we're back to that tired old song," Gloria shook her head.

"Mom, let me decide whom I love and don't love, okay?"

"If you don't love Steve, then quit acting like you do."

"I don't take his calls," Heather snapped angrily. "I don't enjoy his flowers and I don't read his card. I am not acting like I love him."

"You sit around the house moping and watching reality TV," Mom started her own list. "You didn't reclaim your beloved dog. You don't clean your house or do your laundry. You don't paint or read. You haven't been back to work or to church. You don't watch football anymore. You haven't taken his calls but neither have you removed him from your phone. You don't listen to his voice mails but you haven't deleted them either. You didn't throw the flowers or the card in the rubbish. Need I go on?"

Heather just sat there sullenly.

"You think that Steve betrayed your love, kicked you when you were down and stomped all over your heart," Heather raised her head with eyes flashing and Gloria put up a hand to stop her. "And you would be right. You think he doesn't deserve a second chance to win your love. You may be right, but I'm going to tell you a story about a second chance."

Gloria looked around then got up to get the box of tissues from the bar between the kitchen and living room.

"Just in case," she said as she sat back in the armchair. "As far as I know, I'm the only person still alive who knows the whole story. There are a number of other people who have known bits and pieces but only two others who knew the whole story. They're the major players in this story.

"It was about thirty-five years ago. They were young and in love. He was just finishing his junior year of college, she was finishing her sophomore year. During spring break, he asked her to marry him and she gladly accepted. She came back from the break wearing his pretty little diamond and everyone admired it and congratulated them. All except one boy.

"This boy was a little imbalanced. He thought he loved the girl who was newly engaged and he thought she loved him too, even though she had never encouraged him in any way. But he was convinced and one evening when her roommate was gone he forced himself into her room. His intent had apparently just been to compel her to admit she really loved him but she wouldn't, couldn't because she loved her fiancé. The boy forced himself on her and took what she didn't want to give.

"He left her there, crying. When her roommate came home and found her, the authorities were called. They went to get the boy and he jumped from his fourth story window, apparently so ashamed of what he'd done that he couldn't live with himself.

"The girl healed in her body but her heart and soul were deeply bruised. It didn't help that her fiancé didn't look at her the same anymore. She was damaged goods in his eyes. He had held himself pure for his wedding, for his bride, and now the woman who was supposed to be his bride was no longer pure for him. Though he loved her still, he knew they were no longer right for each other. Before finals were over, he asked for his ring back.

"They went their separate ways for the summer just like everyone else at the college, but he couldn't get her out of his mind. Even though she had never been to his home, she popped up everywhere he turned. He saw her in the summer storm, in the rainbow after the storm. He saw her when his mom baked an apple pie and when his dad got out the mower and the smell of fresh cut grass drifted into his room. He began to realize that love is not nearly as easily destroyed as he thought. Oh, he could kill his love for her if he truly wanted to, if he worked hard enough at it but he didn't really want to. Each day he grew more and more certain that she was the woman he wanted to live with for the rest of his life. He went back to school with that ring in his pocket, determined to win back her love.

"It took him almost the entire school year to do it, but he did. He publicly apologized to her, over and over and over again. He wrote corny sonnets for her and went down on one knee while he read them to her. He serenaded her until dogs howled all over town and the dean threatened to throw them both out of school.

"She finally realized that he'd gone through his own fire, that the attack on her had hurt him as surely as it had hurt her. He had just needed a season to heal and grow, time to learn a deeper faith and trust. He had hurt her only because he was himself hurt. Only when he let God heal him from his hurt did he become the man she needed him to be.

"God allowed the fire to burn through their lives because that's how he refined both their characters. He refined their love for each other and for him. That fire heated them both enough to bring impurities up to the surface. When they chose to face those impurities, those character issues, God was able to skim them off and refine both the boy and the girl. He changed them, made them more Christ-like through that fiery season.

"The boy put that ring back on the girl's finger during spring break, one year after the first time he'd given it to her. She wore it the rest of her life. She even took it to the grave with her, quite a few years before her beloved husband died too.

"The girl was Kalea, your mother. The man who betrayed her was your father."

Heather stared at her mom in stunned silence. "No!"

"Oh yes. It was them," Mom said firmly. "I heard the story myself, from both of them."

The story shook the foundations of everything Heather knew to be true. Mom-Kalea and Dad's relationship had been the epitome of what a marriage should be, their love strong and true. Dad was the most stalwart man of God there ever was. In fact, Mom-Gloria had always said that the reason hers and Dad's marriage was so strong was because he'd learned to love so wonderfully in his first marriage. He was so in love with love that he could have married a monkey and had a perfect marriage.

But Dad had failed Mom-Kalea, kicked her when she was down. Then she took him back.

"How?" Heather was surprised to hear her voice crack. "How did she do it? How did Mom take that risk, that Dad wouldn't hurt her again?"

"One of the things she did was to put her own sins on the balance. She saw them sink the scales."

"Her sins? But she was raped."

"Of course, dear," Mom said gently, "and she wasn't guilty of sin in the rape, but we all have sins. Sometimes we think ours are petty and other people's are so much worse."

Gloria leaned forward in her chair and stared intently at Heather.

"Take you for instance," she said. "You know that Steve was wrong in what he said but did you think about how wrong you were that day?"

Heather looked sharply at Mom, ready to defend her actions.

"Oh, I'm not talking about at the school and you know it," Gloria scoffed at the unspoken argument. "I'm talking about in those few moments in that room when Steve stood there dying inside and you clung to your brother's hand. And don't you try to tell me or yourself that you didn't know what you were doing. You didn't want Steve to take your hand because you didn't want him to know how weak and hurt you were."

Heather opened her mouth but Gloria shushed her.

"Don't try it, young lady," she scolded. "I've been mothering you for almost twenty years! You have never wanted anyone to see you weak, not even your family. You've always fought it. You didn't cry at your mother's funeral because people would see you cry and you were only ten years old. You've always had to be as tough as your brothers. No, even tougher!"

Gloria looked at her sharply. "But here's a news flash for you, honey. You're weak just like the rest of us. One of the reasons you didn't want to take Steve's hand is that you would have had to share in his pain and you weren't strong enough to do that."

She stood up and got her purse.

"God uses different seasons in our lives to refine our character. You and Steve grew to love each other in a gentle, beautiful season. Now you're in a season of fire, a refining fire. This isn't the first fire you've faced nor will it be the last. Just like every time, you have the choice, Heather. You can face the character issues that God brought out through this fire and he will help you remove them like dross, changing you to be more Christ-like, just like he's changing Steve. Or you can ignore them and let your heart cool, harden back to what it was with all those issues still intact. You choose."

Gloria leaned over and kissed Heather on the top of her head. "I've given you enough to think about for now. You let that percolate in your brain. You think about how you could be different and quit worrying so much about how Steve hurt you."

She turned at the door.

"I'll expect to see you tomorrow for Thanksgiving. You better be wearing your jersey and be ready for some football."

Chapter 36

*H*eather was glad that her shoulder had healed enough that she was able to put on her Grizzly jersey with relative ease. She didn't want to wear her sling but she knew it was probably wise. She still had trouble remembering not to strain it, like yesterday when she was flopping around on her couch. If she had a hard time remembering, her brothers and nephews would forget easily too, especially when they started getting excited about football. She decided to wear the sling to start and see how things went.

Greg picked up her and Moose because she wasn't driving yet. When she walked out to get in the car, she took one look at Greg's car then grimaced at her dog.

"Moose, I must really love you," she said. "We could have left you at home and taken Steve's BMW convertible but no, we're going in this sorry excuse for an automobile instead."

"Hey, be nice to her!" Greg patted the roof as he opened the door for Moose. "She'd be in great condition if I could find a decent mechanic."

"Punk!" Heather punched him in the arm and climbed into the car.

Greg pulled away from the curb and glanced over at his sister.

"Nice jersey," he commented nonchalantly.

"Oh, this old thing," Heather sniffed regally. "Mom insisted, nay even threatened, that I must wear it."

"How's it feel?"

"Scary!"

"How so?"

"Contrary to popular opinion," Heather said. "I don't like getting hurt."

"I didn't think you did," Greg said.

"But I guess I can seem rather careless about pain."

"Sometimes it does look that way."

"Do me a favor, would you?" Greg raised his eyebrows in question. "If you catch me acting like that, like nothing hurts when you know it does, please let me know."

"Okay," Greg agreed.

"But gently," Heather amended. "I really don't like pain!"

As Heather watched the familiar landscape slip by, she suddenly realized how long it had been since she'd been to Mom's house.

"Greg, have I been anywhere in the last month?" Heather asked quietly. "I mean other than to the doctor."

"Um, nope," Greg said. "Not that I know of."

"Mom was so right," Heather said sadly. "I hate it when she does that."

"You mean the mom thing," Greg groaned in agreement. "Zero in on the thing you don't want to look at then slap it right out there on the table so you can't avoid it?"

"Yeah, that thing."

"So what thing was the thing she hit you with this time?" Greg asked.

"Steve," Heather said.

"Ah, the love thing!" Greg dragged out "love" and sighed theatrically.

Heather gave him stink eye. "Consider yourself punched, punk."

"Ow, I'm telling Mom," Greg grabbed his right arm as he whined.

"Both hands on the wheel," Heather scolded. "I don't want to die today."

"That's good to hear," Greg said emphatically.

"Worried for a while, were you?" Heather blinked back tears.

"Yeah, I was," Greg said softly.

"You know he's been calling?" Heather asked after a short pause.

"Yeah," Greg snorted. "I watched you ignore some of those calls, remember?"

"Oh yeah," Heather said. "He's called thirty-four times now."

"Whew," Greg whistled. "Just since Sunday?"

"I listened to twenty-eight voice mails last night," Heather said.

"No kidding? I didn't know you could get that many."

"I guess you can. I did, and an extra two since then."

"When were the last ones?"

"This morning."

"Why didn't you pick up?"

Heather thought for a while.

"I was mad," she sighed. "Now I'm just scared."

"Of what?" Greg parked on the curb at Mom's, but neither of them made a move to get out yet.

"I guess of messing up again," Heather said.

"Oh Boss, your life is so messed up now, does it matter if you mess it up more?" Greg asked helpfully.

Heather glared at him, trying not to laugh. He wiggled his eyebrows at her and gave her a cheesy grin. Heather burst into laughter. Shaking her head, she climbed out of the car. When Greg came around, she looped her right arm through his left.

"Little Big Man, no one comforts me quite like you do!"

"That's a good thing, right?" Greg grinned proudly.

"Oh, it's a very good thing," Heather said dryly.

THIS THANKSGIVING, THE Grizzlies and the Leopards played the late game which started at three in Hawaii but the Shepherds had to watch both of the earlier games too. The Grizzlies were in a precarious position with a five and five record. Their playoff hopes rested on a combination of not losing any more games and rooting for teams that could take down the ones who had higher standings than the Grizzlies, so the Shepherds felt like they had a stake in both the other games.

Like the rest of her family, Heather was interested in the early games. She enjoyed the groaning, complaining, cheering and arguing over calls. She was happy to discover that she could do it all relatively calmly, never once jarring her injured arm. At lunchtime she took off her sling because it was much easier to eat with both hands free. She didn't think to put it back on because when three o'clock rolled around, she was sleepy from the combination of turkey and football. She expected to watch the Grizzly game in a sleepy haze.

The Leopards won the toss and the commentators announced the Grizzly starting defense. Of course they paused briefly on Steve's picture to comment on how hot he was this year. He's always been superstar caliber, but this year, wow! Heather agreed dreamily even though she didn't often agree with the commentators.

Almost three minutes into the game, it happened. The Leopards had slugged it out down to their own forty yard line but they had third and a long seven. Their running back took the handoff from the quarterback and burst through the line. He juked a defender and was off into the end zone. He went up the left. He juked Steve!

Stunned silence filled Mom's living room.

"Oh no he did not!" Luke said.

"Tell me that wasn't Steve," Heather gasped and sat up straight, no longer sleepy or dreamy.

"It sure was," Mom mourned with them as the replay confirmed it.

"Someone got past Steve," Robert shook his head and looked at Heather.

They all looked at Heather.

"What're you looking at me for?" Heather shrank back into her corner of the couch.

"He's distracted, sis," Tim said.

"We can't have the best defensive end in pro football distracted," Greg said mournfully, patting Heather's knee. "Take one for the team, sistah."

Heather smacked his hand away.

"Leave me alone. It was just a fluke," Heather growled.

But it wasn't. On the Leopards' next possession, the same running back slipped past Steve again. Fortunately, Pete brought him down. Then in the third quarter, Steve hit a wide receiver as he came down with the ball on a short pass, but the man didn't go down.

Fortunately, the Grizzly offense was hot that day and every score the Leopards made, they answered with equal points or more. Late in the fourth quarter, it was a four point game with the Grizzlies on top. The Leopards had the ball on their own twenty-nine yard line. The quarterback dropped back for a pass and Steve came charging in from the left.

"Get him!" Heather leaped to her feet with a scream.

The quarterback ducked under Steve's rush, dancing away and slapping the ball, looking for an open receiver downfield.

"Don't let him get away!" Heather raged.

Steve shifted his momentum back toward the quarterback.

The quarterback saw a man wide open in the end zone.

He drew his arm back for the pass.

Steve hit him like a freight train and they both went down.

"Yes!" Heather jumped in victory. Then she cried in pain, dropping to her knees and clutching her left shoulder.

Suddenly she was surrounded by family, bending over her, touching her, asking her what was wrong, did she hurt herself. Blocking her view of the television.

"Get, get, get," she smacked at them, trying to see the television, still huddled over and clutching her shoulder. "Steve. Did he get up? Is he up yet?"

"Yes," Robert said. "He's up and on the line of scrimmage."

"The Leopards have to go for it," the commentators were saying. "This is fourth down territory."

The quarterback dropped back for a pass. He saw a man open downfield. He threw a beautiful pass. Pete leaped into the air and smashed the ball back down into his face.

"Yes!" Heather clenched her fist in victory and rolled over onto her back. "Someone call the doctor. I think something popped in my shoulder!"

Luke called the hospital and fifteen minutes later the doctor returned his call.

"Don't tell me," the doctor sounded too happy for such a call. "She watched the game."

"How'd you guess?"

"I think I pulled a muscle in my back jumping off the couch when Jeremiah missed the quarterback," the doctor laughed ruefully. "She probably went ballistic."

"Precisely," Luke said. "And this makes you happy because ...?"

"A cheerful heart is good medicine," the doctor said. "If she's cheering again, she'll be healing much better."

He told them to check for bleeding or swelling or numbness and tingling in Heather's hand. She probably hadn't done any serious damage but if she had, those were the signs that would tell them. If any of that started, they should call him directly and take her to the emergency room. Barring that, pack it in ice and bring her by for a checkup tomorrow afternoon.

They also needed to see if they could do something about Jeremiah's apparent distraction.

Chapter 37

*H*eather did not have a good night. Her shoulder hurt like a thousand menehune were tap dancing on exposed nerves. The painkillers only helped for a few hours, then she was up for an hour waiting to be able to take another. The only benefit was that she read Steve's card again and again, memorizing every word. It wasn't a simple little card nor was it a stock bouquet of flowers. Together, the card and bouquet were a very personal declaration of Steve's love for her.

> *Mere words are not enough to express my love for you, nor to apologize for my behavior. I pray that these beautiful roses help to convince you of my sincere repentance.*
>
> *I knew that my heart belonged to you when we stood beside Rainbow Falls and you so wisely advised that we proceed with caution, so the first twelve roses are the colors of the rainbow. They represent the joy we shared in Hawaii.*
>
> *Watching whales at Halona Blowhole.*
> *Decorating my home with your crazy family.*
> *Watching the sunset from the lanai.*
> *Hiking Diamond Head.*
> *Dancing to Phil Collins in the pediatrics ward.*
> *The best birthday I've ever had.*
> *Riding on the North Shore.*
> *Watching you dance for the Lord.*
> *Playing with Moose.*
> *Walking in the rain together.*
> *Holding you in my arms.*
> *Knowing my heart had found its home.*
>
> *The deep red blossom begs you to forgive me for my heartless words and actions. I cannot defend them. I can only say I was very, very wrong to succumb to my fears and to speak to you in such a way. Then I compounded my sin*

*by ignoring you, rejecting your plea for my love. I do not
deserve your forgiveness but I pray that you will extend
grace to this fool and choose to love me in spite of my faults.
    The remaining six blossoms are all white rosebuds,
tipped with the colors of the rainbow. They wait to open and
show us their wonder, just as our relationship waits for its
future. Only God knows what it will be, but I know that if
you are at my side then it will be a truly blessed adventure.*

When she was finally able to take her pain meds again, Heather fell asleep on the couch with the single red rose clasped to her breast. She was in the middle of a good period of sleep when the doorbell rang at the ungodly hour of six-thirty.

Grumbling irritably, she thrust her right arm into her old robe and tried to work the left side up as she stumbled to the door. If it was her brother because he had forgotten his key, he was dead.

She jerked the door open and came face to face with Steve.

He looked out of place in Hawaii with his sport coat, button down shirt, slacks and loafers. His hair and clothes were mussed as if he had been sleeping in them and his chin had an impressive amount of stubble. His shirt was unbuttoned to the third button, framing his Mizpah. His eyes were tired, sad, and hopeful, all at the same time.

"What are you doing here?" Heather gasped in surprise.

"A quarterback sneak," he said with a gentle smile. She looked wonderful to him in her cotton Taz pajamas, buttoned over her left arm, robe half-on, half-off. Her hair was in wild disarray and her eyes were sleepy, sad, and hopeful, all at the same time.

"You're not a quarterback," she blurted out.

"I'm versatile," he reached around her and pulled her robe up over her left shoulder, gently wrapping it around to overlap in the front.

"You jerk," she said, pushing him with her right hand, hard enough for him to stagger back a step. She followed shaking a finger at him. The door clicked gently shut behind her.

"I don't want you here! My shoulder hurts, my house is a mess, I can't fix my hair," she burst into tears and covered her face with her right hand, "and I can't put my Mizpah back on."

"Oh sweetheart," Steve groaned softly and gathered her into his arms. "It's okay. It's all okay."

"No, it isn't," she hiccupped trying to stop her tears. "Because you stole my heart and now you can't even play football anymore."

"Oh that," Steve looked more than a little embarrassed. "I'm hoping it was just a momentary distraction."

"It better be because I can't take another one for the team any time soon."

"Darlin', you sure keep a man wondering. How about we go inside so you can explain everything?" Steve reached around her to open the door. "Heather, where are your keys?"

"On the hook –," she turned around and saw the closed door. "Oh no, it has one of those bolt thingys that's always locked!"

"I don't suppose Moose can open a door?"

"Funny!"

"Back door?"

"The whole house is still locked!" Heather cried. "I just got up. Call Greg or Mom, they have keys."

Steve reached into his pocket and came up empty. He checked every pocket in his pants, shirt and jacket. Nothing. He started to laugh.

"Good thing I called Greg from the airport," he grinned, "since I left my phone on the plane with my coat."

"When's he coming?"

"Probably by about seven thirty or so. I woke him up."

"Well, we can sit at the table in the back," Heather started around the house then stopped and groaned. "Oh no, no, no! We can't do that either."

"Locked?"

"Padlock on the gate. The kids kept going in and messing with Moose."

"And the key?"

"Hanging next to the back door."

"So, you wanna walk down to McDonald's?" Steve asked innocently. She gave him stink eye as she stalked back to the front stoop and plopped down. She put her feet on the first step, her elbow on her knee, her chin in her hand.

Steve sprawled beside her, sitting on the first step with his elbows on the stoop, long legs stretched out on the sidewalk, his right foot crossed over his left. They sat quietly for a moment, both suddenly shy and unsure of where to go next.

"Aren't you supposed to be at practice?" Heather finally asked.

"Yep!" Steve agreed briefly but firmly.

"Don't you have a game Sunday?"

"Yep!"

"So what are you doing here?"

"Courting!" He smiled up at her.

"Why now, today?"

"After the fiasco yesterday that you so gently commented on earlier," Steve said. "I made an audible walking through O'Hare."

"An audible?"

"Yep, I could see the play called wasn't going to work, so I changed the play," Steve swung his right foot back and forth, watching it instead of looking at her. "We walked past an information kiosk and I stepped over to ask about charter services. I just happened to find a great guy, Joshua Wolfe, retired Air Force colonel, widowed, flies just for fun mostly but he was more than happy to fly to Hawaii for love's sake."

"And Coach was okay with this?"

"Nope! But I didn't give him much choice. I called him from the plane just before Colonel Joshua made me turn off my phone."

"Are you in trouble?"

"Oh, big time!" Steve laughed.

"Define big time."

"Twenty-five thousand dollar fine and grounded until we win the game on Sunday."

"Steve!"

He shrugged. "It's all worth it to be sitting here, talking to you."

Heather blushed and looked away. "How is a pro football player grounded?"

"Coach is meeting me at the airport, taking away my phone and putting me under twenty-four hour guard until we win on Sunday."

"What if you don't win Sunday?"

"We'll win." Steve smiled lazily.

"But it's the Stallions and they're undefeated!"

"Trust me, sweetheart. We will win!"

She looked at him doubtfully, but didn't argue. "When are you going back?"

"Colonel Joshua needs six hours of sleep before he can fly back. He said to be back at the airport at thirteen-thirty hours. That gives him time to put his baby to bed before he gets some sleep himself and time to check her over before we fly out again."

"What's that costing you?"

"Here's part of the beauty of the whole thing," Steve said. "If you don't mind, it won't cost me anything this time."

"Me? What do I have to do with it?" Heather asked in surprise.

"He's retired military. He wants to meet you."

"Why?"

"Because there aren't many living recipients of the Medal of Honor wandering around."

"Oh that," Heather said flatly.

"You say that as if it's a bad thing," Steve sat up and turned toward her, still on the lower step.

"I was just doing my job," she whispered. "I feel like a fraud."

"You're not, Beautiful," Steve said. "You're the real deal and you proved it a second time at the school that day."

Heather frowned and looked away.

"I've seen the footage the students took," Steve said softly. "What you did that day was incredible and probably saved a lot of lives. I know Robert's name was on the list they found in that boy's pocket. God put you in the right place at the right time, Heather. You just did what he told you to do."

Heather was still looking away. He saw her blink back tears.

"If I had known what it would cost," she whispered. "I might not have done it."

"It hurts that much?" Steve nodded toward her left shoulder. "It will heal."

"Not there," Heather covered her shoulder with her right hand and then slid it down, making a fist and tapping her heart. "Here." She began to cry. "I missed you so much."

She reached for him with her right arm. He slipped his head and shoulders under her arm and gathered her carefully into his lap, scooting back to sit in the corner of the stoop. His own tears fell with hers.

"I'm sorry, sweetheart, so very sorry," he whispered in her hair.

"You were a jerk," she sobbed, "but you weren't wrong. I was."

"No, you were brave and strong," Steve disagreed.

"I was weak and scared," Heather corrected, "but I wanted you to think I was brave and strong. I always want people to see me as brave and strong. But with you, ... with you, I want to be delicate and pretty and protected and that scares me. It gives you so much power. And I was already scared and you scared me more because you looked right into me and saw what no one else did."

"Shh," Steve laid a finger across her lips, then he lifted her chin to look in her eyes. "What we have scares me too, sweetheart. No one reaches into the places in me that you touch with such ease. Let's just follow God on this."

Heather blinked away tears as she gazed into Steve's eyes. Suddenly the tears began to well up again.

"I might not be able to play golf!" she moaned.

Steve laughed with delight. "Then we'll find something else to do on our honeymoon!"

She blushed and buried her face against his neck. "And I can't watch your games." Fresh tears fell.

"But that's just for a while," Steve promised. "Your shoulder will heal and you'll be back in top form. Until then, you can watch us on TV."

"No I can't," Heather sat up and frowned at him, tears still shimmering on her eyelashes and cheeks. "Yesterday when you let that little rat of a quarterback duck under you ...." She shook her head.

Steve laughed ruefully. "I felt your wrath, my dear, but I made him pay."

"Unfortunately, I paid too," Heather rubbed her shoulder gingerly.

"Ahh, the one you took for the team," Steve now understood.

"I'm not sure whether it was when I jumped up to scream at you or when you finally hit him and I jumped in victory," she wasn't sure if she should be proud or embarrassed, "but when you hit the turf, I felt the pain. It was a nine."

"Will it help if nothing ever gets past me on the field again?" Steve asked.

"Tremendously, I'm sure," Heather said seriously. "It's certainly worth the try."

"Then I'll make it so," Steve promised, "and you do your best not to get into a tiff with a ref so that you'll be all healed up in time for the Championship Game."

"Sounds like a plan," Heather sighed and laid her head back on his chest. Steve was suddenly very glad that they weren't alone inside with only Moose as a chaperone.

Just then, Steve noticed his BMW coming up the street. "And here's Tonto, the faithful sidekick, sooner than expected."

Greg was laughing as he climbed out of the car.

"You two are quite a pair." He shook his head as he grabbed some grocery bags and a small duffle bag out of the trunk.

"I call Steve from the grocery store to see what we need for breakfast since I know what Heather's kitchen looks like." He came up the sidewalk and stopped in front of them. "I don't get Steve, I get his pilot. I didn't even know he had a pilot. So I call Heather and get no answer."

He handed Steve the bags in his right hand and fished around in his pocket for his house keys.

"So I rush over here, praying that the aforementioned facts don't mean that something's going on that neither of you want to happen yet." The relief in Greg's grin was obvious. "What I discover is that my sister locked herself out of her house again. Boss, I told you to stash a key somewhere closer than the shop."

"Just shut up and open the door, punk," Heather reached up with her right hand. "After you give me a hand up."

When she stood, so did Steve, stepping out of the way for Greg to get to the door. As soon as she heard the click of the bolt snapping back Heather panicked, suddenly remembering what her house looked like.

"No," she turned to Steve and put her hand flat on his chest, pushing him away. "You can't come in. Go away for an hour." She looked over her shoulder. "Make that two hours. Then you can come back."

"Sweetheart, I have seven hours in Honolulu that are supposed to hold me over through January, why would I waste a minute of it away from you?" Steve asked.

"Because I ... haven't been myself," she ducked her head in shame, "and my house really is a mess."

"Hey, no shame, Beautiful," Steve tilted her chin up with his free hand, wiping away a tear that trembled on her lower eyelid. "You're back now, that's what matters."

"Okay, but you asked for it," she sighed and swept into the house.

Greg stood there holding the door open, waiting for him.

"She's such a drama queen," Greg said softly as Steve walked up. "It's really not that bad."

Prepared for the worst, Steve looked around when he walked into the house. Greg was right, it wasn't nearly as bad as it could have been. There was a general feeling of clutter about the living room and kitchen which flowed together, broken only by a breakfast bar. Clean clothes were piled in a heap in one armchair. Books, magazines and mail cluttered the coffee table and fell onto the floor with a number of empty foam cups laying amidst them. A pillow and blanket testified to someone sleeping on the couch. A cereal box lay on its side on the floor below the pillow with a single red rose laying on the box. A half-empty bottle of diet cola, a basket of bananas that were ready for bread, an empty pizza box and a diverse collection of other items cluttered the bar. Dishes flowed into the sink and the coffee pot hadn't been cleaned out. But the house smelled like dog, not rotten food, dirty clothes and other much more unpleasant odors that he could still remember from his childhood.

Heather was busy stuffing things into a rubbish bag. Steve cleared a space and set his grocery bags down on the counter then quickly walked over to Heather, taking the bag from her and leading her over to the hallway. He took her face in both his hands and made her look at him.

"Stop fussing, sweetheart," he said earnestly. "My father was an alcoholic and my mother was depressed. I've seen much, much worse. What I see now is the clutter of a person who has fought depression, not succumbed to it."

He kissed her on the forehead and then hugged her tight, albeit gently. "Go get dressed." He turned her and gave her a gentle shove. "By the time you get back, we'll have the kitchen in order again."

Heather looked over her shoulder at him and he shooed her away. She walked slowly down the hall, looking back at him once then disappearing into her bedroom.

As soon as her door closed, Steve ran his hands through his hair and groaned. "I feel like such a heel, having done this to her."

"Oh you're a heel alright," Greg cheerfully gave him small comfort, "but this isn't all your fault."

They started cleaning as they talked.

"She's had nightmares about Robert getting shot and her shoulder was really messed up, especially since it's the same shoulder injured over in Iraq."

Greg stopped and stared down at the rubbish bag he was filling.

"She hurt so bad, in head, heart and body and she didn't want to face any of it. For the first week she was home, she barely moved from the couch at all. The counselor advised us to be around but not to do too much for her, so we quit cleaning, doing her laundry and stuff. We hoped that she would be motivated to do something for herself, but all she did was make sure there was no really nasty rubbish. That was something I guess."

Greg looked at Steve and smiled. "She really started coming back when I brought Moose home last week. Then Mom said something to her on Wednesday and she even washed clothes. She's going to be okay, even without you, you jerk."

"I'm glad you think so, brah," Steve said, "but she's going to be even better because she has me, as long as we both live."

"So are you guys officially engaged?"

"No, but we will be when I come back after the season," Steve grinned.

When Heather came out, the kitchen was cleaned and breakfast was almost done. Steve was scrambling eggs when he smelled pikake and jasmine behind him. He turned with a smile.

Heather now wore a pair of navy capri pants and an orange and yellow oversized shirt, her left arm buttoned up inside it. Her hair was unbound and still damp, the curls just beginning to spring free. In her hand she held her Mizpah, offering it to him with an unspoken plea.

He took the necklace from her hand and she turned, lifting her hair off her neck. His fingers were no less clumsy than they had been the last time he'd put it on her but he managed just fine. When the chain was hooked back together, he laid it gently on her neck, smoothing it then leaning down to kiss her neck. Heather sighed and leaned back against him. He ran his hands down her arms.

"Excuse me," Greg said loudly, "but it's breakfast time. I'm starving."

Steve gently pushed Heather away from him and turned to the stove again. "Why don't you get some plates out while I finish the eggs?"

Greg caught the look that passed between them. Muttering about reinforcements, he went to the back door and let Moose back in.

Chapter 38

*G*reg had brought Steve a change of clothes so after breakfast he used Heather's guest bathroom to shower and change. While he was changing, Greg and Heather cleaned most of the living room and Steve helped finish when he came out.

When they were done cleaning, Steve and Heather sat side by side on the couch and Greg sat in the armchair, talking about inconsequential things. Suddenly Greg got up and squatted in front of Heather.

"When's the last time you took your pain meds, Boss?" he asked gently.

Heather glared at him. Steve shifted his position to look at her more directly.

"I don't know. Three-thirty, four o'clock," Heather shrugged.

"What's your pain?"

She didn't reply.

"Heather?" Steve asked sharply.

"Okay, it's an eight, maybe a nine," she said with tears pooling in her eyes. "Why do I keep crying?"

"It's still that bad?" Steve was surprised.

"It was better until yesterday," Greg explained. "She's got a doctor's appointment this afternoon." Greg looked back at Heather. "Have you checked for swelling? Bleeding? How are your fingers?"

"My fingers are fine," Heather said.

"But you can't check your shoulder very well," Greg stood up and held out his hand. "Come on, Boss."

She just sat there, staring at her right hand, curled up in Steve's.

"Heather," Steve said gently. "Please, take care of yourself."

"But you're only here for such a short time," she looked at him sadly, "and then I won't see you for two months."

"And we'll have a lifetime together," Steve stood and helped her to her feet. "You need to take care of yourself."

When they came back ten minutes later, Greg looked serious, much too serious for him. Heather went straight to Steve, laying her head on his chest and wrapping her right arm around him. He wrapped both arms around her and looked questioningly at Greg.

"There's swelling, maybe even a lump," Greg sighed. "The doctor said it could be a blood clot. He said to put ice on it and bring her in for her appointment this afternoon, but she just took a painkiller so she's gonna be groggy at best. Sorry to have your trip wasted like this."

"She's talking to me," Steve smiled, "so this trip has not been a waste."

Heather quickly fell asleep, sheltered in Steve's arm. Steve and Greg talked for a while until they both fell asleep too. About an hour later Heather woke up with a throbbing shoulder but at least the pain was only about a four. She sat up carefully and nudged Steve awake with a giggle.

"Hey," she whispered, "just who's taking care of who?"

"Whom, my dear," Steve whispered back with a sleepy smile. "Who is taking care of whom?"

"Oh don't be such an English major!" Heather teased him.

"Can't help it, Beautiful." They were still whispering. "It comes with the territory."

Heather leaned back and drew her feet up on the edge of the couch. Steve felt her movement, sensed a sudden thoughtful attitude.

"What?" he whispered with his eyes still closed.

"I was just wondering," she whispered back. "What it's like ... exploring that territory."

"I wouldn't know," Steve whispered, eyes still closed, a blush gently touching his cheek.

"You mean ...?" Heather's whisper was awed.

"Virgin territory," Steve nodded slowly.

"Not just me?" Heather felt a fierce joy rise inside.

"Not just you, sweetheart," Steve rolled his head toward her, his blue eyes bright with his smile.

"Some whispers are loud enough to wake the dead," Greg grumbled. "This is not a conversation I wanted to hear."

"Does it bother you to find out you've been hanging out with the world's largest virgin?" Steve laughed.

"It shouldn't," Heather giggled. "He's the second largest."

"You are?"

"I am."

"He is," Heather smiled.

"Good for you," Steve said.

"Good for all of us," Greg agreed. After a moment's thought he had to ask. "How did you guys do it? It wasn't hard for me because girls never pay attention to me but you two have both been in cultures that glorified and expected ... shall we say vigorous activity."

"Pretty much the same way you did, I guess," Steve answered thoughtfully. "I made a conscious decision while I was still young then stayed as clueless as possible for as long as possible."

"Clueless?"

"Yeah," Steve said. "Don't look for it. Don't listen to it being talked about. Don't watch it in pictures or videos. It's a lot easier to resist temptation if you keep it out of the room."

"How'd you keep the motivation all these years?" Greg asked.

"I knew it was what God wanted for my life," Heather said, "and that was enough. When I got out into the real world, I heard other women comparing the men they'd had and I realized I never wanted to have anyone to compare my future husband to. That pretty much cemented it for me."

"I was backwards from that," Steve carefully controlled his surge of joy at her words. "I started out thinking about being as pure as I wanted my future bride to be. Then when I was a junior in college I dated a girl. One date. She was looking for a rising star to hook up to and she embarrassed me with the lengths she was willing to go to sink that hook."

Steve shook his head and blushed with the memory. "That's when I realized that waiting for my future bride wouldn't be good enough motivation to stay sexually pure. If it was only for her, what would I do if she decided she wanted it before the wedding night? So I decided to remain pure because God is pure and holy, not for my future bride."

Greg thought for a moment.

"So you both did it for God," he finally said. "I've wondered if I'll be strong enough when temptation comes, now I feel more sure. But I don't know if it's really weird or way cool to have had this conversation with my big sister and her wanna-be fiancé."

Heather made a face at him.

"He's getting concerned because he's falling in love," Heather whispered conspiratorially to Steve.

"I am not!" Greg hotly denied it.

"Her name is Beth," Heather told Steve. "She's in a couple of his classes in bible college."

"I barely know her," Greg frowned. "I'm not falling in love with her."

"He informed her she was a girl," Heather said slyly.

Steve roared with laughter.

"Oh yes, you are! Does she have a pair of pretty hazel eyes?" Steve winked at Heather.

"Actually, they're gray," Greg scowled.

"And he barely knows her," Heather giggled, toppling slowly over onto Steve's shoulder and batting dreamy eyes up at him.

"I can't wait to meet her," Steve said with a huge grin.

"Well you're not going to," Greg snapped. "Not until we bring home our firstborn child."

Heather's laughter pealed so loud that Moose sat up and barked.

"I don't mean ... that. I just want to ... protect her from .... I'll shut up now," Greg stood and stalked to the kitchen. "Does anyone want lunch?"

"He sounds like you, love," Steve smiled down at Heather. She had slid down to lay stretched out on the couch, her head on Steve's leg. She rubbed her shoulder ruefully as she smiled back.

"He sounds just like me!"

WHILE THEY WERE enjoying lunch, it suddenly occurred to Steve that the three of them weren't going anywhere together in his two-seater car and the backseat of Heather's car was too doggy. They called in reinforcements. Mom was happy to come over with her minivan, though Steve did grumble about the utter humiliation of riding around in a soccer mom vehicle.

The terminal for private planes was much easier to get to than the commercial terminals and all too soon they were pulling up to park. Steve had called Colonel Joshua and let him know they were coming. The colonel was easy to spot as he emerged from the building, not only because he was the only other person in sight but also because of his obvious military bearing. He was so straight and strong that when he came up to shake Heather's hand, she was surprised to discover that he was no taller than her.

"If this were a corny movie," the colonel said with a gentle smile. "I'd salute you even though you don't wear the Medal yet but we both know that's not how it's done in the real world."

"I deeply appreciate your restraint," Heather smiled back. She immediately liked Steve's pilot. His grip was firm, his green eyes bright and his attitude confident without being cocky. The fact that he still wore his wedding ring warmed her heart. Mom still wore hers too.

"I wish we had time to talk story more," the colonel said, "but I need to get the truant back to school."

"You've spent some time in Hawaii?" Greg caught the "talk story" part of his comment.

"Affirmative. Nine years total at Hickam," the colonel shook Greg's hand too. "The wife really loved it. That's why she's buried up in the Punchbowl."

"She was military too?" Mom asked as the colonel also greeted her.

"Marine. She was killed early on in the desert. Roadside bombing."

"I'm sorry for your loss," Mom said.

"As I am for yours," the colonel gave her a slight bow. At her questioning look, Steve shrugged.

"It was a long flight."

"I've heard quite a bit about the Shepherds," the colonel smiled.

"And yet you wanted to meet us anyway?" Greg was puzzled.

"Wouldn't have missed it for the world." The colonel's eyes twinkled as he turned to Steve. "Are you ready to get this show on the road?"

"About that," Steve said, "do you have anything waiting for you in Chicago?"

"That's a negative."

"Heather has a doctor's appointment at one-thirty," Steve took her hand and looked at her with hopeful eyes. "If she doesn't mind, I'd like to stay for that."

"I don't mind," she smiled joyfully up at him.

"Do you mind if I go off base with you?" the colonel asked. "This place is about as much fun as plucking my beard with tweezers."

Steve looked at Mom.

"It won't be very interesting," she told the colonel. "We'll be sitting in the waiting room but you're welcome to come with."

"Thank you, ma'am," the colonel said with a nod.

"Have you really done that?" Greg was staring thoughtfully at the colonel's chin.

"Done what?"

"Plucked your beard with tweezers," Greg half whispered with curious awe.

"You'd be surprised what I've done, son," the colonel's face lit up with his grin.

"This is gonna be fun," Greg laughed. "I get shotgun."

As he climbed into the front passenger seat, Steve smiled ruefully down at the colonel. "I hope you don't mind sitting in the back of a minivan."

"With such beautiful ladies and a horse's ... backside in front of me," the colonel said with a twinkle in his eye. "I'll feel like I'm Cinderfella on the way to the ball."

"Hey I heard that! Was he talking about me?" Greg complained as the colonel walked around the van to open the driver's door for Mom. "Were you talking about me? He wasn't talking about me, was he Mom?"

"I'm afraid so, son," Gloria sighed sadly but with a smile that denied her sorrow.

Heather went back to the exam room alone while the others sat in the empty waiting room, talking story. The doctor had kept a very light schedule for the semi holiday so it wasn't even fifteen minutes before the nurse came out per Heather's request and invited them all, including Colonel Joshua, to come back for the doctor's prognosis.

They met in the doctor's office rather than the small exam room. Steve sat on Heather's right, holding her hand, with Gloria on her left. Greg and Colonel Joshua stood behind her.

"The news is good and not so good," the doctor said. "The not so good is that there's definitely something in Heather's shoulder. It could be a blood clot or a bone chip. We won't know for sure until we look at it with an MRI. But once we know what it is we can easily take care of it. When we do, the intense pain that she's been experiencing will abate."

"How long will it take?" Heather asked.

"If the technicians are available over at the hospital, we can get the MRI done this afternoon."

"And then?" Steve asked.

"If it's a clot, we'll start dissolving it. If it's a bone chip, we'll take it out."

"When? How long will my shoulder be immobilized again?"

"It won't be nearly as serious as your last surgery. Within a week, you'll be doing physical therapy. As for when," the doctor shrugged. "If the resources are available at the hospital, we can do it this afternoon. It isn't a major surgery."

"You can stay?" Heather asked Steve.

"It may cost me another tiny little fine but yeah, I can stay," Steve affirmed.

"Then let's do it," Heather said.

While the nurse called the hospital, Mom called Heather's other brothers and let them know what was going on. If she did go into surgery, they would be there.

Things moved rapidly because Heather was a favored patient. Everyone was willing to either stay or come back in. When the doctor's diagnosis was for surgery to remove a bone chip, Heather opted for local rather than general anesthesia so that she wouldn't have to spend another night in the hospital.

The surgery didn't take long and by six o'clock, Heather was being wheeled into a recovery room where Steve came to take her hand once again.

"Hey, no pain," Heather smiled up at him.

"Maybe that's because you're on some really good painkillers," Steve suggested.

"Maybe," Heather giggled, "but I can still feel things. I feel your love."

"Always, Beautiful, always," Steve kissed her forehead.

"Oh man, they're back at it again," Tim complained from the door.

"Do you have to do it in public?" Robert joined his brother.

"You don't have to look," Steve said, smiling into Heather's dopey eyes and stroking the hair back from her face.

"Get out of the way, boys," Luke said, "'cause I'm gonna watch."

"Oh me too, me too!" Greg pushed his way into the room.

"Calm down, boys," Gloria warned, "or I'll throw you out. They're breaking the rules for us, so you could behave."

"Is she talking to *my* brothers?" Heather asked Steve with a frown. "Does she really think they could behave?"

"Maybe it's senility," Steve said. "She is getting old."

"I'm not that old," Gloria denied hotly.

"Not too old to love again, right Colonel Joshua?" Heather giggled.

The colonel looked startled and Gloria blushed furiously.

"Ignore her, Colonel," Luke laughed. "She has hoof-in-mouth disease."

"And it get's worse when she's tired, on pain meds or mooning over Steve," Greg raised open hands toward the bed, "and there we have all three."

"I didn't say that out loud, did I?" Heather asked Steve with tears in her eyes.

"Yes sweetheart, I'm afraid you did," Steve said.

"You don't think I scared him off, do you?" she whispered, looking only at him.

"I don't think he scares that easily," Steve assured her.

"Good, 'cause him and Mom should be friends, don't you think?" she still whispered. "They'll be good for each other."

Steve shook with silent laughter, refusing to raise his eyes to his new friend.

"I think you might be right," he choked back his laughter.

"I know I'm right," she said smugly, no longer whispering. "Hey, you know what else?"

"What?"

"You need to go win one for the Gipper!"

Steve threw back his head and laughed.

"That's what I'll do, my dear. I love you, Heather Shepherd."

And he did.

Heather had her arm anchored to her body with both a sling and ace bandages. She wasn't taking any chances during the game. Over in St. Louis, Steve let nothing past him and the Grizzlies annihilated the previously undefeated Stallions, twenty to nothing. Grizzly fans began to have serious hopes for a shot at the championship, especially after they also won their next two games.

Chapter 39

*C*olonel Joshua was not scared away by Heather's recovery room suggestion. In fact, he was instrumental in getting Heather to the White House the week before Christmas to meet the President and receive the Medal. He flew the entire family there in his Gulfstream, from Gloria on down to baby Naomi. Heather didn't have to wait two months to see Steve since the Grizzlies were playing the Washington Generals the following Sunday. He was there for the Friday afternoon ceremony and spent Friday and Saturday evening with them also.

Even though he was a football fan, the President didn't make any fanfare about meeting Steve. He kept the ceremony and reception centered on Heather, leaving Steve in his rightful place as a very close friend.

December in Washington, D.C. is cold, especially for people from Hawaii but they still went sightseeing on Saturday. The colonel had spent many years in the District and he gladly acted as their tour guide. They walked the Mall, saw the Lincoln Memorial, the Washington Monument and the Wall. They had lunch at his favorite restaurant and watched boats on the Potomac. They called it a day in mid afternoon because the cold was starting to bother Heather's shoulder.

The next day was sunny and mild with temperatures predicted in the sixties. Though Heather had gone to D.C. knowing that per the doctors orders she wouldn't be going to the game, she was still sad when the others headed out right after brunch. The colonel had chosen to stay with her and Naomi, assuring Luke and Nalani that he had seen many pro games and would see many more.

When Heather and the colonel got back to the suite with Naomi, they laid her down and decided to take naps with her since the game didn't start until one. The colonel woke to find Heather staring down at the Medal. When they had come back to the suite on Friday, Gloria had put it in its display case and placed it on the side table in the living room. Heather had avoided it ever since.

"I don't deserve this," Heather said as the colonel walked up behind her.

"I disagree," he said, "but I'm curious to know why you feel that way."

"I know there are others who did so much more and got downgraded," Heather shook her head. "Why me?"

"Why do you think you got it?" the colonel asked.

"Because I'm a woman. Because I was already a public figure since I've been dating Steve. Because I just happened to walk into a school shooting on the very day they were going to vote me down on the Medal."

"Why do you think all those 'because' things happened?"

"I don't know," Heather said angrily.

"I think you do," the colonel replied calmly then stood there silent and unmoving.

"But why did God will it?" Heather finally asked. Before the colonel could start his next question, she jumped in and answered it.

"Okay, so he wants me to use it for his glory, but how?" She gave him stink eye and shook her finger at him. "And you better give me a straight answer this time."

"I think you already know your answers," the colonel laughed gently. "You don't really need my advice."

"But I want your advice," Heather sighed and stared at the floor. "I miss my dad so much sometimes."

"From what I've heard, he was a very good man, a good husband and a good father."

"One of the best."

"I'm flattered that you would consider me as an acceptable reinforcement."

"Um, I'm sorry about that," Heather blushed fiercely. "I really hadn't intended to say that. I don't even recall thinking about it before saying it."

"Actually, I was talking about your comment just a few moments ago, about wanting advice," the colonel said wryly, "but I'm very, very flattered that you suggested the other."

"It probably doesn't surprise you that I found out very early on that I wasn't going to be able to make the army a career," Heather sighed and flopped down on the couch, wincing as the flare of pain reminded that she still wasn't ready to do that.

"Tact and diplomacy are necessary skills for military career advancement," the colonel agreed, sprawling in the easy chair facing her.

"I bet your airmen hated to stand in front of you for an Article 15," Heather grinned.

"Some of the highlights of my career were watching them squirm," the colonel agreed.

"Figuratively speaking, I'll bet," Heather said. "I'm sure none of them dared twitch from the position of attention."

"Except for the one who fainted dead away, you would be right," the colonel agreed with a small grin.

"Oh? Do tell!" Heather laughed.

"Not much to tell, I'm afraid. The girl was two months pregnant and she locked her knees. That combination did her in, not my gentle attention," he smiled, "but none of this answers your question."

"Yes. What am I going to do with that thing?" Heather pointed toward the Medal with her chin. "I know I don't really deserve it."

"But how often do we get what we deserve, either for the good we have done or for the bad," the colonel shook his head. "The trick, my dear, is to take your focus off yourself."

"And put it on God where it belongs," Heather sighed and frowned. "I know this. Why do I need to be reminded of it?"

"Because my friend, for all your heroism, you're still just a child," the colonel inclined his head, "as am I also. We're struggling to grow in God, to become more Christ-like. Like a child we toddle along, fall down and get back up again."

"I do a lot of falling," Heather said.

"But your general direction is toward a bold march," the colonel replied.

"But how do I know where to go?"

The colonel thought for a moment. "When you were in boot camp, did you always know where you were going?"

"Ha! Hardly ever."

"How did you get there if you didn't know where you were going?"

"I followed the guy in front of me," Heather smiled, understanding his direction. "Who followed the guy in front of him, who was ultimately following the drill sergeant."

The colonel nodded.

"So all I really need to do is just take one step at a time, as the way becomes clear."

He nodded again.

"When opportunities arise, ask God what he wants me to do, and follow his lead," Heather said. "Thanks, Colonel. You're a good reinforcement."

"It's an honor," the colonel smiled. "Now, are we ready for some football?"

Heather was still wearing her sling except when she did physical therapy. For the games she usually strapped it down well, but today she was caught unprepared to do so since she was on the road. She hoped that she would be okay anyway, what with the sling and Colonel Joshua's calming presence. She was wrong.

The first factor she forgot was the importance of their last two games. If they won them both, they would win the division and have home field advantage the first week of the playoffs. If they lost one and won one, they would still be guaranteed a wild card slot but they might not get the division. If they lost them both, they might not even get the wild card slot.

The second factor that came back to haunt her and every other Grizzly fan was the offense. They had been so good in the last three weeks that some of their talent for ineptitude had been forgotten. Unfortunately, though forgotten it was not dead and it reared its ugly head in a major way.

The third factor, previously unknown, was that the colonel was a huge Grizzly fan and he hated ineptitude.

Through most of the first half, Heather and Colonel Joshua both did very commendable jobs controlling themselves but it was a major strain. The quarterback looked like a second-string high school quarterback, or so the colonel observed with rising ire. He fumbled handoffs, threw into double coverage, lofted the ball with no clue where his receivers were and hung in the pocket way too long. The Grizzly offense didn't earn one first down in the entire half and the only score put up for the visiting team was a punt returned for a touchdown.

The defense was incredible, standing like a wall on the field but the Grizzly offense's failure to keep the ball left the defense out on the field for a grueling twenty-three minutes of the first half. With that many shots at the end zone, the Generals put up thirteen points on a touchdown and two field goals.

During halftime Heather and the colonel both felt the need to cool off and calm down, so they turned off the sound of the commentators and stepped out on the balcony, the door open to listen for Naomi.

"Steve's just fine, Heather," the colonel said when he noticed Heather chewing on her knuckle.

"But he's got to be tired," Heather stared vacantly out over the city. "He's played almost the entire half! How's he going to make it through another half like that without getting hurt?"

"Heather, his life is in God's hands. Relax and let God be God. You don't need to worry about Steve."

Heather didn't reply, still staring out over the city. "Do you think God cares about the outcome of this game?"

"I don't know, but I do know that he cares about how well Steve plays the game, whether he honors God and gives it his best effort. That's what really matters, not the win or the loss."

"You're right, of course," Heather agreed. Then she leaned closer and whispered. "But I really wanna win!"

"So do I, Heather. So do I!" The colonel turned back toward their suite and motioned with his hand for Heather to precede him. "Shall we?"

The second half started no better than the first. The Generals received the ball at the twenty yard line after a touchback and an already exhausted Grizzly defense took the field. Inch by inch, the Generals clawed their way past the fifty yard line, the Grizzly defense digging in but too exhausted to push them back. After five and a half minutes, the Generals finally put up three more points on a field goal from the thirty-one yard line.

The Grizzly offense took the field. On the third down, the quarterback threw a beautiful pass, right to the Generals' safety! The Generals had the ball in Grizzly territory and the visiting fans were livid, including Heather and the colonel. Little Naomi picked that moment to awaken from her long nap, and the colonel and Heather helped each other take care of her needs as they continued to watch the game.

Exhaustion and frustration dogged the Grizzly defense. Yard by yard, the confident Generals pushed back the disheartened Grizzlies. Penalties began to proliferate as tempers flared on both sides. The Generals finally pushed into the red zone and the Grizzlies dug in, forcing them to two third down conversions to get to first and goal from the three yard line. There they stood. The Generals couldn't go over or through the Grizzlies' defense of their goal line. On fourth down, they settled for another three.

As the third quarter ticked away, the Grizzly offense took to the field again. The first two downs were running plays that yielded four yards. They had to go to the air on third down. It was a good pass, enough for a first down. It was into double coverage. It was batted down.

Flags flew in the backfield immediately after the whistle blew for the dead ball. It was a late hit on the quarterback, a fifteen yard penalty and automatic first down. The quarterback was slow getting up, clutching his right shoulder.

Heather knew she shouldn't be glad for the man's injury, so she shoved back the fierce joy that Steve and the defense wouldn't have to drag themselves back onto the field yet. The second string quarterback, Tyler Reynolds, was virtually untried with less than fifteen minutes of playing time in his first two seasons but he couldn't be worse.

He wasn't. He didn't have the flash of the Grizzly starting quarterback but he was rock solid, unflappable and utterly resilient. He ran onto the field and took charge like a maestro leading a world class orchestra, drawing the best from all the instruments in his control. Reynolds was indeed in control on that field.

Coach told him to stay on the field, so he did. Running plays and short passes perfectly placed for the receivers ate up the time as they marched slowly down the field. While time passed, the play clock didn't tick away nearly as fast since the Grizzlies used the sidelines to stop the clock on almost every down.

Even though they were down by twelve and the fourth quarter was relentlessly ticking away, Reynolds would not be rushed. Heather and the colonel read his message long before the commentators picked up on it. He had utter confidence that the defense would not allow another score if he only gave them the time to get their second wind. He was giving them back the hope that they had lost in the grueling first three quarters even as he displayed his faith that they would get the ball back to him with enough time to score again.

Eight minutes and thirty-six seconds showed on the clock when the kicker put up the point after the touchdown, which was a three yard run into the end zone. The Grizzly fans were wild with joy. Hope surged.

A renewed defense took to the field and schooled the Generals' offense. The running back hit a wall in the middle and lost two yards. He hit another wall on the left, lost another yard. Forced to pass, the Generals' quarterback found himself laying face up on the turf, another eight yards back from the line of scrimmage. He was offered a friendly hand up by number ninety-five of the Grizzlies.

As the defense jogged off the field and the offense trotted on, many of the defenders gave their young quarterback high fives and pats on the back, encouraging him as he had encouraged them. He responded by once again taking charge of the field.

After the Generals' punt they had the ball deep in their own territory, perilously deep at the four yard line. Reynolds played as if there were no end zone, either behind or before him, just the next five yards that he needed to get. He took the offense on a leisurely stroll down the middle of the field, stopping the clock as little as possible and forcing the Generals to use all their timeouts. Picking up three to five yards on every play, he rarely got a first down other than on a third down conversion. He gave the fans plenty to dance over, little to cheer about and nothing to groan about. He stomped solidly down the field and gently laid the ball into the receiver's hands on third and goal from the six yard line.

Now the fans, both in the stadium and in their hotel room, did cheer, leaping with explosive joy. Not only had they scored and taken a two-point lead, they also had an excellent prognosis for a win. The two-minute warning was long since passed and the Generals were out of timeouts. They would be hard pressed to put up the three they needed to win the game with little more than a minute remaining.

Fear surged in the Grizzly heart when the Generals' kick returner broke free and was not taken down until the Grizzly forty-five. The Generals only needed ten yards to get into their kicker's field goal range.

A false start put them back five. A short run up the right and out of bounds gave them three and stopped the clock. Then an offsides penalty gave them ten yards, but the running back lost two when he tried to go up the left. Unfortunately, he was able to step out of bounds and stop the clock. A short run up the right and out of bounds gave them the four they needed for a first down, but with only eight seconds left on the clock they didn't have enough time to do anything but go for the field goal. They were in their kicker's range.

The ball was snapped. The kick was up. At the extreme edge of his power, the kicker knew he had to kick it lower to go the distance and split the uprights. It rocketed off his foot and into the upraised hands of a six foot eight defensive end whose vertical leap intersected the ball's trajectory.

Heather had wisely laid her little niece in her travel crib behind the couch. She and the colonel were perched on the edges of the couch. When Steve erupted into the air, so did they. With fierce shouts of joy, they raised hands in victory, jumped and hugged and did their victory dances.

Heather finally collapsed back onto the couch, laughing happily and groaning miserably. Pain shot through her shoulder, maybe even a seven but not more. She hadn't hurt anything, it was just used much more than the sore tissue desired. Right then she made a secret decision. She would be healed enough to go to the Championship Game because the Grizzlies *were* going to make it, but she was going alone. She didn't want to risk the pain of the full contact, excessive celebration that she obviously couldn't control when she was with her loved ones.

Chapter 40

*T*he Shepherds and Colonel Joshua met Steve at the airport Sunday evening. They were spending Christmas in Chicago and watching the last regular season game, a home game, before returning home.

Heather's pinched look testified to her need for pain meds even before she confessed to it. She laughingly told Steve that the colonel's calm and restraint totally disappeared when he watched the Grizzlies play. She also ruefully admitted that she was going to need some better bindings before the next game, which she would still have to watch from home.

Steve suggested that they could sit in the team's family box but Heather wasn't ready for that kind of scrutiny yet. She wasn't sure if she ever would be.

Heather took her pain meds as soon as she was sure no one would have to carry her onto the plane. She fell asleep with Steve's arm around her, feeling his laugh rumble under her cheek as he told how Reynolds had apologized to the defense for leaving so much time on the clock after the last score.

She awoke in Steve's arms as he carried her from the plane. A cold Chicago wind brought her out of her sleep but drove her deeper into the warmth of Steve's embrace. When he felt her snuggle closer Steve laughed and tightened his grip.

"It's snowing," he said.

Heather had spent three winters in Fort Drum, New York and two in Germany, so she'd already seen plenty snow. This snow had a special magic that she'd never known before. She slipped one slender hand out from beneath the blanket that Steve had wrapped her in and reached out to the downy flakes, now falling gently as they'd stepped into the lee of the building. She smiled up at Steve and he too felt the special magic though he'd seen snow every winter for all his thirty years.

Heather and Gloria stayed with Jenni and the girls while the rest of the family bunked over at Steve's. Early Monday morning, Kara and Ana woke the women, insisting that it was time to go to Uncle Steve's. They were invited for breakfast, so they trouped on over. Even though it was seven-thirty, Nalani and the children were the only ones already up.

"Too much testosterone," Nalani shuddered. "They were up with their chest-pounding, male-bonding silliness until the wee hours of the morning. Please take me away!"

"It wasn't silliness, woman, it was manliness," Luke grumbled as he emerged from the hallway, "and no one is taking you from me."

With Naomi snuggled in her left arm Nalani went into his arms for a kiss.

"Silliness and manliness," Heather said, "are equivalent terms."

"Are not, Boss," Greg disagreed as he emerged with their younger brothers in tow. "I'm starved. What's for breakfast?"

"This is a well-stocked kitchen," Jenni said, "so we can have whatever we want but I don't recommend that anyone go beyond the coffee that's already brewing until the master chef puts in his appearance."

"Where is our illustrious host?" Luke looked around.

"Probably dead to the world after the whipping I put on him last night," Greg said confidently.

"You put a whipping on him?" Tim laughed. "That's not how I remember it."

"Me neither," Robert agreed. "Seems to me you were the one he had pinned."

"I see what you mean," Heather said to Nalani. "You do need to be rescued."

Luke just tightened his hold on his wife and glared at his sister.

"Do we raid the master's kitchen," Greg said, "or beard the lion in his den?"

"We'll beard." Tim looked at Robert as if he were crazy. "Awe come on Tim, it'll be fun!"

"Fun! He weighs more than both of us put together," Tim complained.

"Oh, I don't think he's *that* big," Jenni said confidently.

"Weapons. We need weapons," Tim said nervously.

"Nah, you only need interference," Greg corrected him. He pushed Heather forward.

"Me! I'm not running interference!"

He shoved a cup of coffee at her. "Then be the carrier for this."

"Please," Robert pleaded. "This'll be a whole lot more fun if we don't get killed."

"Ya think?" Luke said sarcastically.

"Oh, okay," Heather took the cup from Greg with a frown, "but Steve better not get hurt!"

"Him!" Tim almost wailed. "What about me?"

"You're the one looking for trouble," Heather said. "He's innocently sleeping and vulnerable."

"Vulnerable? Steve?" Greg laughed.

"We need weapons," Tim insisted.

STEVE WAS SOUND asleep, dreaming of Heather smiling at him in the falling snow. Suddenly a clump of snow hit him in the back of his head, then another.

It shouldn't be snowing in my bed, Steve thought as he struggled to wake up. It wasn't snowing, that was snowballs. Two more hit him on his torso and he pushed himself up with a roar, spinning as he leapt to his feet. A pillow hit him from behind, staggering him before he could grab Robert who swung an uppercut with his pillow.

Steve threw his right arm up to block Tim's next hit and lunged for Robert, ignoring the pillow. He wrapped both arms around Robert and lifted him in a bear hug. Tim pushed him from behind, and with his footing not level Steve fell over with Robert still firmly in his grip.

Robert popped an arm free as they fell and he flailed around until he found another pillow. He weakly flopped it at Steve but Tim jumped to the rescue with two pillows, battering Steve rapid fire.

Steve made the mistake of letting go of Robert to go for Tim. Both boys quickly double-teamed him, pushing him off the bed. He rolled and flipped to his feet, taking off after them as they ran through the door.

Suddenly a slender shapely hand was blocking the doorway. He slammed into the doorframe with a hand on either side, stopping himself with his bare chest just inches from the hand. He smelled pikake and jasmine.

Steve watch the hand gently touch his chest and feel around briefly at the muscles still flexed with his arms pushing against the doorframe. Just before the hand disappeared, he thought it blushed.

The hand reappeared with a cup of coffee.

"Make yourself decent and get into your kitchen," Heather said. "We're all perishing from hunger, master chef."

He slid his right hand down her arm as he reached to take the coffee from a now trembling hand.

"Your wish is my command, fair maiden," Steve said softly. Then he stepped back and closed the door.

Five minutes later he emerged from his room having traded his pajama bottoms for jeans and a long-sleeved polo. His hair was still wet and his cheeks unshaved.

Pete must have been waiting for the smell of breakfast because he rang the doorbell as Steve flipped the first pancakes. Kara and Ana ran to hug Uncle Pete and soon he was playing with Matt, Jeremy and the girls even while he loudly complained about having to wait for breakfast.

Steve's griddle was big but not big enough to fix pancakes for such a large group all at once. Heather helped him pass out plates as he filled them, and everyone settled in to eat while the food was hot.

Amid the noise and laughter, busy with his breakfast preparations, Steve stole a look at Heather. She was staring at his cheeks and chin.

He rubbed his face with his left hand and shrugged. "You seemed in a hurry, so I skipped it for now."

"As far as I'm concerned," Heather smiled. "You can skip it for the rest of the day too."

"You like?" Steve asked with a raised eyebrow.

"Oh yeah, I like," Heather blushed but didn't look away. Steve was glad that their ohana was gathered around to keep him from taking her in his arms and kissing her until they were both breathless.

"So is this," Steve rubbed his stubble again, "an ordinary kind of way that I can romance you?"

"Oh yeah," Heather sighed. "It sure is."

"'Somebody's watchin' you,'" Greg sang from behind Steve.

"They always are," Steve said dryly.

"Thank God for that," Heather sighed, not sounding particularly thankful.

THROUGHOUT THE WEEK they were watched. There were so many family activities that Steve and Heather hardly had any time to themselves. Steve and Pete had practice during the day most of the week, except Tuesday and Christmas day, but Colonel Joshua often joined the rest of the family for snowball fights, ice skating and sledding in the parks. They went up the Sears Tower, compared Lake Michigan to the Pacific and tried to find scenes from Harrison Ford's *The Fugitive*.

On Wednesday, Grandma and Grandpa Shepherd came up from Normal. They were spending the entire weekend and Steve easily convinced them to stay in his penthouse, especially since baby Naomi was there. Greg, Tim and Robert moved across the hall to Pete's place since he was complaining about the imbalance of visitors – Steve, eight, ten if the grands stayed with him; Jenni, two; Pete, zero.

"Hey Greg," Steve slipped into Greg's new room, "your Grandpa's black."

"He is?" Greg looked around in surprise. "How come no one told me!"

"Your grandma doesn't look like she's black, is she Mexican?"

"Yeah mostly, but she's African, Cherokee and Irish too. Grandpa's also Italian and Irish," Greg looked at him strangely. "You didn't know this?"

"Well I sure knew you all weren't haole, but I thought you were typical kamaaina. You know, Polynesian, Asian, Filipino with some haole maybe."

"You were part right. We're all that and then some. Does this bother you?" Greg sounded wary.

"Bother me?" Steve was surprised. "No! It's just that I never thought to ask. It just surprised me when I saw your grandpa. I realized that I wouldn't be able to tell my kids anything about their heritage."

"Hey yeah, you'll be giving me some niephews, won't you?" Greg grinned. "They'll be African, Irish, Mexican, Italian, Cherokee, Japanese, French,

Hawaiian, Chinese, Filipino and some kind of Scandinavian from our side of the family. What about yours?"

"That's so much of everything that it's not much of anything!" Steve laughed. "I always had the impression that we were English."

"But you don't know?"

"Never really cared."

"What about your grandparents? Didn't they ever tell you anything?"

"I only knew my father's mother and she didn't talk about family at all. Neither did Mom. I don't even know my mother's parents' names. Come to think of it, I'm not even sure Uncle Joe was actually my father's brother."

"That's really weird, brah," Greg stared at him in disbelief.

"It is, isn't it?" Steve shrugged. "But it wasn't like my father ever had a real conversation with me about anything. And Mom never talked about her past or her family. I always thought she was an orphan with no siblings but she never actually said that."

"So you could have family out there somewhere," Greg said.

"I suppose," Steve didn't seem very interested. "Does it matter?"

"It might not to you and Jenni anymore," Greg said thoughtfully, "but it might mean something to Kara and Ana. It's not like they have any heritage from their fathers."

"But does it really matter?" Steve asked seriously. "Isn't it enough to have God in your life?"

"I'm not so sure it is," Greg replied. "God made a big deal about family in the Old Testament. Your status as a child of God is obviously the most important relationship but I think family is really important to all of us. If we don't have family, we're alone, even if we have God. He intended us to be in relationships with each other as well as with him."

"You certainly have a point," Steve said. "I'll have to think about it. Maybe I'll put that investigator back to work again."

"Or you could just take an ad out on TV," Greg suggested drolly. "'Hi, I'm Steve Jeremiah, of the Chicago Grizzlies, and I'm looking for anyone who might be related to me. If you think you are, please call one-eight-hundred-sucker.'"

"Wow Greg! That's an awesome idea," Steve said sarcastically. "That would help me so much and it wouldn't bring out any crazies."

"Something to pray about, brah," Greg grinned slyly. "I'm always looking for ways to help out ya know."

"In my opinion, brah," Steve grinned back. "You need to get help, not give it. I think Nalani can squeeze you in at two."

"I don't know why I like you," Greg frowned.

"Sure you do," Steve smiled slyly at Greg's questioning look. "I'm taking your sister off your hands."

"Not yet you aren't," Greg sighed, "and not soon enough."

"You know, that's one I can't argue with," Steve sighed too and threw his arm over Greg's shoulder as they headed back to his penthouse. "It sure isn't soon enough."

CHRISTMAS EVE THE whole family attended the children's service at church where Kara was part of the angel choir. When they went back to Steve's for a Christmas Eve party, somehow an impressive array of presents had appeared under the tree.

The children were enthralled, especially Kara and Ana who had never before seen such abundance. Steve said everyone could open just one present tonight. When everyone had opened their gifts, Ana crept up to Uncle Steve with tears in her eyes.

"Uncle Steve, Santa forgot you and Mommy." Her little lip quivered and she dashed away the tears falling on her cheeks.

"Santa didn't forget us," Steve said, picking up his niece and kissing her. "He gave me my Christmas present way early. It was you and your sister. But he didn't forget your mommy either. He just didn't put her present under the tree. Let's go see if we can find it."

Heather watched curiously as Steve disappeared with his niece. Suddenly she heard a squeal of joy from the vicinity of Steve's bedroom. Steve came back out with a squealing child in one arm and a squirming Rottweiler puppy in the other.

"Mommy, Mommy," Ana clapped her hands. "Look what Santa brought you!"

"Oh! He's so cute," Jenni took the puppy from Steve's hands and held him up to look at him. He tried to lick her face and they all laughed. Kara ran up to see the puppy and Jenni knelt down next to her. Ana demanded to be put down so she could join her mom and sister and their new puppy.

"You bought them a puppy for Christmas?" Heather hissed.

"No, Santa did," Steve slipped his arm around Heather but she didn't snuggle against him.

"It's a real bad idea to give puppies and kittens for Christmas presents," she whispered fiercely.

"I know that," Steve whispered back.

"Then why'd you do it?" Heather hissed angrily.

Steve stood up and pulled her up with him, fairly dragging her through the kitchen and into the laundry room. He picked her up and set her on top of the dryer, then closed the door. He placed his hands on the dryer, bracketing her knees and he leaned down with fire in his eyes.

"Heather Nohealani Shepherd," he said clearly and calmly. "Please never do that again."

"What?" She shrunk back against the wall with doubt in her eyes.

"Don't try to pick a fight with me when other people are around," Steve said.

"I didn't –"

He interrupted her by simply raising an eyebrow. "Okay, maybe, but –"

"But nothin', darlin'," Steve drawled. "Trust me at least long enough to drag me to some private place before you try giving me a scolding, please."

"Okay," Heather said meekly.

"It just so happens, sweetheart," Steve pushed himself away from the dryer and leaned against the folding table on the opposite wall, crossing his arms over his chest. "That this time, while you're right, you're also wrong."

Heather just looked at him, waiting to hear his side.

"It is a very, very bad idea to give puppies and kittens as Christmas presents because it's usually an impulse buy, like most of our Christmas presents are. They end up neglected and untrained, and often get taken to the Humane Society before spring arrives. That is not the case here."

Heather was listening carefully and Steve gave her a small smile.

"Jenni and I have been talking about this for a long time, ever since she revealed that she has a ... let's call him a nemesis. Pete and I can't be around all the time and as good as Jenni has become with self-defense, she isn't good enough to take care of herself and the girls if necessary. A well-trained Rottweiler who loves the girls will be a blessing to her family and it will ease Pete's and my worry when we have to be on the road."

He saw the question in her eyes and anticipated it.

"I already have training lined up. Would you like to know the date, time, and name of the trainer?" He leaned back on the dryer, this time with a smile. "We've been vetted by the breeder, Beautiful, and we're ready for this puppy. We even followed their suggestion that the puppy not be given to the girls but to Jenni. That will keep either of them from having a proprietary interest in him and help him stay a family dog. No feelings will be hurt if the girl who didn't get him as a present becomes his focal point."

Heather stared into intense blue eyes, focusing on them so she wouldn't see the warm, firm lips so close to hers. Lips that she hadn't kissed yet because this man was a very careful, cautious man. Danger was not part of his life, except on the football field and even that he was well prepared for. He would never bring a potentially dangerous dog into his sister's life without thoroughly studying the subject. What had she been thinking?

"Are we okay now?" Steve asked.

Heather smiled and nodded.

"I'm sorry. I should have trusted you," she said, pushing off the wall and leaning toward him. "Please forgive me?"

"I forgive you, love," Steve leaned his forehead against hers. "Shall we go back out now before your brothers come in to defend your honor?"

As they walked toward the living room, it was obvious that the family was trying out names.

"Brutus," Robert said.

"Toto," that was Greg.

"Spike," Luke said.

"How cliché," Nalani scolded.

"That's not a name, 'how cliché,'" Greg frowned.

"Flower," Ana said.

The puppy looked at her and barked.

"You can't name a Rottweiler 'Flower'!" Pete cried in horror.

The puppy barked again.

"Sounds like you can," Luke laughed.

"Flower," Ana said again. She giggled as the puppy barked again and bounced into her lap, trying to lick her face.

"Steve," Pete looked up at his friend, leaning against the wall, laughing. "Tell your niece that 'Flower' is no name for a Rottweiler."

"'You can call me Flower if you want too,'" Steve replied with a commendable imitation of the skunk in *Bambi*, even batting his eyelashes. "Sorry, brah. *Bambi* is her current favorite movie and Flower is her favorite character. Looks like we're stuck with it."

"Can you see yourself with him at obedience school?" Pete frowned and mimicked the frustration of someone trying to train a puppy. "Flower, *sit*."

Flower barked and sat and everyone laughed.

Pete snatched up the puppy and glared at it. Then he did a quick check.

"He's a boy," Pete grabbed at one last very logical argument. "You cannot name a boy dog Flower!"

Flower barked happily and licked Pete's face.

"Flower it is," Jenni laughed. "Sorry Pete."

"That's really going to strike fear in a prowler's heart," Greg said. "Flower, attack!"

"It might not strike fear in their heart," Steve said wryly, "but they're still going to get bit in the – oof!"

Steve bent over as Heather elbowed him hard in the gut. Still bent over, he turned to her.

"That," he croaked with a weak smile and a wink, "was a *good* call. Thanks."

"So happy to help you," she said with a smile and a slight bow.

Flower it was. Pete grumbled mightily when Steve handed him the leash to walk the puppy home to Jenni's apartment.

"Carrying Sunshine will ease the embarrassment if not the indignity," Pete said as he picked up Ana. "At least people can make the very correct assumption that she was the one who named the dog, but don't even think

285

I'm going to drag that dog around the neighborhood without her. 'Flower, come. Flower, heel. Flower, don't shishi on the flowers.' Man that will be so embarrassing. You do know that people recognize me!"

"Relax, brah," Steve said as they followed Pete's grumble out the door and to the elevator. "Maybe you'll get lucky and a visiting offensive lineman will see you with Flower. Then he'll be tempted to laugh at you on the field and you can take his head off."

"Yeah, instead of 'Gator-aide's better than water,' he'll be saying, 'You've got a dog named Flower,'" Heather was very helpful in her comfort. "It worked for *The Waterboy*. Just think what that will do for your game, Flower-boy."

"Don't say that," Pete looked around as they stepped into the elevator. "A name like that could stick with a guy, especially in this family!"

"You all behave and leave poor Pete alone," Gloria scolded.

"Thanks, Aunty Gloria," Pete said.

"He has enough trouble being stuck with a Flower on a leash," Jenni couldn't resist the tease.

Heather noticed that Pete didn't seem very bothered by Jenni's tease and she looked up at Steve with a question in her eyes. He gave her a small smile, a nod and a shrug. Ah, Pete was dreaming but Jenni wasn't biting yet. That would be an interesting project once she moved to Chicago.

Chapter 41

*T*he Grizzlies tore through their opponents for the next four weeks. They totally annihilated the Coyotes in the last regular season game. They not only shut them out but they also put thirty-five points on the board as Reynolds continued to control the field. In the first week of the playoffs, they redeemed their loss to the Sharks with a thirty-one to nothing win. Then they went to the Rebels and took them out with a twenty-four to zero win. The last game, giving them the conference and sending them to the Championship Game, they beat the Boars forty to three.

Steve took a lot of ribbing from the Shepherds over that field goal. They refused to let him claim redemption because he had a safety. They all joyfully prepared to head for Atlanta the first weekend in February. Steve was as eager for the post-game festivities as he was for the game itself. Whether they won or lost the game was much less important to him than Heather saying yes to his proposal after the game. He checked his preparation for that event as much as he did his preparation for the game.

Luke and Nalani decided that going to Atlanta was too much travel for the children too soon after their last trip to the Mainland so Nalani and the children stayed in Hawaii but the rest of the family went to Atlanta. Matt and Jeremy weren't happy to be left behind but they were comforted knowing that Uncle Steve and Uncle Pete were coming home the next week. Gloria decided it wouldn't hurt Tim and Robert to miss a day of school, since they were flying out Friday night and coming back on Monday. They weren't flying commercial. Colonel Joshua had insisted on coming to get them.

Jenni and the girls were meeting them in Atlanta, staying with them in the same suite. Just as Nalani had not wanted to disrupt her children's lives again so soon after the trip in December, Jenni had hesitated to bring the girls. Two factors convinced her to bring the girls with her to watch her brother in the Championship Game. She had no one she really trusted enough to leave the girls with, and the short flight and two nights in Atlanta would be much less disruptive to her girls than the trip from Hawaii would have been for Luke and Nalani's boys.

Heather tried very carefully not to lie outright when she sent her family and Colonel Joshua to the game without her. They were sitting in their normal places, to the left of the fifty yard line and three rows up. She was sitting twenty rows behind them and well to the right of their seats. She didn't expect to be seen because no one would be looking behind them.

When she watched the unreserved exuberance of her brothers, Heather was sure she had made the right call in going to the game by herself. They would have done a good job of controlling themselves for a while, being careful not to hurt her with their vigorous hugs and back slaps but she didn't want them to have to restrain themselves. This was the Championship Game and they should buckaloose. If she was with them when they did, she would hurt afterward and she had hopes for the post-game show that didn't include an aching shoulder.

She had regained almost full range of motion and was able to put on a jersey with her left arm in the sleeve, on the outside of the jersey wearing a sling that strapped around the waist as well as around the neck. She debated on the jersey because she knew people had started to recognize her as Steve Jeremiah's girlfriend. Wearing it certainly did increase the odds of someone noticing her but she just couldn't go to the game without it. She had also debated over the sling since she didn't really need it anymore but it would encourage people to be more careful around her when they saw it. It would also help her to not get too exuberant in her own celebrations.

The Raptors won the toss and elected to receive. When she saw Steve trot out onto the field a fierce pride surged through Heather, giving her chicken skin. She tried to watch the ball but she could barely take her eyes off Steve. He stood there so fierce and strong, so ready. The Raptor center snapped the ball and Steve was in motion. With power, speed and grace, he plowed through the offensive line and hit the running back almost before he even had the ball.

So the game began. The first quarter was a regular slugfest. Both offenses gained yards but neither defense gave up points. In the second quarter, the Grizzlies' punt returner took the ball all the way into the end zone. The crowd was electrified and the Grizzly defense didn't mind at all going right back out onto the field.

Or maybe they did. On the second play of the Raptors' possession, Steve hit the running back hard. Pete scooped up the resulting fumble and took off for the end zone. Then the Raptors' kick returner took the ball all the way. It was a fourteen-seven game.

Reynolds and the Grizzly offense took the ball eighty-two yards and put up another seven. In the last few minutes of the first half, the Raptors tried to score but Steve started punishing the quarterback. He hurried him for incomplete passes, batted down passes and sacked him for a major loss of yards. The first half ended twenty-one to seven.

When Steve started to harass the quarterback, Heather could not contain her delight. She started to get puzzled looks from some of her seatmates. At the start of halftime, a young man in front of her turned around and stared openly at her.

"Oh man, it's you! You're her," he looked back down at the field where the teams were still jogging off to the locker rooms. "You're Jeremiah's girlfriend. I saw you on TV."

"Wow! It is," his girlfriend agreed. She pointed to the sling. "Hey, is that from the school shooting? It still hurts?"

Now Heather wished she hadn't worn the darn thing. She sank deeper into her seat.

"Yes, that's where I got shot," Heather said kindly. "No, it doesn't hurt much anymore, only when I strain it too much. I wore it today so I wouldn't strain it."

"You're one of the true American heroes, young lady." That was an elderly man behind her. "I'd be proud to shake your hand."

Heather could see her family down below. No one was looking this way, but would they see the strange gathering and wonder? No matter, as long as she was sitting they wouldn't see that it was her in the center of the small crowd. Even Greg wouldn't be curious enough to climb up the twenty rows to see what was going on. She thought fast and hoped that what she came up with was better than normal for her.

"Look guys, I appreciate your enthusiasm for me but I've got to make a confession," Heather prayed that this would work. "See, I didn't tell Steve I was coming. He thinks I'm still back at the hotel watching the game by myself and taking care of my shoulder. I didn't want to take any chance of distracting Steve from playing well today by thinking about me so close, watching him."

She took a deep breath and plunged on.

"I think he's already planning to ask me to marry him after the game." *Oh God, I hope I'm right.* "That's distraction enough. So I don't want him to see me. So I'm not going to stand up during half-time because someone will spot me since I'm so tall." *Am I rambling now? Please stop me Lord.* "So I'm just going to sit here and if you want to talk to me or shake my hand or, or, ..., well, you're just going to have to come around front and be my shield." *Like that won't draw attention!* "But not too many at once. I don't want attention. Act cool, please?"

It worked. For the first ten minutes of the halftime, she signed autographs, had her picture taken with her seatmates and answered an endless array of questions but no one outside her small section to the right of one of the stadium entrances had any clue what was going on. A small screen of people always blocked the view as they nonchalantly looked around the stadium and watched the festivities down on the field.

Finally Heather begged for a break. "I really gotta go ... answer the call of nature and I'm dying for nachos and a diet cola."

"You go take care of nature," the elderly gentleman and his wife said. "We'll get you that snack."

With the press in the stadium, Heather didn't get to slip back into her seat until the second play of the half. She wasn't too concerned because the Grizzlies had the ball at the start of the half so Steve wasn't on the field anyway. She had plenty of time to enjoy her nachos and diet cola while Reynolds coolly marched down the field with the offense, using five minutes on the clock and putting up another seven.

Reynolds was solid but Steve was electrifying. Nothing went up the left. The quarterback began to live in fear for what was coming from behind him. No one could stop the big man and time after time, Steve took down the quarterback. After being sacked twice in one series, he took to tossing up the ball as quickly as he could but often it wasn't quick enough and Steve was hitting him even as the ball was being released. He finally threw right to the Grizzlies safety who brought it back into Raptor territory. The offense scored a field goal with insulting ease.

As the third quarter wound down and the Grizzlies had put up thirteen unanswered points in the third quarter alone, the tempers on the Raptors' side were beginning to flare.

With one minute, thirteen seconds left in the quarter, Steve pushed the Raptor running back out of bounds, almost casual in his lack of effort. Suddenly, after the play was dead and Steve was turning to go back to the line of scrimmage, the Raptor tight end hit him hard from behind. Totally unsuspecting, Steve went down like a log. Whistles blew furiously, flags flew vigorously and fans screamed angrily. Steve didn't get up. Heather stood with her right hand fisted in her hair, a scream building in her chest, eyes wide in horror. Silence began to fall across the stadium.

Slowly the big man's arms moved. His elbows went back and up, and his right leg drew up under him. He rose to his feet and turned slowly toward the Raptor who had hit him. He stared down at the man for a few long seconds. Teammates raced up to take his arms and drag him back from the fight but he shook off their hands and stared down at the other man. Finally he said something then turned and walked away, back toward the line of scrimmage.

The second string defensive end ran up to him but Steve shook his head and kept walking. The man grabbed his arm and Steve stopped and turned. He looked over at the bench and the coach, shook his head and trotted to the sidelines, pulling his helmet off as he stepped off the field.

Heather got a good clear look at his beloved face, knew he was fine, and she fainted. Fortunately, her new friends grabbed her and guided her into her seat, patting her hands and handing her diet cola to her.

"Put your head between your knees for a minute, dear," the elderly lady behind her patted her on the back. "That helps tremendously. Hurry dear or you won't be ready to watch again when they let him back out."

The Raptors got a fifteen yard penalty for the hit and the young man was ejected from the game. It was now third and twenty-two from their own forty-three yard line. The Raptors went nowhere on the down. They had to punt.

By the time Reynolds finished his leisurely stroll down the field, putting up another three, Steve was back out of the locker room and ready to play. He ate up the offense. On the next Raptors possession, he hit the quarterback as he was drawing his arm back to pass, popping the ball out easily. He stepped over the downed Raptor to pick up the ball and trotted into the end zone. The Raptors got the ball back and on their second first down Steve met the running back with a bone-jarring hit. The ball popped free and was recovered by the Grizzlies. After the offense played around for a while, going three and out, they gave the ball back to the Raptors. In their final possession, Steve sacked the quarterback two out of three downs and he made it look easy. The Grizzlies won the game with a score of forty-four to seven.

Chapter 42

*H*eather stayed in her seat throughout the postgame festivities. She knew that her family would be allowed on the field along with the players' families and that many other fans from the lower deck would manage to slip onto the field. Right now, however, she had no desire to be down amidst the noisy throng when she could sit up here and see Steve so clearly.

Even among his teammates, Steve stood out, easily the tallest man on the team. Even without his pads and jersey, he still looked huge. His sweat-soaked t-shirt clung to his body and enhanced those muscles that made her heart flutter. His hair was sweaty and rumpled under his brand-new championship cap. He looked wonderful to her. She saw his happy smile as he spotted Jenni, the girls and Heather's family heading his way. Before they got to him, as one of the defensive captains he had to climb onto the dais where the championship trophy would be awarded.

When the microphones were pointed his way after the presentation, Steve spoke simply. "Today was an awesome day. The whole team played incredibly well. I thank God for giving me the opportunity to play this game with these guys. They're great."

When it was time for the presentation of the MVP trophy, Steve was already heading off the dais. He seemed genuinely surprised to hear his name announced as the MVP. Again the microphones were shoved in his face.

"I don't think I'm the one who should be getting this trophy. I've been playing with the pros for eight years now and this is my second appearance in the Championship Game. I should have played well, but Tyler Reynolds is a man who inspired us all. This is his, what, fifth full pro game? But he plays football like a ten-year veteran. He's the one who really was the most valuable player for the Grizzlies!"

Steve turned to go but the reporters stopped him for the standard question. "So, Steve Jeremiah, you've just won MVP of the Championship Game. What are you going to do now?"

Steve was surprised by the question because he'd never expected to be asked it. Defensive players don't get MVP in the Championship Game.

Thoughts chased each other through his mind. Joy because he knew what he was really going to do. Worry about what Heather would do if he said it to the reporters. Awareness that if he said anything other than the truth, it would sound false.

"Honestly?" he asked with a slow smile and an upraised eyebrow.

"Honestly!" the reporters chorused back.

"I'm going to go back to Hawaii and marry my sweetheart, if she says yes." Then he turned and made his way to the family waiting for him on the field.

Heather felt the blush creeping up her cheeks as her new friends all looked at her. She grinned like a fool.

"I guess there's going to be a wedding in Hawaii," the young lady to her right said. "I'd sure like pictures of that!"

"Give me your address and you'll get some," Heather said, overflowing with love.

"Seriously?" another woman asked.

"Seriously," Heather said with a little laugh. "In fact, all of you, give me your address. I want to thank you for being so good to me today."

Soon Heather had a collection of addresses on business cards, napkins, the backs of receipts and scribbled in the margins of her program. Since the presentations were over, her friends all soon drifted away, giving Heather cheerful good-byes and congratulations.

Much of the lower tier was already cleared out. Many had been family and friends allowed onto the field and those who weren't had no reason to hang around after the trophies were awarded. Heather took off her sling, stuffed her game trophies in it and rolled it then stood up and went down to the walkway. She stood there, briefly wondering if she should just go or if she should wait for her family to see her.

The Grizzly players were beginning to drift toward the locker room. Steve handed his trophy to Jenni then loped off. He glanced up and looked around the stands casually, eyes sliding past Heather. Suddenly he stopped and turned, looking again. She saw his grin. Everyone was surprised when Steve threw his cap in the air and ran back across the field. He jumped on the wall, grabbing the top with both hands and pulling himself up and over.

Heather sat down on the top step of the lower tier, knees up, arms around her knees and her chin on her knees, grinning happily. Steve ran up the steps, taking three at a time, slowing as he came to her. He smiled as he flopped down beside her, just as he had on her front stoop on Thanksgiving weekend. This time however, it was a much smaller space there between the rows of seats. He crowded her but she scooted still closer.

Heather saw their family wandering over to watch them. She blushed.

"You came," Steve said with a happy smile which he tried to turn into a frown, "but that means you lied to me."

"I did," Heather sighed her confession. "I'm sorry. I shouldn't have lied, even by omission. Please forgive me?"

"I'll think about it if you answer a question for me," Steve smiled and felt his heart begin to hammer at his chest.

"But you have to forgive me because I already forgave you," tears welled up in Heather's eyes.

"For what?" Steve said in surprise.

"For scaring me half to death," Heather blinked at the tears.

"Oh that," Steve smiled ruefully. "Sorry about that Beautiful."

"Why did you just lay there?" Heather stared across the stadium and frowned.

"Because I was unconscious," Steve shook his head. "The doc says I hit the ground so hard that it knocked the wind out of me with such force that my brain instantly sensed oxygen deprivation and shut down. But it was only for a few seconds."

"Do you know how long a second can be?" Heather whispered.

"Yeah, I do," Steve sighed.

"I think I can understand a little how horrible you must have felt by the time you got to the hospital that day," Heather said softly. "What I felt for five seconds went on and on for hours for you."

"On the other hand," Steve smiled sadly at her. "I had plenty of time to give up my fear and to trust in the Lord."

"We're learning," Heather hugged her knees tighter. "So, what did you say to him?"

"To whom?" Steve asked.

"To the little rat who hit you."

"Him," Steve laughed a little. "When I first came to, I was really ticked off but by the time I got to my feet and turned around I was just thankful to be alive to serve God and love you for another day."

"And you said ...?" Heather prompted with a small smile.

"I said, 'I forgive you, but they won't.'"

"They being ...?"

"The refs, of course," Steve smiled.

"I forgive him too," Heather said.

Suddenly Steve sat up straight so that he was in front of Heather instead of beside her.

"Hey, unhook my Mizpah, would you?" he asked.

"But why?" Heather was shocked at his sudden request.

"Just trust me sweetheart, please," Steve said urgently.

Heather reached up with fingers suddenly cold and fumbled for the clasp. Steve had grasped the charm and was pulling the chain over his shoulders as soon as she freed it.

"I was going to do this part in the room, before I went to pick you up later. My fingers are so clumsy with that tiny clasp. I don't want to run the risk of dropping it and losing it. It would have been bad enough at the restaurant but a whole lot worse here. But I didn't want to lose it somewhere in a hotel or forget it at home so this seemed the best way to keep from possibly losing it."

Heather only half understood his ramblings but she thought she understood the feelings behind them. He sounded a lot like her when he made her nervous.

Steve half turned and handed her the Mizpah again.

"Here, put it back on please?" He turned around and leaned back towards her. This time the clasp worked much easier.

Suddenly he was turning on the step below her, facing her, left knee down, right knee up with his right forearm resting on it.

"This isn't really a romantic setting and I'm not dressed for romance, all hot and sweaty, smelling like I've been wearing pads for the last four hours because I have. But you're the one who wants romance in unromantic ways so I guess you get what you ask for."

"Steve," Heather interrupted him with a finger to his lips. "You're rambling."

"I am?" he asked, surprised. "I am. I sound like you."

"Yes you do," Heather smiled.

"I want to go golfing," Steve said abruptly.

"So do I, but there's something you need to ask first," Heather smiled.

"I didn't yet?" Steve seemed surprised.

Heather just shook her head.

"All that rambling and I didn't ask?"

Heather grinned broadly and shook her head again.

"Then, Heather Nohealani Shepherd," Steve took her left hand in his right. "My sweetheart, my love, will you do me the honor of becoming my wife?"

She nodded, tears spilling from her eyes.

"That does mean yes, doesn't it?" Steve leaned closer. "The nod says yes, but I'm not sure about the tears."

"Yes, you jerk," Heather smacked him lightly on his left shoulder.

She felt him slipping a ring on her left hand but she couldn't take her eyes off his adorable face. When Steve looked up from his happy task, she threw both arms around his neck with such exuberance that he was hard pressed to keep from being bowled over.

He slowly stood, wrapping his arms around her, pulling her up with him and stepping closer. She lifted her face to his and his lips descended on hers.

The kiss was sweet, tender and passionate. It was all they'd hoped for and all they'd feared.

Steve suddenly felt weak in the knees.

"Next Sunday," Steve suggested.

"You have the Superstar Game next Sunday," Heather murmured rubbing her cheek against his.

"Oh yeah," Steve kissed her again. "How about tomorrow?"

"Ticker tape parade."

"Oh that," Steve sighed "Valentines' Day?"

"Too cliché." Another kiss.

"How about Thursday?" Heather suggested. "I always wanted to get married on Thursday."

"The girls and I can't be there by Thursday," Jenni complained as the family came up the steps, surrounding them with smiles and laughter.

"Sure you can," Steve kept his arms around Heather, his eyes on hers.

"I don't have class on Friday," Greg suggested helpfully.

"Yeah, but we do," Tim and Robert complained.

"How about Saturday?" Jenni said.

"That's the prayer breakfast and practice," Luke nixed Saturday.

"Let's let them figure it out," Heather smiled as she leaned closer to Steve. "Kiss me again."

Aloha Reader,

This story was borne out of the desire to show that a successful marriage requires a lot more than just sexual purity before you marry. Many people who remain pure until they marry still don't have a successful marriage even though they may never divorce. To make a marriage truly good, you need to be much more concerned about God's place in your life than you are about your spouse, and you need to be more concerned about meeting your spouse's needs than you are about getting your own needs met. Heather was indeed wise when she didn't want to manufacture romance to foster love. There is enough romance in everyday life to keep a marriage strong but you really do need to learn how to look for it. Can you keep loving your husband if he never brings you flowers? Can you love your wife if she isn't a good homemaker? Absolutely! Love is a choice to see the best in your spouse and to encourage them to be all that God created them to be. Marriage isn't about changing your spouse, it's about being changed by God as he uses your spouse in your life.

I hope you have enjoyed meeting the Shepherds as much as I have. Heather and Steve were a lot of fun to work with, as was the rest of the family. When I started writing, I didn't know I would meet so many interesting characters. If you have found them as interesting as I did, then be sure to look for Greg's story, *A Gilded Sky,* which will be out in a few months.

I welcome your comments and questions. Please come visit me on Facebook and check out my website, www.cherylokimoto.com.

Mahalo and God bless,
Cheryl Okimoto

Notes

Arigato - Japanese for "thank you"

Brah - short for "braddah," not just a male sibling, but any male, especially a friend of similar age or younger. Older males will usually be called uncle or tata (but not used as often as tutu for females).

Brok' da mout' - a particularly delicious food

Chicken skin - called "goose bumps" on most of the Mainland

Directions in Hawaii - directions are told by local landmarks not points of the compass. Everywhere on the islands, mauka (mountains) and makai (ocean) are used as two points in the Hawaii "compass" and they are always opposite each other like north and south are. The other points change based on where you are. In Honolulu, you can go "Diamond Head" in a generally eastward direction between the mountains and the ocean or you can go "Ewa." Diamond Head is the distinctive tuft volcano to the east and Ewa is the major town on the leeward coast. If you are in Ewa, the directions that cross mauka and makai are "town" and "Waianae." In Kailua, they're "Waimanalo" and "Kaneohe."

(Luke) Guys - the pidgin way to say "Luke and his family"

Halau - a Hawaiian dance troupe, particularly hula but for many local churches it also includes sign dance

Haole - technically means "stranger" or "foreigner" but has come to mean a white person

Haupia - a creamy coconut desert

Honu - Hawaiian sea turtle

Huhu - grouchy

Kamaaina - local people, particularly those born and raised in Hawaii

Kapu - forbidden

Keiki - children

Kii - small wooden statue, probably an idol in ancient times

Kine (da kine) - kind, kind of. Da kine is also a general catch-all word when the specific word escapes you. "Did you get da kine?" Amazingly, most locals very easily figure out what is being talked about

Lanai - balcony

Lolo - someone not too bright, even a little crazy

Mahalo - thank you

Makai - ocean

Make (pronounced mah-kay) - dead

Malihini - newcomer, especially one who knows nothing about Hawaiian culture

Mana - power

Manini - little

Mauka - mountains

Melicious - (mom-ism) extraordinarily delicious

Menehune - Hawaiian little people, kind of like Irish leprechauns

Monku - grumble

Musubi - Japanese rice balls. In Hawaii it has come to mean a block of sushi rice (rice, vinegar and sugar) with a piece of meat on top, usually Spam, and a strip of nori (seaweed in sheets) wrapped around it

Niephew - (mom-ism) niece or nephew

Ohana - family

Omiyage - gifts, usually food, presented to family, friends and co-workers after a trip

Ono - delicious

Pau - done, finished

Salt & Light aloha wear - the shirts Gloria gives Steve for his birthday (Chapter 22) are real. Go to www.saltandlightdesigns.com to see them.

Shaka - wave showing the back of the hand with the thumb and pinkie finger extended and the other three curled toward the palm

Sistah - not just a female sibling, but any female, especially a friend of similar age or younger. Older females will usually be called aunty or tutu.

Stink eye - glare at someone